FATED DREAMS

BOOK ONE: Anna and Hayden

Author Vicky Low

Book One: Anna and Hayden.

summary

My name is Anna Harris, and I am a human with the gift to shapeshift into a wolf, not any ordinary wolf, a much stronger powerful version. My Dad is the Alpha of the pack I am from, we are named after the town we come from. As the Ashwood pack, my mum is our Alpha female as well as our healer and works for the Hospital in town helping all the residents of Ashwood town to be healthy. Our pack helps to protect all residents from unsafe animals and creatures that we share our world with, each town, and city have a pack to protect its land. We have coexisted with our human counterparts without them knowing what we are. We live as humans most of the time and run with our pack during the full moon in the forest that belongs to our pack. I have three best friends Cara, Jade, and Zoe, who are my sisters from another Mr. We have grown up in our pack together and we have always had each other's backs. We go to school together, we have a group of human friends, we are all taking our final exams as we have two weeks left before we each take our own paths in life. and we finish in two week's time. Cara and I have our eighteenth birthday party in a week's time and as we both were born on the same day. It's at this age when we could find our fated mate, I have been dreaming about mine for weeks, my girls and I have battles that need to be fort, while we look for pack members who have been taken. Loyalty and love for each other will help us battle the tougher times ahead, new friendships will form, and mates will be found. My girls will be taken, and I will not let the evil of one sick human leader and his followers take my sisters. With my mate by my side, we will do whatever it takes to win this battle from prejudiced human arsehole who thinks he is powerful because he has learned what we can do and the technology he has created that nobody else has yet.

My name is Hayden Hawk, and I am a human who has the gift to be able to shapeshift into a wolf as I am next in line to be Beta, to my pack I am more extensive than the other wolves of our pack. The Alpha is the biggest of us all. I am from the city and my pack is named the Darlington pack after it. We protect a large area of our land from keeping the beast at bay to protecting the more unique species like unicorns. My role in our pack is to travel on missions my Alpha has given me, I am also good at fighting and being able to track and hunt. I live alone in a beautiful town house, close to my parents' home. I have a younger brother, Leo, who joins me on each mission. We have two younger sisters, Maisie, and Jess, and I will protect them at all costs, along with my dad, our current Beta. Being a male shapeshifter, we are not only protective, but we are also known by our female mates to be possessive. Which can cause tension, as are just as fierce as the males. We coexist with the residents of our city and have always coexisted with them from the beginning of time. My best friend's Tommy, Sam, Delia, and my brother Leo, we grew up together and have always worked well together. I work doing missions with my team, and we uncover an Alpha's murder, a kidnapped child, and many obstacles of kidnappings, to realization of an island we thought had no more living pack members. My pack, alongside all the other packs, will help protect our kind at all costs from fear from being used in deadly games and defeat the human arsehole who we discover has secrets of his own. I find my fated mate and as I get to know her, and her crazy friend's, things will become clearer the more we uncover, the worst is hard to swallow. Can we each find love and help protect what our nature is made for? Protection, I will protect my pack, and all the packs who come together will defend our lands and our way of life to root out this evil. Will I be able to survive the outcome? I will not stop until I have her, my fated mate back in my arms, where she belongs. Alongside her father, and brother's, the packs, and the help of new friends, can we help those taken and bring them home?

I plan on releasing a series of books with each story the journey will keep unfolding. Along with love, there will be laughter. Along with pain, it will lead to joy. Journeys of each fated mate characters. Who are loveable, annoying at times, and will make you laugh with them, or cry for them. It is easy to fall in love with each character as they make each book come to life.

Acknowledgements

Dedicated to my brother in law r.i.p you are missed. This book has been a journey of my love for books. My favourite pastime is to lose myself in a story. I love imagining the characters as if I am there with them. I hope you enjoy reading my first book. Thank you to my husband for giving me time between our full workdays and family life. I could not have done this without your support. To all my children who have kept me grounded and have inspired me to be better, I love you all you are my world. Shout out to my best friend Lauren, who has helped me follow my passion and, on the days when I was frustrated or needed encouragement was always there to offer it., I love you. My other friends Jenna and Dingle, who helped me with positive vibes and just being there for me, you are all fantastic. I love you and thank you. To all who have fully supported me with everything I have done in life, I will always appreciate it thank you. To anyone who has not felt good enough, or life gets too hard. Do not give up.

About the author

I live in the United Kingdom from England in a county called Yorkshire. It has four parts to it: the north, south, east, and west. All parts have beautiful places to visit, from the hills of the countryside to the historic places with castles, museums, and old buildings. We have many places to visit, from zoos and restaurants, from theme parks, to shopping centers and country pubs, beautiful lakes, and rivers. To the smaller villages with grade two listed buildings with history from our Viking days and history kept buildings. A place where you can travel to the coast or to the countryside. I love where I am from, and I love how we speak, though we are a small country, but we have an array of regional accents. Our accent has been portrayed in tv shows to film. We are known for and joked about as a region that cannot say the letter T when we speak. I love that you can travel a few miles away and the accent changes, from broader

Yorkshire to a more subtle range. Yorkshire is known for being friendly, and if you are in the region, most will say good morning, good afternoon, or good evening. Which is spoken with phrases like "hey up," which means hello, we do ask how you are. Which is phrased with 'ya alrite?' or asked by saying" how are ya?" in Yorkshire accent. Another friendly term used as a phrase is 'na then,' which means "hello" to someone you have not seen in a while. More personally, I have been married for over 26 years, we met as teenagers and have been together for 30 years. I have a busy home life, between looking after a large family and working. I multitask by juggling many plates.

PREQUEL

Jimmy and Julie Sanderson.

CHAPTER ONE: Jimmy
CHAPTER TWO: Julie
CHAPTER THREE: Jimmy
CHAPTER FOUR: Aiden Huntsman
CHAPTER FIVE: Alpha Max

CHAPTER ONE:

Jimmy

I come from the Ashwood pack which is the name of the town that I live in with my family. Julie, who is my fated mate, and my wife too. I am a peace enforcer for my pack and my mate and I travel from the packs collecting data. As shapeshifters, we change shape from humans to majestic wolves. We are bigger than normal wolves, but we still follow in their footsteps by marking our mates by biting them during sex. Which binds us together as bonded, Julie is my fated mate. The bite is the wolf's way of marking what belongs to them, that mates are ours. We also get married in the human way, which is how you bond as human partners as husband and wife. We make love just as humans do, we don't mate in our wolf skin, we are created as protectors of each island we live on to keep all who live amongst us flourishing and safe. We change shapes in the blink of an eye, we shimmer gold, and we switch between each shape, between human, then wolf and back. We do pack runs in the forest that we own, and during each full moon, we stay in our human shapes the most. All our kind are protective, but we can be very possessive, the males are the worst. We ensure we are bonded in both the mating bite and the human ceremony of marriage. We want and need full commitment to each other. We want the world to know that we belong to each other. She is mine in all ways, as I am hers. Julie is my world, she is my everything, I love her with all my being. I know that I am a lucky shapeshifter. Julie is a peace enforcer as well, we met at a gathering fifteen years ago, I was twenty-four and Julie was twenty. We have been together since the day we met; I moved packs. I come from the Sanderson pack. My brother is the Alpha now. He took over from our dad, after he died, my mother died two years ago. We had their ashes scattered into the sea; we had a lovely ceremony to connect them back together after death. My dad died four years prior to my mother; they had my brother and me later in life. They didn't find each other until they were both almost thirty. My mum and dad met at the last gathering they attended; it took a while for islands that were further away to travel over, and each trip was long. The gatherings only happened every four years back then; we now do them every year. My dad was the host of the one where he and my mother met; he was at the docks. As he greeted each member from each pack, he saw my mother and he ran towards her and held her as each of them said mate. My mother came from Bear Island, which is the furthest island away from ours, which is Griffin Island.

They have been together ever since, from that day forward. Now as time has evolved, so has our technology. We have ships that can carry more of us between each of the islands, boats that are smaller and carry each of us quicker than the boats did back when my dad was younger. We will soon have radios that will work from island to island. We can talk to each pack on our own island, but we haven't been able to transmit the signal further than it is now. When my dad died my mother was heartbroken, but she knew that they would reunite in the other world. My mother used the time she had left to help build the pack my dad had left behind to continue to help it flourish. She helped my brother become a good leader and helped his mate perform the duties expected of an Alpha female. My mother made sure she was there to help when needed and spent each day helping the pack and spending time with each of our children, she was content, and it made her happy. When she died, it was with a smile on her face as we heard her say my dad's name, followed by.' You came'. She told us that dad said he was proud of us and that he would always watch over us. Then, Mum's eyes closed as she took her last breath. My brother took over as the Sanderson pack's Alpha, and I came with him to Ashwood, where I met Julie, who was so beautiful my breath caught in my throat; I felt a snap click into place, and I couldn't stop staring at her. I moved here to the Ashwood pack to be with her, we are now parents to our own children. We have a daughter called Jade who is twelve, and our son Ethan who is three. Julie is heavily pregnant with our third child, and I am so blessed. When we have to leave for our missions, we both work as peace enforcers for our pack and travel the islands. We collect the data from each pack, from how many members, the number of deaths, and any new births to report, as well as mating's. For those who are newly mated, and those who have yet to find mates, all new births and any who have turned eighteen and wish to go to any of the gatherings. We also collect data on the creatures known as the beasts; they are two-headed, large and aggressive; they are at their most dangerous when they are looking to mate or have young. We have had to relocate some away from civilization as they will attack and maim; in most cases, those who are attacked tend to die as the injuries obtained are severe. We have Neeman Lions; they, too, can be troublesome. All the data collected helps us track numbers and if they have moved too close to any built-up areas. We tranquilize them to be able to relocate them. Some of the older shapeshifters had to battle them to scare them by using their wolves and working together to bring them to heal. Or they would try to catch them with cages and traps to move them to another area away from residents to a place where they could be free without hurting anyone. Where they can breed, eat, have a water supply and make shelter. We have herds of unicorns we keep protected from humans taking them and trying to use them like horses, they are not to be ridden on. They have a horn on their heads for a reason to use when feeling threatened. Their horns can kill if they target the heart or lungs; they can stomp on them or cause injury to any who are too close. We also have others we track, and we also gather information on any new shapeshifters, we have our young when they turn thirteen until they reach their fourteenth birthday will go through a month of changing from human to wolf. We call it the growth phase and the Alphas, alongside the Betas from each pack, will help each teenager learn to transform. To teach them how to control each shape. The Alpha and Beta are the only members of our pack that can sense the growth phase, as their wolves are the strongest of our kind. They can scent each teenager when the time has come, and they need to step in and help with the transition. I am excited to see my daughter as she turns thirteen soon. Her wolf will come out between then and her fourteenth birthday, and we will be able to run with each other on full moons with her as a wolf. We have this last mission before we have time off to prepare for our new arrival. We always leave our children under the watchful eye of our Alpha and his mate and wife, Annabelle. We know our children will be well cared for and it makes our job as peace enforcers easier by not having to worry, as we know they are in loving hands. As Julie and I are due to leave, we are at the pack house dropping our children off. When we turn to leave, we tell them both to be good, and how much we love them. If they behave themselves, we might fetch them a present each. Jade hugged each of us goodbye and ran to play with her best friends, Anna, our Alpha's daughter, and Cara and Zoe. They have been friends since birth, they are together every day and have many sleepovers. Jade spends more time here at our Alpha's home than at our home. She has her own suite here, as do each of the girls in our home. Each parent in the pack has a bigger home, and we have spare rooms in case we have guests visiting from other packs. If our own pack wishes to stay over as we like to stay close to each other, and our children like to share a sleeping nest with their friends who they have grown up with, it helps them settle and sleep easier. We have an extra-large bed that they use, and they have their on-suite bathroom. We enjoy that our children get along so well; wherever the girls stay at our home or Cara's home, the Alpha's sons and some friends tag along with them as they are older; they tend to be overprotective and watch them like Hawkes. We've often had them all stay in another suite beside the girls. Adam is the oldest brother. He will be eighteen soon and has his first gathering next month. Adam wants a mate immediately, knowing he will take over our pack as its Alpha after his father. He would prefer his mate to be ready once he turns of age, to be able to learn alongside him in their roles before his parents retire. Abel and Zara, who is Zoe's big sister, she and Abel are close. They are always competing and trying to outdo each other. Zara is almost seventeen, and Abel is almost sixteen. They like to spar in combat and train and race with each other. They do go at it without holding back. Cara has a brother the same age as Adam; he and Callum are the worst. They drive the girls crazy, and Zara helps keep them off their backs as much as possible. She is the buffer between them. She, too, is protective, but not where the girls can't grow and learn as the rest of the pack must. Many times, Gerald, our Alpha, has told me he has on many occasions butted heads with Adam as Adam is just as powerful as being an Alpha himself; he won't back down. Gerald understands he is protective, as are we all, but he must let them breathe. Then we have our son Ethan, who turned three a few weeks ago. Gerald and his wife spoil him rotten, as do the girls. Ethan loves spending time here; he gets so much attention. The boys teach him how to spy on the girls and protect them. "He's like a sponge, my son. He takes in what all the boys tell him. But he loves the girls more and has many times gotten angry and had to kick Adams in the ankles. We all laugh as Adam pretends the kick caused damage. Ethan always walks away with his chest puffed out. I ruffled my son's hair like my wife, and I hugged him goodbye. Alpha Gerald has arranged for us to go alone as we have a perfect relationship with the Vale Islands, and Alpha Max is a gentleman. We say our goodbyes and head out to the port to travel by ship; we have the technology, boats, and ships that take us where we need to go. We also have buses and cars and are still building train tracks. The Keel Islands have designed those with a train that can carry containers and trade from each port to the cities and towns. We use radios to communicate between ourselves. We all have one in each Alpha's home to contact each other. We prefer to travel and speak in person; it's a better way to form stronger ties. We stay more connected to each other being together the more we adapt to the changing times. The more we adapt, the more we can help each other. My mate has been given the all-clear to travel with my mate, due in a few weeks. This will be our last job for a while; we have another child to add to our family. We catch the boat over to Vale Island, where we will meet Alpha Max, and we will meet his daughter Ali. She will be seven now; she is a remarkable child. Max adores her. He lost his wife during childbirth, and it was hard for him to lose his mate. As Alison laboured their child, they both couldn't wait to meet, and to have joy and sadness it was tough. Max got to say goodbye to his wife, but Alison knew she wouldn't make it. She told Max to love their child as she would watch them both from the other side, to give their child all the love in the world. Alison didn't want her child to regret being conceived or from being born, as giving her own life for the sake of her child's wasn't a choice she would ever regret. She would happily give it, to allow their child life. In each pack, we have healers, and hospitals, but unfortunately, the healer didn't arrive in time. Alison went into labour a few weeks earlier, than predicted. The nurse managed to get there but couldn't stop the blood flow. The wolf couldn't heal until the baby was born safe. How Alison managed to stop her wolf changing proves how much control she had. We always have a healer in each pack. The one who oversaw the Alpha's wife's care had been stuck in a car accident and had to help the injured. The backup was stuck in the same accident as the third had changed into his wolf and ran from the other side of the city to reach her; it was already too late. She died from losing too much blood. It was challenging for Max to have joy, and sadness was a lot to bear. We had a mourning period of three months for Alison, and we all felt Max's pain. One of our many fears is losing each other. We can all die. We are not indestructible. Once we arrive at the port, we are driven up to the Alpha's home. Max greeted us at the door. It was good to see you both. How was the trip? I shook his hand and told him it was pleasant. He hugged Julie, my mate and wife, asking her how her pregnancy was going. I am a little tired, and my back is killing me, but other than that, I am happy to be here. Where is Ali? Max said she is playing inside and is awaiting your visit. She has a picture she has been working on to give to you. We are led inside and taken up to our suite, to rest for a while. I have matters to attend to; I will see you both at dinner later. After leaving us both to settle in, I ran a bath for Julie; I helped her in. You relax; I will bring you a drink and a bathrobe. I leave Julie in the bath, pouring us both a drink each; I have whiskey and hand Julie an orange juice. I massaged her feet and washed her body with the loafer. I never get tired of seeing my mate naked. Knowing my child is growing in her belly, she looks stunning, which makes my wolf preen. I want her, and I always do. She allows me to care for her. I dry her using a giant fluffy towel, then wrap the robe around her as I pull the sheets off the bed and lay her down. She opens her arms. Come here, mate, and warm me up. I do a lot more than warm her up; she is so responsive that she moans my name as I make her climax from my tongue. I placed her on her hands and knees as I lined myself up at her entrance. I start to move as Julie gives as good as me by pushing herself deeper into me. I pinched her nipples as I pulled her back towards my chest. I keep up the pace as I feel her clench around me as she climaxes; I shudder as my climax hits. Afterwards, I wet a cloth and cleaned us both up. I lay beside my mate. Her head rests on my chest as I stroke her hair while she sleeps. I love these moments when we can be together; I left her to rest until dinner. We don't want to be late for dinner when Julie wakes up. We both get dressed, and we are about to leave our suite. I can't help but take Julie into my arms and give her a slow, sensual kiss. I love you so much; I told her you are everything. I love you too, Jimmy. Let's eat. I am starving. I hope there is pudding. When we entered the dining room, there were Ali and Max "Good evening"," I have one of our healers coming over in the morning, Julie, just to check that all is well." "Thank you, that would be great." I hear you have drawn a picture for us, Ali. I will show you. I just finished it before dinner. I have drawn it to take home with you as a gift. Ali pulls out a painted picture of a unicorn with her children. She is also pregnant with another unicorn. My dad took me there last week. There is a whole herd of them in the fields, near the woods. I love watching them run around. Max begins to tell us about how the herd is safe and hidden in the fields close to the woods. They have been watching them for a while now. They have the largest herd in the area, and their numbers are improving. You and Julie should visit while you're here, there are no creatures nearby that can harm you, and I have enforcers checking around the area at regular intervals. We might do that, Max, before we leave; thank you. "No problem," Max said as we talked about everything during the meal, catching up on events and how the gathering arrangements are going as Max is the host this year. We have taken down all the numbers of new mating's, births, deaths, and all who will attend the gathering next month. I have arranged all the data for you including the beasts and other animals. I have jotted and collected all the numbers and information you will need to bring back with you. I had my peace enforcer gather the data for you. You can read through it after dinner if you would like. I have a few pack members who will attend the gathering to see if there are any new age pack mates. Thank you, you have saved us a lot of work. I hope it will be another successful gathering next month. After dinner, we followed Max to the office, and we went through all the information. The beasts had increased their numbers, but no attacks were reported. Everything looks to be in order. It all looks good. We have a few thunderbirds the humans have named them. The lightening birds as we like to call them. Yes, they have kept us all lit up most of the winter months when we're running with the pack. It's amazing watching the moon as the birds spark huge lightning bolts as they fly. I will leave you two with it. Everything you need is here; I am going to read to Ali and get an early night. We will read all the data collected and check it alongside the earlier data. What we have is good news: more of our kind have found their mates. The unicorns have flourished, and the other animals are away from humankind and have been homed away from civilization. They have found mates and started families, and the data is promising. We both went through the whole data. It took a few hours, but we got it all in order, and everything was good. Afterwards, as it was late, we headed up to bed. Max has done our job for us; he is a good man. The next morning, we got ready and went for breakfast. We spent time talking with Ali and Max, and we all had to draw a picture of a unicorn. Ali was the judge, and she picked the winner. I am not particularly good at drawing, but as Ali enjoyed watching us pretend to be artists, we kept trying. She chose Julie as the winner. Her drawing looked like a unicorn, mine and Max's looked funny. The healer and nurse came to check Julie over. They did her blood pressure and urine test, and the healer said all was well; the baby's movements were good, and the blood flow and heartbeat were perfect. Our baby is happy, and the mother and baby are doing well. Max joined us afterwards; he suggested we use this time to relax; you have all the information you need and deserve a little rest before returning home in two days. Go on and enjoy all the city has to offer. I have my driver out front; he will take you wherever you wish. We hugged him as we left as we decided to have some much-needed alone time. We decided to have a look around the city, where we visited the sites and went for a walk around the shops. Julie bought each of our children an outfit and Ethan another car. He likes to collect them. Every place we visit, he asks for another car. Julie bought a few items we needed for the baby. We bought a couple of outfits and a few cuddle toys. She even bought a painting set with paper and an axel for Ali. Our driver took them back to the house and agreed to come back in a few hour's time to collect us. I took Julie out for a late lunch; it was a stunning place; we were seated near the back in a quiet spot that was owned by the pack. So, we got to order the chef's special, and the food tasted delicious. We went towards the theatre to see the show I had booked for us. We were both shown to our seats and as we sat, we were looking forward to seeing the show as the curtains opened. The show started with some comedy moments; it was a fantastic production; the actors had created a good story using added comedy. Each performance had the audience laughing throughout the entire show. Julie and I had to wipe our eyes because we had laughed so much that we each had tears in our eyes. After the show had finished all the audience stood, cheered and clapped. Julie and I enjoyed every minute. We came out of the theatre in such good spirits. The driver had returned to collect us, we were driven back to the house. Julie was feeling tired, so we went upstairs towards our suite. Why don't you go downstairs and spend some manly time with Max? She reassured me that she would be fine on her own as she just wanted a nap, as she began to stripe to her beautiful naked self. I am tempted to lay beside her and not sleep, but I can see how tired she needs her rest. After going downstairs, knowing nobody was there, I decided to join in with the late afternoon training. After a few rounds of boxing and combat training, I showered and checked on Julie. I left her to sleep. She shouldn't wake up now until morning. I found Max, and we played snooker before dinner. We grabbed a few beers and watched the match on television. Ali is sitting watching with us, shouting ref. Open your eyes. I can't help but laugh as she shouts at the screen instructions to the referee. I didn't know you liked football. "I do, I enjoy it," Ali said, "I play at school; I am good; I scored two goals in last week's game." After the game had finished, Max took Ali to bed, and I said goodnight and went up to my suite. I get into bed and cuddle into my mate. I can hear the baby's heartbeat, and I touch my mate's belly as I hold her close. I can feel the baby kicking my hand. I love how the baby responds to my touch; That they know I am here, and how much they will be loved knowing that I am their father as I feel the baby kicking and moving around against my hand. I remove my hand after a few minutes of touch as I don't want the baby's movements to wake her mother. I pull my mate close to me as she reacts to my touch, she moves closer to my heated body and nuzzles in as I wrap my whole body against her as I fall asleep beside my beautiful mate.

CHAPTER TWO:

Julie.

I woke up early and checked my watch. It was 4.30 am, and I needed to pee, as the baby was kicking my bladder. I tried my best not to wake up Jimmy; as I climbed out of bed, I needed to use the bathroom, so I walked towards the on suite. As I take care of business, I clean my teeth, take a shower, and wrap a huge fluffy towel around myself. I slept all through dinner, I am starving, and I really would like to see the Unicorns this morning. Alpha Max has cut our stay in half by doing our jobs for us, he is such a wonderful man, and he is a good leader. He cares for everyone, and he takes care of all the pack's needs. He has protected the city, kept all the creatures safe from harm and let their numbers increase away from civilization. To give them their own space to grow with enough food sources and water nearby. They get to grow their families without being in contact with people. I adore being here; we feel like we have had a mini holiday before the baby arrives. When I opened the bathroom door to get dressed, Jimmy was awake waiting for me. As he smiled at me, "morning beautiful," he said. "Why are you up so early?" Jimmy, I slept all through dinner, and all through the night. I thought we both could enjoy a moment alone and go to the fields to see the herd of Unicorns as the sun rises. I was going to leave you in bed to catch up on some sleep while I prepared a picnic to surprise you. I am awake now Julie, and I have a need that only you can ease. Why don't you come back to bed for a while? I missed you, then we can both prepare a picnic together and go to see the sunrise together. He pulled the covers back, and I could see he was ready for me; I could not deny him anything, as I, too, wanted him just as much as he wanted me. I take my time removing the towel. Jimmy watches from the bed. He never removes his eyes from the way my hands slowly unwrap the towel to the way I walk towards the bed as I join him. These moments are rare with having children, we need to be more inventive. As I climb into bed Jimmy kisses me hard, and as he slowly moves from my lips to my neck he nips, and trails kisses all the way to my breast, he licks nibbles and takes each nipple into his mouth, as he works from one breast to the other. He travels down my body, kissing all the way to my pussy. Where he blows warm air on to my most intimate part until he has me coming apart on his tongue. We make love, and my mate knows how to have me panting as he takes care of all my needs. Jimmy is passionate, as much as he likes to be the boss in the bedroom. He likes to take care of me, and he makes sure that each time I am screaming his name, once is never enough. He has me coming apart as many times as he sees fit. Even if I think I can't take anymore he likes to prove me wrong. As we both come down from our earlier lovemaking, we both take a shower, and as we begin to wash each other. Jimmy has other ideas as he teases my most intimate parts. I am horny, and he knows it. Hands-on the wall, bend over, mate, while I take away the ache. "Open your legs" he said. I do as I am instructed, as Jimmy lightly grabs my hips, pulling me further back towards him. Once he is satisfied that I am in place, he thrusts inside me like a man possessed, he pistons his hips in and out as skin hits skin. He does not let up until I feel him, he is close. "I need you to come Julie now "I need more," I told him in return. Jimmy turns me around and he takes a hold of my leg as it's lifted and pinned over his arm. My other leg I am using to help me balance, he presses his legs to hold me steady. As his thrusts begin to deepen, I gasped and enjoy the way he kept up the pace, he adjusted my leg, and he used his hand to pinch my nipples. I am so sensitive there, I come moaning his name. Jimmy rode me through my release. Open your eyes now. I do as I am told, as he picks my other leg up, leaning my back against the tiles. "I need one more." He spoke. Is he crazy? "I can't," he does not let me finish my sentence before he kisses me. Demanding my submission as he thrusts slower, more leisurely than earlier, he pinches my clit hard, between strokes. He mimics the movement with his tongue as he continues to kiss me. I feel so many different touches and each one takes me higher as I come again. Jimmy loses control and joins me as he bites into my neck as he releases inside me. Jimmy eases himself out of me with a smug look of pure satisfied male, he finishes washing himself and then helps me too. Once he helped me dry off, he helped me dress too. My legs feel like noodles after all the love he has given me this morning. Once were both ready and we have a romantic sunrise to watch while enjoying seeing the herd of Unicorns. I can't wait to see them. They are the most beautiful creatures, they are free, and we protect them to keep them that way, they are a gift to be around them and to watch them is a pleasure. As we arrive in the kitchen, we pack up pastries and tea in a flask. We take a few blankets from the pantry and place all our breakfast picnic into the basket. We walked towards the front door and bumped into Max. "Good morning, where are you going so early"? "We thought we would take your advice and see the herd of Unicorns during sunrise, before we go home tomorrow." That sounds like perfection to me. I will get you a map of the area and circle where to go, take one of the buggies. Jimmy goes to the garage to retrieve a buggy as Max hands over a map he has circled, with the fastest route and where the enforcers will be when they check the fields. They have a rota; they follow and check every few hours so you will both have privacy. 8 am is when the enforcers will be around to check the fields that all is well, which should give you enough time alone. We thanked him, and we headed out towards the buggy, it was such a warm morning. I can hear the birds singing and smell the clean air. Jimmy loads everything onto the back of the buggy, secures the basket and starts up the engine as I hold onto my mate. We drove the roads Max gave us, enjoying the fresh air and hearing nature. Jimmy parks roughly a mile away and we walk the rest of the way as the noise from the engine will scare the herd away. Jimmy carries the basket and takes a hold of my hand as we begin the walk towards the area Max marked out for us when we have walked about halfway. We can hear noise further ahead. Max said nobody was in the area, we walked closer, being as quiet as possible, as we got closer to the field, we both could hear voices that were giving orders. Loading up the pregnant mare we have enough for now, let's hurry this up gentlemen before anyone hears us. What is going on? I ask Jimmy to be as quiet as I can "I don't know, Julie but stay close beside me I don't like this." I hold my mate's hand as we sneak even closer once we are a few yards away. We chose to use the trees and bushes nearby to hide behind as we took in the scene in front of us. Watching as a group of humans with large vehicles are loading up cages with trapped Unicorns inside. Jimmy, what are they doing? This is private land that belongs to the pack, I could not believe what we are seeing. I don't know Julie, but I did not like it one bit as they have loaded up a few of the younger ones.

We can see one of the pregnant Unicorn sleeping on the ground, as they begin to loop rope around her neck and legs. The one in charge as he begins barking orders at the team of men in front of him. If the male starts charging, tranquillize him. We have two already loaded up take those back to base now. Keep them under use another Tranquillizer if needed, these are to be used as an attraction so we can use those two as rides for the visitor's kids. We will make a fortune using them for the tourist to ride on, and we can put the others in the zoo that the boss is creating. He has many ideas and wants to use as many species as possible to make the zoo open successfully. I am disgusted at what I witnessed, and what I am hearing as they speak amongst themselves with plans of capturing and using these creatures for greed. Humans who think that they can take the creatures we have been created to protect and put them into a zoo. What other creatures are they planning to take if they have any already? The numbers we have collected show that none are missing though. What have we stumbled across? "Jimmy, what shall we do it's just the two of us"? I "It is our job to protect them. We could not leave" I know love. We need a plan. We need to be careful; I did not like the look of them. "I will change into my wolf and try to scare the herd away" "I could not risk anything happening to you or our unborn child." I want you to walk back to the buggy. I will meet you there, but if I am not back after a few minutes. Go, and get help from the pack, and tell Max that we stumbled upon humans, who are up to no good that they have come onto his pack's land. Tell him everything we have witnessed. I will open the gate to change shapes to my wolf form. Scare the herd into a panic so they can run away. It will help to confuse the men. So, I can escape. I will catch up, I will run as my wolf, we can alert the pack for help. If I am held up, you know what to do. "Ok," I said, "but please be careful they have tranquilizers and if they take you, what will I do if you are taken?" I will be careful I promise." Now go," I do as Jimmy told me. I try to blend into the trees and walk away as quietly as I can. I look back at Jimmy and mouth" I love you be careful." He mouth's "back I love you too." As I get further away from the area and closer to where the buggy is parked. I can hear footsteps behind me, I could not smell anyone, though as my heart is beating loudly, I am hoping it is my mind playing tricks on me. I am frightened for the first time in my life. As I turn around to check who could be there, I am backhanded hard across my face. I land on the floor with a bump, as I look up, I see men, who have now surrounded me "Who are you? What do you want"? "Ahh sweetheart the older one said with a sneer on his face "I want you." "Now we can do this the straightforward way," or, I did not allow him to finish his sentences." I act I need to get home to my children, and I needed to protect my baby, and alert the pack. I was back on my feet, and I did not give them time to respond the cocky man who sneered at me, he was my target as I kneed him in the balls I spun around and kicked another. I hit, punched, and kicked. Until a needle hit my neck and I fell into blackness.

CHAPTER THREE:

Jimmy

I waited until the last second, I wanted to give Julie enough time to get away. I can see that they have a pregnant unicorn on the floor, and I see that they have rope tied around her. They are reversing a truck as more men get out to help move her; I hope Julie managed to get back to the buggy as we need help. I am a good fighter, as is my mate. However, I am not willing to cause any harm to my mate and I am not stupid these men could drug us there are too many of them. They have tranquillizers. If I get shot with one, I would not be of any use to the Unicorns or be able to gather any help. I could not help but feel fear, as I know what is at risk, but I have a duty to these creatures to help get them out of danger. To do that, I need to scare them away. The fenced area is open as the vehicle reverses to gather the female that they have hogged and tied down. The man in charge has already given orders for the others to take the one they have captured already. I have the plate memorized. I have a plan in mind, and as I am about to put it into action, another smaller vehicle comes into the field. An older man my age gets out and starts to shout out into the area, come out, come out, wherever you are. We have someone who belongs to you. Others around the area who? "Not you," you idiots I am asking for the man hiding who thinks he can outsmart me, he is the mate to this one." I see him open the door at the back of his vehicle as he lifts my woman onto his shoulder as he shouts out again. The mate who has a plan. Isn't that right, Jimmy? Men he is in the woods hiding, he has plans to change into a wolf. "Yeah, right, what have you been smoking, Aiden?" "Shut up, you idiot." He shouts as he hands my mate over to another man who takes her from Aiden and carries her over to a clearing as he dumps her hard on the ground. She is not responding and as this dead man walking hurls my mate, I see red, I don't think; I react. I come out of the woods and Shout, "hey, arsehole, leave my wife alone." She is pregnant, who the fuck do you think you are? Why is she knocked out? you sick bastard! I brought my wife here to see these beautiful creatures." "Now you think I am what a wolf, are you mad?" Do I look like a wolf to you? My pregnant wife, does she look like a wolf, how dare you"? You see this? He interrupts my rage. He is holding in his hand some sort of device. It is so small, "I could not see properly from over here. No, what is it"? I asked. I am hoping by keeping them talking, it will be long enough for the pack enforcers to walk by and help us. Max said they patrol around this here at 8 am and I hope they hear us and come to the rescue early. The older guy Aiden pressed another device and that is the moment I can hear Julie and I as we discuss a plan to help. Aiden has advanced technology I have never heard of or met. Their leader, Aiden, after he had played the device to the crowd, gathered smiles my way as he handed the device to the areshole who dropped my mate. Aiden turns my wife to face me as he bends down and strokes her face. Ahh, she is a pretty one with a child as well." When is she due?" I lock my lips together I am not telling him anything, he looks and smells pure evil. "Why"?

I asked instead. Because I was wondering whether to keep her or not. You know, as she is so pretty, I can see her in a cage while I invite people to watch her birth another of, your kind. I can then kill her and keep the child as my pet. I am trembling with pure hot rage; the man and my wolf want to tear this man's throat out. Touched a nerve, I see, as he caresses my wife's stomach. Julie chooses that moment to open her eyes and headbutts him, breaking his nose. She acts with speed, and I follow her lead as she rolls, sweeping her leg out to tumble the guy close to her. I kick out, knocking another man back into a tree, knocking him unconscious, as another tries to grab me. I punched him, breaking his jaw. I know if I stop fighting, we are both dead. I try to get closer to her as I kick another man. She is holding her own, and that is when I see Aiden holding tranquillizer gun as he aims it at Julie. It hits her as she slumps to the floor. "No! I scream out "have you no honour." I am taken and held, as the youngest man who aims a gun at me" Do not move." Aiden holds on to my mate, and he shouts over to the men" Hold him "Don't take your eyes off him." Let us see if we can convince him to change, "That is when he stands up, and kicked my mate in the belly. I lose it, I change on the fly and aim for the fucker's throat that is when I am hit with the tranquillizer and fall into darkness alongside my mate.

CHAPTER FOUR:

Aiden Huntsman

We have devices that we can listen to if anyone is nearby, as we are rounding up from the herd of Unicorns, which has a patrol near the area. This will help my team and I; we will be able to tell when the best time is to go and collect. The devices planted around each place I want to take from I have installed my invention it means that I can hear conversations from anyone nearby. I have been watching this area for over a month and I know the times when I see others walking in and around the area. I have a team watching the owner of the land these creatures have found homes on. He has teams that guard the area. Early morning is our best shot at capturing the youngest herd members and the mothering Unicorn. My team have thirty minutes in and out. I have big plans. I want a zoo with more of the rarest creatures. I have captured a few Thunderbirds, and I have managed to trap a Griffin. That cost me two of my men as they were killed, it took thirty of us to take it down using tranquillizers. It is now in a large field trapped with no way to get out. Unicorns are my next plan to raise more money as little girls will want to ride upon them and parents will be willing to pay for them to have the chance to. I run holiday camps. I am a businessperson and I started it up, by myself from scratch. Over the years I have added onto it, now I have hunting parties, each who takes part enjoys feeling the power of being known as the ultimate hunter, to show off to family, and friends. They like to add danger by being able to hunt Lions, Tigers, and Bears and with each hunter who wins each battle. As I pit ten hunters into each package deal. They must track by living off the land and find each animal I place on the list. Each kill, they can keep the spoils. They can take their heads and mount them on their walls at home to show them off. They can do whatever they want if I get paid. I make sure each has a radio to update the head office on tracking, how they are coping, if any have been killed from the list given. Updates on who is winning all of it. They have a time limit to do so in as each hunter likes the challenge of not only hunting but being able to have competition. Knowing they have beaten another hunter helps them feel powerful. I have regular rich clients on my books. I offer cabins for their families where they have a swimming pool and nature all safe and away from where the real action is. As with all businesses, they tend to go stale. I need more unique creatures for the zoo we have that already houses the usual animals. We have a petting zoo with Rabbits, Goats, Sheep and Pigs with a play area. I am planning to extend a newer version of the zoo with unique rare creatures. As my team has already loaded and set off with the young, we have already collected this morning there is just the pregnant one to load up, that is when I noticed that my invention has picked up a conversation between a couple in the area. I heard him say he would change shapes into a wolf. I could not believe what I was hearing. After listening in and hearing their plan, as I was on my way from delivering those, we had already captured to the main road where my team was ready to transport them to my land. I spotted the buggy earlier as the conversation took place a woman was on her way here. My men and I hid our vehicle and set up a trap we had scent blockers on and waited in place. We knew she would pass and waited for her name I heard mentioned was Julie, as she got closer to my men and I, they moved in as I saw her shake her head and turn around o check I reacted with speed, I backhanded her hard she didn't give up easily she fort but after she kneed me in the balls that bitch was going down. I shot her knocking her out, I knew she would sleep a while with the dosage we gave her. I had a plan formulated in my mind, now was the time to put it into action. I left my son in charge at the field where the herd was found along with the husband of this one, I had captured she will be baited to lure him out of hiding. Once she was loaded up, the short drive up to the others was not long. Pulling her out of the vehicle onto my shoulder into the clearing. I felt her child moving inside as her belly was laid against my chest. I gave her to my son who threw her down onto the floor. I was going to tell him to be careful, as I had formed a plan on the drive up, but it seemed to work, as her husband came out once she was dumped hard onto the floor. After I baited him stroking her face, she surprised me by waking up they put up a fight I had to act fast and put her back to sleep. I saw that Jimmy needed more as I played back the conversation my men listened in, I think they thought, their boss had lost his mind. Well, I soon changed it, as I could tell my recording was not working, I used violence instead. I kicked her in the belly as I knew he would react. He did, as I saw him change before my eyes in the blink of an eye was not a man but a large wolf type of creature, he was huge. I reacted fast before he could rip my throat out and I shot the tranquillizer gun, and it is now lights out for them both. I instructed my men to clean him up after I ordered him killed, make it look like he was killed by a wild animal. I remembered that I had some of Bert's clothes in the back of my vehicle, using some of the clothes in the back. We collected from the hunt that night. I had torn clothes from a hunting party with the scent of lion who almost killed Burt, he is one of my rich clients, he was lucky another was nearby to finish the kill. He got cocky and decided to play with it, by thinking he would slowly use a weapon at a time he had wounded it but that had only pissed it off. The joke was on him as the lion had torn into him as it leapt on his back about to tear him to pieces. At least I can use his soiled clothes to mask this mess up. I ordered my men to use a scent blocker after rubbing as much blood from the lion as he was shot in the back, going all over Bert's shirt. My team and I were in shock when Jimmy was shot with the tranquilizer, he changed back into a human just like us around him. I know time is running out and I needed a plan fast. I needed to cover our tracks. I instructed my men to wipe away any traces of blood, all the footprints and mask away any scents using the scent blocker. We have a lab where I have the best scientists working for me. They have helped in creating scent blockers, it helps us hunt better. I have a dream and I will build upon it. I then look upon the woman, she would not have cooperated. I can see how hard she fought me; she would rather die than give in. I am a sick bastard as I take out my hunting knife as earlier the plan that form in my mind takes place. I called my son over and asked him to bring me some blankets and have the nurses set up and tell them we have a baby coming in who will need medical treatment. He gets on with the task I set for him and comes back with Blankets "All is arranged, Father." Now I am going to cut the baby from her. I need you to clean the scene afterwards to make it look like a beast tore her baby from her womb. I cut her open, tearing through flesh and muscle as I carefully cut closer to the sack of fluid holding the baby, who is human. I pop the fluid and pull the baby out I cut the cord and tie it off wrapping the baby who is a girl into my arms as I wrap her up, and I take her to my truck. I told my driver to step on it. I will let my wife Anya look after her, bring her up, and take care of her as she grows until I can work on what I am good at. I have control over my woman. I allowed Anya too much freedom, I let her in, I showed her how much I loved her, I gave her anything she wanted and how did she repay me? She tried to leave me and take my sons with her. I had her followed, when I was not around or with her, I had my men watching over her every move, and on one of her ventures out she had plotted. She had planned to leave me and move away to her sister's place in Deadwood. I found out about it from my men. I took care of it the only way I know how. By taking control, I confronted her about it, she tried to lie I told her about the conversation she had with her sister that morning. How she told her that I was cruel and that she had men following her. How she had packed and was ready to leave. She had to wait until I left for work, and she could take the boys. She cried and said it was not true. I found the bag she had packed as I told her the only way, I would ever let her go was if she died and I had no intentions of losing her. I love her, she is mine, and as I showed her how much I loved her by carrying her to our bed. Where I worshipped her body, as each tear fell from her eyes I kissed them away, as she screamed, that she hated me. I made her body come repeatedly. She swore to me she would find a way to leave, I made sure she never got the chance to. She is guarded, and I make sure I love her body every night, each night I hold her I make love to her, I make sure she comes every single time. She belongs to me; Anya is the only woman I have ever touched. I will not let anyone near her. She has her suite with a kitchen, bathroom and living space. I have guards on duty. All who dare touch her will die; I am that sick. She is mine! Hopefully, this child will give her life purpose and make her see sense. That everything I do is for her and our sons, they see it, and she will. After I had her sister killed, and her parent's died in an accident while travelling. She has me, she has our sons now she will have this baby as our own. I will teach her to obey me, like I have done with my sons. My word is the only one that matters around here, and Anya knows that now.

CHAPTER FIVE:

Alpha Max

My enforcers alerted me that both Jimmy and Julie were found near to the herd dead. I was shocked to my core; I did not waste any time I sent a crew to meet me there and I drove up to the fields. What I found there was distressing. I saw Julie with her bump ripped open. She has had her womb taken, it looks like a beast came by and tore into her abdomen. My pack sniffs the area and has concluded that they can smell the herd of unicorns and a Neeman Lion as they run the scene in wolf shape. I look at Julie first and my heart is breaking for her children, her beautiful soul has left and only tragedy is here instead. I know this will devastate her Alpha and pack mates. She has two children who have now lost their mother. I touch her, laying her neatly on the ground. As I check her over for any other wounds. Her hands have small markings like she punched something. I checked her nails and found a little bit of blood under them. I ask for a bag as I clip her nails to see if I can get any traces of blood. I took off her shoes and checked her feet and she had bruising on her right foot. Strangely, as I look over her abdomen, I notice that the area has jagged teeth marks around it, and I can see benign her the floor is moist. Blood and water mixed into the earth below as if she had been laid on the ground and lifted or moved away. I couldn't understand what had happened. I sniff the ground beneath her body as I carefully turn her over. I can smell metal, but it is faint there is just a hint of it, which has been hidden beneath her with some kind of scent blocker. We are in the warm season and nothing about this scene makes any sense, she looks as though she has been torn open. I sent a team out to all the creatures around the area to see if any have been nearby, I check and track any footprints in and around the area to see if any belong to Julie or Jimmy. Afterwards, I asked my men to fan out and check the trees and the grass the bushes nearby. The herd needs checking, has any gone missing? have any been killed? I ordered my team to look everywhere. I look upon Jimmy next and he has had his throat torn out by looking at his neck and he has wounds as though he was mauled. He is further away from his mate. If Julie had been attacked first, he would have gone into a rage, and changed into his wolf. There would be blood everywhere from the attacker and Jimmy. I could not put my finger on it, but my gut is telling me something else happened here. We have no creatures nearby according to all the data I had my pack collect all were in the areas we had moved each pack of creatures to. There are no normal animals, Lions or Tigers Bears that can inflict damage to our kind. We are too tough, we can beat them easily. Even if one did come here my pack would have noticed, we have patrols all over the perimeter. I told my Beta, who is ready to retire soon, to arrange a watch over the area until further notice: I have another one of my team Brock, he is only twenty-two, he has a mate and has a child on the way. He has been chosen by the pack and I, to take over when it is my time to retire unless Ali is strong enough after her growth phase which we have plenty of time to discover. Brock is the strongest wolf we have, he is growing in strength and becoming a good replacement for me when it is my time to hand over the reins. He has been my shadow since he mated and has been learning the ropes. His father is one of my head enforcers, he is a good fighter and helps train the pack. The Beta son is strong and will be a good beta, for Brock when the time comes. I asked Brock his thoughts" What do you think"? "I can't smell any beast tracks in the area," "The animal has the scent of a lion, but no lion could take out a wolf or do this type of damage. It looks like an attack, a Neeman lion, or ordinary lion, a stray one we have not noticed yet" Good, I praise him. I can see it in his face he is as baffled as I am, he must be feeling fearful as he has his mate with a child to protect. "Brock, I want you to leave here and go and spend time with your mate and seek comfort from each other.""This scene is the worst scene our kind has ever seen. I want you to take time off to be around your mate and wait until your child is born, she has not got much longer left. I know that when I need to break the news to all the packs it will be hard on you both. I would like you to stay in the pack house though until I think it is safe for all of us to be alone," As Brock leaves, I send another team member to arrange that each with children under fourteen and with any who are with child to move into the pack house and the Beta's home where we have more of us for protection and comfort. I want the suites set up ready. I could not allow any of our pack to lose their mates. "Yes Alpha, it will be done." I need to take care of the bodies and arrange for them both to have a traditional service as I do not want to transport them home. It is too dangerous for our kind to be exposed. I will not rest until I find out who or what is responsible. I need to now make the radio call to the families. An Alpha task, that I am dreading, but I will have to inform Alpha Henry that his brother and sister-in-law are dead and that they lost their loved ones to a creature attack and how saddened we all are. Their pack Alpha Gerald that he has lost his peace enforcers in horrific circumstances and that he will have to break the news to both children that Jimmy and Julie worshipped. I would like to supply proof if this is not as it seems. I will order extra patrols and make sure all my pack stays in our forest only. No wood walks just to be safe pack runs will be in our forest and all training will be held at the centre. Guards will patrol the city and I will place the team on patrol once I have the creature's numbers alongside the Unicorns, maybe a clearer picture will be more clear. I will not stop until I am satisfied, I will never ignore my gut as it is never wrong. I have a moment to allow myself to feel the loss, the morning before they both left, I am devastated, and I know I will weep there loss as will we all. I will hug my baby girl Ali tighter tonight as I must shield her from what has happened today. I Kiss Julie and Jimmy on top of their heads as I vow to them both I will uncover the truth, and I will try to get justice for each of your children, your families, and your pack. As I allow each of them to be taken to help arrange their funeral my team and I focus on finding out as much as we can from the scene and area. When I moved to where the buggy was found I walked around the whole area taking in the footprints that belonged to both Jimmy and Julie as well as the path they took to get to the herd. I am taken to an area uncovered by my beta, where he has found land that has had a scuffle or fight in the area. Once I reach the land I can see the way the branches have snapped, the leaves are placed as though it had been fort on, and the scents have been messed with to trick our senses. I scented the whole area of the floor.dirt and as I moved some of the leaves I found something my first clue. It is a small piece of technology that I have never seen before I pocket it to add into my safe, as something of interest I know that whoever did this has done a very good job at hiding what happened. I know I now have a lead, and I will find more and until I have answers I will keep searching until my last breath.

FATED DREAMS: BOOK ONE
Anna and Hayden.

CHAPTER ONE. Anna
CHAPTER TWO. Anna
CHAPTER THREE. Anna
CHAPTER FOUR. Hayden
CHAPTER FIVE. Anna
CHAPTER SIX. Anna
CHAPTER SEVEN. Hayden
CHAPTER EIGHT. Anna
CHAPTER NINE. Hayden
CHAPTER TEN. Anna
CHAPTER ELEVEN. Hayden
CHAPTER TWELVE. Anna
CHAPTER THIRTEEN. Hayden
CHAPTER FOURTEEN. Anna
CHAPTER FIFTHEEN. Anna
CHAPTER SIXTEEN. Hayden
CHAPTER SEVENTEEN. Anna
CHAPTER EIGHTEEN. Hayden
CHAPTER NINETEEN. Anna

CHAPTER ONE

Anna

My name is Anna Harris, and I am a member of the Ashwood pack. My world consists of several islands we call them the Wolf Islands. We believe that our creation is to protect, and we still follow on with that belief as our ancestors did. We exist to keep all those in our world safe, we are the only ones who have the gift to be able to change forms. I am from the Griffin Island, which is one of the five that we travel between, using ships, and boats. With time we have gained more knowledge, and we have built strong relationships with all who live on each of the Islands. We have built good relationships with each pack and help protect all residents from the dangerous creatures and the animals that live there. The islands are called Flame Island, Keel Island, Bear Island, Beast Island, and Vale Island. I am from a town I live in Ashwood. All the packs across the islands are named after the place they live in. My Dad is the Alpha of our pack, and my mother is known as the Alpha female. I am a shapeshifter, and I can switch forms between my human body into the body of my wolf. Our wolf has been part of us since birth, we only start to fully shift forms after the growth phase, also known in human terms as puberty. During the growth phase, for a whole month, we start to be able to shapeshift. Once the growth phase is over, we stabilize and can carry on as we did before just with our wolves being free. Our Alpha, and Beta, help each of us learn how to control our shapeshifting from our human shape to our wolves. We find it hard to control as we tend to shapeshift a lot during the growth phases. We must learn how to control it with practice, enabling control when we can shift. During this time when we stay on pack land, it helps keep us away from being exposed and protects us from any attacks from the creatures as during this time we are more vulnerable.in our forest and the Centre to be with others of our kind to gain better knowledge of our changing shapes, it helps as we get to learn, play, walk, run and how to hunt how to track and how to hide if needed and how to switch quickly. We stay there to help keep our secret away from any humans as well. Anyone who is seen in fear, when we have so many dangerous creatures, we share our world with, which puts us in the category of dangerous, because we shapeshift. We have lived amongst humankind since the dawn of time. We believe we exist to protect as we have many dangerous creatures that share our world. We are the only ones who can battle the creatures and keep them away from entering civilizations. In our history books, we have always called ourselves protectors of all kinds. We are strong and kind. We live and work like all humans do, we all go to school to learn, and we have jobs, and we help build. As time has gone on, we have adapted and learned alongside our human neighbours. We go shopping, we have holidays by visiting the coast. As we live amongst humans, we are also human, we limit ourselves to doing pack runs once a month. We do have the ability to change whenever we feel our wolf needs to be free, we will go on pack lands to do so. We have a huge forest which has a training centre we use for training and controlling our Wolves in the growth phase. We have many lakes, trees, and lots of diverse types of nature. We have rare, varied creatures that live amongst the other animals, all are important, to keep nature's balance. We have normal wolf packs that run with us each month they enjoy joining us, it's fun. We have Deer, Rabbits, Hair, Boars, Horses, and Unicorns those are rare, but they do exist, we have small herds we have been hiding. To keep their numbers from dying out, humans want their little girls to have them to ride on, but they are not like normal horses they are wilder and like to be free they can use their horns as a defense to protect that can be harmful, especially young children. We have Bonnacons, they are like wild bull creatures with horns. If they are in large packs when frightened, they can hurt you. Especially if they charge at you and fall you can lose a limb or bleed out. Chupacabra are like our bears but are smaller than usual bears, and they are hairless beasts that could become hostile if provoked. We have bears of all distinct species, and we have some bigger, wilder bears who you do not want to come across; we call them Callisto. They are large, and they are the worst to fight off, especially if they are mating or have cubs. We have many types of birds. Thunderbirds. They can shoot lightning. They are big, and often seen more when we have heavy rain. They tend to add these white strikes of light across the sky. That's why we call them lightning birds. Humans named them Thunderbirds. We have Neeman lions, and we have many lion species, but the Neeman ones are tougher than the normal lions. We've had a few scuffles on pack runs with these beasts. They are stubborn and hard to fight off alone. You must be a strong enforcer, a Beta, or an Alpha, to take them down. We try not to go near their territory, but they have been known to hunt humans and we do our best to protect them. We have Griffins that live further towards the sea, we have an area where no humans live, and we leave them there to be free. We have patrols check on them as they only attack if they feel threatened; if they like you, they will let you ride on them. I have never had the pleasure, but my dad had when he was a boy my grandfather took him. Many years ago, one of the Neeman lions had settled closer to where the humans like to hike and enjoy nature. My dad had to rehome him and his mate. The beast had injured a human who was hiking in the woods around the town when he came across one. It charged and bit his leg trying to drag him away from his territory. Luckily, Dad was nearby looking at some land to build log cabins for tourists as we have a beautiful lake that has plenty of land surrounding it. Humans like to fish there and have boats and fun races, like paddle boarding and rowboat races. Dad heard the animal as our hearing was heightened thanks to our wolves. Dad just managed to tranquilize the animal, and he sent Bradley, our beta, over to collect the beast and its mate. He took them back to our forest. The Neeman lion was only protecting his mate who was heavily pregnant with cubs. They now live in the caves near a lake right at the end of our territory. So far, we have had little contact. It is the young males looking for mates that give us the most trouble, we must work as a pack to move them along. They are annoying at times but that's nature. We have Snakes, amongst many other species like Lizards and Frogs, Toads, Reptiles and all the usual types. Our other rarest creatures we have are Phoenix's, they come out more in the summer months like now is our hot season and if you are lucky enough to see them, we are honored they showed themselves to us. The worst and most dangerous are the beasts we picked that name. Humans are useless against them, they are two-headed huge creatures with fur, and teeth that can easily rip you apart. They have large paws with huge claws that hold you in place. We rehomed the beast on our land in the mountains, far away from us and Humankind. We have patrols check on them, and we make sure they have a food source and that they have water and can make a nest inside the mountains. We normally move them deep in the mountains, it takes a lot of tranquillizer guns and plenty of teamwork to handle these creatures. We like to call ourselves Wolf shifters or shapeshifters, I live at home with my father who is our pack Alpha, Gerald Harris. My mother Annabel and my brothers, Adam and Abel, who are my protective, pain in the arse, typical older brothers. They drive me crazy; they think I am still five years old and need constant babysitting. One of my best friends and pack member Jade lives with us as well as her younger brother Ethan. They both lost their parents due to an accident over five years ago. They are both part of our family unit now, I love them just as much as the rest of my family. My other packmate and best friend is Cara, she and I were both born on the same day, both of our mothers are best friends, and they work at the local hospital. They also keep the pack healthy by running clinics just for our kind in the hospital, only wolf shifters work on the ward that houses the clinic. We can suffer monthly cramps like all girls, and we can get injured, hurt or even killed. But as for normal human illnesses, we don't catch them. Our wolves help us battle any infections. Cara and I are both excited as we get to travel to the city and catch up with friends and family. We are spending two nights in the city, relaxing as much as we can away from taking exams at our school. There have been a lot of revision tests, and we are trying our best to do well. There have been endless studying and sleepovers as we have all been testing each other. My girls are my family too, we are all pack mates as well as my best friends we have all grown up together. We do have friends from school who are fully human. Lisa, Becca, and Ellie. As well as Natalie and Simon, who is also my dance partner at school, his girlfriend Becca is so sweet, they are both in our year at school. It was Becca who helped me find Simon as my partner in the dance, he has a good natural ability in hip hop, and he can perform all the major moves. He has taught me well and with my gymnastics background, we have a cool hip-hop routine to show our year and all our loved ones. Simon introduced Dale to Jade. He is good at contemporary dance. He has helped Jade express her grief through the art of dance. They became friends in the first year of high school, thanks to Simon. I think Dale has helped her a lot, he has her focus all her pent-up emotions on her dance, but I also think he would date her if she ever saw him as anything other than a friend. She is an amazing dancer; she puts a lot of her heart and soul into it. We all have a big show on our last day at school, we have individual pieces. Zoe and I are doing gymnastics, a floor-based routine, and then we each have a dance routine as we have a paired performance. Zoe will team up with Luke. Luke and Dale are best friends. They met each other through junior school and became friends with Simon who they met through dance school. They introduced all of us to Mattio.

His parents own a dance school, and he has been dancing since childhood. He knows all styles of dance, he helped the guys with their routines as they grew into stronger capable dancers. "They all met when we enrolled. We were teenagers, and my dad thought it might help Jade deal with her loss. We all needed to focus our minds on all the pain, it was tough as we all felt the loss. Matteo has helped bring Cara out of herself and out of her comfort zone. It has taken him time, but he has shown her how to express herself by using her hips and sensually moving her body. They have a Latin dance that they are performing, she is short with red hair," he tells Cara all the time, "to bring the fire." you may be short, but you are strong. Zoe, my other packmate and best friend, is tough, she is a firecracker, and she gets us all into trouble as she has issues with being told what to do. I blame her sister Zara. Both are trained fighters, and their dad owns the gym where he runs fights on the weekends. Zara is now a co-owner. Zoe does not take any shit; she has learned to be more graceful as Luke has learned her control. He lifts her a lot as they do swing dancing and rock and roll, which is an old dance from the early 20's and 40's, but the two of them have made it their own by adding in their moves to update it to a more modern age. Zoe introduced Luke to our friend Ellie, who had a rough experience with her ex-boyfriend. He was taught a lesson by my bestie Zoe. She was the one who helped Ellie move on by introducing her to Zoe's dance partner and friend, Luke, who is one of the best guys. Her solo performance will be gymnastics like mine. It will be graded as our P.E. choice as we get to choose what we wish to present at our event. Another event is working with another in partnership, then we get to perform as a team. We have drama doing a play after our dance show. We have a full-on week of sports and drama in the last week of school. It will be fun. Our teacher Miss Fields, who is human, and Mr. McBride, who is from our pack, will be there to help cheer us on as they have taught us P.E. Cara and I turn eighteen on Saturday we are so excited, and as we get to spend time with our friends and our family as well as our pack. Our whole pack helps us celebrate each year, we also bring any friends from school as we like to mix our worlds to fit in with our fully human neighbours. On Saturday when we both turn eighteen, we are planning to have our party in the city called Darlington. It is where our best friend Jade's Uncle lives with his family. Henry Sanderson is the Alpha of the Darlington pack Wendy his mate and wife is Alpha female, they are both Jade's and Ethan's uncle and aunt. They have two twin daughters who are double the trouble. The twins are called Sara and Sally. Henry lost his brother Jade, and Ethan's, dad Jimmy Sanderson, whose mother was called Julie, they both sadly died just over five years before some sort of accident. Julie was pregnant at the time, and she was okayed to travel. Max had a healer and nurse on duty after he lost his wife during labour. He had everything prepared if Julie labored early. He vowed it would never happen to anyone on Vale Island again. Where he is the city's Alpha they travelled over, just checking on the number of packs and if any mating's were found. Checking in before the gathering was due to take place the following month. Sadly, after it happened, all the packs went over for the funeral. We don't know the full story, but I have heard my parents talking. They know Max has taken their loss hard as it was an accident involving the Neeman lions who attacked them. We know that it leaves a hole in all the packs, losing any pack mate is hard, especially as it's rare. We see Jade and Ethan's Aunt and Uncle regularly as well as their twin daughters, as they often will holiday with us in the summer months. They are lovely, warm, kind, and honest. They are family and much-loved pack members. Their pack is called pack is named Darlington as the territory is known as the city of Darlington. Our mothers and Jade's aunt and cousins have planned everything, alongside our other friends Zoe, and her older sister Zara. The past few weeks have been busy, we all have our final exams over the next two weeks of our school term. My friends and I have been trying our best to get in as much studying as we can on top of training at the gym, and dance practice making sure our routine is performed perfectly. We try and train together at least three times a week at the gym, we dance and do partner work most Sunday mornings along on Friday after school we do our solo practice. We spent the whole weekend at my house studying, the girls normally stay over. As pack mates, we like to sleep at each other's homes, and we try and get together as much as we can. We always fall asleep in my room or the family's pool house which has a huge bed. We like to cuddle up and talk about boys away from my brothers who like to eavesdrop, as much as they can to annoy us all. We come out here and we get a lot of schoolwork completed as well as a lot of chatting in, we do sit upstairs in the main house either in mine or Jade's bedrooms. We try to relax and chill afterwards with a movie we even let Ethan stay with us, as we enjoy spending quality time with him. All the girls wanted to see their parents and decided to spend the night at home. I'm about to go to sleep as I have school tomorrow. I set my alarm just in case, Jade normally barges in as usual to wake me up. Jade is sleeping in her room tonight after she has done reading to Ethan knowing Jade, she probably will just stay with him. It's an important part of your pack life to bond via comforting each other, touch is important to us, and a sleep pile is the best way to feel the love of your pack mates. We all do it, especially us girls. It helps strengthen our bond as a pack, but also as best friends. The past few weeks whenever I have fallen into a deep sleep, I keep having the same dream each night. I am always in the woods at the back of our house I am always alone, I see him, he has started to become my everything, his scent teases my nose, my wolf relaxers whenever she feels he is close, she feels he is important to us. I lay down and closed my eyes, I fell asleep not long after my head hit the pillow. I am back outside behind my house walking on the pathways in the woods, I love the scent of the trees, and I can smell all the wildflowers that grow in the fields nearby. The path is a solid path made from the land it has small grass patches and hardened soil.

With leaves that have blown from the trees crunching beneath my feet. There are bushes and grass between each tree, with patchers of large leaves that give the woods their scent. Hearing the leaves swaying in the breeze, I love being able to walk and take in the sounds. I always hear the animals going about their day the sounds they make talking to each other. In the woods in the spring, when new life is born, you can hear the babies crying for food their mothers hunt to find, while their fathers stay guard. I can hear bugs, bees, and birds, my hearing is heightened as I am part wolf shifter, and my hearing is better than a typical human. My wolf half allows me to change and be able to enjoy what a wolf enjoys. The freedom of being able to be free amongst nature, to run, hunt, play, and be carefree. I do not hunt, as in a way to kill another animal although I could, we can cook and buy food. I eat enough in human form, my wolf is never hungry enough, but it does still enjoy the ability to hunt. To track, to fight, to learn to use my nose to smell, not only animals but even humans and us shapeshifters leave scent trials behind. I love spending time enjoying life experiencing friendships, going to school, and learning to become whatever I want to be as I am human too. Even with the history of our ancestor's knowledge, that we are incredible hunters who hunted to feed their families and pack, we used to do pack hunts and share the spoils from the hunt, using fur for warmth, and meat for food. We would trade the spoils that we had spare, for other items that the pack needed. We have moved forward, and as time has moved forward, we are much more civilized nowadays, than our past ancestors. We grow as evolution has grown, with our kind, alongside humankind. We grow the same as humans have grown and developed, we are much more advanced with each century that passes, we adapt learn more skills, and technology advances and we progress with it. There are more humans than there are our kind, but we have managed to coexist, for hundreds of generations. To let all our pack mates know who each child belongs with, as with fated pairings we bite to say here is my wife, we are mated, she is mine, and I am hers. We as a pack use our runs to play and hunt to bond with each other as pack mates. We mark our land to warn away any dangerous predators and to let them know we are pack, and we have ownership of these lands. We are all trained on how to fight, in case we may need to protect If we have a dangerous creature in our area that needs to be put back in its place, we learn to work as a team to keep harm away from civilization. We believe we are created for the protection of the Wolf Islands, for all who live on them. Any issues that do arise between us will be dealt with by our Alpha and Beta teams who will help resolve any problems within our pack. Our young are cared for as all children don't get their wolves until after puberty. That is why we have patrols and caregiver enforcers, they will take our children to school, and pick them up, we have teachers who work in the schools as well as humans. Caregiver enforcers are strong, they will fight to the death if it's required to protect our children and any human children who are in any danger. We have a few centers that provide childcare services for working parents and families. We do this as humans know there are dangerous animals in the woodlands, and they know that we teach each child with safety talks and provide fighting classes as part of our childcare program. We integrate our children alongside our human neighbours, and it helps us be a community where we take care of each other. If any issues or resources are needed each pack tries to offer some form of help. Travelling around each pack, sending well wishes, our kind is needed to carry on protecting our world from the beasts that only our kind can kill if needed. We try to keep track of the worst beast, the others, a much feared two-headed beast that hunts humankind and our kind we call them the beast. They are homed away from any civilization. They are too dangerous to be near any of us. I am walking along the pathway enjoying the beauty of the day, I have now reached the middle of the woods. The sun has risen it shines brightly in the sky above, I see we have fresh leaves regrown from the fall. I am always walking in these woods. I normally walk in these woods with my pack friends, my sisters from another Mr. Cara, Jade, and Zoe. Sometimes our friends from school will join us. When it's hot we all go swimming in the lake, with its fresh water and mini waterfall it's a perfect place to relax in. We have patrols nearby to protect us from any of the animals or the creatures that may venture nearby. It feels strange being here alone, I am enjoying the heat on my face. Looking around at the wildlife, enjoying the scents of the trees, grass, and wildflowers. Listening to the sounds of the creatures rustling, in the grass, hiding amongst the bushes, it is always so peaceful. I love the way my wolf calms, and just allows my human half to be able to walk at a leisurely pace. I can hear the birds in the treetops talking to each other, singing their morning songs. I can hear the bugs flying around. The horses in the fields further ahead, the unicorns further up the river stomping and playing. The trees are swaying in the light breeze, the grass is rustling, and I can hear the roar of the river flowing down into the lakes. Strange, it feels like someone is out there, watching, waiting, yet I can't see anyone visibly nearby. After staying still, listen for any movement. After holding my breath for a few seconds, I still cannot hear anything out there. I decide to continue walking, my pace picks up. My only intention is to reach the river. Normally I would see my brother Abel there, with his friends. The pack runs patrols, nearby to where I am walking. Our territory normally has patrols on duty. I could hear them earlier just walking, I could smell who each pack mate was and who was on duty. Now I hear nothing, smell not one single member of my pack, and my heart rate starts to increase its speed it has picked up in both dread and fear, after I started to resume breathing normally again my breathing seemed so loud to my ears. I checked over my shoulder one last time, and when I turned back around, I ended up faceplanting into a solid, hard chest belonging to a male not from my pack, not a regular human either, he smelled incredible like heat, home. I take another deep breath in, I smell the most heavenly scent, it smells of crisp, spicy, warm, safe comforting scent. It is like my whole-body shudders, I want to roll around in this intoxicating scent. It smells strong, powerful, of pure strength and pure heated male. I feel my wolf has become more alert like she knows him but hasn't figured out what or who he is to me. As I am about to look up, to see his face, I hear a voice in my head, which says 'soon.' I jolt awake. I am sweating, my pajamas are soaking in sweat, and I feel my heart beating a little erratic as if I have been running. For the past few weeks, I have been having the same dream. Most nights I am always in the woods near my house, they lead from the back of our garden towards the bigger more denser parts of the woods. I never see his face, I smell him, I always try each time I dream, to hold onto his scent, to see if I recognize the scent from another pack so far, I haven't been able to find it. I stretch out my body and blink away the sleep from my eyes. I checked the time on my alarm clock it is 7 am time to get ready for school. As I head towards my bathroom, I relieve myself and turn the shower on, while I await the water to get warm. I brush my teeth, and after my shower, I like to moisturize my body. I have a slim curvy body, with slightly smaller breasts than the other girls. I tied my straight light brown hair up into a high ponytail. I apply eyeliner across the top of my eyelids, with slightly thicker ends to tick. Which helps to make my blue eyes pop, I brush a touch of mascara across my lashes and apply pink gloss to my lips. I spray my favorite perfume on the back of my wrist and behind my ears. Picking out my uniform for school. My uniform is simple. I wear Slim black trousers, with a white shirt and part of the uniform includes a blue tie. I slipped my feet into some comfortable low-heeled black shoes. We are in the middle of the summer term, and in two weeks my friends and I will have taken all our exams. It has been hard to practice and to make sure I have done as much as I can to pass all my subjects. I want to enjoy the summer holidays before working at our family business. We have all been helping each other as we all have dreams of what we would like to do after school finishes. My friends and I are in the same year group, we have most of our classes together. We are the same age, just a few weeks apart. Cara and I have our birthdays on the same day. Jade turned eighteen last month, and so far, she hasn't been ready to find her mate just yet. Zoe is the youngest of our group she isn't eighteen until after exams finish which is two weeks after mine and Cara's but hey, it's still two weeks younger than us. Jade always teases how much younger she is compared to us three even though it's a few weeks. We are like sisters, we are always together, from birth, and we love each other. We may not be blood relatives, but we are pack, we are family. Cara is our responsible friend, the voice of reason, that one friend who would not suggest breaking the rules. She can be shy and when she gets embarrassed, she blushes beetroot red, she has the kindest heart and she gives good advice, the kind of advice Zoe should follow not to mention Jade with her pranks. Cara makes us all laugh, she has brains, she can type at speed, has good communications with others, and has a gentle personality, a girl next door beauty, her body is soft, yet she has feminine curves. With her long wavy red hair, she has the most beautiful hazel eyes, she is an intelligent, softly spoken, classic beauty that shines throughout. She has freckles across her nose that are so cute, and her skin is pale, but she can tan if the sun is out, she is like me in that way my skin is tanned. She has a stunning booty with boobs that are at least a C cup not too large, just perfect for her figure. She will be an amazing asset to my dad's company after graduation. She always follows our Alpha and Beta rules without questioning my dad Gerald Harris or our pack Beta, Bradley Anderson. She used to also follow whatever Adam said, whenever he said no to us, or asked me where I was going. Cara would break, he always asked her if I wouldn't tell him or if we all were going which was all the time none of us would say we would pinky swear. but Cara ended up not being able to when he asked her. She would break and reveal all he knew she would. He will become our pack's next Alpha when dad is ready to retire. He always managed to manipulate Cara into telling him he would use the fact he was going to be her Alpha soon and the fact she is vulnerable and not able to use her shapeshifting as a protection against all the dangers. She would put the rest of us in danger as we would protect her at all costs endangering us all further. We never made her feel bad as we blamed Adam. Cara over the past few months, has started ignoring him, she has started to not give in no matter how hard he tries, I think we have all rubbed off on her he gets so annoyed at her as he used to be able to manipulate her and now, she is stronger and more confident she knows we all are tough enough to protect ourselves. Matteo, her dance partner, has helped her grow. He has brought her out of her shell a lot more given her encouragement and confidence to be a beautiful woman using Latin dance and the moves they use. It's taken years but these past few months she has put in all he has taught she now uses her sex appeal that is needed to pull off her dancing. Matteo has been building her confidence and helping her perform through dances to be herself, to express herself and who she wants to be, not what she thinks she must be. She has always been shy and meek hiding her body keeping her head down and not breaking any rules been a goodie for two shoes. She is still working on it, trying to be more confident. Cara has not been able to shift into her wolf, but she does have the gene in her DNA she has the strength, speed and agility of a shifter. We believe it is a birth defect that is due to our wolf side, we believe it is a wolf defect. What we have learned so far from our history books, is that once she finds her fated mate. Once she is bitten during the mating process, it will trigger her wolf to be able to appear, to enable Cara to switch forms, to be able to switch from human to wolf to be able to be part of the enforcers who protect our land. She is classed as a child in the sense that she is vulnerable to some of the animals we have, especially the beast, as we call them. To be fully free to feel the rush of letting our wolves run, chase, and play is such an exhilaration to have that ability. She has struggled, especially when we all changed, and she couldn't. Zoe is our group's Gossip she never stops talking either. Zoe likes to kick butt just like the males in our pack, she has a major attitude especially when it comes to authority. She has the same courage and attitude as my brother Abel. She never quits, and she is one of our strongest fighters. Her Dad John and Sister Zara own their gym in town, it is where we all go to learn to fight in our human forms. It has an M.M.A. cage, a boxing ring, a combat studio and a modern gym are all on the first floor. Up on the second floor is a whole space for running laps and learning self-defense and varied fighting techniques. Downstairs is where our pack fights, we fight each other to make it more fun we will fight for Cash with the other town's packs. It is an effective way to learn more skills while fighting stronger, faster opponents. We all like to place bets, on who will win they always let us attend it helps us learn more effective fighting skills as well as be able to form bonds with each pack. We are wolf-shaped shifters, our wolf part needs that balance to be allowed to fight, to keep calm and to burn off any excess energy and aggression. It also helps keep our fighters safe, especially with the dangers we fight against to protect our pack and humankind. We have fights where human fights take place on Saturdays, and we all like to watch and bet on those, we have seen some good levels of skill, and it is fun to be able to live and fit in as one existence. We also do mixed fights where just our human form is used, and no skills from our wolves are allowed. This helps us stay balanced with regular humans. It helps us blend in more, by slowing down our bodies to fight and learn in our human shape but also helps humans get better at fighting. John makes sure you're evenly matched up to the correct ability when fighting in mixed fights. When we fight packs in human form we can use our wolf's strength, endurance, speed, all the ability and agility of our wolves in those fights. We have pack matches on different days when the gym closes. We stay in our human form more often than our wolf form especially where there are more populated areas of humans. We must be able to coexist for our survival to remain hidden and still be able to protect our wolf forms to help keep the land and our territory safe, we keep our wolves out of sight and hidden from humans. Zoe has long curly blonde hair, with deep brown eyes, and her skin is pale. She has a feminine curved booty with boobs and incredibly toned abs. She has a beautiful heart. She is protective, but she is just as fierce as the males are, Zoe is just as protective even with the girls in our school who are both pack or who are regular humans. Zoe does not react well to any guys, mistreating any of the girls in our school. She has ways of making the guys involved pay by exposing them, for who they are. If they cheat, she will get them back by pinching their clothes after sports. She takes everything and dumps them. It's funny as they just have a towel to hide away their bodies. If they hit another girl, they are dating by being abusive in any way at all. She takes them down by sparring at her family's gym. She offers them the prize money her share, as well as their own if she loses. She never loses, that's her fighting skills she is not using her wolf for help, but using the skills she has learned being pure human. We can sense human arousal. We can scent who the person is, and their girlfriend's scent blends with their boyfriends. If we smell another female's scent on a male, who is in a relationship we know via that scent if it has been intimately. We know that this guy has been unfaithful. The male wolf shifters smell arousal, it can be embarrassing for us female wolf shifters. At least as a human, you are not aware of it. You can have an attraction for another and not even know you smell interested. When we are aroused the males in our pack can smell it. We females can only smell it on regular humans. It is the hormones they produce during sex; we also can smell if the human is married, or in a relationship as the hormones and scents mix. Like our kind, when we mate it is for life we blend into each other's scent, each mated pair have their scent. It can be very awkward, for us female wolves, but as it's part of nature to us we have learned to tone the scenting part down. It's about being able to shift through scents and learning to ignore the scent of arousal to the other scents in the room instead. If we are in heat, which is the most fertile time to produce a baby with our mates, we can want to mate more often as we have a burning desire, to produce, if not stated, it can be painful for the female. We can only have children with our Fated mates. Most produce children who can shift, in rare cases like Cara's condition, to be unable to shift after puberty. Our only way to protect ourselves from pregnancy during the heat is for the male to wear a condom or use the pull-out method the male must make the female orgasm for the heat to settle and soothe the pain the heat can cause. Luckily the heat only lasts two days a month. If our Fated mate dies, the other who lives can choose to mate again with another, who has suffered the same fate. But unfortunately, they can't produce children they can be in love and can bond and stay belonging to each other. Our healers do their best to try and save as much of our kind as they can, but we can die especially if we get injured fighting some of the creatures or with the beasts. If a healer arrives in time, we can be saved but if we lose a limb, it can't be grown back. If we fall in love via our human half after losing our Fated mate and choose to get married to be content being human, we can't produce a child, but we can be happy. Normally a mate connection is better for our wolves as they can keep being part of the pack. It is hard to not accept your fated mate, once you find them your wolf won't allow you to keep hurting them. If the human half fights the bond, which some do, as they want to enjoy the freedom of being human and crave that need to choose for themselves. Eventually, the wolf will be forced to bite and mark the mate without sex. It's how the wolf lets the female wolf know they will be together, once the human part stops being an idiot. Zoe will be like her sister Zara, a good enforcer for our pack. They are both strong, skilled fighters, they are both able to take down men twice their size using purely human strength, with their wolves' help they are good. I can't wait to see what she will grow up to become. With John as their dad, they will be skilled assets to our pack alongside our highest-ranking enforcers. This is all Zoe wants to be known as, not just for her looks as she has a stunning figure, she has had to prove to even some pack members she may be small, but she is also mighty. She has been training from being little like her sister, they are both protective towards us all even our human friends and fellow neighbours. Zoe is the one you want in your corner she always looks after the females she hates that the guys in our pack think they can do as they please, but do not allow us the same freedom. She stands up against authority if she is passionate enough about it. Sometimes it gets her in trouble, she is a hellcat, and she has claws when they are needed. Yet she has such a good heart she would rather her suffer than another. I love her for it.

CHAPTER TWO

Anna

Zoe's favourite topic now is to talk about is Mr. Anderson, who is our pack Beta. Mr. Anderson's first name is Bradley. Who is to me and my friends the ultimate hottie, he has not found his fated mate just yet. Once we reach thirty if we still haven't found our fated mates by then, the records will be looked at to see who has died, the age at which they died, and when and what happened. That is why our peace enforcers are important, all this information is shared and stored in the records providing information that is needed. We found out through our history records that a pack member has died. If another pack member has not been able to find their fated mate, then it is a perfect way to enable happiness to be found via a mate bond. This happened a lot in our history, in the earlier years when packs didn't know other islands and other packs existed. When we learned to travel and meet others like us, we built relationships with one another. As our kind almost died out, without fated mates no offspring could be born. With the creatures we were killed off, we needed each other to form fated mates and to breed and grow back our numbers. This is why we started trading between packs, why we fight to protect against creatures and the beasts, why we decided to get along, our packs must do regular gatherings. For each pack to be able to travel between packs to look for fated mates, by the time you reach thirty you will have interacted with every single pack around the world. The biggest age gap between fated mates is twelve years, normally eighteen is the earliest a fated mate is found as that is adulthood, by thirty most of the fated mates have met, and know they are each other's fated, even if one-half is not ready to bond just yet. They still know their mate is alive and awaiting the mating process. Bradley has only just turned twenty-seven, and the chances are he will find his mate in the next two years at most, as more of the pack's females become of age. He is tall, and muscular in the way that you see in another who has dieted and trained hard, he is naturally muscular. His arms do it for me, we daydream about him when we are all together even Zara joins us when we discuss Bradley. He has short mousy brown hair, he has blue eyes, he is tall, and he can fight. He is a strong, skilled fighter, he spars a lot with Adam as he is going to be one tough Alpha. Bradley will be a good beta for Adam when it's time for Adam to take over. Bradley's dad was our Beta, but he stepped down six months ago. He lost his leg during a scuffle he had with Neeman Lion. It was a male looking to steal another male who had found a mate, the other male was trespassing on his territory. Trying to steal what was his ensuring a fight would take place. Our Beta got caught in the crossfire as the beast hadn't come alone, it had a friend. He's fine but decided he wanted to enjoy being less action-filled. He and his mate now run the cabins my dad has built they look after the guests and keep the area in good condition. We have had no major creatures out that way, they have all been relocated. Bradley has joined in the gatherings they are done every year; each pack hosts one. So far, he has not been lucky enough to find her. He's been dating and hooking up now, as Zoe, our gossip queen, has seen him and our P.E. teacher Miss Kelly. She swears she heard them having sex in his office. Zoe has gotten a lot worse since Bradley started teaching our math class. He is covering our pack member Mrs. Jones who is on maternity leave. Ever since he took over, she will do anything in her power to annoy him or try to see how he reacts. We are not savages, any time Bradley has ever punished Zoe, he has done it the same way he punishes any student. On pack land, any rules that are broken or any situation where misbehaviour is new or can expose or be seen as threatening to our kind, or towards each other. The Alpha, or Beta, gets to put a punishment in place. It ranges from being a child taking a toy or banning them from playing for a day or two. Older kids can have cleaning duties to litter picking. As teenagers, it can be washing all the cars the pack has and I mean all the cars. Shopping for our elderly, helping them clean their homes, babysitting kids while their parents have a date night. Adulthood by then we are more able to not mess up. I would not like to piss either my dad or Bradley off. You can sense their wolf's power, in wolf form they are bigger than the rest of the pack. The enforcers are bigger, they sense the power of an Alpha, their first-born son, and Beta and their first-born son are a lot bigger, stronger, faster, tougher. Jade is our glamorous girl, she has dark skin with bright green eyes, and her hair is long and wavy. She is tall, has a booty you could slap, she has bigger breasts than the rest of us, and boy, do we know it. She will show off as much cleavage as she can get away with. Half the guys in school have their tongues hanging out. She is always trying to dress me and Cara up, she says we are too boring with our choice of outfits, and we need to try to push our style choices from the brink of 'nunhood'. We need to bend the rules and live a little. She is also our prankster, she is always getting our group into trouble. She likes to keep us all on our toes. She once swapped out our shampoo with blue rinse extra strong hair dye. Wolves right, you would think our sense of smell would pick it up. She said, "She knows her way around a science lab." She is incredibly good at mixing different ingredients to block scent. It made us look utterly stupid, we were all so mad, but after a while, we learned how to embrace it. We're laughing about it now. The best one so far is the one she pulled on my dad, our Alpha. I never thought she could outsmart my dad, but she got him good. She filled his car up with a strong form of an odour that was so powerful it smelled like sewerage. The smell lasted for over a week. Dad had the car valeted he could not get the smell to clear. How she managed to pull it off, without him knowing as he has a good sense of smell being a shifter. Jade and Ethan live with us, I love having another girl in the house, she always tells my brothers off. Jade is loving, kind and thoughtful. Ethan is the same, he was only three when he moved in with us. They have grown up in our house for just over five years now. They used to stay with us whenever their parents had pack duties. They would drop them over to our house, and Mum and Dad always let the pack stay at our home. It has many suites that have their own living area, bathroom and bedrooms in each. They are for packs, and any visitors so each has their privacy and can bring their children along with them. We have our suites upstairs for the family. Mum and Dad have a private suite that has a spare bedroom. Ethan used to sleep in their suite, but he now has a bedroom with his on suite near Mum and Dad's, and as he gets older, he will have a suite like mine and the others. We all have a bed large enough for multiple people to sleep in, and we have a living area and bathroom, with a walk-in wardrobe in each of our suites we all have our own. Adam, Abel, Jade and I have our suites next to each other. On the left wing, we have a large library and Dad has an office and a large meeting room he uses for pack meetings. His gym in case he can't get to John's gym. We have a swimming pool and a pool house where me and my girls hang out if we want privacy. It is also used for any hookups my brothers may have. Most of our rooms are soundproof and allow privacy. My brothers are nosy especially when my girls are over. Even Zoe's sister Zara comes and stays it helps our wolves, we enjoy being able to see each other and sleeping in the same bed helps when our wolves want to feel safe and loved. Jade likes to sleep in here sometimes with me, but last night she wanted to comfort Ethan, they were reading bedtime stories. She must have fallen asleep. Speaking of Jade, she comes barging into my bedroom, nearly giving me a heart attack." Hey girl what's up"? I was in my mind thinking about my dream, about him, his smell, his muscles, the fact he is tall. I had not even heard her come in. "Hello, Earth to Anna", "Sorry Jade", I was miles away thinking, you know, how I keep having the same dream, but this time he said the word "soon". Not to my face, but into my mind! Last night was the first time he has spoken to me. "He always smells so good Jade" I want to roll around in it. I want to roll around with him in it. My wolf feels warm, secure, and safe, and I feel protected and loved. Jade replies with, "Girl, you have had the same dream the past couple of weeks." You are seriously putting out arousal vibes. You always dream about him, but you can never see his face." You can never look up, why"? He never speaks in this dream of yours. I do not understand why each time you get to the best part of being able to look up. I mean he might be ugly, or old or just not what you imagine him to look like. I mean, what if he has the body of an angel but the personality of an arsehole? I wonder what all these dreams mean if they are trying to tell you something. It could all mean he may just be a fragment of your subconsciousness, with it getting closer to your birthday. I don't know, perhaps he could be your fated Mate, or is he just your mind making up a scenario? "Because you're horny"." Jade, I interrupted really, are we going to have this conversation with our brothers listening"? Jade carries on the conversation as if I never said a thing. It could be your wolf hoping for a hottie, or your wolf is the horny one, or both halves are horny. "I mean, have you ever orgasmed in your sleep about this guy"? With your birthday coming up maybe I can buy you a little friend to help you along in the orgasm variety." Jade really, you must always lower the tone". Jade responded with a "yes well maybe it was what you were both feeling"."Horny"! You girls need to stop being prudes, you need to be able to talk to all of us girls, who will happily help you with your imagination if you know what I mean. At this point Jade wiggles her eyebrows, I can't help but laugh, her favorite subject to talk about is sex or mating, if he brings the goods to make you scream. "If he is a hottie though, where will he come from"? As she pretends to think. I decided my best option is to suggest we head down to breakfast. I can smell Mum's cooking from here, my mouth is watering. Jade said "Okay, let's go eat before Abel and Adam eat it all." Mum has made fresh pancakes with bacon and fresh toast with scrambled eggs. I grab my bag, my dad owns and runs a building company that helps build new energy-efficient houses. They also build hotels, casinos, lodges, and factories. Dad has worked hard building up the family business, adding more types of buildings, hiring more staff and making it as big as it can be. The business has been in our family for two generations. Adam works with Dad, and he knows the ropes, as does Abel. Mum works as our pack's healer, she also works shifts at the Human Hospital in town. Deadwood, the next town over, have to travel to Ashwood for any trips to the hospital their town hasn't got one. Deadwood residents can travel by car, or they can catch the bus. We now have a train service that can take you to each of the towns. They are a new invention that Keel Island developed. We managed to finish all the tracks two years ago and we now can travel faster. We have no stops other than the towns and coastal towns. Each pack has a few enforcers travelling on them in case any beast attacks the tracks or the train. Ashwood our town is full of amazing views and green spaces, and it has plenty of woods and forest, mountains and fields, and our town is large. We have a college. It is beautiful, we have large, wooded areas all over the outskirts of town too. A huge forest that is private and owned by our pack in the center holds our training grounds for our wolf forms. It's huge and has a lake where we hang out, our pack runs there every full moon. A large river which runs through all the towns, towards the coastal towns. Deadwood is slightly smaller, having less land but for humans, has the best nightlife, club's pubs and shops have a lot more varied places to visit than our town does. The other town is Barrington, which is a town much like our own. Then there is Bromwich, another town nearer to the mountains, it has a large pack too as well as beautiful mountains you can ski there as it has a huge ski lodge, the local pack runs. It gets a lot of human visitors, it also has beautiful lakes and woodlands, so the pack gets to enjoy all aspects of their land. Many humans in and around the area live in smaller villages. It has a vast part of valleys in and around the area where the Forest surrounds it with beauty and nature. breathtaking views of the mountains, the pack is large and more able to protect the humans from all the nasty animals that live there. We have a town called Riverton where there is more water. Lakes and Rivers also has a huge natural waterfall Mum and Dad holiday there, and for time alone it has natural springs, the pack there is friendly and offers holiday venues. It has log cabins around the area so all humans and shifters can book to stay. It is how they make money, to look after the pack that lives there while protecting all who live there. We have a large city called Darlington it has everything, hotels theatres, clubs and restaurants, a standard city where you have a lot of buildings. The pack there is Jade's uncle, he has made the outskirts where the pack lives, it has woods, scattered trees, lakes, and valleys, he has the enforcers patrolling the whole area the city has the biggest pack they need the numbers to keep the land safe the city clear of any threats. We also have a coastal town, Clayton Bay, where we used to have holidays there when we were younger, it has many fields, and a nature reserve where you can walk miles and not see a single person, the pack has kept it safe for centuries from having packs of the more dangerous animals. The coastal area has vast amounts of dunes and sandy beaches, it is heaven on earth, the smell of the ocean, and wildlife. Then there is Castleton Bay with lovely beaches and a forest with surrounding woodlands. Large lakes surrounded by trees and fields of untouched valleys. Luna Bay, which is like the other coastal areas, is the port area where our largest coastal town, Shipland Bay, is close to the City of Darlington. The last coastal area is Griffin Bay where nobody lives. It's where the Griffin can live in peace, nobody is allowed near there as it is protected. We arrive in the kitchen and mum has a large kitchen table full of food. I make myself and Jade a coffee, mum already has one made and is sitting down eating her plated-up breakfast. Ethan and dad must have already had their breakfast with my dad having to be at work by 8 am. It must be dad's turn to take Ethan to school on his way to work. Ethan starts school at 7.30 am and finishes at 2.30 pm. When my mum is on shift at the hospital my dad likes to take

Ethan, we have members of our pack who are called caregivers they would normally take the children to and from school. Mum and dad like to do the honours as they enjoy taking him, as that is their time with Ethan, to catch up with him and check how he is doing at school. After school has finished, the caregivers who are highly trained enforcers of our pack watch over the younger members. They get to go on trips, mixing with human residents in town, and they go to the leisure Centre, where they can learn to swim. Learn to swim by having swimming lessons with the other children both from our pack and humans. Ashwood has an ice-skating ring, and bowling, movies playing at the cinema all our children have plenty to do here. Our caregivers take the youngest members of our pack on trips out to help socialize and remember the gift they will receive via the growth phrase, as we are human as well. We know how hard it is once our gift comes in to have a good relationship with all who reside on griffin island. They also get to go on camp trips and hikes, they teach them how to hunt, and they learn about all the dangers of some of the more dangerous animals, especially the beasts. When they do become wolves, how it is pain-free, how it is fun to play with our pack members by chasing, racing, playing fighting, tag and even hide and seek. I loved my time at the Centre, we all loved it, as children it was the best childhood you could ever dream of. When my dad takes Ethan to school, who is only eight. Mum has more time to get ready and have the morning with us before we have to leave to go to school. Her shift at the hospital normally starts at 10 am, she works until 10 pm twice a week. She chooses to work, as she enjoys meeting people, and likes to help keep them healthy. She also looks after the pack's health, doing check-ups on pregnant shifters and delivering any birthing mothers. We do not get human illnesses, but we can break bones, open wounds, or have internal bleeding or bruising. We can be injured from the fights we may get into with the animals that we try to keep away from civilization. The females in our pack can still bleed out when delivering babies. It is important to have a healer to help calm the wolf to help ease the birth and to make sure all is well with the mother and baby. If a healer is not there when the labour pains become too intense. The wolf in us can force the change, thinking it will protect us and the baby inside. What happens is the wolf form can kill the baby. We do not change forms in pregnancy, the male mates know before the females if we are carrying their offspring. Having a healer helps speed up the healing process. Female shifters also have monthly cycles, like all human females we have cramps and can have pain. We suffer like our humans do, as we are half-human. Mum is not the only healer, we have five others in our pack, three females and two males. Cara's mum is a healer too as she helps the pack a lot with healing. She is also a trained midwife, who attends births of all humans and our kind. With advanced learning we have now advanced in medicine. We have midwives who can, cut a baby out of the mother's abdomen, we have named it an operation. In an emergency, if the baby is stuck, or the heartbeat drops, they can perform this operation and it helps deliver healthy babies and save more mothers from bleeding out. She has delivered a lot of babies. Alpha Max, from Vale Island, had this idea after he witnessed something similar, he had his healers, and the nurses all learned about it. Within a year he had nurses who trained in just the care of mothers and their babies. He helped after what happened to his wife and losing Jade and Ethan's parents. He used the money needed to advance technology to help assist in deliveries. It has been a game changer for all who now have a person who can take care of them during this special time. Mum asked how we both slept, and Jade mumbled "Great", as she had already stuffed a full pancake in her mouth. Mum holds a laugh behind her coffee cup, just as Abel comes rushing down into the kitchen like his arse is on fire. He makes no noise being a wolf and an enforcer he is good at hiding the sounds he makes. That is why we stay in the pool house on sleepovers as I do not trust him. He grabs a cup, makes himself a coffee, and sits beside me on my left, while Jades is at my right." Morning Abel, you sleep okay"? I was on patrol with Zara last night, Mum. "Zara has got hormonal issues like her period coming in". She has been a nightmare these past few weeks, she is a pain in my arse she has to be the best, it is down to her female mood swings. "Abel! You two honestly, it is as if you both like to annoy and irritate the other." Mum then asked him, "Are you sure you weren't the moody one", as you put it. The other day you said Zara was in a mood, have you ever thought Abel that you might be the reason she is in a bad mood? Ever since you both started working patrol together and having to spend more time as enforcers together, it is like you both hate each other, which confuses me and your father as you both have always been in each other's lives, been pack mates you were always so close. She is your closest friend. "Why not apologise and make up?" We hear the back door slam shut, it is Adam he walks in from our utility room, where our back door is which leads into the kitchen. The back door leads from our garden into the woods around the back. He is so loud, he yells out the loudest "good morning" ever, as he enters the kitchen and starts to then rub my head. He then has to go and ruffle Jade's too, messing with her hair that she has styled ready for school. Jade gave Adam the death glare and asked him to leave her hair alone. Adam walks awachuckling as he walks over towards the chair across from me. I said, "Good morning!", back in a loud voice, to see if he likes it. The conversation changes from Abel moaning about Zara who may I say has to have the patience of a saint working alongside Abel. I asked Adam, "Have you been out for a run? Why"? He asked me back. I see this as a perfect way to tease him for rubbing my hair. Please go shower, your stink is killing my nose. Jade cracks out laughing, spitting out the rest of the pancake bits she had just demolished all over her face. Abel and Mum started laughing along too. Adam glares at me, it serves him right, he acts like he is our dad all the time messing my hair up. Adam drives us crazy the girls and me, he never knocks on your door he just makes out that it is too quiet, and he had to check we were okay. It was quiet at the time as we were all studying, he knew that but no, he couldn't help himself anything to make us all aware he was in the building. No funny business, no boys and no sneaking out, no going anywhere without a watchdog. He is so annoying; we have had this bullshit from him and Abel is just as bad they spy on us all the time. Jade and I can't even go to Zoe's house without them following us. Callum, who is Cara's brother, and Adam are like a spy club. When we were at Cara's house, they made sure that they had the room next door. They even tried to send Ethan to see what we were up to. Lucky for us Ethan told us who sent him and why? He is our double agent, he will do anything for us, especially Cara, he adores her. Adam is almost twenty-four, and Abel turned twenty-one a few weeks ago he and the guys went to a strip club and had lots of sex according to our spies Zara and Zoe. They have such double standards. Our friendship groups are all in the same year at School after the next two weeks of exams are over. We are going to a party! the only time we ever got near a party. Yes, we are underage, we just finished the spring term and wanted to let out some frustration before exams started. Thankfully Zara covered for us with our parents, she sorted out the food, and music, and bought the alcohol. She allowed us to have it at her place. Which is above the gym, she has the whole top floor as hers. It's huge she has made it into a trendy loft with three bedrooms, a beautiful, styled kitchen with a breakfast bar in the centre big enough for ten people. A huge living space with the biggest sofa, large flat screen, a log burner with a fluffy rug, all the floors are wooden varnished in a dark stain. She has an amazing view from the floor-to-ceiling windows. It lets in natural light, the ceramic views of the woods, and the town it is breathtaking. We have watched many movies and had just as many sleepovers. Zara is twenty-two one year older than Abel who shares his birthday in the same month as Zara's. She and Adam have become close friends, and she and Abel have been close friends most of their lives but this past year. They are butting heads more often, they are completely crazy and when training together they do not hold back. They are both enforcers, dad doesn't like to interfere he just lets them work it out between themselves. Cara got so drunk that night, her body was struggling to burn it off, as fast as the rest of us did. Zara stepped in and cut off her alcohol supply. We had the best time, all of us were dancing, we made up a few dance moves too. Our singing got more out of tune than the drunker we got. Good times. Adam is leaving the kitchen to get showered, he will be meeting Dad at the office soon. We finished breakfast peacefully after Adam left. Abel offers to drive us to school. We pick Cara up on the way she only lives a ten-minute drive away from our house by car. It's a nice walk, through the woodlands at the side of our house. There is a shortcut, it takes ten minutes if we use our wolf forms, by sticking to the thicker terrain of the woods where humans don't walk. Abel drives us down the road, where the houses are not as secluded, but still private. The closer you head towards town, the houses become more closer together. Typical streets of the suburbs, as you get into town there are a lot of townhouses. Abel drives us to school, while me, Jade and Cara catch up, with our plans for later as we're going to Zara's self-defence class. We enjoy training, it helps to keep our wolves happy. Jade is sitting in the front seat, she likes to mess with Abel, she likes to put her feet on the dash, or play around switching the radio stations. Abel ignored us when we started chatting. If it is not about the girls that have moved into the college campus dorms, which are right at the top of Beach Street it is a huge campus, that offers lots of different teaching programs. He will only join in our conversations when we talk about the new girls we have seen in town. He says he is not ready for his fated mate yet, he likes the freedom of random sex before he gets stuck with one person for the rest of his life. As we drove closer towards Town, we spotted Zara pulling her motorbike out of the garage attached to the gym. The gym sits on the outskirts, enjoying the best of both worlds, nature, and town. Zoe gets onto the back of the motorbike, and both of them enjoy the freedom of the fresh breeze, hitting their bodies. Zara and Adam, drive motorbikes. Zoe wants one too but must save up to be able to buy one. She has been getting lessons from her dad, who taught Zara. Their mum works as a nurse, with my Mum in town, at the Human hospital. Their Mum, Tanya Sullivan, is short like Zoe, she has softer features her body is curvy more soft but sexy. She is always more delicate, she does not like fighting, she likes to work at the hospital as she is more of a natural caring soul, she helps to deliver and cares for labouring mothers, and their babies she is also one of our pack healers. John Sullivan is over six-and-a-half feet. He is another of our pack enforcers, he is fast, powerful and has the best knowledge of the types and varied styles of fighting. He is good at fighting with any of the worst animals. He teaches all our enforcers how to fight them. That is why he made Zara their gym co-owner. Our pack trains there three days a week. Abel can't help but increase his speed, here we go again, and Zara is going to compete again. Those two have started driving us all insane, me and the girls just do not understand why they have started to hate each other, it must be their human half, as pack take care of each other. As Abel's speed increases, Cara and I are flung back deeper into our seats and Jade grabs the front seat of the shit bar. I see Cara reach for the back seats, oh shit bar. Zara will have sensed us all coming as we all can smell each other's scent, not to mention we have a stronger hearing. Abel has a blacked-out car with dark-tinted windows, and his own number plate says NO1KING, he bought it as a birthday gift to himself. He is such a show-off Zara waits for Zoe to put her helmet on before she picks up speed, I am so ready to get out of this car. Zara speeds by as she finger salutes Abel, oh now she has done it. Abel has his eyes set, his forehead scrunched up, he is not going to let Zara win, this round. He revs up the engine and steps on the gas, he takes a sharp right towards the back of the shops and other places of businesses. "Short cut he shouts", wait until Adam hears about this, and he will personally kick Abel's arse." Abel takes the next left at the end of the road, barely missing a truck parked in the delivery bays, around the back of all the shops and cafes. The roads are for deliveries, so staff can park their cars away from the main streets. It is not far from normal traffic to use, its purpose is to help keep our main roads clear from parked lorry's, trucks, and vans. I swear he loves to make Cara go green, she is not good in the back seat, especially knowing Abel is driving. Abel takes the next road to the right, heading towards the main road. It is a traffic sign, do not use these roads. Delivery, owners, or if you live above the businesses. Abel speeds through, these roads like he is a racing car driver. The last road leads towards the main road. I grab onto the oh shit bar on my side of the back seat. He is so dead when I got out of this car. We finally pulled out into the main road, at the back of the school. Where: The school staff park. Mr Anderson is just standing near the Gates with fury in his gaze. He will see Abel later, by the way he is looking over at Abel he will be having words with how he drove us to school. There will be a pack meeting later where they are held on a daily basis with the top-ranking wolves, just to check in. We drive towards the front of the building where the student's car park is. In the summer, most of the students who live closer to the school like to walk or cycle. As I undo my seat belt, Cara opens the door on her side of the car, and she starts dry heaving onto the floor where the student parks their cars. Jade heads over to help Cara by rubbing her back. As I grab my door I hear the purring of Zara's motorbike, as she pulls in on my side of the car. Abel stayed in the driver's seat, staring ahead like butter would not melt. It was as if had driven us in a perfectly safe way. I am so mad at him that before I got a chance to close my door, he began revving the engine to go. I slammed the door as he sped off. Zoe was taking her helmet off as Zara let her get off the motorbike. As soon as Zoe was off, she popped the helmet under her arm. Walked around to check on Cara who was still dry heaving across from us. While Jade was stroking her back. Zara shakes her head as she removes her helmet and asks us girls if we were ok, "that brother of yours Anna is a pain in my arse, I have to go. I have to help Dad with the gym. I will see you all at training, enjoy your day", Cara, "I hope you feel better soon. I would tell him off for you, but he never listens to me anymore. I will talk to Adam later to see if he can have a brother-on-brother conversation about not driving like his arse is on fire." "See you soon girls gotter go" She puts her helmet back on and drives away at a much steadier and safer speed than Abel did. I wish those two would sort out whatever beef they have lately. Zara is a little less extreme compared to Abel who just does what he feels in the moment. I walked over to the girls and at that moment we heard Cara fully throwing up. We all ask at the same time" You, ok"? Cara gives us a thumbs up. We hand over tissues, and Zoe gives her some breath mints. Jade hands over water so she can rinse her mouth and get rid of the taste. She has not enjoyed Abel's bad, driving me crazy, or his ego having to beat Zara.

CHAPTER THREE:

Anna

When can hear when the morning bell rings, we know we must start our school day, it's time to start our morning lessons. I have an exam this morning and a math revision this afternoon. We take exams mostly in the main hall as we all start to enter the school, we move towards our classrooms. Half of us have revision this morning and the rest of our group have an exam. My sister and pack friend Jade and I, along with our human friends Lisa and Simon, and don't forget Matteo. Who normally brings some fun to our group, he is such a nice guy, he is honest and open, and he has a good sense of humour. He has helped Cara this past year by using dance to help her put her feelings into her routine, it's her way of releasing all the pent-up emotions and frustration she feels at not being able to change shapes. She has had to deal with a lot. Going through the growth phase and having all her friends be able to change shapes into their wolves, while she had to wait until her fourteenth birthday knowing she had a defect hit her hard we all felt guilty as she always wanted to become an enforcer and her wolf not being able to fully come through was awful for her. Dad, Adam, and Bradley had to look through all our history books to locate all they could on her condition. How they could try to help her through it. It's good news that her mate could help her change, which gave her hope, but alongside hope, there was the added pressure of finding a mate. We don't know if she will be able to tell who her mate is or if he needed to be the one who looks for her. She also will feel more pressure once she turns eighteen as she wants her mate to want her for who she is, not to feel sorry for her but to be proud of her without her being able to shapeshift. That she, too, is strong, capable and can fight right alongside him. Her whole family have their wolves. We have no others that we know of yet who have been born like her. The last was one hundred years ago. This past year, as her eighteenth birthday approaches, she has been struggling more. We are hoping she will open up soon and tell us what is bothering her as we all love her dearly and we know we can help her through anything were sisters, were pack, and were best friends and we stick together. As we part ways, we wish each other luck. This morning went by fast, my focus was to answer the questions as best as I could and try to answer them in the time given. Even Matteo knuckles down. We are not allowed to talk during the exam as soon as we enter the hall, we find our seats and once the teacher starts the clock they will say begin. We have a clock to allow us a certain amount of time to complete the exam. We all just want to do our best and we all will miss not being together as often, as we all have different paths ahead of us. Once the time has run out, we must leave our papers face down and leave the room quietly. Once we were outside the hall, we all asked how each of us thought we did. I told them I managed to complete all the questions, there were two I was not confident with, but the others I knew. We all part ways at lunchtime Cara, Jade, Zoe, and I have our little routine we like to sit close to the wooden area, and some of the humans go into the small woods on the school grounds to kiss and sneak out to bunk off school they like to use them to mess around in. We have some woodland animals that like to visit the patch of grass where we have bird baths and food out for them. It's nice to see it, we also come out here in art class we can sit outside and sketch them, those classes are always the student's favourite. Jade and I head towards the ladies' bathrooms, and we go take care of our bladders. After washing our hands and freshening up a little bit. We met up with Cara and Zoe for lunch. Some food and fresh air always get us through the afternoon lessons. Jade and I went over to the lunchroom, which was a little earlier than normal. We don't have the rest of the school to compete with today we each walk to our areas to grab our lunch. As I walk towards the food part of the dining room, Jade walks towards the drinks section. After we pay, we walk over towards our favourite seats, the ones closest to the woodlands. I bought each of us a meat and potato pie, with fresh potatoes, vegetables, and gravy. We always work in pairs one pair gets the lunches, while the other pair saves our favourite table. Cara and Zoe are already seated and waiting for us as we sit down across from them. The conversation at lunchtime is about training tonight, Cara may not yet be able to shapeshift, but she still has all the ability and agility of the wolf inside her and she gets just as much benefit from training as we do. Some shapeshifters want to wait to find their Fated Mates. Some, like my brothers, choose to date humans. Our kind does not date each other because that would not be a good thing, for when we find our fated mates, fights would occur as we will not tolerate the knowledge that another has been near what is ours. but humans, yes. Just some of our kind do, as the human side likes to have a choice, those where the wolf and human part are willing and wish to wait. It takes both halves of that soul to be ready before the mating bond snaps into place. If one half is ready and knows who the other half is, for it to work the other half must be ready too. I like to think about mating bonds in the human term of marriage, both people must want the union when both are ready to bond to be together once you mate you can't change your mind, that is it. Once you do wish to bond, it is the most amazing love you can ever find, so we are told by others who have mated. Your mate will never cheat, will never hurt you, they will never leave you. We are protected and we are loved. Males can be more possessive than most females, which can drive their mates insane. Each bond is unique to each couple, no one has the same story, we all have unique ways of finding each other, some can be lucky to meet and boom that is it there fully ready and willing. Some can take a while as I said, but it is like human relationships sometimes it's about timing. We agree on what our plans will be after school finishes. I started to tell the girls about my dream that I had again last night and how he was able to 'mind speak' with me. They listen and ask questions; each of my girls think that he could be my mate. Cara hasn't had any dreams like mine of a guy in the woods, or in her favourite places she likes to visit. Cara is different, we are not sure how she would find her mate, she is a rare case, hopefully, her mate will find her first as maybe it will be harder for her to spot her mate, who knows, either way, me and my girls will help her through it as best as we can. I just hope my mate isn't as bad as my brothers when it comes to being protective, I hope my mate sees me as a strong capable woman. We ate up and headed towards the math block we all had math revision together and I already knew it would be entertaining. It has nothing to do with Bradley. No, it is because Zoe turns into a total pain. It's what she enjoys the most about being at school lately, as he is our beta, she likes to be the biggest annoyance out of the whole class. Even Matteo can't take her crown for most detentions, she has had him beaten in spades, especially ever since Bradley has had to take over. Zoe tries to get us in trouble alongside her when we are all together, she has called it bonding time. Doing a little crime together will help keep Bradley from having a bigger head than he already has. Mr. Anderson has put Zoe in detention so many times, that I have lost count he has gotten wiser about her scheming though. He has finally seen how she deals with involving the rest of us to achieve his attention. It makes Bradley late to leave school, which means he has to stay behind with anyone who has detention. The teachers do put all who are in trouble in the main hall, one teacher will stay behind. But as Zoe is the only one causing the trouble, these past few weeks everyone else has grown up and knuckled down. No, not Zoe she just loves making him sweat it gives her the most fun ever. She says when she feels his temper rise it makes her laugh, it is funny, she will say. I can see he is dying to punish me pack-style, but he can't on school grounds. With an evil little laugh, as she does while rubbing her hands together. Jade encourages her the most as our prankster, they have so got a prank planned before school ends for the summer. I know Bradley is our Beta and she swears she has caught him in a compromising situation. As our beta he has a lot to do with our pack, he has duties he has to take care of especially keeping all of us safe. Our pack also keeps rarer animals safe, like our unicorns and the Phoenix birds, and we have others too that we protect from being hunted or preyed on by the beasts. He oversees the patrols, he does all the rota and paperwork. Checking the numbers and keeping an eye on any breachers is our beta job. While he is teaching, he does have a lot of other responsibilities. Zoe just enjoys adding more pressure to his already big plate. I am sure though, after putting up with Zoe for two months now, he is ready to smack her arse red. Over a couple of weeks now, she has tried to provoke a reaction. She is always spreading rumours about Bradley; her latest creation is that he and our P.E. teacher, Miss Kelly, were having sex in the female changing rooms when we were all at lunch. She told as many girls as she could she heard them in his office while in detention, she swore he left her doing mini-tests and said you had until I returned, he would then lock her in to make sure she never left. All of this started when we were in P.E. Miss Kelly is extremely attractive, she smells good she has an amazing female shape sexy, big shapely breasts a strong but feminine upper body, long toned legs, and that long dark hair up high in a ponytail. For a human, she has the perfect body girls would love to have. She is blessed in the chest department, which is why half of the guys like her lessons. She always gives Miss Kelly a tough time. It was around the time she caught her, and Bradley, in a compromising situation on a game night our school was playing. I am sat in math revision as the girls, and I are waiting to see what Zoe has planned in today's class. "Here we go" I mouth to my girls," she whispers to Ellie, Mr. Anderson, "he is a total fuckboy." I saw him on a date with Miss Kelly on Friday, they were holding hands and kissing in the street as I was on my sister's bike and saw with my own eyes. On Saturday, I saw Mr Anderson again tongue fucking another girl who my sister knows from college. Afterwards, I saw the same girl a few hours later in the bar drunk, showing her goodies to any man with a pulse. Zoe winks at us all as she takes her seat. Ellie said: "Really, I am not surprised I wouldn't say no he is one hell of a man," he has made this class more of a revelation if you get my meaning." I heard Zoe laugh, he probably has caught a std with using his dick too much on lame-arsed pussy. Here we go, that should get a reaction as I am waiting for Mr Anderson to interrupt her. Especially with that last remark it should do the trick, let the fireworks begin. The pack can hear her, every word she just said as I heard them suck in their breath. Like me, I can hear them as they whisper, "oh shit." I sneaked a glance at Bradley, he so heard her, he is acting as though he has not heard her, as so far, he has not reacted. It was a disrespectful dig at our Beta, the only sign he has given that he could hear her was because he had his left fist clenched. He continued to teach the class without any reaction. Zoe was expecting some sort of reaction, not an aloof response. Her facial expression is one of bafflement. Looks to me like our Beta has chosen the high road today. I am impressed, he continues the class as normal while we all try to listen, we are all taking notes, trying to cram in as much as we can as this will be our last lesson before our final exam. During the last few minutes before the class is due to end, he asked Zoe to come up to the front of the class and solve the equation he just wrote on the board. It's a complicated sum, Cara is good at math's she gets the answer in seconds, Jade and or breaking the sum down in our notebooks as we are trying to figure it out. Zoe descends towards the board at the front of the class. When she looks over at the puzzle Bradley has written down, I see her taking a deep breath as she quickly began to solve the equation. Cara had just completed the sum in the time it took Zoe to walk to the front. Jade and I are still trying to figure it out. Zoe seems satisfied with how she has answered and completed the puzzle by turning away from the board, giving Mr Anderson a smart-arsed smile, with a little nod and strutting back with a pleased smile on her face. Mr Anderson is burning holes in the back of her head as she retakes her seat beside us. Ellie and our friends planned an ice-skating trip after school finished, to shake off the stress from today. We have training and could not go with them. Once the bell rings to end our school day as we all wave goodbye to Ellie. As we begin to pack up our belongings, I am feeling more confident. Bradley has gone through everything expected of us as we finish packing up to leave. Bradley aka Mr Anderson has snuck up and is right in front of Zoe's desk, I did not even hear him move. By the shock on Zoe's face neither did she, Zoe covers it well by saying "Mr. Anderson, what a pleasant surprise, we didn't even hear you approach, can I help you sir?" She sure can play nice now he is standing in front of her. Mr Anderson has a look of irritation on his face as he stares down at Zoe." Actually yes, Zoe, you can help me by following me to my office right now." "I would like to have a little discussion, on how you knew the answer to the equation. I am intrigued by how you managed to pull off not only was the answer correct, but it was also done textbook accurately." Zoe does not miss a beat, "sir, I do not have time for this little discussion." I have a date, oh, right about now, as she pretends to look at her bare arm for the time. "Oh sir, will you look at the time, I would love a chat sir, as I can see my brain power has surprised you." "I will not take offence by reporting you for telling a very bright student that she isn't bright enough." "I wouldn't want you reprimanded in front of these witnesses Sir, who can verify the accusation?" Implying I cheated somehow, or I have not gotten the smarts to answer the equation correctly. You asked me to solve it in front of the whole class. Mr. Anderson, sir I have things to do. I sit there with my mouth open; she is good, she knows how to make trouble and how to get out of it. She did not give him a chance to respond, with speed, by using her wolf for help, she summersaults her way over a few desks and is out of the door to the classroom in a few seconds flat. Jade, Cara, and I sat there as we took in Bradley's face, knowing she had used her Wolf power during school. Which has broken our Alpha's rules which means she is dead; The Beta, has witnessed it therefore he can now punish her using pack rules. Great, now Zoe could be doing the centre all summer, as well as working at the gym as she is taking over from Zara in the holidays. I swear I just saw Bradley smile with a knowing twinkle in his eyes, he must have known how she would react he was hoping for it. We get the hell out of there before he remembers we are going to see Zoe in five minutes time. I do not want to have to pass on a message, I bet the conversation he will have with my dad will be explosive. I know Bradley has had heated discussions with my dad about Zoe before about her endless disrespect. Jade, Cara, and I hurried out of there as quickly as possible. Bradley turned away and started packing his things away ready to leave for the day.

CHAPTER FOUR:

Hayden

For the past few weeks, every time I go to bed to sleep. I have the same dream, it's always in the woods behind a large home. I end up being on a footpath behind a girl, I don't know. I hide behind the trees and watch her, to check that she isn't a threat. Each time I track her, I know she isn't a threat to me or mine, she is just innocently walking and enjoying nature. I follow her, and as I get closer, I can't help it, I want to roll around as her scent is so intoxicating. I breathe her in, and each time that I do I am more and more intrigued by her. She has the most delicious scent that stirs up my wolf where he chants on repeat in my head, she is mine, mine, mine. I am cautious in the first few dreams that I have. I spend each dream just watching her, seeing where she walks to, watching as I take in her beauty. I notice each of her little traits, the tilting of her face, the way her hair flows free down her back, the curve of her body, the shape of her breast. The way her eyes lighten with the sun as it rises beyond the horizon. Each time I dream it's always about her, I always see her in the same woods, behind a huge house, walking along the path which has naturally formed from being walked upon. I started to show myself to her, as the time went on, and I enjoyed the moment she knew that I was there with her, she always looks behind her shoulder, and I always stepped in front of her each time that she did. She would always bump into my chest each time she does I feel so relaxed and at peace as I breathe her in. I know now after dreaming about her for so long that she is meant to be mine. I try to show her my face, but each time that I have tried too, she always wakes up. Tonight, though it is different, as I dream about her, I notice that her scent is a lot stronger than it has been before. I sense her in a way that I am aware of where she is, and what she is doing as she bumps into my chest. This is the dream I know what she will be to me, she will be mine. I know now that she is my fated mate. I know exactly when she is about to wake up, and I yell into my mind "Soon", as I know I will find her. I won't stop until I have her in my arms with me, where she belongs. I wake up feeling lighter, as I know my dreams have a meaning, they have a purpose that she is meant for me. My wolf has known all along, my human brain took a little bit more time to catch up. Once awake, I start my day by taking a shower and going to meet my Alpha Henry Sanderson. I live alone which is away from the hustle and bustle of the city. I live in the city of Darlington. I belong to the Sanderson pack, we help protect humans from the rougher, more dangerous creatures we have, as we are a city with many humans living here. We have managed to keep most of the creatures at bay, as they find the loud noises of the hotels, casinos, theatres, and lots of traffic too much. Most of our pack live further away from the city centre, my parents, my brother Leo and my two sisters, Masie and Jess, live nearby. My dad is the Beta of our pack, and he lives closer to the Alpha's home. Henry, our Alpha must make sure we have enough enforcers protecting our land as our territory is larger than any of the towns and villages we have on our Island. My best friend Tommy lives next door to me. He and I normally spend time together when we are both free. He moved in a month ago. He was ordered out of his family home, due to his disrespect to his mate. Who he hasn't excepted as his mate just yet, he is still living in his Playboy phase. He is one of our enforcers, he is strong, fast and good at his role. He and I like to practise our training together in both forms. Tommy has nice qualities, it's just a shame he is pushing Sophia away, who is his mate. I try to stay out of it, as I have tried so many times to talk to him. I don't know what else to do other than kick his arse in training for each occasion. I've seen how it affects Sophia. How much it is hurting her, having a mate who is not ready just yet to commit to her. Sophia is masking her pain from everyone else. We have many enforcers in our pack, all are dam good at it, they have to patrol a large area, and we work in rotations. My pack role will be Beta once my dad retires or wishes it to be. I like to sit and tease him like saying thing's," hey dad you want to handover the position you have a ton of grey hair coming through, and I swear you have slowed down as time moves on." He always comes back with a when you can beat me, then I will be happy to hand my position over. I love spending time at home, especially as I can joke with my parents, my dad will always have a comeback to everything I joke to him about hanging up the Beta role. The last one was when my dad said, "who knows maybe me, and your mother can find a way to enjoy the time together?" I always laugh, as I know my dad loves my mother so much when I see them together, I see nothing but devotion and love for each other. I want to find that love that both my parents have who wouldn't, they are a good match they have shown my siblings and I how amazing a mate bond that is fated to you is such a gift. My dad has been a constant in our lives, he works hard to help our Alpha run the pack, occasionally he travels on missions with me and my brother Leo, he likes to use that time to spend time with us it helps to bond us closer together as shapeshifters we spend a lot of time with our pack, we stay stronger and comfort one another. My current job role for our pack is to run a team that includes my dad David Hawk, who is beta to the Sanderson pack, and he only joins us when we travel to other islands on missions. With a Beta joining us it helps with building trust; he has expertise with the creatures and how best to deal with them. My Dad is a strong fighter, he is trained well using weapons and he is a tracker. My friend Delia and her Dad Phillip Moss, they both have joined me on many missions. Phillip has a lot of skills including taking down a beast, he had a scar on his leg when he was bitten by one during a mission he did with my dad when we were little, he was evaluating tranquilizers. What is the correct dosage as each one has different shapes, and sizes. The same strength for one may not be strong enough for another. The only way to evaluate the tranquilizers out is to use them in the field and time how long each dosage lasts for. He had a close encounter from one of the tests, one creature woke up much quicker than expected, he survived it. He likes to call it his war wound for the good of all who live amongst them. Delia works as hard as anyone, she does the radio and has been working with Sophia since they were not out on the field. They are both good with trying to learn technology, they collaborate with a team. We have a base that our Island shares with all of the packs, we have six members from each pack that help with developing better ways to communicate. Trying to innovate ideas to help with transport amongst other things to help advance moving around and being able to help with hospital equipment. My brother Leo is good at both tracking and hunting, he is quiet and has been able to merge into his surroundings, he is a perfect match to help me as we work so well, we don't need words, we just know what the other is thinking. Which helps when we have to track the worst of the creatures, we have to be quiet, we have to work well together and most of all not get hurt. We are a good team collaborating well with each other. Tommy normally comes along but he has been on rotation and needs to help the boarders with patrolling. Our Alpha is hoping by keeping him grounded he might get his shit together. Sam is my other best friend, and he has been helping his dad out with the family business. They run a security firm. They look after humans watching the bigger clubs and casinos, from any trouble, drunk humans can become aggressive and do tend to start trouble, sometimes getting handsy with the females. Sams family work to minimise any damage. Sam has the best nose I have ever come across, his dad was the same, he learned all of us how to track. Were better now, as he taught us all he knew and now Sam does the training. His Dad is in his sixties, him and his wife have two children, Sam, and Hope, they miscarried twice, I think her wolf broke free on the pack run wanting to run free with the rest of us. The second time was because the baby hadn't developed properly, and her wolf rejected it. After having Sam, they were happy they finally had a child, it was a joyous occasion and an unexpected surprise when they fell pregnant late in life with Hope. She is doted on, and her family have allowed her to join in the family business as she is nineteen her. I think they liked her in sight, and this was the only way they knew how. They had a tough few years but thankfully they were so close to each other, they all run the family business it helped them overcome a lot by having a focus. Henry our Alpha suggested it as he needed to make each business safe and help keep tourists happy without any crime being committed, we do have holding where we can put humans to sleep it off, we also cut them off if they are too drunk that they are a hazard. Sam has helped run it they now have many of the packs who earn good money from it and it helps our pack with having less to worry about. We have a large city and the last thing we need is humans causing damage to property or on each other we have a force called the community peace. It is made up of pack members and humans, who want the same things. To keep the island from creature attacks, and to keep all who live amongst us safe from harm. From certain individuals who wish on harming others or committing crimes against society. The peacekeepers have a large building in the center of the city that our Alpha chairs. It's a new thing that Henry came up with. We have evolved as civilization has, we have made some beautiful ways to substain ourselves. We can move about more freely than ten years ago. With transport, from the invention of buses, vehicles, and larger transport vehicles to load up produce and goods from place to place. Now we have a railroad that has taken decades to build. Trains are helping with a better way of life. We patrol the rail roads to make sure none of the creatures attack them. Each pack makes sure every patch is protected, the trains stop at each town and have so far been untouched, the noise it makes and the whistle help to frighten any that would dare to approach. We have ships that we use to travel between each of the islands. Rules were made because they were needed to allow for peace and not to have any hunting of the creatures we share our world with. Each

Alpha help provides, safety as well as making sure all have provisions and homes. My dad, Delia, and Phillip are good at watching our backs during the hunts, they help discourage any larger packs of either the Neeman lions, or the Bonnacons from living too close to civilization, when they work on each mission, they have eyes on any other threats. As a pack, any of these creatures can cause damage even to us shapeshifters. I have noticed that since the dreams started, I have become restless, I am ready to find my fated mate, so far, I have not found her, I have been to a few gatherings with no luck. I am twenty-five, and I have some time to spare, but after my last dream I know I will soon meet her soon enough. I have waited as many of our kind do, some will choose to if their human half wish to explore and grow first. I have chosen to wait I want my mate to know that I have not dated. I have wanted to find my mate since I turned eighteen to know that now is my time I know her hair is light brown, long and straight it touches past her shoulder blades, her eyes are blue, she has an amazing figure, her lips are like wow, each time I see her lips I want to kiss them, nibble each of her lips I want to taste her on my tongue. She is breathtakingly beautiful. My wolf wants to bottle her sweet flowery scent up. To be able to roll around in it each day, we want to explore her body to leave our mark on each part of her with licks, kisses and my bite. To see her, knowing she is mine and I am hers. After we have finished this current mission, we will go looking for her. Once I smell her nearby, I will hunt her down. I make myself some breakfast as my thoughts are just re living my dream, I need to see my family. I travel over to my parents' house, it's not far from my own place. My parents live on the other side of a small, wooded area, where you can see the alpha's home not far behind with it's vest surrounding forest. We have lakes with endless landscapes of fields and farmland. We have a river that runs through our land. It's further north where it connects to all the towns on our Island towards our coastal towns. We have three coastal towns, alongside five large towns and many villages as well as the city where I live with my pack. Our land we all live on is The Griffin Island. We have a four-hour boat ride to Vale Island which has the City of Evergreen as it's capital. This is where we will meet the new Alpha of Evergreen, Brock Steel. He has been made the new Alpha of the city as the last one Max died. We just don't know any details; we know that the new Alpha has had a lot to deal with. Each of the Alphas have given him time to settle into his new role. Our mission is to gain information the new Alpha couldn't tell us over the radio. It has to be in person as the details are delicately classified. An agreement was made amongst the leaders that my team and I would attend. We need to know what happened to Max, how he died, and how the new Alpha is coping being the new Alpha. How is he settling in? As I parked my car on my parent's drive, I saw my brother taking both our sisters to school. It's Monday morning and they have only two more weeks left. I wave them off and go inside mum is in the living space my mother is beautiful she has a kind soul, her long brown hair tied into a bun with her workout clothes on. Hi, mum are you going for a run or are you at the center watching over the kids? My mum works protecting our children from any danger, especially as the creatures we have found tend to hunt our most vulnerable pack mates thinking they are easy pickings. My mum is forty-nine and she is still able to fight any creature who dares to stalk our children or any from our city we all have talks and safety instructions to follow. The children are taught to protect themselves, how to hide, how to cover their scent. I loved my time at the centre, I met so many friends from having such good memories from the camping trips, the days out football, tag all of it. Good times. My mum replies "I have a day off and I am going to combat training with a few of my team". We have a trip coming up, we are taking the kids camping and we have received warnings of more Neeman lions around. I like to make sure we are ready just to be safe". "Haven't the enforcers moved them away yet?" I spoke. They normally have them rehomed further away from all the resident's it is not normal for any to be around close to where most of us live. My mother said, "I know it's been strange they seem to be coming in with no scent trails."It has everyone stumped so we have been told to be careful and when we do go camping Henry has asked for all the staff to go". I am a little shocked, I know I haven't been home much this past month. Hearing my mum speak about the Neeman lion's that have been spotted closer towards civilisation, I only got back last night from tracking the other side of our city. Closer to the port, where we've had reports of a Griffin flying around the area. Which isn't normal behaviour for those either, they too have been moved away from civilization. My Dad enters the living space, "where are we going son?", We have orders, we need to visit Evergreen to see the new Alpha. He has some information he needs to share. We will leave in the morning. I have a few errands to run. Can you tell Leo?"" Yes, he will be back soon. I will let him know." I will see you tonight for dinner. I have missed your cooking mum. You be safe, I will see you tonight. My mother said "I will make your favourite dinner" if you will make a dessert, for afterwards. I love your desserts, anything with chocolate in it would be appreciated Hayden. "You have a deal", see you later. After running a few errands in the city, I bumped into Sam. Hi Sam, tough night? we had a few drunk people to deal with and a few sore losses, but it was all dealt with, and nobody needed to be taken in by the peacekeepers. We decided to go to the coffee shop to catch up. We talked about what each of us had been up to. Sam is my height, he has long black hair, he ties it up into a man bun, he has stubble and looks tired. He has hazel eyes with a tanned skin. He likes to be in the sun as much as possible. Sam has got the best nose in the pack, he can smell from a few miles away if he has to. He can focus on his wolf abilities, hone them in and follow up on the source of the scent. He is one of my best friends alongside, Tommy, and Delia, he has been having a tough time these past few weeks he has bags under his eyes like he is carrying the weight of the world on his shoulders. Sam enjoys training daily, it helps him deal with his wolf as both him and his wolf are unsettled. Sam has been waiting for a mate a lot longer than me. He will be turning thirty next year. He is worried that maybe he has lost their fated mate. May I ask Sam, "are you sleeping?" I do get some sleep, though my wolf is driving me hard lately. It's like he knows something, that is important. I don't understand what it is, I can't figure it out just yet. He is frustrated. I know that I want to find my mate too. He wants his mate found today. Like, I haven't tried, I have attended most of the gatherings, I have met most, if not all the females the packs have to offer. Still nothing, I have not been able to locate her. I am so frustrated, and even when I do sleep, all I see is a place I don't recognise and a pack I've never met. I can't make sense of my dreams, my wolf gets pissed at me because he knows what they mean, and I don't as I wake up each time, I think I'll see what my wolf wants me to see. I don't know Hayden," I'm beginning to lose hope." He has other gatherings coming up. I hope he finds her this time as he will have met every single pack member and all the newly aged females. He has been in a relationship seeing the same human on and off for over two years now, which is unusual for our kind. He mentioned dreams, maybe he is having the same ones that are similar to mine. Where his mate is there, but maybe he hasn't figured it out just yet. So, I tell him about the dream that I've been having. Sam "I too have been having dreams like you have". Each night they are always set in the woods, there is a house in the background, and at first, I just watch her as I have never seen her before. I don't recognise the setting either as the dreams have been happening more often, I have managed to gain more knowledge. Her scent, how she looks, her hair colour, the colouring of her eyes, the way she tilts her head. Last night it had changed it was a lot stronger, my wolf has been going crazy at me frustrated, as if he knew all this time. It has been a few weeks of the same dream with her in it and last night I finally figured out who she is." She's my mate Sam, my fated mate". I just have to find her, but my gut is saying that it will be soon. He listens to every word I say, as if he too has had these dreams. He seems to be thinking, about what his dreams mean, as he has gone quiet. I hope I have given him hope by sharing my situation. We have many females turning eighteen, according to our records. If she isn't ready, he will mark her as a warning, so that his wolf settles, and his mate knows that he is hers and she is his. He is ready and I don't think he will allow his mate to run or live a little. It's going to be interesting, I can tell. He and I part ways, and I tell him not to give up and to use his gut instincts. If he has been having dreams, he knows she is here somewhere he just has to find her. I tell Sam to go and find her, remember the dreams and to use them to try and locate her. Use the land you see, is it a place you recognise? what stands out? Do you remember any of the scents? what noises can you hear, what can you see? Could it be a familiar place where you could have seen when riding across the sea? Are there any beaches or creatures around that you recall from previous visits? The smallest detail could lead you to where she is. She has to be around; I believe your dreams are trying to show you. "Thank you Hayden," you have given me back a little bit of hope back. Knowing Sam, he will find her wherever she is. We hugged goodbye and agreed to see each other once I returned. I feel lighter myself talking to Sam and how he's dreaming too, it has helped my own determination on finding my own mate. I need to focus on this mission and find the rest of my team. I need to find out where Delia is, we have a training session planned. She will most likely be at the Centre. As I thought she was already here, warming up. Hey Hayden, what took you so long? I bumped into Sam, and we caught up. "You ready for a beat down". In your dreams, Hayden" I will be the one beating your arse." I laugh we always like to annoy each other in a fun way she is a warrior, and she enjoys training it helps her clear her thoughts, it helps me too. Delia wants to run off some energy first, we both decide to have a run in our wolf forms and practice our skills. We switch forms near the center, being able to shapeshift into a wolf is easy, it's like magic we glow a second and then were in wolf form, it's strange during the growth phase as you switch forms constantly. One moment you can be eating dinner the next a wolf. You can be walking along on two legs and then flash into a wolf. Once our leaders the Alpha and Beta teach you to control it, life resumes as normal. You learn that just before you shift your wolf becomes stronger, it's up to your human shape to control if it's safe to switch and allow your wolf the freedom to run. With time it becomes easier to control, as you and your wolf learn the danger of being exposed. How we protect each other is the key to becoming balanced together. We are in our forest that belongs to the pack, it's private, and we have high fences with patrols all around them. We do have a few Neeman Lions and Bonnacons nesting inside our land, and we have the areas sealed off to help keep them away from hunting our own kind, especially on pack runs when we all participate. We have a few Bonnacons families, they are up by the lake further south where there are good hunting grounds for them, and they have caves they use as nests to protect their young. We have our stronger enforcers watching over the Neeman lions, those are tough fucker's they can cause a lot of damage to us, we have them guarded as they are intelligent and the males are aggressive we have a few families that have formed a pack we have them in the mountain area where they have everything they need to survive food, shelter and water. When mum mentioned that some have been near the camp sites it's worrying it's not normal behaviour. I trust our Alpha no doubt he will make sure to keep all our city safe. Delia is up front running and hiding trying to attack me without me knowing we are hiding and masking scent. This is a good way for us when we are tracking, we have to be able to blend into our surroundings. We run laps around the forest we fight in our wolves to practice honing our skills. Once we have completed our wolf training we head back towards the centre. We have training facilities and the intense course we do in human form. After we switch back to humans, Delia pushes my back saying, "You ready for more Hayden, it feels like you're out of shape?" really Delia I could have sworn that you were eating my dust. We are both laughing as we start our human training doing laps. The center has a killer workout program where we have large obstacles to climb and jump over. We have a shooting range where we use crossbows, throw axes, and shoot arrows. We have an area where we learn how to use tranquilizer guns. We have to learned how to be able to shoot into a moving-sized shapes, as if we are in the field. We have to be able to hit small targets and the bigger targets. We have to be able to hit each target accurately, some of the creatures and animals have thick hydes and the only way to enable the tranquilizer to work is to hit underneath in there most vulnerable areas. We have an outside crawling station full of mud water and spikes, there are bushes above us that we find around our land we have to be able to get into small spaces to hit our target that might include jumping into water or hiding in bushes up a tree anywhere that hides and can help make it easier to put the creature to sleep. The training helps you adapt to any possible sinero. To finish the course, we jump across water into another obstacle course to climb up the last wall, which is high. Once you manage to complete that part of the course, it's a race to the finish line. As I am catching my breath Delia finishes behind me. I crossed over the finish line first as I will become our pack's Beta, I am naturally stronger and faster. Delia is tough, she has trained as much as I have. We stretch out and begin walking towards the facility to shower and clean up. We are meeting up with Sophia and Tommy for lunch we haven't seen much of each other in over two weeks. Tommy has a lot of muscle, he is good at being an enforcer, his fighting skills are fast he has quality styles he uses and switches between each one during combat. He is just as skilful in his wolf form, he has grace as a fighter and when you watch him engage in training he mixes it up to confuse each oppunate. He has blonde hair, he wears it up in a man bun, his hair is long, he likes the wildness of it, it suits his roaming ways. He has blue eyes and a little stubble; in his words the stumble helps to tickle and pleasure my dates. His words not mine, he has been holding off from mating. He has dated many, especially these past six months, as his human half knows time is running out. He was given a gift Sophia is his Fated mate, yet he refused to bond yet he has told her he isn't ready he is too young to settle down. Soon though his wolf will take over, as he has been a real player his human half is stubborn and has been the stronger of the two. He has decided and argued that he wants freedom. He doesn't need a mate, he is happy as he is single and living life the way he has chosen. Sophia tries to ignore all of his playboy ways, as she has tried to be understanding she knows he isn't ready. She has given him time hoping he will come around, for her. He is it for her, she wants him, she has been loyal she hasn't been interested in dating, she has always wanted the real thing the commitment of a mate who will love you and never hurt you like her parents when they met it was love and they mated straight away as did Tommy's parents. We have never really had anyone who has blatantly refused to mate, and not only is he lucky his mate comes from the me pack like him. She is stunning, she is kind and caring, she deserves to be treated as such, a gift. Why Tommy chose not to see this is confusing for the rest of us. When we enter the restaurant, Sophia looks defeated, Tommy smiles and looks carefree I can feel the tension building as Delia gives Sophia a smile and completely ignores Tommy this is going to be awkward. Delia says hi and sits herself next to Sophia as Tommy is sat as far away from Sophia as he can. I greeted Sophia first, giving her a hug and whispering in her ear so nobody but her can hear. I whisper do not let him see you break, show him you are are unaffected. You say the word and I will take you with us tomorrow to get some distance. Sophia gives my cheek a kiss and smiles as she sits down. Sophia has brown eyes with long curly dark hair, she is short for a pack mate and has a softer famine look. She is more a lover than a fighter she prefers to heal than to fight. Our pack Alpha Henry thinks she is an omega, the rarest of our kind. She is the first we know of that has been born in centuries, she is shy and more reserved. She is softly spoken and is a healer for our pack, she has calming abilities and has a fantastic way with the children if they get hurt. Sophia has been learning more about what she is and what gifts she has compared to other pack members. Tommy has treated Sophia poorly and he needs a kick up the arse Sam would kill to have what he has. Maybe that's why those two don't hang out as much anymore. Delia has told me they haven't been hanging out as much as they used to, Sam is dating and has dated, he had waited until he was my age, twenty five before he decided to date. He probably sees Sophia hurting and wishes he had her as a mate. Sam and Sophia have a good friendship and he has become protective over her as most of the pack are. We all feel her power, and she calms us down naturally. I don't know how, but I do remember when our Alpha became grief stictened having Sophia nearby helped him focus. He healed, he was able to see through the pain and be there for his pack. Tommy is acting like an arsehole, he has to know she is in pain, and his actions are hurting her. I am confused why his wolf hasn't taken control and bitten Sophia. We all talk about what each of us have been up to over the past two weeks. We each order and enjoy being together, the only one of us who has been abnormally quiet. She has not spoken, she has expressed interest but hasn't said a word. I want to hug her and tell her he is a fool again. Anything to help her as she has us. I see Delia, who is thinking of something. I know she is planning, as she takes a hold of Sophia's hand and takes her to the bathroom. I have to say something, to Tommy he has to be able to feel what I felt, even Delia felt it. "What are you doing Tommy? You're hurting your mate!" are you willing to destroy the woman that has been gifted to you? "I know" Tommy said "my wolf is getting harder to control". I have just turned twenty-two. I need time Hayden, I need to make sure we are both ready. I am fighting it, I just can't explain it. I interrupted him before he gives me an excuse, Sophia has waited for you, she has saved herself for you!, she could have behaved the same way as you. How would you feel? What more is it going to take? By the time the girls come back I can see Delia, giving off you will be sorry vibes towards the direction where Tommy is sat. Delia is best friends with Sophia, and as a pack we all grown up together. Everyone is drawn to Sophia, she is special. When she turned eighteen six months ago she told Tommy, thinking he would be happy about it. Normally, when both partners are ready, the bond snaps into place. You know that they are yours and you are theirs. Sophia had found out on her birthday that she and Tommy would be mates. She found Tommy and told him. He has done nothing but sleep around ever since. I know why he moved in next door to me, his parents wouldn't allow him to bring hookups back as they had an inkling Sophia might be his. He has two brothers, I think if he had sisters like me, he wouldn't want to hurt them, and he would see what a blessing he had been given. His wolf will take over soon, he will bite her and force the man inside to take his mate his wolf knows she is as a gift, and he will not allow the man to hurt his mate. I reckon Tommy knows this and has been much more of a player than normal. After the food is eaten Delia decides to put her plan into action, I work with her and I know her so well she has got a plan goodluck Tommy you are going to need it. Hayden, I will meet you tomorrow with my Dad to board the ship, me and Sophia have plans tonight. We are going out with the twins tonight, one of them has received an invitation to the new club that Marcus is opening up. Marcus is human, he has another club on the south side of the city, this new place he is opening is in the center. Marcus's big party is risky, normally the weekend pulls the crowd in, it's Monday today. Marcus knows what he's doing. Most of those who are not working will be there, he has a fantastic club already it is popular he has a waiting list. He knows by opening another he will fill this one too. even the visiting packs will be there, it's the club, it's one of the best places to hook up. Tommy perks up, oh yeah! he is so used to

Sophia being a goodie two shoes. She has always followed him around, she has made her feelings clear. she has understood and has allowed him to be free and come to her when he is ready. Maybe she has had enough, especially with the smile she gives Tommy Good for her, Tommy needs a reminder of what he could lose. Delia will make sure he gets that lesson. Delia says to Tommy, "I hear you're on duty tonight sucks to be you" See you tomorrow Hayden, as she takes a hold of Sophia's hand and for the first time, Sophia doesn't look at Tommy with adoration in her eyes. If you see anything it's pure disappointment. "Oh boy Tommy you're in deep shit," see you when I'm back." I leave Tommy sat there stewing. I'm driving home and making dessert for dinner tonight, while it's baking in the oven I pack for Evergreen. Once I have packed I return to the kitchen and take out my apple pie after leaving it to cool. I decided to take a nice soak in the bath until it's time for dinner. Walking over to see my family, mum has almost finished dinner and it smells good. Dad was watching a game on the television in the living space. Hi Dad, where is everyone? Well, Masie has gone out with her friends, she has a party. One of our pack members has a visiting cousin over she is fetching a few friends along to help celebrate. Dad, did you know Marcus is opening up his new club tonight? "I do," Dad responded, "I told him she would be high-jacking the guest list to get inside." "I know," Dad replies. If you know then why isn't she here then? My dad responded with son I am the packs Beta. I know everything that has to do with the pack, I know she will be there, I also gave her strict instructions to not drink any alcohol. Leo is heading there with a few of the pack to keep an eye on her. Dad you sent Leo and his friends, she will not react well, she is most likely going to drink just to piss him off. "I know, that's why I'm telling you, because you will be there too." He is right I will now I know my sister is going. Jess is the youngest member of our family. She is only eleven, and she comes into the room, barreling in with a bundle of energy. Hey little sis, "what have you been doing while I've been away"? She begins to tell me all about her activities, her friends and school, how she is going on the camping trip with Mum and the rest of our caregiver enforcers next weekend. I know Dad will put extra patrols on, he won't risk our youth nor will our alpha. I listen as she tells me more of how her and Masie are going on an adventure. I see, where are you going? Maisie will be helping with the camping trip, we are going to hide in the woods and sneak up on the others who think they can hide from us. Maisie has told me we have to beat all the others so we can win the prize. What is the prize? I asked, She whispers in my ear as if she has a secret. We win a hamper filled with goodies to enjoy round the fire. Well then you have to win, I bet there is choclate and biscuits with marsh mellow. Jess smiles I love camping it's fun, we can watch the sky and listen to a story by the fire. Mum, dinners ready, we hear her say, we all sit down at the table as we listen to my sister Jess. How she is enjoying her last year at junior school, she starts high school after the summer holidays, After kissing my mum and sister good night I tell my Dad I will see him tomorrow morning. I head back to my house and swap clothes. I put on a pair of black dressy jeans and my boots with a short-sleeved shirt. I reached the club around 10 pm, it's been open for an hour, I ordered a drink and let my eyes roam around the club, it is tastefully decorated. Marco has dancers on stage warming the crowd up. He has a fire-breathing artist blowing and dancing with batons as they twirl the burning batons in the air and show off their skills with tricks for the crowd. I My brother is at a table sitting at the back of the club with some of his friends, a mixture of human and pack members. I see Marcus, he is upstairs in the V.I.P. lounge watching from above. I can't scent my sister just yet, as I take in deep inhales to see if I can track her down, she has a friend who is dam good at masking scent they are homemade nobody sells things like scent blocker. We have packs who learn to make things but nothing like that is in any of the shops. I walk around the club. It's dark and has flashing lights loud music that messes with my hearing. I use my natural defence by blocking the noise to a bearable level. We as shapeshifters are able to adapt. We wouldn't be able to live in towns and cities if we couldn't. While checking with my eyes and using my nose Leo hasn't moved, I notice as I am walking around that he was looking upstairs but I couldn't see from the bar earlier. I find the staircase and walk up towards the security, both are pack one whispers she's up there. He knows I am looking for my sister, she is smart arse her trio, have defiantly added grey hair to my dad's head. Constantly pushing boundaries, they are trying to see how much he can take. The last time they pushed my dad there punishment was that they had to clean all the cars at our pack's hotel, daily for a full week that was during the spring holidays. She has herposse around her with human bad boys, alongside a couple of the girls from school. I notice in the far corner drinking and partying hard is Sophia she is sitting on someone's knee, I try not to make it obvious I want to turn around and look. He is human Delia is with them a few more females of our pack, and they are surrounded by men. I head over to my sister and she knows I'm here, she is currently giving Leo the finger salute. Maisie, what a surprise how you sweetly talk yourself in here, that would be telling,' she whispers in my ear. You know Dad is aware of your antics, yep, I promised Mum I would not cause trouble and I will only drink juice. Here, can you smell any alcohol in my glass, I can't but I noticed a few of the boys are wasted. Be careful, I know you hear me pack mates no drinking, no kissing, no trouble. As I leave, I get to see the guys around my friends, Delia is in her element, she had her mouth on one of the guys full on zero shits given. I think seeing her best friend waiting and being treated like dirt has made Delia not want to be in the same situation. Sophia is battling her wolf I feel it, her wolf doesn't want to betray their mate, but for once, Sophia is fighting and not letting her wolf win. She has a seat on a man's knees, he was nuzzling her ear, which is our most sensitive spot, where we scent our mates. He is a big guy, he trains, I can see it he has a tight white shirt on, he is a little older, maybe thirty, but boy he is aroused, I can smell the hormones in waves. I walked over to see Marcus, we started talking and he told me how busy he has been getting the new place open and ready to make sure tonight went well. Marcus is a good guy, he has a wife that he adores and they have two daughters. He keeps the business running so smoothly, as he has staff he trusts working alongside him. He even hired a security team that Sam's dad owns, they are the best in the city and have helped with his other club with protecting the customers who don't allow drugs, we have plants that humans have learned they can use to make into a drug, apparently its used to help them loosen up. If taken in high amounts they can pass out and need hospital treatment to pump it out of their systems. After chatting with Marcus for a few minutes I want to see my brother who is still sitting at the table. I walk over towards him and he moves over so I can sit with him. "Hey, I say she enjoys pushing your buttons". I know Leo said" she is trouble with a capital T." She sure is, I said back. We laugh and catch up, it is nice the music is good a girl asks Leo over to dance. He gives me a nod and his eyes go up towards our sister. He gets up and starts dancing, I see the girls dancing, Delia and Sophie are dancing, I think they see the bad boys drunk and are protecting the younger females, that's what we do as a pack, we watch out for each other. I need the bathroom so head over tapping another pack enforcer to keep an eye out. When I return I hear my brother and a few pack members running towards the second floor. I thought it was my sister, so I ran up the other stairs closest to me. I see Delia holding back a raging Tommy, he is meant to be on duty. I hear Masie whispering to Sophia it is ok, you did nothing wrong, he is the arsehole who has pushed you away he sees you sitting on a sexy man's knee. Who smells like he wants to stamp your V card Sophia? Sophia is laughing she is drunk, it takes a lot to get us drunk. But she was drowning her sorrows. The guy in question politely asks hi can I cut in, Sophia I don't know who that boy is but are you ready for a real man I assure you, I will make sure you enjoy riding my dick. Fuck me, Leo is on the verge he is holding back but the dick comment did it, luckily Leo has his arms around the back of Tommy Delia in front. For the first time, Delia takes the guy's hand and says yes please, I've never ridden a dick before why not. Shit! Tommy loses it he manages to get a hold of Sophia, he picks her up over his shoulder and smacks her butt hard in front of all of us. The guys all laugh while Delia the devil high-fives him, thanks Jack you were fantastic You did put on a great show even my friends were fooled you're a star. Jack hugs her, and says, "You ready baby, you promised me the ride of my life, if I helped your girl out I recall you saying later tonight." "Most of us just stood there, in shock with our mouths hanging open," Masie claps and says, "Well played." Leo laughs and we are all ready to leave. I saw Jack take Delia and whisper you kissing Rodger turned me on baby, I wanted to drag him off you and take over. I know babe but I needed my plan to work, let's get out of here you deserve a reward. After that performance, I made my way over to apologise to Marcus who said he already knew he was in on it. He likes Sophia and can't stand seeing her hurt because Tommy keeps breaking her heart. Marcus says he doesn't realise that finding a woman like Sophia is a blessing he would be a fool to let her go. I agree but I still feel with it being his opening night it was a performance he could have done without. He laughs and we shake hands, you are a good man Marcus, that could have gone wrong in so many ways. I need to go as I am leaving Leo's offer to give me a ride home. We are all talking about Tommy Masie sitting in the back, she is telling us how Tommy needed a kick up the bum, he has been an idiot let's hope he starts grovelling on his knees. I agree, I just hope he hasn't taken Sophia to where he takes hookups as she deserves more. It's midnight and I see Tommy hasn't come home. Knowing him, he most likely dragged Sophia to the nearest hotel. To right the wrongs, he has committed. I get ready for bed I fall asleep instantly and there is my angel I always see her first, and I like to watch her as she is carefree. Walking along the path admiring the sounds of nature. Her hair is down and she always has a thoughtful expression on her face, I take deep breaths each time memorising her scent. I want to be able to track her to be able to find her. She gets more and more beautiful each time I see her, she has a summer dress on with sandals on her feet. The sun is bright it is making her hair glow I can see the lighter shades giving her a sunkissed look. Her body has a tanned look of sunbathing. I can see her taking deep breaths as she keeps walking forward. I see her stop and look over her shoulder and by the time she turns back around I am in front of her. She always tries to look up to see my face but each time she tries she wakes up. I can't wait to meet her to get to know her, to give her love and support the memories we will make together, I can't wait to make her mine. I already feel she is mine, I won't allow anyone to touch her, I will not let her live a little unless it's living a little with me. Once I complete this mission, I will ask my Alpha for leave to find her. To go on a mate hunt, we all go to the gatherings, but we are allowed to travel and have a few days with each pack to check we didn't miss anyone. For the past few weeks, every time I go to bed to sleep. I have the same dream, it's always in the woods behind a large home. I end up on a footpath behind a girl I don't know and I hide behind the trees and watch her, to check that she isn't a threat as I track her as she walks further away. Each time I follow her I breathe her in, and each time that I do I am more and more intrigued by her. I can track her by following her scent, she has the most delicious smell that stirs up my wolf where he chants mine, mine, mine, on repeat in my head. I am cautious in the first few dreams that I have. I spend each dream just watching her taking in her beauty and her little traits, the tilting of her face, the way her hair flows free down her back, the curve of her body, the shape of her breast. The way her eyes lighten with the light of the sun as it rises beyond the horizon. Each time I dream it's always about her, I always see her in the same woods behind a huge house walking along the path which has naturally formed from being walked upon. I started to show myself to her, as the time went on, and I enjoyed the moment she knew that I was there with her she always looks behind her shoulder and I always stepped in front of her each time that she did. She will bump into my chest and I feel so relaxed and at peace as I breathe her in.I know she is meant to be mine. I try to show her my face, but each time that I have tried she always wakes up. Tonight though as I dreamed about her something seems different, her scent is a lot stronger than it has been before. I sense her in a way that I am aware of where she is, and what she is doing as she bumps into my chest. this is the dream where this I know what she will be to me, she will be mine. I know now that she is my fated mate. I know exactly when she is about to wake up, and I yell into my mind "Soon", as I know I will find her. I won't stop until I have her in my arms with me, where she belongs. I wake up feeling lighter, as I know my dreams have a meaning, they have a purpose that she is meant for me my wolf has known all along my human brain it took a little bit more time. Once awake I start my day taking a shower and going to meet my Alpha Henry Sanderson. I live alone which is away from the hustle and bustle of the city. I live in the city of Darlington. I belong to the Sanderson pack, we help protect humans from the rougher, more dangerous creatures we have, as we are a city with many humans living here. We have managed to keep most of the creatures at bay, as they find the loud noises of the hotels, casinos, theatres, and lots of traffic too much. Most of our pack live further away from the city center, my parents along with my brother Leo and my two sisters, Masie and Jess, all live nearby. With my dad being the packs Beta, and my Mum being the packs female Beta, they live closer to our Alphas home. He helps keep the beasts at bay, my Dad and Henry who is our Alpha. Both make sure we have enough enforcers protecting our land as our territory is larger than any of the towns and villages we have on our Island. My best friend Tommy lives next door. He and I normally spend time together when we are both free. He moved in a month ago. He was ordered out of his family home, due to his disrepect to his mate. Who he hasn't committed to just yet, he is still living in his Playboy phase. He is one of our enforcers, he is strong, fast and good at his role. He and I like to practise our training together in both human form and wolf form. He has nice qualities its a shame he is pushing Sophia away. I try to stay out of it, as I have tried so many times to talk to him. I don't know what else to do other than kick his arse in training for each occation I've seen Sophia hurting, but masking it from everyone. We have many enforcers in our pack, all are dam good enforcers, they have to patrol a large area, and we work in rotations. My pack role will be Beta once my Dad retires or wishes it to be. I like to sit and tease him like, hey Dad you want to handover the position you have a ton of grey and I swear you have slowed down. He always comes back with a when you can beat me then I will happily hand my position over. I love spending time at home who knows maybe me and your mother can find a way to enjoy the time together. I always laugh my dad loves my mother so much when they are together, I see nothing but devotion and love for each other. My dad has been a constant in our lives, he works hard to help our Alpha run the pack, occasionally he travels on missions with me and my brother Leo, he likes to use that time to bond as he just has boy time except when Delia's around another member of my team. My job role where I do a lot off is to run missions, my team includes my Dad David Hawk, he comes along when we are attending missions overseas. Being a pack Beta helps with building trust, and he has expertise and knowledge of the different types of creatures. He knows best on how to deal with them, he is also good at fighting, weapons and tracking. My friend Delia and her Dad Phillip Moss, they both have joined me on many missions Phillip has a lot of skills including taking down a beast he had a scar on his leg when he was bitten by one during a mission he did with my Dad when we were little, he was testing tranqulizers out on strengh as what dosage may work on oe creature, might not work on another he was bate He survived he likes to call it his war wound for the good of all who live amongst them. Him being bate enabled us to be able to mix up a better tranqulizer that worked. Delia works as hard as anyone she does well working on the radio and has been working with Sophia when they are not out on the field. They are both good with trying to learn technology, they work with a team we have a base that our Island shares with all the packs we have six members from each pack that help with developing better ways to communicate by inventing new ideas. My brother Leo is really good at both tracking and hunting,he is quiet and has been able to merge into his surroundings, he is a perfect match to help me as we work so well we just don't need words, we know what the other is thinking. Which helps when we have to track the worst of the creatures we have to be quiet, we have to work well together and most of all not get hurt. We are a good team. Tommy normally comes along with us but he has been on rotation and needed to help the boarders with patrolling. I think our Alpha is hoping by keeping him grounded he might get his shit together. Sam is my other best friend and he has been helping his Dad out with the family business, they run a security firm. They look after humans watching the bigger clubs and casinos, from any trouble, drunk humans can become aggressive and do tend to start trouble, sometimes getting handsie with the females. Sams family work to minimise any damage. Sam has the best nose I've ever come across, his Dad was the same, he learned all of us how to track. Were better now, as he taught us all he knew and now Sam does the training. His Dad is in his sixties, him and his wife have two children, Sam and Hope. They suffered a miscarriage with the first two pregnancies, I think her wolf broke free on the pack run wanting to run free with the rest of us. The second time was because the baby hadn't developed properly and her wolf rejected it. After having Sam they were happy they finally had a healthy child, which was a surprise when they fell pregnant late in life with Hope. She is doted on as she will be nineteen now her Dad allowed her to join the family business if she wanted, I think they liked her in sight and this was the only way they knew how. They had a tough few years but thankfully they are so close to each other, they all run the family business it helped them overcome a lot having a focus.Henry our Alpha suggested it as he needed to make each business safe and help keep tourists happy without any crime being commited we do have holding where we can put humans to sleep it, off, we also cut them off if they are too drunk that they are a hazard. Sam has helped run it, they now have many of the pack who earn good money from it and it helps our pack with having less to worry about. We have a large city the last thing we need is humans causing damage to property or on each other we have a force called community peace. It is made up of pack and humans who want the same to keep the Island from beast attacks and to keep all who live safe from harm, or harming anyone else. We have a large building in the center that has our Alpha who is in charge of it. It's where humans go when any crime is committed, most are fine and commit little crime. On the odd occasion that do are punished by a team who decide what the punishment will be it's up to them to be fair, the punishment has to fit the crime. It's a new thing that Henry came up with as we have evolved, so has all our surroundings, we have alcohol, we have vulnerable humans who deserve to be able to walk the streets and not be harassed or hurt as they do so. To make sure the Unicorns are free and not locked up, little rules are in place that help all exist without being cruel or causing problems. The Alpha of each town and city entall that all humans alongside there pack, have jobs, homes, schools,were building more hospitals we now have a rail way to be able to travel from each place. We have ships that we use to travel from and to each of the Islands. Rules were needed to allow for peace and to make sure each place had enough to substain a comfortable life. My Dad, Delia, and Phillip are good at watching our backs during the hunts, they help by discouraging any larger packs of either the Neeman lions or the bonnacons from living too close to civilization, when were on a mission they have eyes on any other possible threats. As a pack, any of these creatures can cause damage even to us shapeshifters. I have noticed that since the dreams started I have become restless as I am ready to find my fated mate, so far, I have not found her, I have been to a few gatherings with no luck. I am twenty-five, and I have some time to spare but after my last dream I know I will soon meet her. I have waited as many of our kind do, I have not done any dating, some choose to depending on their human half if they are ready to settle yet or not. I chose to wait I know she has long light brown straight hair, blue eyes, and has the most amazing figure, her lips I look at them and want to be able to kiss her. She is breathtakingly beautiful, I can smell her. She has a sweet, scent. My wolf wants to bottle that sweet flowery scent up to roll around in it all day long. I tell myself after we finish this current mission, we will go looking for her. Once I smell her near I will hunt her down. I make myself some breakfast as my thoughts are just re living my dream I need to see my family. I travel over to my parents house, it's not far from my own place. My parents live on the other side of a small, wooded area, where you can see the alpha's home not far behind with it's vest surrounding forest. We have lakes with endless landscapes of fields and farmland. We have a river that runs through our land. It's further north where it connects to all the towns on our Island towards our coastal towns. We have three coastal towns, alongside five large towns and many villages as well as the city where I live with my pack. Our land we all live on is The Griffin Island. We have a four-hour boat ride to Vale Island which has the City of Evergreen. This is where our mission is to meet the new Alpha Brock Steel. He has been made the new Alpha of the city as the last one Max died. We just don't know any details, it's just that the new Alpha has had a lot to deal with and all the Alphas have given him the time to settle into his new role. I am to go over with my team as he has some information to share that is delicate and he doesn't want to use the radio to discuss the matter. It was agreed that

I would go over this with my team and see what has happened to the last Alpha and how everything is going. As I parked my car on my parents drive I saw my brother taking both our sisters to school. It's Monday morning and they have only two more weeks left. I wave them off and go inside mum is in the living space my mother is beautiful she has a kind soul, her long brown hair tied into a bun with her workout clothes on. Hi, mum are you going for a run or are you at the center watching over the kids? My mum works protecting our children from any danger, especially as the creatures we have found tend to hunt our most vulnerable thinking they are that think our young are easy pickings, my mum is forty-nine and she can still fight any creature who dares to stalk our children or any from our city we all have talks and safety instructions to follow. The children are taught to protect themselves, how to hide, how to cover their scent. I loved my time at the centre, I met so many friends from having such good memories from the camping trips, the days out football, tag all of it. Good times. My mum replies "I have a day off and I am going to combat training with a few of my team". We have a trip coming up, we are taking the kids camping and we have received warnings of more Neeman lions around. I like to make sure we are ready just to be safe. Haven't the enforcers moved them away yet they normally have them rehomed further away. I know it's been strange they seem to be coming in with no scent trails it has everyone stumped so we have been told to be careful and when we do go camping Henry has asked for all the staff to go. I am a little shocked I haven't been home much this past month, I only got back last night from tracking the other side further to the port where we have had reports of a griffin flying around the area. What isn't their usual behaviour, we have a coastal area that we moved them to taking them away from civilization. To allow them to replenish their numbers and live in peace. My Dad enters the living space, "where are we going son?". We have orders from Henry and we need to visit Evergreen to see the new Alpha, he has some information he wants to share. We will be leaving in the morning, I have a few errands to run in the meantime. Will you ask Leo, to be ready to leave in the morning please?" he should be back be back soon, I will let him know". Okay thank you Dad, I'll see you tonight for dinner. I find my mother filling up her water bottle ready for her workout, I'm leaving, but I will be back tonight for dinner, I have been missed your cooking mum. I will make your favourite Hayden if you make a dessert . "You have a deal, see you later." I kiss my mother's cheeks as I need to go into the city, to run errands. Once I have finished, I bumped into Sam. "Hi Sam, tough night?" hi, Hayden you could say that I had a few drunk people to deal being sore losses. I dealt with it and nobody needed to be taken to see the community peace centre last night. "Good," I haven't been back long, I have to go back out again tomorrow do you fancy grabbing a coffee we can catch up".We decided to go to the coffee shop across the street. We caught up about what each of us have been up to. Sam is my height he has long black hair he ties it up into a man bun, he has stubble and looks tired he has hazel eyes with a tanned complexion he likes to be in the sun as much as possible he can scent a few miles away if he has to, he can focus his wolf abilities hone them in and follow up to the source of the scent. He is one of my best friends alongside Tommy and Delia, he has been having a tough time these past few weeks he has bags under his eyes like he is carrying the weight of the world on his shoulder's. He likes to train daily, it helps him deal with his wolf he has been waiting for a mate for longer than me. He will be turning thirty next year. His wolf is worried they may have lost their fated mate. May I ask Sam if he was able to sleep? I get some sleep my wolf is driving me hard lately like he knows something important but I can't figure it out just yet. He is frustrated he wants his mate found, like I haven't tried I've been to most of the gatherings met most if not all the females the packs have to offer but nothing. I'm feeling the frustration and even when I sleep I see a place I don't recognise and pack, I've never met. It's so frustrating as I can't make any sense of it my wolf gets pissed and I don't know Hayden I'm losing hope. He has other gatherings coming up, I hope he finds her this time as he will have met every single pack member and all the newly aged females. He has been in a relationship seeing the same human on and off for over two years, which is unusual for our kind. He mentioned dreams maybe he is having the same ones like mine where his mate is there but maybe he hasn't figured it out yet so I tell him about the dreams. I've been having dreams like you seem to be having and each night they are in the woods, a house in the background and at first I just watch her as I have never seen her before, I don't recognise the setting either. As the dreams have been happening more often I have managed to gain knowledge of her scent as last night it had changed, it was a lot stronger, my wolf had been going crazy as if he knew all this time. I didn't and last night I figured out who she is, she's my mate Sam, my fated mate. I just have to find her, but my gut says it will be soon. He listens to every word I say as if he too has had these dreams. He seems to be thinking, about what his dreams actually mean, as he has gone quiet. I hope I have given him hope by sharing my situation. We have many females turning eighteen, according to our records. If she isn't ready, he will mark her as a warning, so that his wolf settles, and his mate knows that he is hers and she is his. He is ready and I don't think he will allow his mate to run or live a little. It's going to be interesting, I can tell. He and I part ways and I tell him not to give up and to use his gut instincts. If he has been having dreams he knows she is here somewhere he just has to find her. I tell Sam to go find her, remember the dreams, use them to try and locate her on the land you see, if anything is familar any landmarks, anything that you would have seen before having travelled all the Islands. She has to be around, if there are no death recordings she has to be out there, use the dreams as they are clues to where she is. "Thank you Hayden", you have given me hope I know Sam and he will find her wherever she is. I need to go to bed and sleep I'm tired maybe I can try to understand more what the dreams mean, or what they are trying to tell me. We hugged and agreed to see each other once I return. I feel lighter myself talking to Sam and how he's dreaming too, as helped my own determination on finding my own mate. I need to focus on this mission and find the rest of my team I need to find Delia, we are due a training session she will most likely be at the Center. As I thought she was already here, warming up. Hey Hayden, what took you so long? I bumped into Sam and we caught up. "You ready for a beat down". "In your dreams Hayden." I will be the one beating your arse." I laugh we always like to annoy each other in a fun way she is a warrior and she enjoys training it helps her clear her thoughts, it helps me too. Delia wants to run off some energy first, we both decide to have a run in our wolf forms and practice our skills. We switch forms near the center, being able to shapeshift into a wolf is easy, it's like magic we glow a second and then were in wolf form, it's strange during the growth phase as you switch forms constantly. One moment you can be eating dinner the next your a wolf. You can be walking along on two legs and then flash into a wolf. Once our leaders Alpha and Beta teach you to control it, life resumes as normal. You learn that just before you shift your wolf becomes stronger, it's up to your human shape to control if it's safe to switch and allow your wolf the freedom to run. With time it becomes easier to control, as you and your wolf want what's best, the danger of exposing and protecting each other is key to becoming balanced together. We are in our forest that belongs to the pack, it's private, and we have high fences with patrols all around them. We do have a few Neeman Lions and Bonnacons nesting inside our land and we have the areas sealed off to help keep them away from hunting our own kind, especially on pack runs when we all participate. We have a few families of Bonnacons they are up by the lake further south where there are good hunting grounds for them, and they have caves they use as nests to protect their young. We have our strongest enforcers watching over the Neeman Lions, those are tough fuckers, they can cause a lot of damage to us, we have them guarded as they are intelligent and the males are aggressive, we have a few families that have formed a pack, we have them in the mountain area where they have everything, they need to survive food, shelter and water. When mum mentioned that some have been near the camp sites it's worrying that it's not normal behavior. I trust our Alpha he no doubt he will make sure to keep all of our city safe. Delia is up front running and hiding trying to attack me without me knowing we are hiding and masking scent. This is a good way for us when we are tracking we have to be able to blend into our surroundings. We run laps around the forest we fight in our wolves to practice honing our skills. Once we have completed our wolf training we head back towards the center. We have training facilities and an intense course we do in human form. Delia pushed into my back and said: "You ready for more Hayden, it feels like you're out of shape?" really Delia I could have sworn that you were eating my dust. We are both laughing as we start our human training doing laps. The center has a killer workout program where we have large obstacles to climb and jump over. We have a shooting range where we use crossbows, throw axes, and shoot arrows. We have an area where we learn how to use tranquilizer guns. We have to learn how be to able to shoot into moving-sized shapes, as if we are in the field. We have to be able to hit small targets and the bigger targets. We have to be able to hit each target accurately, some of the animals we relocated have thick hydes and the only way to enable the tranquilizer to work is to hit underneath in there most vulnerable areas. We have outside a crawling station full of mud water and spikes, there are bushes above us that we find around our land we have to be able to get into small spaces to hit our target that might include jumping into water or hiding in bushes up a tree anywhere that hides and can help make it easier to put the creature to sleep. It's easier than having to fight them if they sense you're there. The training helps you adapt to any possible sinero. To finish the course we jump across water into another obstacle course to climb up the last wall which is high once you can manage to complete that part of the course its a race to the finish line. Delia and I completed the whole course, I completed the course first as I was catching my breath Delia finished. I am stronger, and faster, being the pack's next Beta. Delia is tough, she has trained as much as I have. We walked back to the facility to clean up. We met up with Sophia and Tommy when we hadn't seen much of each other for over two weeks. Tommy is mates with Sophia, he has a lot of muscle, he is good at being an enforcer, he has good fighting skills, he has blonde hair, he wears it up in a man bun, his hair is long, he likes the wildness of it, it suits his roaming ways. He has blue eyes and a little stubble, in his words the stumble helps to tickle and pleasure my dates. That is what he said, he has been holding off with Sophia from forming a mate bond via mating. He has dated many, especially this past year like his human half knows time is running out. Soon his wolf will take over, as he has been a real player his human half is stubborn. Sophia tries to ignore it, as she knows he isn't ready, but when we meet up it's been two weeks for me. I can feel the tension building Delia could have given me a heads up, awkward. We are all caught up I feel that Tommy has treated Sophia poorly he needs a kick up the arse Sam would kill to have what he has, maybe that's why those two don't hang out as much. Delia has told me they haven't been hanging out as much as they used to, Sam is dating and has dated, he had waited until he was my age before he decided to date. He probably sees Sophia hurting and wishes he had a mate Tommy is acting like an arsehole he has to know she is in pain, after telling each other what each of us has been doing. Sophia is quiet, she has not said a word, I want to hug her and tell her he is a fool. I see Delia, she has a plan she takes a hold of Sophia's hand and takes her to the bathroom. I have to say something, what are you doing Tommy? You're hurting, you're mate, are you going to destroy the woman that has been gifted to you? I know Tommy says my wolf is getting harder to control, but I am only twenty-two she is twenty-six I need time Hayden I need to live a little my human is fighting it I am fighting it I just. I interrupt Sophia has waited for you, she has saved herself for you!, she could have lived a little how do you think you would feel? What more is it going to take? By the time the girls come back I see Delia, she is not having this, she gives off the vibe Tommy will pay dearly for hurting his mate, and she will make sure of it. Sophia is pretty, she has short, bobbed hair with waves she puts in, she has deep blue eyes has a softer shape than Delia as Sophia is a chef in the best hotel in town, she has a natural talent she can cook. She trains with the pack, she does all the workouts and practices so if she's ever alone she can handle it. We have all our pack mates and members trained to do so. Delia is her best friend, she knows Tommy is younger, but he is being an idiot, he has a mate, so why wait? I know that's why he moved in next door to me as his parents wouldn't let him bring hookups back as they had an inkling Sophia might be his fated. He has two brothers, I think if he had sisters like me, he wouldn't want to hurt them, and he would see what a blessing he had been given. His wolf will take over, he will bite her and force the man inside to man up and take his mate as he will see her as just a gift, and he will not allow the man to hurt his mate. I reckon Tommy knows this and has been much more of a player than normal. After the food is eaten Delia decides to put her plan into action, I work with her and I know her well she has got a plan goodluck Tommy you are going to need it. Hayden, I will meet you tomorrow, me and Sophia have plans tonight we are going out with the twins tonight one of them has received an invitation to the new club that Marcus has opened up. Marcus is human, he has another club on the south side of the city, this new place he is opening is in the centre. Monday is not a normal day to open a club Marcus's big party is risky, normally the weekend pulls the crowd in, but Marcus knows what he's doing. and I bet half the packs will go tonight, those free anyhow, even the visiting packs will be there, it's the club, it's one of the best places to hook up. Tommy perks up, oh yeah! he is so used to Sophia being a goodie two shoes. She has always followed him around, has made her feelings clear, she has waited and agreed to give him time, it's been four years and maybe she needs to let loose. Good for her, Tommy needs a reminder of what he does she can also do maybe Delia will make sure he gets that lesson. Delia says to Tommy, "I hear you're on duty tonight sucks to be you.'See you tomorrow Hayden, she takes a hold of Sophia's hand and for the first time, Sophia doesn't look at Tommy with love in her eyes, if I see anything it's pure disappointment. "Oh boy Tommy you're in deep shit, good luck, I'll see you when I'm back." I leave Tommy sat there stewing, I feel he has taken advantage of the fact that he has a mate right there ready for the taking, yet he has gotten a little used to knowing she has given him time, maybe that's why Sam had not bothered hanging around with him. He acts like a typical human guy who wants his cake but likes to try a few mouthfuls of different flavours first. Sophia looked ready to go along with whatever Delia had planned, Sophia must have lost hope as Tommy did seem to be pulling away further, instead of moving closer to mating. I drive back home and start to pack for my new mission. I decide to soak in the bath before dinner tonight I might even drop in at the club to see what Delia the little minx's is up to. I go over to see my family, mum has almost finished dinner it smells good. I had a beer with dad and we talked a little. I asked why is the house so quiet where Maisie was? she had plans tonight with her friends, and at some sort of celebration, one of the pack cousins was over. Fetching a few friends to help celebrate. Dad, did you know Marcus is opening up his new club tonight? "I do," my dad responded, "I told him she would be high-jacking that guest list to get in." "I know," Dad replies. Why isn't she here then? My dad responded with a son I am the pack beta, I know everything that has to do with the pack I know she will be there I also gave her strict instructions to not drink any booze. Leo is heading there with a few of the pack to keep an eye on her. Dad really, she would not react well, I know that's why I'm telling you, because you will be there too. He is right I will be, my sister Jess is the youngest member of our family she is only eleven, and she comes in just at that moment barreling in with a bundle of energy. Hey sis what have you been doing while I've been away? She fills me in on all her friends and her school, she is going on a camping trip with Mum and the rest of our caregiver enforcers next weekend. I know Dad will put extra patrols on, he won't risk our r youth nor will our alpha. After spending time with my family having dinner it was good especially my sister Jess she has been enjoying her last year at junior school she starts high school after the summer holidays she is telling me how many friends she will make and how she gets to play with Ethan soon as he will visit his aunt and uncle our alpha is his family, He is visiting for two weeks in the summer. They have a trip planned they are all going with the mums to the seaside my mum tells me she and Wendy want to give his parents his adopted ones a break and have booked a large house for all of our pack kids to go while we all have patrols and other things we have to do. They have arranged to take a few enforcers along, with the caregivers as well as taking their mates. The kids will love it, I remember when my mum and Wendy would take us and all the pack kids for two weeks every summer. It's a pack holiday where all the kids get to be just kids. After kissing my mum and sister good night I tell my dad I will see him tomorrow morning. I head back to my own house and change clothes. I put on a pair of black dressy jeans, and my boots, with a short-sleeved shirt. I have toned arms, I will show them off. I reached the club around 10 pm, it's been open for an hour, I wanted to wait and see if my sister was trying to get in. I ordered a drink and let my eyes roam around the club, it is tastefully decorated, and there are dancers on stage warming the crowd up. He has fire-breathing artists and dancing using batons that are on fire, they throw them in the air and catch them while they move to the music. It looked amazing with each performer doing different tricks. My brother is sat at the back of the club with some of his friends, most are pack mates. He has a few human friends, sat at the table with him too, and they are attracted to a few human females. Some of them get up to either the bar for drinks or onto the dance floor. I see Marcus, he is upstairs in the V.I.P. lounge watching his successful launch by the looks of it. I can't smell my sister just yet, she has a friend who is dam good at masking scent they are homemade as we don't sell them in our country or any others that I know of. I took a walk around checking the place out. It's a cool place, there is a large dance floor with a stage and some cages filled with dancers each doing tricks I can tell it will be a good investment for Marcus. Leo hasn't moved from where he has been sitting since I came in, he hasn't taken his eyes from the second floor as he is watching an area upstairs. When I was at the bar earlier I couldn't see the staircase leading up to that floor. Walking up towards security, both are pack members," one whispers to me" she's up there." My sister Masie is smart. She and her best friends from our pack, who we call the treble trio, have defiantly added grey hair to my dad's head. They always find trouble, or try their best to push boundaries, by trying to see how much they can get away with seeing how we all react to each time they have pushed us all. Leo bites the most out of my dad and I. The last punishment they all received was to clean all the cars for free at our pack's hotel, every day for a full week. That punishment was during the spring holidays. So far they have behaved, but I know those three it won't be long before they pull another stunt to push boundaries. Maisie has the same group around her, the human bad boys with a couple of the girls from school. I notice that in the far corner drinking and partying hard is Sophia, who is sitting on someone's knee, I try not to make it obvious that I want to turn around and look. Delia is with them, alongside a few females from our pack, and they are surrounded by human men. I head over to my sister and she knows I'm here, she is currently giving Leo the finger salute. Maisie, what a surprise how you sweetly talk yourself in here, that would be telling,' she whispers in my ear. You know Dad is aware of your antics, yep, I promised Mum I would not cause trouble and I will only drink juice. Here, can you smell any alcohol in my glass, I can't but I noticed a few of the boys are wasted. Be careful, I know you hear me pack mates no drinking, no kissing, no trouble. As I leave, I get to see the guys around my friends, Delia is in her element, she had her mouth on one of the guys full on zero shits given. I think seeing her best friend waiting and being treated like dirt has made Delia not want to be in the same situation. Sophia is battling her wolf I feel it, her wolf doesn't want to betray their mate, but for once, Sophia is fighting and not letting her wolf win. She has a seat on a man's knees, he was nuzzling her ear, which is our most sensitive spot, where we scent our mates. He is a big guy, he trains, I can see it he has a tight white shirt on, he is a little older, maybe thirty, but boy he is aroused, I can smell the hormones in waves. I head over to see Marcus, we start talking and he has been busy making sure tonight went well, he is a good guy, he has a wife he adores and two daughters. He keeps the business running smoothly, and he hires a security team, that Sam's dad owns, they don't allow drugs, we have plants the humans make into a drug, and it makes the humans loosen up. If taken in high amounts they can pass out and need hospital treatment to pump it out of their systems. I head towards my brother's table and he moves over so I can sit. Hey, I say she enjoys pushing your buttons, I know she is trouble with a capital T. She sure is, we laugh and catch up it is nice the music is good a girl asks Leo over to dance he gives me a nod and his eyes go up towards our sister. He gets up and starts dancing, I see the girls dancing, Delia and Sophie are dancing, I think they see the bad boys drunk and are protecting the younger females, that's what we do as a pack, we watch out for each other. I need the bathroom so head over tapping another pack enforcer to keep an eye out. When I return I hear my brother and a few pack members running towards the second floor. I thought it was my sister, so I ran up the other stairs closest to me. I see Delia holding back a raging Tommy, he is meant to be on duty. I hear Masie whispering to Sophia it is ok, you did nothing wrong, he is the arsehole who has pushed you away he sees you sitting on a sexy man's knee. Who smells like he wants to stamp your V card Sophia? Sophia is laughing she is drunk, it takes a lot to get us drunk. But she was drowning her sorrows. The guy in question politely asks hi can I cut in, Sophia I don't know who that boy is but are you ready for a real man I assure you, I will make sure you enjoy riding my dick. Fuck me, Leo is on the verge he is holding back but the dick comment did it, luckily Leo has his arms around the back of Tommy Delia in front. For the first time, Delia takes the guy's hand and says yes please, I've never ridden a dick before why not. Shit! Tommy loses it he manages to get a hold of Sophia, he picks her up over his shoulder and smacks her butt hard in front of all of us. The guys all laugh while Delia the devil high-fives him, thanks Jack you were fantastic You did put on a great show even my friends were fooled you're a star. Jack hugs her, and says, "you ready baby, you promised me a ride of my life, if I helped your girl out I recall you saying later tonight." "Most of us are just stood there, in shock with our mouths hanging open," Masie claps and says, "Well played." Leo laughs and we are all ready to leave. I saw Jack take Delia and whisper you kissing Rodger turned me on baby, I wanted to drag him off you and take over. I know babe but I needed my plan to work, let's get out of here You deserve a reward. After that performance, I made my way over to apologise to Marcus who said he already knew he was in on it. He likes Sophia and can't stand seeing her hurt because Tommy keeps breaking her heart. Marcus says he doesn't realise that finding a woman like Sophia is a blessing he would be a fool to let her go. I agree but I still feel with it being his opening night it was a performance he could have done without. He laughs and we shake hands, you are a good man Marcus, that could have gone wrong in so many ways. I need to go as I am leaving Leo's offer to give me a ride home. We are all talking about Tommy Masie sitting in the back, she is telling us how Tommy needed a kick up the bum, he has been an idiot let's hope he starts grovelling on his knees. I agree, I just hope he hasn't taken Sophia to where he takes hookups as she deserves more. It's midnight and I see Tommy hasn't come home. Knowing him, he most likely dragged Sophia to the nearest hotel. To right the wrongs, he has committed. I get ready for bed I fall asleep instantly and there is my angel I always see her first, and I like to watch her as she is carefree. Walking along the path admiring the sounds of nature. Her hair is down and she always has a thoughtful expression on her face, I take deep breaths each time memorising her scent. I want to be able to track her to be able to find her. She gets more and more beautiful each time I see her, she has a summer dress on with sandals on her feet. The sun is bright it is making her hair glow I can see the lighter shades giving her a sunkissed look. Her body has a tanned look of sunbathing. I can see her taking deep breaths as she keeps walking forward. I see her stop and look over her shoulder and by the time she turns back around I am in front of her. She always tries to look up to see my face but each time she tries she wakes up. I can't wait to meet her to get to know her, to give her love and support the memories we will make together, I can't wait to make her mine. I already feel she is mine, I won't allow anyone to touch her, I will not let her live a little unless it's living a little with me. Once I complete this mission, I will ask my Alpha for leave to find her. To go on a mate hunt, we all go to the gatherings, but we are allowed to travel and have a few days with each pack to check we didn't miss anyone. For the past few weeks, every time I go to bed to sleep. I have the same dream, it's always in the woods behind a large home. I end up on a footpath behind a girl I don't know and I hide behind the trees and watch her, to check that she isn't a threat as I track her as she walks further away. Each time I follow her I breathe her in, and each time that I do I am more and more intrigued by her. I can track her by following her scent, she has the most delicious smell that stirs up my wolf of where he chants mine, mine, mine, on repeat in my head. I am cautious in the first few dreams that I have. I spend each dream just watching her taking in her beauty and her little traits, the tilting of her face, the way her hair flows free down her back, the curve of her body, the shape of her breast. The way her eyes lighten with the light of the sun as it rises beyond the horizon. Each time I dream it's always about her, I always see her in the same woods behind a huge house walking along the path which has naturally formed from being walked upon. I started to show myself to her, as the time went on, and I enjoyed the moment she knew that I was there with her she always looks behind her shoulder and I always stepped in front of her each time that she did. She will bump into my chest and I feel so relaxed and at peace as I breathe her in.I know she is meant to be mine. I try to show her my face, but each time that I have tried she always wakes up. Tonight though as I dreamed about her something seems different, her scent is a lot stronger than it has been before. I sense her in the way that I am aware of where she is, and what she is doing as she bumps into my chest. this is the dream where this I know what she will be to me, she will be mine. I know that she is my fated mate. I know exactly when she is about to wake up, and I yell into my mind "Soon", as I know I will find her. I won't stop until I have her in my arms with me, where she belongs. I wake up feeling lighter, as I know my dreams have a meaning, they have a purpose that she is meant for me my wolf has known all along my human brain it took a little bit more time. Once awake I start my day taking a shower and going to meet my Alpha Henry Sanderson. I live alone which is away from the hustle and bustle of the city. I live in the city of Darlington. I belong to the Sanderson pack, we help protect humans from the rougher, more dangerous creatures we have, as we are a city with many humans living here. We have managed to keep most of the creatures at bay, as they find the loud noises of the hotels, casinos, theatres, and lots of traffic too much. Most of our pack live further away from the city centre, my parents, my brother Leo and my two sisters, Masie and Jess, live close by. My dad is the Beta, of our pack, and he lives closer to our Alpha's home. To help keep the beasts at bay, he and Henry must make sure we have enough enforcers protecting our land as our ory is larger than any of the towns and villages we have on our island. My best friend Tommy lives next door. He and I normally spend time together when we are free. He moved in a month ago. He was ordered out of his family home, due to his total disrepect to his mate. Who he hasn't yet commited too, he is still living in his playboy phase. He is one of our enforcers, he is strong, fast and good at his role. He and I like to practise our training together in both human form and wolf form. He has nice qualities its a shame he is pushing Sophia away. I try to stay out of it, as I have tried so many times to talk to him. I don't know what else to do other than kick his arse in training for each occation Ive seen Sophia hurting, but masking it from everyone. We have many enforcers in our pack, are all dam good enforcers, they have to patrol a large area, and we work in rotations. My pack role will be Beta once my dad retires or wishes it to be. I like to sit and tease him like, hey Dad you want to handover the position you have a ton of grey and I swear you have slowed down. He always comes back with a when you can beat me then I will happily hand my position over. I love spending time at home who knows maybe me and your mother can find a way to enjoy the time together. I always laugh my dad loves my mother so much when there together I see nothing but devotion and love for each other. My dad has been a constant in our lives, he works hard to help our Alpha run the pack, occasionally he travels on missions with me and my brother Leo, he likes to use that time to bond as he just has boy time except when Delia's around another member of my team. My job role, which I do a lot of, is to run missions. My team, dad, joins us when we leave our island as our Beta he enjoys helping and making sure each pack is well. It helps with building trust, he has a lot of knowledge when the creatures are involved. How best to deal with them, he is also good at fighting, weapons and tracking. My friend Delia and her dad Phillip Moss, they both have joined me on many missions Phillip has a lot of skills including taking down a beast he had a scar on his leg when he was bitten by one during a mission he did with my dad when we were little, he was testing tranqulizers out on strengh as what dosage may work on oe creature, might not work on another he was bate He survived he likes to call it his war wound for the good of all who live amongst them. Him being bate enabled us to be able to mix up a better tranqulizer that was strong enough to work. Delia works as hard as anyone, and she works on making sure the Radio's are up to date. Sophia and Delia are our inventors, they are both smart and have worked hard to enable us to communicate long distances. when they are not out on the field. They are both learning technology, they work with a team we have at the base that our Island shares with the packs we have six members from each pack. Helping with developing better ways to communicate. My brother Leo is really good at both tracking and hunting, he is quiet and has been able to merge into his surroundings. He is a perfect match to help me as we work so well we just don't need words, we just know what the other is thinking. Which helps when we have to track the worst of the creatures we have to be quiet, we have to work well together and most of all not get hurt. We are a good team, Tommy normally comes along but he has been on rotation and needed to help the boarders with patrolling. I think our Alpha is hoping by keeping him grounded he might get his shit together. Sam is my other best friend and he has been helping his Dad out with the family business. They look after humans watching the bigger clubs and casinos, from any trouble, drunk humans can become aggressive and do tend to start trouble, sometimes getting handsie with the females. Sams family work to minimise any damage. Sam has the best nose I've ever come across, his Dad was the same, he learned all of us how to track. Were better now, as he taught us all he knew and now Sam does the training. His Dad is in his sixties, him and his wife have two children, Sam and Hope, who miscarried her first two pregnancies. I think her wolf broke free on the pack run wanting to run free with the rest of us. The second time was because the baby hadn't developed properly and her wolf rejected it. After having Sam they were happy they finally had a healthy child, and she had an unexpected surprise when they fell pregnant late in life with Hope. She is doted on as she will be nineteen now her Dad allowed her to join the family business if she wanted, I think they liked her in sight and this was the only way they knew how. They've had a tough few years but thankfully they are so close to each other, they all run the family business in security it has helped them overcome a lot, having a focus. Henry suggested it as he needed to make each business safe and help keep tourists happy without any crime being committed we do have holding where we can put humans to sleep it off, we also cut them off if they are too drunk that they are a hazard. Sam has helped run it, they now have many of the pack who earn good money from it and it helps our pack with having less to worry about. We have a large city and the last thing we need is humans causing damage to property or on each other we have a force called community peace. It's made to help maintain peace if anyone commit's a crime that is deemed unsafe to others, or deemed dangerous. They will spend time in the facility, until a vote is made for each case if they have learned a lesson or not. I have noticed that since the dreams started I have become restless a lately as I am ready to find my fated mate, so far, I have not found her, I have been to a few gatherings with no luck. I am twenty-five, and I have some time to spare but after my last dream I know I will soon meet her. I have waited as many of our kind do, I have not done any dating, some choose to depending on their human half if there ready to settle yet or not. I chose to wait I know she has long light brown straight hair, blue eyes, and has the most amazing figure, her lips I look at them and want to be able to kiss her. She is breathtakingly beautiful, I can smell her. She has a sweet, scent. My wolf wants to bottle that sweet flowery scent up to roll around in it all day long. I tell myself after we finish this current mission, we will go looking for her. Once I smell her near I will hunt her down. I make myself some breakfast as my thoughts are just re living my dream I need to see my family. I travel over to my parents house, it's not far from my own place. My parents live on the other side of a small, wooded area, where you can see the alpha's home not far behind with it's vest surrounding forest. We have lakes with endless landscapes of fields and farmland. We have a river that runs through our land. It's further north where it connects to all the towns on our Island towards our coastal towns. We have three coastal towns, alongside five large towns and many villages as well as the city where I live with my pack. Our land we all live on is The Griffin Island. We have a four-hour boat ride to Vale Island which has the City of Evergreen. This is our mission to meet the new Alpha Brock Steel. He has been made the new Alpha of the city as the last one Max died. We don't know any details just that the new Alpha has had a lot to deal with and all the Alphas have given him the time to settle into his new role. I am to go over with my team as he has some information to share that is delicate and he doesn't want to use the radio to discuss the matter. It was agreed that I would go over this with my team and see what has happened to the last Alpha and how everything is going. As I parked my car on my parents drive I saw my brother taking both our sisters to school. It's Monday morning and they have only two more weeks left. I wave them off and go inside mum is in the living space my mother is beautiful she has a kind soul, her long brown hair tied into a bun with her workout clothes on. Hi, mum are you going for a run or are you at the center watching over the kids? My mum works protecting our children, from any danger, especially as the creatures we have found tend to hunt our most vulnerable, thinking they are our young are easy pickings, my mum is forty-nine and she can still fight any creature who dares to stalk our children or anyone from our city we all have talks and safety instructions to follow. The children are taught to protect themselves, how to hide, how to cover there scent. I loved my time at the center, I met so many friends from having such good memories from the camping trips, the days out football, tag all of it. Good times. My mum replies "I have a day off and I am going to combat training with a few of my team". We have a trip coming up, we are taking the kids camping and we have received warnings of more Neeman lions around. I like to make sure we are ready just to be safe. Haven't the enforcers moved them away yet, they normally have them rehomed further away. I know it's been strange they seem to be coming in with no scent trails it has everyone stumped so we have been told to be careful and when we do go camping Henry has asked for all the staff to go. I am a little shocked I haven't been home much this past month I only got back last night from tracking the other side further to the port weve had reports of a griffin flying around the area. Which isn't their usual behaviour, they have a coastal area that we moved any residents away from to allow them to replenish their numbers, and live in peace. My Dad enters the living space, "where are we going son?", We have orders, we need to visit Evergreen to see the new Alpha he has some information he needs to share we will leave in the morning, I have a few errands to run can you tell Leo?" Yes he will be back soon, I will let him know", I need to let the Mosse's know I'll see you tonight for dinner I have been missing your cooking mum. You be safe, I will see you tonight I will make your favourite if you make dessert I love your cooking too son. You have a deal, see you later. After running a few errands in the city I bumped into Sam. Hi Sam, tough night? we had a few drunk people to deal with and a few sore losses, but it was all dealt with and nobody needed to be taken in for a rest. We decided to go to the coffee shop to catch up. We talked about what each of us had been up to. Sam is my height he has long black hair he ties it up into a man bun, he has stubble and looks tired he has hazel eyes with a tanned complexion he likes to be in the sun as much as possible he can scent a few miles away if he has to, he can focus his wolf abilities hone them in and followup to the source of the scent. He is one of my best friends alongside Tommy and Delia, he has been having a tough time these past few weeks he has bags under his eyes like he is carrying the weight of the world on his shoulder's. He likes to train daily, it helps him deal with his wolf he has been waiting for a mate for longer than me. He will be turning thirty next year. His wolf is worried they may have lost their fated mate. May I ask Sam, are you able to sleep? I get some sleep my wolf is driving me hard lately like he knows something important but I can't figure it out just yet. He is frustrated he wants his mate found, like I haven't tried I've been to most of the gatherings met most if not all the females the packs have to offer but nothing. I'm feeling the frustration and even when I sleep I see a place I don't recognise and pack I've never met. It's so frustrating as I can't make any sense of it my wolf gets pissed and I don't know Hayden I am beginning to lose hope. He has other gatherings coming up, I hope he finds her this time as he will have met every single pack member and all the newly aged females. He has been in a relationship seeing the same human on and off for over two years, which is unusual for our kind. He mentioned dreams maybe he is having the same ones like mine where his mate is their but maybe he hasn't figured it out yet so I tell him about the dreams. I've been having dreams like you seem to be having and each night they are in the woods, a house in the background and at first I just watch her as I have never seen her before, I don't recognise the setting either. As the dreams have been happening more often I have managed to gain knowledge. Her scent last night was stronger, my wolf had been going crazy as if he knew all this time. I didn't and last night I figured out who she is, she's my mate Sam, my fated mate. I just have to find her, but my gut says it will be soon. He listens to every word I say as if he too has had these dreams. He seems to be thinking, about what his dreams actually mean, as he has gone quiet. I hope I have given him hope by sharing my situation. We have many females turning eighteen, according to our records. If she isn't ready, he will mark her as a warning, so that his wolf settles, and his mate knows that he is hers and she is his. He is ready and I don't think he will allow his mate to run or live a little. It's going to be interesting I can tell. He and I part ways and I tell him not to give up and to use his gut instincts. If he has been having dreams he knows she is here somewhere he just has to find her. I tell Sam to go find her, remember the dreams, use them to try and locate her the land you see, if it's familar or is there any landmarks, anything that you would have seen before having travelled all the Islands. She has to be around, if there are no death recordings she has to be out there use the dreams as they are clues to where she is. Thank you Hayden", you have given me hope I know Sam and he will find her wherever she is. I need to go to bed and sleep I'm tired maybe I can try to understand more what the dreams mean, or what they are trying to tell me. We hugged and agreed to see each other once I return. I feel lighter myself talking to Sam and how he's dreaming too, as helped my own determination on finding my own mate. I need to focus on this mission and find the rest of my team I need to find Delia we are due a training session she will most likely be at the Center. As I thought she is already here, warming up. Hey Hayden what took you so long? I bumped into Sam and we caught up. "You ready for a beat down". In your dreams Hayden, "I will be the one beating your arse." I laugh we always like to annoy each other in a fun way she is a warrior and she enjoys training it helps her clear her thoughts, it helps me too. Delia wants to run off some energy first, we both decide to have a run in our wolf forms and practice our skills. We switch forms near the center, being able to shapeshift into a wolf is easy, it's like magic we glow a second and then were in wolf form, it's strange during the growth phase as you switch forms constantly. One moment you can be eating dinner the next your a wolf. You can be walking along on two legs and then flash into a wolf. Once our leaders Alpha, and Beta learn you to control it life resumes as normal. You learn just before you shift your wolf becomes stronger, it's up to your human shape to control if it's safe to switch and allow your wolve the freedom to run. With time it becomes easier to control, as you and your wolf want what's best, the danger of exposure and protecting each other is key to becoming balanced together. We are in our forest that belongs to the pack it's private, and we have high fences with patrols all around them. We do have a few Neeman Lions and Bonnacons nesting inside our land we have the areas sealed off to help keep them away from hunting our own kind, especially on pack runs when we all participate. We have a few families of Bonnacons they are up by the lake further south where there is good hunting grounds for them, and they have caves they use as nest to protect their young. We have our stronger enforcers watching over the Neeman Lions, those are tough fuckers, they can cause a lot of damage to us, we have them guarded as they are intelligent and the males are aggressive, we have a few families that have formed a pack we have them in the mountain area where they have everything they need to survive food, shelter and water. When mum mentioned that some have been near the camp sites its worrying its not normal behavior. I trust our Alpha he no doubt he will make sure to keep all of our city safe. Delia is up front running and hiding trying to attack me without me knowing we are hiding and masking scent. This is a good way for us when we are tracking we have to be able to blend into our surroundings. We run laps around the forest we fight in our wolves to practice on honing our skills. Once we have completed our wolf training we head back towards the center. We have training facilities and an intense course we do in human form. "You ready for more Hayden it feels like you're out of shape?" really Delia I could have sworn that you were eating my dust. We are both laughing as we start our human training doing laps. The center has a killer workout program we have large obstacles to climb and jump over. We have a shooting range where we use crossbows, throw axes, and shoot arrows. We have an area where we learn how to use tranquilizer guns. We have to learn how be to able to shoot into moving-sized shapes, as if we are in the field. We have to be able to hit small targets and the bigger targets. We have to be able to hit each target accurately, some of the animals we relocated have thick hydes and the only way to enable the tranquilizer to work is to hit underneath in there most vulnerable areas. We have outside a crawling station full of mud water and spikes there are bushes above us that we find around our land we have to be able to get into small spaces to hit our target that might include jumping into water or hiding in bushes up a tree anywhere that hides and can help make it easier to put the creature to sleep. It's easier than having to fight them if they sense you're there. The training helps you adapt to any possible sinero. To finish the course we jump across water into another obstacle cause to climb up the last wall which is high once you can manage to complete that part of the course its a race to the finish line. Delia and I completed the whole course, I crossed the finish line before the course first before Delia being the pack's next Beta. I am bigger in wolf form and I am fast as well as I was naturally born to be a Beta. I am stronger, and faster, being the pack's next Beta. We walked back to the facility to clean up. We met up with Sophia and Tommy when we hadn't seen much of each other for over two weeks. Tommy is mates with Sophia, he has a lot of muscle, he is good at being an enforcer, he has good fighting skills, he has blonde hair, he wears it up in a man bun, his hair is long, he likes the wildness of it, it suits his roaming ways. He has blue eyes and a little stubble, in his words the stumble helps to tickle and pleasure my dates. That is what he said, he was holding off mating with Sophia. He has dated many, especially this past year like his human half knows time is running out. Soon his wolf will take over, as he has been a real player his human half is stubborn. Sophia tries to ignore it, as she knows he isn't ready, but when we meet up it's been two weeks for me. I can feel the tension building Delia could have given me a heads up, awkward. We are all caught up I feel that Tommy has treated Sophia poorly he needs a kick up the arse Sam would kill to have what he has, Maybe that's why those two don't hang out as much. Delia has told me they haven't been hanging out as much as they used to, Sam is dating and has dated, he had waited until he was my age before he decided to date. He probably sees Sophia hurting and wishes he had a mate Tommy is acting like an arsehole he has to know she is in pain, after telling each other what each of us has been doing. Sophia is quiet she has not said a word, I want to hug her and tell her he is a fool. I can see that Delia has a plan. She takes a hold of Sophia's hand, and takes her into the bathroom. I have to say something, "what are you doing Tommy?" You're hurting your mate, are you going to destroy the woman that has been gifted to you? I know Tommy says my wolf is getting harder to control, but I am only twenty-two she is twenty-six I need time Hayden I need to live a little my human is fighting it I am fighting it I just. I interrupt Sophia has waited for you, she has saved herself for you!, she could have lived a little, how do you think you would feel? What more is it going to take? By the time the girls come back I see Delia, she is not having this, she gives off the vibe Tommy will pay dearly for hurting his mate, and she will make sure of it. Sophia is pretty, she has short, bobbed hair with waves she puts in, she has deep blue eyes has a softer shape than Delia as Sophia is a chef in the best hotel in town, she has a natural talent she can cook. She trains with the pack, she does all the workouts and practices so if she's ever alone she can handle it. We have all our pack mates and members trained to do so. Delia is her best friend, she knows Tommy is younger, but he is being an idiot, he has a mate, so why wait? I know that's why he moved in next door to me as his parents wouldn't let him bring hookups back as they had an inkling Sophia might be his fated. He has two brothers, I think if he had sisters like me, he wouldn't want to hurt them, and he would see what a blessing he had been given. His wolf will take over, he will bite her and force the man inside to man up and take his mate as he will see her as just a gift, and he will not allow the man to hurt his mate. I reckon Tommy knows this and has been much more of a player than normal. After the food is eaten Delia decides to put her plan into action, I work with her and I know her well she has got a plan goodluck Tommy you are going to need it. Hayden, I will meet you tomorrow, me and Sophia have plans tonight we are going out with the twins tonight one of them has received an invitation to the new club that Marcus has opened up. Marcus is human, he has another club on the south side of the city, this new place he is opening is in the centre. Monday is not a normal day to open a club Marcus's big party is risky, normally the weekend pulls the crowd in, but Marcus knows what he's doing. and I bet half the packs will go tonight, those free anyhow, even the visiting packs will be there, it's the club, it's one of the best places to hook up. Tommy perks up, oh yeah! he is so used to Sophia being a goodie two shoes. She has always followed him around, has made her feelings clear, she has waited and agreed to give him time, it's been four years and maybe she needs to let loose. Good for her, Tommy needs a reminder of what he does she can also do maybe Delia will make sure he gets that lesson. Delia says to Tommy, "I hear you're on duty tonight sucks to be you.'See you tomorrow Hayden, she grabs Sophia's hand and for the first time, Sophia doesn't look at Tommy with love in her eyes if I see anything it's pure disappointment. Oh boy Tommy you're in deep shit, good luck il see you when I'm back. I leave Tommy sat there stewing, I feel he has taken advantage of the fact that he has a mate right there ready for the taking, yet he has gotten a little used to knowing she has given him time, maybe that's why Sam had not bothered hanging around with him. He acts like a typical human guy who wants his cake but likes to try a few mouthfuls of different flavours first. Sophia looked ready to go along with whatever Delia had planned, Sophia must have lost hope as Tommy did seem to be pulling away further, instead of moving closer to mating. I drive back home and start to pack for my new mission. I decide to soak in the bath before dinner tonight I might even drop in at the club to see what Delia the little minx's is up to. I go over to see my family, mum has almost finished dinner it smells good. I had a beer with dad and we talked a little. I asked why is the house so quiet where Maisie was? she had plans tonight with her friends, and at some sort of celebration, one of the pack cousins was over. Fetching a few friends to help celebrate. Dad, did you know Marcus is opening up his new club tonight? "I do," my dad responded, "I told him she would be high-jacking that guest list to get in." "I know," dad replies. Why isn't she here then? My dad responded with a son I am the pack beta, I know everything that has to do with the pack I know she will be there I also gave her strict instructions to not drink any booze. Leo is heading there with a few of the pack to keep an eye on her. Dad really, she would not react well, I know that's why I'm telling you, because you will be there too. He is right I will be, my sister Jess is the youngest member of our family she is only eleven, and she comes in just at that moment barreling in with a bundle of energy. Hey sis what have you been doing while I've been away? She fills me in on all her friends and her school, she is going on the camping trip with Mum and the rest of our caregiver enforcers next weekend. I know Dad will put extra patrols on, he won't risk our youth nor will our Alpha. After spending time with my family having dinner it was good especially my sister Jess she has been enjoying her last year at junior school she starts high school after the summer holidays she is telling me how many friends she will make and how she gets to play with Ethan soon as he will visit his aunt and uncle our alpha is his family, He is visiting for two weeks in the summer They have a trip planned they are all going with the mums to the seaside my mum tells me she and Wendy want to give his parents his adopted ones a break and have booked a large house for all of our pack kids to go while we all have patrols and other things we have to do. They have arranged to take a few enforcers along, and the caregivers along with their mates will all go. The kids will love it, I remember my mum and Wendy taking us the twins and all our pack kids for two weeks every year, they do a pack holiday where all the kids get to be just kids. After kissing my mum and sister good night I tell dad I will see him tomorrow morning. I head back to my house and switch clothes. I put on a pair of black dressy jeans and my boots with a short-sleeved shirt. I have toned arms, I will show them off, I reached the club around 10 pm it's been open for an hour, I wanted to wait and see if my sister was trying to get in. I ordered a drink and let my eyes roam around the club, it was tastefully decorated, and he had dancers on stage warming the crowd up. He has a fire-breathing artist blowing and dancing with batons they throw in the air and catching them while they move to the music. It looks good. My brother sat at the back of the club with some of his friends, mostly pack mates. He has a few human friends, and they are attracted to a few human females. Some of them get up to either the bar for drinks or on the dance floor. I see Marcus, he is upstairs in the V.I.P. lounge watching his successful launch by the looks of it. I can't smell my sister just yet, she has a friend who is dam good at masking scent they are homemade as we don't sell them in our country or any others that I know of. I decided to walk around checking with my eyes and using my nose Leo had not moved he was watching an area upstairs I couldn't see from the bar. 'I see where the staircase is and walk up towards security, who are both from my pack. One whispers to me "she's up there". When I see her, she is with her two best friends Gemma and Voilet, both are members of our pack, they are inseparable, the terrible trio have defiantly added grey hair to my dad's head. They are always pushing boundaries, they are pushing, trying to see how much we can take. The last punishment they received was to clean all our cars for free at our pack's hotel, daily for a full week during the spring holidays. They are surrounded by human bad boys, with a couple of the girls from their school. What I noticed in the far corner drinking, and partying hard, was Sophia who was sitting on someone's knee. I tried not to make it obvious, as I wanted to turn around and look. He is human, from his scent, and Delia is with them alongside a few females from our pack, and they are surrounded by men. I head over to where my sister is as she knows I'm here. She is currently giving Leo the middle finger salute. "Maisie, what a surprise to see you in a club, how did you sweetly talk yourself in here then?" 'Dear brother that would be telling,' she whispers in my ear. You do know that dad is aware of your antics. Yep, I did promise our mum I would not cause any trouble, and I would only drink juice. Here, can you smell any alcohol in my glass? "I can't but I noticed a few of the boys are wasted. Be careful, I know you hear me pack mates no drinking, no kissing, no trouble". After giving them all my warning as they know I will drag there arses out of here if they break any rules. As I leave them to enjoy the place, I can see the guys around my friends, Delia is in her element I can see the glow in her eyes, as she starts to kiss one of the guys as she is looking over at Sophia and the guy she is with. In full on view of the top floor audience giving zero shits given vibe to those staring there way. I think her seeing her best friend waiting for her mate to choose her and finally commit to the gift he has been given. Having seen how Sophia has been treated, like dirt as though she is a curse, not a gift. Has hardened Delia, she has been pushing hard to not want to be in the same situation. Sophia is battling her wolf I feel it, her wolf doesn't want to betray their mate, but for once, Sophia is fighting her and not letting her wolf win. She has a seat on a man's knees, he has been nuzzling her ear, which is our most sensitive spot, where we claim our mates. He is a big guy, he trains, I can see it he has a tight white shirt on, he is a little older, maybe thirty, but boy he is aroused, I can smell the hormones he is throwing in waves. I head over to see Marcus, we start talking and he has been busy making sure tonight's launch went well, he is a good guy. He has a wife he adores and they have two daughters. He keeps the business running smoothly, and he hires a security team, that Sam's dad owns, they don't allow drugs. We have plants growing all over the island and humans, being ever evolving, have learned how to make them, it helps to make the humans loosen up. If taken in high amounts they can pass out and need hospital treatment to pump it out of their systems. After my conversation with Marcus, I returned downstairs to my brother's table. Leo moves over so I can sit besides him." Hey, I say she enjoys pushing your buttons, I know she is trouble with a capital T." Leo response with "She sure is" we both started to laugh. Leo and I are catching up, it is nice to chill out and we are listening to music. Which is good, a girl comes towards our table and asks Leo to dance. He gives me a nod as he takes the girl's hand and his eyes go up towards where our sister and Gemma and Voilet are. I can see the girls dancing, Delia and Sophie have joined them, I think they see that the bad boys are drunk and are joining forces, protecting the younger females, That's what we do as a pack, we watch out for each other. I need the bathroom, as I am walking towards the sign where they are I tap another pack enforcer on my way over to them, I ask him to keep an eye out. When I returned it took me a while as a cue had formed I heard my brother with a few pack members running towards the second floor. I thought it was my sister in trouble, so I ran up the other stairs that were closest to me. I can see Delia holding back a raging Tommy, he is meant to be on duty tonight. I can hear Maisie comforting Sophia whispering to her it is ok, you did nothing wrong, he is the arsehole who has pushed you away. Remember all the pussy he has had, and he sees you sitting on another man's knee. He can smell the desire, that sexy, handsome specimen of a man who wants you. Personally Sophia, I would hump him like a tree, he would totally be able to stamp your V card giving you the best memory of your life Sophia think about him ripping your clothes off as he kisses you and burys himself inside you. As I am listening I really can't unhear the words my sixteen year old sister is saying I know all of our pack up here can hear her as well. I can hear Sophia laughing she is drunk I can tell, it takes a lot to get our kind drunk. However Sophia was knocking them back she was drowning her sorrows. I am about to tell my sister to watch it and tell her those things should not be coming out of her mouth. The guy in question politely asked "hi can I cut in, Sophia?""I don't know who that boy is hovering near you or why he is mad at you sitting on my knee. Let's get out of here, I'm so done having half the club watching you are you ready for a real man, baby? I assure you, I will make sure you are cherished and that you enjoy riding my dick. "Fuck me," that is really going to kick off a raging Tommy, although I am intrigued to see what he will do. Tommy is on the verge of holding himself back, but the riding my dick comment has rage filling the room, luckily Leo has his arms around the back of Tommy and Delia is in front of him. For the first time ever, Sophia opens her mouth while taking the guy's hand and answers with a "yes please, I've never ridden a dick before why the hell not. "Shit! Tommy loses it, he moves fast, he breaks free off Leo while dodging Delia's hold and he manages to get a hold of Sophia. He picks her up, throwing her over his shoulder. You want to ride a dick baby? as smacks her hard on her butt, we all hear the slap. It was a dominant move he has played in front of all of us. The guys around us all laugh as Tommy storms out pushing everyone out of his way. Our kind can hear him loud and clear when he says to Sophia "I want you, and I will take you, you are mine!" You want commitment, you have it. I am not letting go of you. So stop wiggling you started this here tonight baby, and I am going to finish it? You hear me, Sophia? "I hear you, you are an arsehole!" After that they are drowned out by the music and by the antics of the area I am stood in. Delia the devil high-fives, the guy who was wanting to hook up with Sophia, thanks Jack you were fantastic! You did put on a great show and even my friends were fooled you're a star. Jack hugs her, and says, "You ready baby, you promised me a ride of my life, if I helped your girl out tonight. You said " jack I need a favour, I need you to pretend you want to fuck my friend," as I recall you

134

also saying that later tonight. As Delia puts a hand over his mouth before he finishes his sentence." "Most of us are just stood there, in shock with our mouths hanging open," Maisie is clapping and said, "Well played." Leo laughs out loud and asked "if we are all ready to leave?" I I have no idea what the hell is going on as I see Jack take a hold of Delia's hand and whisper "you kissing Rodger turned me on baby, I wanted to drag him off you and take over." I know babe, but for my plan to work I needed you horny, and to look interested the only way I knew how to do that was to kiss Rodger while you watched. Now let's get out of here, you deserve a reward after that performance. They left as I realised that all this was Delia's plan all along and it has worked a treat. I made my way over to apologise to Marcus, as my pack had caused drama on his opening night. Once I am about to apologise for my friend's behaviour, Marcus cut me off with. It's okay Hayden, I already knew. Delia, came in earlier and told me her plan, she told me there wouldn't be any issues just a wake up call for Tommy. Marcus, likes Sophia and he can't stand seeing her hurt because Tommy keeps breaking her heart. Marcus said "Tommy, doesn't realise that finding a woman like Sophia is a blessing, he would be a fool to let her go." I agree with him as we talked but I still feel with it being his opening night it was a performance he could have done without. He laughs and thanks me for caring as we shake hands. I told him "you are a good man Marcus, that could have gone wrong in so many ways." I need to go, it is getting late I have a busy day tomorrow. As I am leaving Leo offered to give me a ride home. We are all talking about Tommy on the ride home, Maisie is sitting in the back. Maisie is telling us that Tommy needs a kick up the bum, he has been an idiot. Let's hope he starts making it up to Sophia by grovelling on his knees. "I agree," I just hope he hasn't taken Sophia to where he takes his hookups. She deserves so much more. It's midnight, when Leo drops me at my home, Tommy hasn't come home by the looks of it there is no fresh scent of him or Sophia. Knowing him, he most likely dragged

Sophia to the nearest hotel to right the wrongs. I get ready for bed and I fall asleep instantly, and there she is my angel. I always see her first, and I like to watch her as she is always so carefree. Walking along the path as she likes admiring the sounds of nature. Her hair is down blowing lightly in the gentle breeze, and she always has a thoughtful expression on her face. I take deep breaths each time I do I am memorising her scent. I want to be able to track her to be able to find her as quickly as possible. She gets more and more beautiful each time I see her, she has a summer dress on with sandals on her feet. The sun is bright, high in the sky it makes her hair glow. I can see the lighter shades giving her a sunkissed look. Her body has a tan, she must have been in the sun often, sunbathing. I can see her taking deep breaths as she keeps walking forward. I see her stop walking, and look over her shoulder and by the time she turns back around I am in front of her. She always tries to look up to see my face but each time she tries she wakes up. I can't wait to meet her to get to know her, to give her love and support. I look forward to the memories we will make together, I can't wait to make her mine. I already feel like she is mine already. Each dream I have the closer I feel towards her, I don't want any others to touch her, I will not let her live a little. unless it's living a little with me. Once I complete this mission, I will ask my Alpha for leave, to find her. To go on a mate hunt, we all go to the gatherings, but we are allowed to travel and have a few days with each pack to check we didn't miss anyone.

CHAPTER FIVE

Anna

After finding Zoe, who had been waiting for us at our seated area. I tried to find out what just happened with Mr Anderson our Beta, who was not going to let her get away with today's antics. Zoe, what were you thinking? 'He will want to punish you as a pack Zoe," Jade finishes off by saying, "All this with our Beta you girl have balls of steel." I do not want you on car cleaning duty on mine or Cara's birthday. Zoe, I can't help it Anna, I see him and how he acts around women in town and I see red, every single time! I understand how you feel but he is our second in command he will want to punish you he will push for it, I just hope my dad can hold him off again. She hates it, the way the guys in our pack are always flirting and being "man whores" that is a man who thinks he can sleep around and be a player. Zoe said" he is, a man whore he has gotten worse this past year like he has forgotten that he has a mate, she is out there he just has to be patient a little longer, he's being an arsehole." He reminds her of Abel, who too has turned into being a selfish prick these past few years, especially with how he is with her sister. He annoys Zara the same way Bradley, our Beta has been annoying Zoe. I see where she is coming from, she is so protective and has always stood up for the females of our pack. Zoe adds, "I wish I could explain it better to you all, but he drives me crazy, each time I smell another woman on him. I mean, what happened to just waiting, you know girl's for your mate. I see him in town care free and enjoying other women's company, and then I see him in school with our teacher, it's okay for him he leaves when we do. But while I'm at school I have to smell him everywhere I go, I know he is a grown arsed man and can do as he pleases, until his mate shows up, I don't know he just pisses me off. Adding Abel in on how he treats my sister and I honestly could throat punch the both of them." We understand, Cara and Jade nod in agreement we all feel the way Zoe does. That's how we are, we are very much loyal to a fault. As we want to wait for our mates. I changed the subject and asked her. How did you answer that question? Oh, that I broke into his office earlier while he was teaching, I went, when I asked to use the bathroom during revision this morning. I used a scent blocker and sprayed the room as I left, hoping it would help mask my scent, so I changed my clothes too. I stole some spare clothes from Tim's locker, he deserved it. You know who I mean, him from last week. He pissed me off by hurting Natalie who had broken up with him. Well, I kept them for emergencies, and I knew Bradley the arse hole would try to get one over on me. So yes, I broke into his office. I also found a pair of Miss Kelly's underwear. I see her pull them out of her bag and show them to us all. Yep, they have her scent all over them. I rubbed those all over his desk to help with my little mission too. Zoe is so damn protective we all joined in hugging her, we understand but honestly he will find out. He is like a ninja, he will find the smallest detail and he will sneak up on you and you won't even smell him. We don't want you to miss our party, let's hope Dad helps you out. We all have her back. We love her so much. She and Zara are two of the same. They each hate the guys being able to hook up while the girls are meant to not do the same. She seems to have calmed down a little bit after our hug fest. We all decided what we needed was a good workout to help clear the day away. We walked out of school into town and towards the gym. I am so ready to be able to loosen up and Zoe really goes full pelt, at training today. Today has defiantly effected Zoe's stress levels. Zara, senses our mood as soon as we walked in, she really pushes us tonight she knows us too well. Zara can tell we all need that beasting, afterwards our whole body shakes . My body feels like I had been hit by a truck, I feel exhausted. Me and the girls stretched out, I thought Zara was going to kill us all. I never want to do a hundred kicks on each leg, as well as running twenty laps, to repeat the process ten times that was just the warm up Zara said. We all punched elbows, kneed, kicked, and used all our ability to not fall on our arses. It was brutal, I had no doubt in my mind as I told the girls that this had Abel all over it. He must have pissed Zara off today or last night on patrol. With Zoe wanting to make our Beta pay for disrespecting his future mate, and Zara wanting to do the same to Abel, it's been a tough session. The Sulivan sisters are definitely a dynamic duo today, Zara gets us she is tough on us, today being the toughest yet. It has helped, after showering we all feel our mood is lighter. We all talked about our plans later tonight, while we were showering and while dressing Zara is with us. She asked how our day was, and we all told her. Zara said " I remember those days, it's hard girls just know I am here for you all." Zoe hugs her sister and thanks her for being the best big sister ever. We decided that a sleepover at mine and Jade's house is needed. Zoe and Jade are up to something I can see how they keep looking at each other with a smile like they have a plan, I don't know what it is nor does Cara, as we have both asked repeatedly, what are you two up to? they won't share what it is, they just say we will be at yours, just wait and see as they both grin and hi-fived each other. Zara is also smiling as though she knows what it is. It's just me and Cara who are in the not a clue club. Zara said "this will be fun." I can't wait until we all meet up tomorrow and we can all reminisce." Zara is laughing as she leaves us four to it. Now I really want to know what the pranksters are up to. Jade said "so we will study a little, then chill out and watch a movie, maybe jump in the pool and swim as it's sweltering today". We have a few more days left at school before Cara and I have our birthday party at the weekend. We are all going shopping tomorrow after school, I have allowed Jade to pick out my outfit. I want to look my best, and I know this is Jade's favourite thing to do. She loves makeovers, all of us are going tomorrow. On the bus home, we made a deal to make the guys pay. We are going to spend the next two weeks having fun! no more saying no to dates, no more waiting, we will not sleep with any dates, but we will date. Let's see if they like seeing us girls on a date. As we start to walk up the long driveway the sun is still bright in the sky, so we decide to go for a swim and relax a little on the lounges. Dad and Adams' car are on the driveway close to the front of the house as we enter through the front door. Ethan comes running towards us happily telling us about his day, Jade picks him up and gives him a spin around before landing him back on his feet. He giggles, it warms my heart to hear him giggle, it's so adorable. Ethan then jumps into Cara's arms, with him losing his parents, my parents became his and Jade's guardian. Cara is his favourite out of the three of us. Ethan begins telling Cara what he has been doing, asking questions of if she would be staying over? as we all walk towards the kitchen, Ethan carries on asking Cara about different topics. Dad and Adam are sitting down at the table talking about work stuff. Dad turned around midway through talking with Adam, to ask us all how our day was. Zoe doesn't miss her chance, she started by telling my dad, how Abel his son is the spawn of Satan How he drove her girl squad by almost killing them Abel started racing against Zara who was driving her to school on her motorbike. Mr. H. Abel has lost his mind, are you sure he wasn't dropped on his head as a baby? I can't help it I laugh out loud at that comment even my dad is trying not to smile. "He needs a punishment or a clip around the ear he had Cara throwing up". He had Zara and me scared that we wouldn't see our pack mates, make it to school without an injury. Speaking of being dropped on their heads, what is wrong with Mr Anderson?" he is our teacher covering our Math class. He has been dating our other teacher who takes us for P.E. Isn't school meant to be a place of learning? He is acting like it's a place to hook up and mingle with all the women who teach at our school". "Why can't we retire him and find a replacement?" He needs a punishment especially as he is meant to be showing an example, him being our pack's Beta. I am genuinely concerned for the male species in this pack, they are acting like most of the guys I go to school with, immature arseholes. "They are all hooking up, everywhere I turn, as though their future mates won't find them, and find out that they have meant nothing to them as they intend to hump anyone who has a pulse!" I call double standards Mr H all the males from this pack get to travel, they can go out with nobody following them, they can go wherever they want, and are allowed the freedom to do so. Pardon my pun, Alpha, but they are like dogs humping anything that moves." We as female wolves from this pack, are expected to stay inside, and not experience anything, as we are too delicate to be able to protect ourselves, but to become submissive wives and mates. I am protesting for equal rights!" Us girls need these so-called "mature male pack members" to be just that by acting as mature. Mr. H. Alpha, Sir,"I am doing my exams. I am working hard and soon I'll be eighteen Jade, Cara and I have had it with the guys in this pack. Not all, but the ones we look up to Adam, Abel, and Bradley and others I mean I could add in more names, but you see my point. They follow us everywhere. I agree with her as I listen to what she is saying to my dad, she isn't wrong. We need things to change, around here we all offer our support by saying "preach sister". Ethan looks confused, as he looks around the room at everyone. Adam, he looks ready to interrupt by saying something, even if he has, he won't get the chance either. Zoe is on a roll and she is doing well as she continues telling my Dad. Who is listening intently? He hasn't said a word, he listens to every word Zoe has to say." I even caught our Beta, my maths teacher, being a total man whore Mr. H. He is always hooking up! I told you what I saw a few weeks ago, how he was humping our P.E. teacher! "I walked in on them as he was mid hump, I can't un see what I saw". I need some support, especially after what I have seen, we have two weeks left at school. I am a young woman. I will be eighteen soon, and I may find my mate, as might my best friends. We are preying that we are not lumped with the males from this pack! Either. Mr. Anderson, Bradley, or Beta, whichever title he wishes to use, whenever it suits his agenda. He has mentally scarred me. Zoe continues ranting to Dad, as Adam is openly looking at her, with a face that clearly shows. You can rant all you want I will be your Alpha one day, and this shit will not be tolerated. I asked if anyone would like a coffee, and Adam and Dad replied yes, please. Zoe then asked "Have you got something stronger, with the day I have had I need it." We all cracked out laughing, she has the best sense of humour and the comedy timing was perfect. After making everyone a drink, I handed a coffee to Zoe her drink first. It was my way of showing her that she has my support. She took a minute to compose herself Alpha, Mr. Anderson has yet to find his mate, and he should at least try to be discreet. Jade joins in and tries to help by adding, "I mean dad the guy is a total man whore according to what Zoe has heard, and witnessed. Not to mention any names but cough, Adam, cough Abel, cough the twins, cough. While Zoe calms down, allowing Jade to say her part, she sips her coffee. Cara and I have to agree, though, that the guys in this pack guard us to the point of nunhood. While they prance around town, satisfying their needs. Jade told Dad that during class today, Bradley overheard Zoe telling our friend Ellie she had seen Mr Anderson in town with different females. "It's not Zoe's fault that she has a teacher with wolf hearing," she was whispering trying to keep her voice low. Zoe said "maybe I shouldn't speak about him at all, knowing he is a wolf and he can hear me, I am sorry I should have known better, I will apologise for it." I can't help that I am a protective female, you know it's not my fault that the actions of the males in this town act like utter morans. Knowing the pack I'm from acts in the same way is disappointing as us girls deserve better, don't you agree? Ethan needs males around him like you, Mr.H. Alpha, sir, loyal, strong and willing to show him how having fated mate and waiting for them to bond, is worth the wait. Dad always allows us a little bit more leighway, especially as he knows the females in his pack do tend to wait for their mates. I hope I'm around to see their faces when their mates do come along. Maybe their females had a lot of fun too, as they wanted to have experiences and sleep around. How I will drink to that day, watching as they know that another has touched what belongs to them. I hear a growl, just as Ethan runs towards the doorway of the kitchen, jumping up for Bradley, the man in question, to catch him. Adam is all smiles now Bradley has entered the kitchen as he gets more comfortable folding his arms. Zoe has her back to him as she is still facing towards my dad. We are all sat the opposite way. Dad knew Bradley was here, that's why he allowed her to keep on speaking without interruption, Adam knew too, that's why he was watching and wanting to say something, would he have warned us I doubt it by the beaming smile he is potraying now. Bradley was here all along and he was listening in. Adam breaks the silence by saying all of you smell of pure rage, as soon as you entered the house. We all smell your frustrations and how you want the males to what, to be banned from living. I have to say something. The situation is frustrating for us all I said, "Dad, you knew he was here, the both of you knew and you allowed Zoe to get angry and keep on telling you more. I'm sorry but I agree with her, we do get treated unfairly, and we are almost eighteen, in our world we are adults, not little girls that need babysitting." Jade is eighteen now, and we are still treated like we are kid's who are still five. One day one of us, or all of us, could meet our fated mates, bond during sex and be mated. We know that the guys follow us around wherever we go, and we are tired of it, we just want to be treated more fairly. Bradley walks further into the kitchen and stands still right behind Zoe's chair, as I am talking to my dad. If I may interrupt Gerald, Zoe has gone still her back has stiffened up. Adam loves this, he is openly chuckling behind his hand. Jade's gaze holds the repercussions as she stares daggers at Bradley and Adam. "Zoe here has made each class I teach, with her in it, as uncomfortable as possible. I have told you this before today. She maybe almost be eighteen, but she acts like a child. I say we treat her as one." The fact is that for weeks now I have had to put up with her gossiping about my personal life, which has nothing to do with her. I have had enough of her blatant disrespect for me as her Beta, and teacher, and for the treament of Miss Kelly." Who has received nothing but whispered words from other students as well as funny looks from them. Due to a little girl, who says and acts like she protects women. When she has done nothing but spread vicious, rumors and pull her female teacher down. I want the right to perform a pack punishment, but of my own choosing. Today she used her wolf to escape my classroom, Zoe opens her mouth to argue but Bradley rests his hands on her shoulders. He hasn't finished. I will accept your apology for embarrassing Miss Kelly with your endless rudeness your remarks make her out to be a wanton woman. You say you want to be treated equally like the males of this pack. Yet the girls you whisper to isn't just about Miss Kelly but others I have spent my time with. If they weren't free to do as they pleased, we wouldn't have women who we pleasure now, would we? Because each person I do sleep with, I make sure she receives as much pleasure as possible, which is why I get asked for repeat performances! Cara, while Bradley lets rip at Zoe, has picked Ethan up and covered his ears. I am shocked dad has remained silent, especially after the last comment. Dad has a secret he knows something, he has allowed both to speak freely, he is an Alpha after all there is nothing that has ever gotten by my dad. Mr. H. "Do you see what I am talking about?" she stands up, shrugging Bradley's hands off her? She is mad, as her face turns red when she blows her temper comes through. The Zoe I know and love, will always get the last words in. She stands face to face with Bradley, she may be short, but she doesn't cower, which I have to admire. "Ok, Mr. Anderson oh mighty Beta, I am allowed to spend time with whoever I want, fact one." The women you sleep with are human!" I am not sorry! I am not sorry for calling you out. I am not sorry that anyone who sleeps with you means nothing to you but as you said pleasure! This is why you are a male wolf shifter, not a male human! One day, I hope it's soon just so I can comfort the woman who ends up being yours! unlucky for her to get stuck with you, and your man whore ways. Your fated mate will know that the town she will end up living in as she becomes your mate, will have to meet these hookups, the ones you pleasure repeatedly! Knowing that you have dabbled in half of the pussy in town, how do you think she will feel? "you can rub it in my face all you want, I mean all the female faces in our pack." I hope that she too has been pleasured many, many times. Unlike us, I hope her pack has given her more freedom to do as she pleases too. I can't unsee what I have seen you hooking up during school hours with my teacher. You, sir, are a disgrace to your future mate. I hope that in three weeks' time when I do turn eighteen, my mate is a far better man than any of you! I'm sorry Alpha, for my outburst. I can't stand to be around these arseholes any longer. She storms out of the kitchen, it looks as though Bradley is about to follow her, but he stands still and watches as Zoe, ruffles Ethan's hair and says "your sweet Ethan, you stay that way for your mate, I promise she will appreciate the fact that you waited for her." She runs out and up the stairs, I can feel the sadness pouring out of her, as though she is about to cry, we hear the slamming of the door, it rattles all of our ears. Dad asked Ethan if he would go upstairs and give Zoe some of your hugs to try and calm her down. "I will Dad," just before he leaves, he walks over to kick Bradley's shin and says, "You hurt my sister," he runs away as fast as he arrived. Bradley sits down in the chair Zoe vacated. He rubs the back of his neck as he says "Look, I understand some of her feelings, but I am almost twenty-seven and I am a human male as much I am a male shifter," I am asking as the Beta of this pack to be able to punish her as is my right as her leader." She has broken the rules that are set to protect us, she has been the biggest pain in my arse for weeks now. I have run out of solutions and nothing I do is working. I want to throttle her at times, to smack her butt like a pertulant child, I want to I don't know but something needs to be done, She has done her best to provoke me, undermine me, and has done so knowing that the pack in her class have heard her. She has zero manors for my pack status; whoever my mate will be, I am not doing anything wrong and I expect my mate to understand that I have been looking everywhere for her since I turned eighteen. That of course I want to find her but I am also an adult and have needs too. Zoe doesn't see that, what do I do here? Carry on allowing her to be disrespectful, I want her to learn not to mess with me in or out of school. I am her Beta and I deserve the same respect my father had when he was Beta. If I let her get away with her behaviour others will follow suit and my position will not be as respectful as my fathers were. You know this as much as I do. My Dad looks at each one of us and says "Bradley let her get these two weeks over with at school, she will be eighteen in three weeks." Come on, let's go to my office and we can discuss your plan of action without an audience. I agree with you, let us come up with a suitable punishment. Once they left the kitchen, us girls sighed in relief, Bradley's power was stifling his wolf was pushing it into the room as his temper rose. He was that angry. When Zoe mentioned the mate stuff at the end before storming out his wolf seemed hurt, I don't know I could just sense a lot of male cockiness too. My Dad knows that Zoe has done enough to warrant a pack punishment, we can all hear as Bradley our Beta has continued venting to Dad that Zoe is the most annoying, infuriating young woman he has ever had to teach, and if she steps one more toe out of line, especially using her wolf, he would tan her bloody Hyde! I mean it Gerald. Zoe turns eighteen in the week after school has finished, maybe Dad has a plan. He would never undermine his Beta so maybe he has a trick of his own up his sleeve. Let's hope Zoe finds her mate and can elope to his pack but then I'd want her to stay here with us, Who knows I know my girl, she will find a way I know her too well. Jade said "well that was tense, I thought he was going to blow a gasit." Cara replies' with "at least she can attend our birthday celebrations." silver lining. I remember he had a twinkle in his eye earlier and I caught a sly smile, what was he thinking about? He has already got a punishment in mind. It must be horrible, like washing cars or cleaning his bachelor pad knowing that it would piss her off. I don't know, but I have a feeling Dad has it figured out. He knows Zoe like we do he too will know she will find a loop hole somehow. I wish we all knew what the hell was going on around here lately. The males in our pack are acting like arse holes exhibit A) When Adam asked how our ride to school was with a knowing smile, Cara began to turn red, I say to Adam, "it is not funny, that Abel drove like he is a race car driver." 'Cara was ill afterwards." I heard,' Adam said," heaving in front of all the students in the car park how classy". Cara would normally just laugh along or go quiet. Cara told Adam "it wasn't even busy with students hanging about, most had already gone inside by then. As clearly Abel loves Zara to the point that he took the back roads and almost crashed into a parked lorry! He could have injured us all! or anyone else with his stupid driving. By the way Adam, I am fine, thank you for asking. You are no better than Abel and Bradley. You are all hypocrites, you have the females in this house on leashes we can't go anywhere, or do anything, without you following us. Yet you can do whatever you want with no guards watching your every move. FYI, we all know you are just as much of a man whore as most of the males in our pack. I think you all could do with growing up, and not let your human side be so distracted by human pussies!. Zoe has a point you guys are Dogs! I can at least admit I am younger, but I am not a dumb arse like you idiots." She stands up and storms out of the kitchen and heads up the stairs to my room. Adam sits there with a face like thunder, being called a dog is a really bad insult, it's the ultimate bitch slap. Serves him right, he just had to have his say and upset another one of my sisters. Yes, we were pack and were best friends but we are just that sisters. We watch out for each other and so far three dumb males have upset our group in one day. Jade and I followed after Cara had left, and after that last little showdown we left before any more males turned up to piss us off. Just as we are about to enter my room, Ethan comes running out and down the stairs like he has a mission just before I shut the bedroom door, I hear Adam say ouch Ethan what was that for. Chuckling to myself, I close the door and ask "Cara, are you ok?", yes, "Zoe you, ok?" "I am just Peachy. What have I missed?" I told her everything that had happened after she left including Cara's rant at Adam. Cara added to the conversation: 'He just got under my skin, I swear he likes to make my cheeks burn just for the fun of it. He always seems to go out of his way to make me feel embarrassed. I know one day he will become my Alpha but I can't stand how they watch us all the time. It was cute when we were children. I used to admire him, you know like I did with Callum, they were looking out for us. Protecting us as, we were vulnerable back then, we are not now. We are growing up, becoming women, they are still trying to control us. Yet they're the ones who need a leash, as they are constantly like two bitches in heat!" Me and the girls can't argue with that, as she is right as we said on the bus things need to change. Zoe said "I hear you, men are always thinking with their dicks." We all say "probably" at the same time. Let's just forget about the morons and get on with doing some revising, we all get comfortable and hit the books. After reading the source material we begin to start testing each other, we get a lot of work finished. We are all still annoyed, we just whizzed through all of it with speed. We are all feeling more confident as each of us answered each question correctly. Once we pack up our books it's still only 6 pm so we decided to take that swim. We don't want to be anywhere near the guy's in the house as we need to relax. Putting on our swimwear, we each take a robe with us as we head to the pool. We put on some music as we each take a bottle of water and lay a towel on the loungers. After we set up, we take our robes off. I am wearing a black two-piece costume. Cara is wearing a red one that pushes her breasts up she looks great. Jade has a white one on that is a wow factor "Jade when did you buy that it's stunning?," I asked her "I bought it with the one Zoe has on Now." Zoe is short, but she has an amazing figure. She has one with a triangle top that just covers her breasts, and the bottoms she has on have her butt on display it's a thong. I didn't notice her butt was out until she started doing a butt wiggle. Jade bought it for me, do you like it? "I do you look fantastic in it". Jade adds that "Zoe needed to show off her assets, as it's the perfect revenge. By showing Bradley that her butt is out, and that he won't be coming anywhere near it, Zoe said, "I am sure our Beta is catching the perfect view, of my cheeks he would love to smack." I know your dad's office has a large window facing the pool. We all began to laugh loudly, if they didn't know we were out here, they will know now with how loud we are as Zoe turns the volume up loud enough for the town to hear as she starts to dance making sure her butt is involved. We all joined in just loosening up, being silly you know after earlier it has made us release we have always got each other and we need some fun. We danced with each other, as we sing along to every song. I know we are being watched, we all do, but we just don't care any more we have had enough. We all then dive into the pool after half an hour of dancing im sweating with the heat. We play a game racing each other, then knocking each other, of another's shoulder taking it in turns. We all feel lighter by the time we have dried off and sunbathe until the sun went down. We all take a shower in the pool house and put on the matching pyjamas we have the black ones on with fluffy sheep. We headed over to the main house as we promised Ethan we would watch a movie. Dad ordered us a takeout as we all sat in the living space and we let Ethan pick the movie. Dad and Adam watched the movie alongside us, Cara refused to acknowledge that Adam was even there, even after he tried to offer her some popcorn. She pretended she didn't hear, as she carried on talking with Ethan. Ethan always snuggles into Cara, I think as she is normally shy, and at times feels like an outsider. Ethan relates to her, especially with his parent's death. He must feel a kindred spirit with Cara Wolves' soul. He always falls asleep when he lays resting on her shoulder. After the movie has finished we say good night. Zoe and Jade wanted to sleep in the pool house tonight, so we all walked back over to the pool house. We each take turns in the bathroom cleaning our teeth, combing our hair getting ready for bed, it's 10 pm and we are all sat in the living space talking, when we hear Abel, who is yelling where are they? Dad asked, "Who?" What is wrong"? I will tell you in a minute, Adam" Yes, what is it"? this best be good, you will end up waking Ethan up. Dad said. Abel lowers his voice but only a fraction we can all still hear him. Have you seen this? Whatever they saw, Dad was laughing and Adam was too. Have you checked your car Adam? Adam said, "no, why? I put it in the garage earlier just before I went on my motorbike to clear my head earlier on." If I were you Adam, I would go into the garage and check. Because if mine has been revamped yours will have too with those four involved. That is when Zoe and Jade lock the door to the Pool house, making us all hide in the bedroom with that door locked too. Listen, Zoe said, "I will tell you about it, but wait until they go back into the house, until then pretend we're asleep." Even out your breathing. Your dad will come here first, once he checks and lightly knocks he will tell the boy's to leave us until morning, by morning I have a plan shhh he's heading our way." We all lay in pure silence as dad knocks on the front door of the pool house after nobody answers. He tries the door, knowing it's locked he tries the handle, and he uses his spare key and unlocks it. He walks towards the bedroom where he stands for a few minutes listening and walks back towards the front door and re-locks it. and we all hear him, tell the guys to shhh, tone it down the girl's are sleeping they have exams in the morning and you are making too much noise. Let's go back into the house and sort this out tomorrow. We can hear both Abel and Adam cursing. Dad my car is missing! I parked in when they were all here and while they were upstairs I moved my car to the garage and went out on my bike. So if they were all here, how the hell could my car be missing dad? Abel's car is covered head to toe in condoms, with bright red paint calling him a man whores little bitch! If they have done that to his car, what the hell would those little minxes have done to mine? I don't know dad replies "I know the girl's didn't leave, Bradley and I were in my office and heard them leave and have a pool party by how loud the music was, I was going to ask them to turn it down." But after how they were reacting earlier I thought it was best Bradley and I let them blow some steam off, at least they were here on the property. Abel then asks them both to look inside the car," look here and see what else those feral beasts have done!" Adam yells at Dad, "I don't care if they are sleeping, this is not funny."We hear two lots of footsteps running to the pool house door, Girls we know you aren't asleep, you wait we will get you for this that's a promise. Oh, and the girls we know you had help! Adam yells "I know you had your friend's help, and Jade you and the scent blocker you mixed, will not mask who did it either. I swear I will bend you over my knee and make you not be able to sit down for a week! and if I find out Cara, Zoe or Anna helped that includes you three as well and I will use my Alpha to make you lay still and not move!" you are so dead. Adam! my dad shouts out "you will not be smacking those girls". "Do you hear me, I will not allow you to punish my girls like that". Then we heard footsteps walking away. Then we heard Abel who was still lurking outside as he whisper "he never said I couldn't do what Adam suggested" you know how many saw my car looking like that in town, you think that you are smart?" I know Zara helped do you think I don't know you all by now. I swear I will get you back just sleep with one eye open from now on. Sleep well. "Shit, what did you both do?" I said. Zoe whispers, "I will tell you when Zara collects us in the morning she has strict instructions to be here early before your dad or brothers wake up, now pack a bag we are having breakfast in town and we will be walking to school." Zara is picking us up to go shopping afterwards, the guys will have chilled out by then and they deserve it. We all pack a bag and get an early night. After falling asleep quite quickly. I awoke to find Jade whimpering in her sleep, she must be having a bad dream. I snuggle closer to her, as it would help ease her wolf. It was really early so I cuddled into her and slept a while longer.

CHAPTER SIX

Anna

When we awaken the next morning, we all feel relaxed and ready for another day at school. Zoe and Jade are rushing Cara and me out of the pool house down the drive and into the waiting car Zara is in. Hi, girl's how were the guys this morning as she steps on the gas and drives away laughing her head off. We park and go into Eddie's cafe for breakfast. He is human, and the place is full of humans this morning, those who will be going to work. We order and take a seat away from the windows incase my brothers are looking for us and find us, spill I say as our food arrives. Jade starts by telling us she roped the girls in to help her, Lisa, Natalie and Ellie. I had their keys cut off from Abel's and Adam's car keys a few weeks ago. They had been away for a few days with dad, I saw my perfect opportunity and took them into town to get cut just in case. Lisa and Natalie have their own cars and all three can drive as they are all eighteen and had passed their driving test. They agreed to wear the clothes that belonged to the boy's. Zara agreed to use her flat to wash them all after they were worn. I met the girls and gave them each a set, I had used a scent blocker that I made in chemistry you all know I aced that class. Then Zara agreed to get all the condoms we needed. We then had to plan on how to get a hold of Callum and Bradley's keys. Cara, said "you took Callums car aswell are your crazy now we will have them all out for blood." Zoe carries on filling us in without answering Cara's question. She told us that she and Jade had planned this payback for over four weeks. We had each of their cars covered in condoms. I may have used a special glue that may not come off without damage. Bradley was a last-minute thought though, while in his office yesterday, I saw the underwear in his drawer, I don't know what came over me, I was so mad. I just looked at the keys as an idea formed and I put them in my hand to take with me as I knew he had a meeting during lunch. I had to leave math class as I had to get the keys back from Lisa, she snuck out during her free period to get them cut for me. I had them back in place before he noticed. Jade finished by adding 'oh' and we wrote 'Man whore on all three cars. We didn't do that to Callum' as he is loyal to whoever his mate will be. I just had his car sprayed with a fish scent and he won't be able to get it out for days. Inside the three man whore cars, I arranged for their seats to be filled with jock straps after the guys wore them for rugby. I had arranged to steal them, as drum roll please, I had the seats recovered in pictures of man-shaped private parts that were drawn by a friend. They come off though, so I glued them down. "No, you didn't", Cara said. I can't believe you did it to both Callum and Bradley's as well o.m.g today is going to suck. As Bradley was an added addition, I couldn't add those in, but the condoms and words are enough revenge, oh and the scent of fish too. "No! we are now going to be playing dodge the guys all week. "How are we going to pull it off?" I said. Zoe answers "we are staying over at Zara's tonight." They will think she is on duty over the next two nights and they won't look. Jade finishes by saying "Abel, Dad and the other two are not here for the next few days." Dad and Adam have business meetings, and Abel has to go down to Browich for building work with Callum as dad has a big job on. He has a new housing estate to build. Bradley is hung up between schools and the fact is, he has to run the pack until dad and Adam are done wrapping up their meetings. Hopefully, by then they will have calmed down enough to see the funny side. Zoe adds that her dad will cover Zara as long as someone is there to patrol it shouldn't matter. Not only do we get to shop, we can go for drinks afterwards so it's a win-win. Zara has arranged for our dad to go in tonight with us, and has said we have plans afterwards that we are all visiting her friends having dinner and coming back to hers afterwards. My dad will do my shifts and I will come down with cramps tomorrow, Zara answers. I am stunned, but I can't help it I laugh so hard then Cara joins in by the end of breakfast. We all have each other's backs, we will not say who was involved and we will deny any wrongdoing. We shake on it and say goodbye to Zara who has work all day. We walked to school and as we're just turning the corner of the school entrance. We bumped into a few guys from the football team. The tall handsome one, he is called Andy, he has light brown hair like mine, but he has brown eyes. He has long hair tied into a man bun. He is quite tall for a human. He is as big as Adam, tall and muscularly built. He hasn't been at our school long since he moved here this spring. He asked Jade if she would like to go out sometime, as he thinks she is cute, he would like to take her somewhere special. Either into town or travel to Deadwood if she is free would she like to go with him? Zoe jumps in and speaks for her, we are having a party on Saturday it's an eighteenth birthday party, for Anna and Cara why don't you and your friend come along? At the same time, Andy is asking Jade out, another guy who is called Liam is asking Cara out. He too is cute he isn't as tall as Andy, but Liam has blonde hair tied up into a manbun, he has green eyes and has a silver stud in his ear. Zoe's hand goes into her school bag, as she pulls out some invites, and hands them to the guys. Each has a location and time to arrive, do not tell Cara or Anna where it is as it's a surprise. Both guys asked if the girl's would meet them tomorrow night in town for a date. Both girls say yes, and they iron out all the details. After we all part way's, Jade and Zoe start heading towards the science lab, as they both have that class together, me and Cara can hear them talking about what Jade will wear for her date, as they walk further down the corridor to their lesson. We both have art, it is mine and Cara's favourite lesson, we love being able to create art. We both appreciate putting our thoughts and feelings into our projects that will be marked as our exam pieces. In this class, we do not talk much, as we are so engrossed in what we are creating. I am finishing, my masterpiece, I have been drawing and painting the woods, where I meet him from my dreams. I have added deeper darker colours for the sky, The trees are in a darker light, as if we are going into late evening, with a full moon that enlightens the woods around us. It is darker than it is in my dream, where normally the suns out and the woods are shining in the sunlight. I think I have gone for the darker shades as I feel frustrated that, I still have not seen his face. Why speak the word "soon" I do not understand what it all means. Who is he, and why am I dreaming about a stranger? It is beyond weird, I know I have a fated mate out there, and I hope he is mine as I can't stop thinking about him. My mind remembers every last detail, each time I dream I remember a little bit more. Were in no rush to settle into mated bliss, just yet. Yet him from my dreams, whose face I haven't yet seen, the darkness is my view point each time I look at it the dream I see darkness not in a bad way but in the way that I haven't a clue what is happening. Am I going to be able to look up next time I sleep and fall into my dream will I see his face? Am I going to find him in my room one day or am I just imagining the dream has a meaning and really it has no meaning at all? it's just that a dream. Cara is in the far corner of the room with her exam piece, and it is a sculpture. She spends all her focus adding detail, each time we enter the room she adds more details and it is already taking shape. We have a few weeks left before the art project is graded. Cara has used steel, and she is handy with a blow torch. She is building it into a shape. She has been bending the steel. It looks like a wolf now she has built it up over the past few weeks. Cara, has added so much detail it is a huge piece of artwork, it is beautiful. She could make a living being an artist, she has the skill set. I can see the other students who are watching her as she continues to build this masterpiece, with pure joy on each of their faces. They know art when they see it, and appreciate the talent that Cara has. If she does not get an A, then I will be shocked. My work is good, as most of the classes are just as good, as mine is. But Cara has that glow: when you are in a trance just putting your heart and soul into your work, she continues creating even though she has a crowd gathering to admire her work. After a lunch break, we each have a few more hours left as Cara and I head back into the art studio to finish each of our projects. Jade and Zoe have a free period so they can revise. The last bell of the day sounds, and we head out of the classroom, and outside to meet the others. Zara is waiting for us, we are travelling to Deadwood to buy some outfits for mine and Cara's birthday party. We all get into Zara's car playing music as we drive to Deadwood, we all just enjoy dancing and singing along with the songs. After we arrive and Zara parks the car, we are all walking and looking into the windows of some of the shops. When we arrived at one of Jade's recommended shops that has all the latest fashion. The shop assistants great to us, and we are all taken towards the dressing rooms at the back. We are all separated into cubicles to change, and each of us receives three items of clothing to try on with heels. Zara, hands over the heels, while Jade passes us all three different dresses each. Try this on, and come out in outfit number one, she and the lady who owns the shop insist that we each come out after a countdown once were all say were ready. In three, two, one. I open my door and Zara slips a mask over my eyes. Cara has the same, but it is the shop owner who slips her mask on. Zoe gets to see herself first. I feel my hair being styled and I get told that I can remove my blindfold. Cara has hers removed as well, we all look at each other, wow we all say. I see myself in the mirror and I know this is a good match for me. I look really good, with my hair and shoes it finishes the look off perfectly. Both girls look just as beautiful. We repeated the process two more times. I really like two of my outfit choices. Cara has fallen in love with all three of hers, and Zoe really likes the first one, she tried on. We all vote on which one we should each buy and wear this Saturday, the lady of the shop has the final say once the votes are in. We come back out with the choices that were voted on, and we have our hair styled roughly how we should wear it in the evening. We all look hot, I come out at the same time as the others do, into the part where the mirrors are floor-to-ceiling high, the lighting is perfect. I am wearing a deep red dress that hugs my figure in all the right places, it's above my knee has no straps and fits perfectly over my body, Jade has loosened my hair and then tucks it behind my left shoulder, she asks me to close my eyes and then she hooks a necklace around my throat and puts earrings in. I open my eyes and wow I look elegant, my hair looks beautiful the jewellery finishes the dress off nicely. Jade puts my feet into a strappy healed sandal that has mid-heel gold shimmery shoes it goes with the jewellery with the clutch bag the lady hands me. I am speechless, all the girls agree, and I bag Jade's choice on the first go. Jade and the owner help the other girls find their perfect outfits. Cara's third outfit was finally chosen after we voted for her eighteenth birthday, she looked stunning elegantly grown up and with her hair colour it just stood out. She has on a dress in a deep shade of green, it makes her eyes pop and her hair has been put up into a high raised up do. Silver earrings that covered her lobes, filling her ears with diamond detail. Her shoes are silver heels, a full shoe her dress is a one-shoulder short mini dress, with her legs she will blow her date's mind. She looks radiant and sexy, but classy. We then look at Zoe who has on her first choice we all voted on, she has on a pink patterned marble effect strapless mini dress with a pair of really high heels, with a high heel that length she gains inches in height. Wow, her long blonde hair has been braided into a fishtail that hangs over her left shoulder and she looks absolutely stunning. Zara has on a jumpsuit strapless outfit which has a corset fitted top that lifts her boobs up, giving her a bigger-looking chest. It gives her body the perfect hourglass shape, her hair is not as long, as our hair. She has it down but curled it to lose waves. Wearing a gold jewellery belt, which added a little bling, she puts on matching gold glitter heeled sandals with her toes painted and on show. Jade's outfit is already in a bag picked out as she heads towards the changing rooms. When she comes out, she is wearing a knee-length dress, it fits her body like a glove and it pulls her in at the waist. It has a corset-style top half that shapes her boobs and pushes them up. Dropping into a flowy bottom half, the colour makes her dark skin glow, it is a beautiful white and has gold encrusted pattern flowers on the corset part. Wearing gold high heels with gold dangling earrings, her hair was also in a fancy updo. We are going to turn heads, that is for sure. We leave with our purchases and put them in the car. We are off to meet Zara's two friends Talia, and Racheal both are in our pack and are Zara's closest friends. One is Adams's age and the other was in the same year as Zara. We meet them at a beautiful restaurant. It is posh inside and is decorated in red and has gold-trimmed chairs. It's run by the pack that lives here. We all order and chat throughout dinner, we order some wine which tastes fruity and fresh on my tongue. After we have finished, we ask for the bill Talia pays saying "my treat ladies. I know you have school tomorrow but do you want to go try the new cocktail bar, my Mate recommend it. He said a few of his workmates have been there, and tonight it's two for one today." Why don't we show off those fabulous outfit's, it would be a shame to waste the opportunity. At the shop we each bought a dress for tonight with strappy sandals, mine is a pattern mini skin tight in blue, and Cara has a red bandore dress that shows her cleavage which enhances her shape. Zoe has on a little black dress. It's shorter than ours. Jades is white with a black mesh over to give it an elegant look but hers is mid-thigh length, as mine and Cara's is a mini length. We were all dressed to impress, no guard dogs, no drama, just us girl's having fun. We are greeted by the waitress as she leads us to a booth near the window where we all order the same cocktails, and Rachael orders us each a shot. It is student night so the place is starting to get busy. It has a retro vibe, it's classy it has mirrors on the walls, black and gold wallpaper, with gold-trimmed around the mirrors. The dance floor has a black surface with disco lighting around the edges that makes the dance floor look brighter. The music playing is good behind the dance floor is a stage it has equipment set up ready for a band. When our drinks arrive the waitress informs us they have a band playing soon, that they are really good and they are handsome, so expect it to fill up. We are asking Talia what she has been up to and she and her mate have just returned from a holiday over at the Keel Islands. She said how golden the beaches were, and that they had a lovely time with lot's of sex. What's it like to have sex? Zoe asked. I wanted to know too, but I didn't want to come across as being nosy. Let me order another round and I will do my best to explain. We all ordered another two more drink's each, as its buy one get one free As well as another round of shots each, with the wine at dinner Cara is feeling it a little. Our drinks are coming, and as Racheal is about to pay. The waitress said "no need, the guy over in the corner said you are too pretty to pay." She turns and serves at the next booth, as we each look the way she nodded. He is wearing a suit, he looks all business across from him are two other men with their backs to us. He nods his head our way, Cara answers "wow, who is he?" I have no idea, but he is handsome. I wouldn't say no. Racheal said we all laughed with her, as she wink's, and blow's a kiss to the guy in the suit. Talia begins trying to tell us about her first time with her mate. As she said "I didn't wait, he wasn't my first" I waited until I was twenty two, and one evening I saw a cute bar man I was on a girls night with colleagues from work. I let him take me to bed, as my employment is mostly human, and I wanted to have fun too, you know. I did it once and never repeated it. I wish I had waited looking back on it now, he was selfish, he never warmed me up first. After a few kisses from me, he took my clothes off quickly. I made him wear a condom too. I know we can't catch diseases, or get pregnant, but I didn't want to give him that. I held that back for my mate, he wouldn't have that privilege. He was on top of me, kissing my lips, and he just rammed his dick hard into me. He didn't even last long, after a few minutes it was over. I left straight after and never saw him again. I felt pain at first, as it stings but to be honest I didn't get a chance to feel anything else because after he pumped into me a few times, he grunted and came. He pulled the condom off, rolled off of me and said you can leave. Now my mate Harry he is wow, I feel wet even thinking about him. Zara said "way too much information Talia as we all giggled." The waitress came back with another round of drinks that we hadn't ordered. "you ladies are pulling some major male attention tonight. These are from the group of guys in the booth over on your left." She leaves after placing our drinks on the table, as we look over to our left to see who has bought these drinks, "Omg it's my mate Harry." He smiles at her, and nods his head at the rest of us. He mouths "enjoy ladies". Racheal saved her by changing the sex conversation, clearly her mate had heard her, she looked totally mortified, bless her. Racheal tells us all about the gathering coming up in two months time, how she might miss it, and hide as she is too young and she likes not having a shadow following her. We all hi five her and giggle, apart from Talia who just adds "wait until you find him you won't care he will fulfill your every desire. He will make you come so hard, so many times, you will never ever want to get out of bed. Harry is my everything and I love him so dam much. Girls you will never regret it," I promise you that. Harry came over, just after hearing his mate gush about him,. He asked " Are you ready Talia?" "I know you have plans" he leans in and whispers in her ear, so we can't hear what he said with the noise around us. But Talia goes pink and jumps out of the booth so fast she almost knocks her drink over. "Sorry ladies I have to go, I will see you soon." Racheal decides to stay with us as we say goodnight to them both. Zara pays for the next round of cocktails as the band sets up. I am having a blast, there aren't any wolves in here since Harry left with his group. The place is getting busier, as we wait for the band to play, we each visit the bathrooms in pairs. On our way back, I'm with Cara as a guy taps her on the shoulder. We turn around and see the guy in the suit with his two friends. Zoe and Zara walk over to us, you two okay? Hello, ladies my name is Carl, here on my right is Jordan, and on my left is Mathew. Sorry, I wanted to get your attention. "Well, you have it", I said. We just wanted to say we haven't seen you around and wanted to ask what you think of this place?. Our boss owns it, he wants us to inform him on what you think of the band? If you like the set up? What do you think of the drinks menu? If you could take this form and fill it out I'd be grateful. You're in with a chance to win a family vacation for up to six members, a two-week stay on Flame island. Zoe calms down and takes the form from Carl, thanks we willl. Oh and for touching my friend, without her permission how about a round of drinks. "No problem, again I am sorry I didn't think you would be able to hear me over the music, that the group next to your table didn't." He points at the booth next to ours. There is a group that is a mixture of older women with younger women. "Would you mind handing them, these forms?" Zara answers him "sure", she grabs our hands and pulls us through the place, it's so busy. Zara talks to the next booth next to us, handing them the form to fill out. They thanked her, and when she returned she asked if Cara was okay? "Yes I am fine he was right though its loud in here, I can just hear you with how loud the music is." Zoe says lets forget about it, he meant no harm and we do have some more drinks heading our way. We do as Zoe said and just carry on enjoying our evening. The band introduces themselves on stage and start playing. They are good, the lead singer has a really strong range, on his vocals as he hit's every single note. The waitress is back with another round of different cocktails with another shot each. The waitress said this round is from Carl. He said " to tell you sorry and to enjoy" Thank you we all say it together." Jade picks up the shot and gives us all a count down in 1,2,3 drink, we all slammed it back." wow that is lethal" its so strong. We drink up the first cocktail then decide to dance off the effect's. We are in the thick of the dancefloor each with a cocktail in hand. As the dance floor started to get busier we ended up slamming them back. With more students at the venue filling up the place, especially with the band playing. We are all cramped in on the dance floor enjoying the music while we all find our own little area to dance in. The band is amazing, they are really getting the crowd going, I need to pee, as do my friends we each hold one another's hand as we make our way through the venue to where the bathrooms are. Were all are standing in line waiting, Cara is feeling slightly drunk as she does a jig dance because she needs to pee. Racheal is leaning against the wall crossing her legs I need to pee so bad, we are all doing the jig dance after a while because we have been in line for almost ten minutes. Why is it that every time there is a female bathroom there is always the longest cue? While the guys there bathroom isn't as busy they are in and out. When we see the male bathroom is empty and a few girls go in there to pee. We all think the same, why don't we all go into the men's and relieve ourselves. We all enter the men's bathrooms while each of us take turns and guard the door. We are all heading back out into the corridor when we bump into Carl and his two friend's," hey girl's why is it that the females bathrooms always have a cue, while the men's always seem to be empty? "I answer probably because we must sit and pee, while you guys can use whatever those smelly things are. "That is true, well ladies if you don't mind, we kind of need to use those smelly things?" "Sure, erm of course sorry", we all rushed out and started laughing as we went back to dance. I have sweat dripping down my back. "Drink" I said as I was about to grab us all some water, as we were all hot from dancing when some guy's came over and said to our group "Hi there, you girls look hot?" do any of you like a drink? Where are you ladies from"? Jade answers for us, were from Ashwood, Anna here is going to get us all a drink, and thank you we do look hot don't we. When the band begins to play a slower song. Well then ladies, how about this dance then? "Okay", Jade answered" but no funny business", each of the guys takes a hold of each one of my friends, who are taken for a spin with their new admirers around the dance floor. Zara and I, sit down at the booth leaving them to it. Zara signal's to get the waitress's attention as she comes over to take our order. "Six bottles of water please". Once the waitress returns with our order we move away from the booth and start to push through the crowd, to find our friends. I noticed that Jade and Racheal are kissing their dance partners, meanwhile Zoe has moved her dance partner's hands off her as she begins to pull away. Cara has her dance partner who is trying to kiss her neck, where our mate will bite us during mating. Cara is trying to pull away as she shouts, "hey get off me". Zoe has managed to push her guy away and is stepping in to help Cara escape her dance partner's clutches. That's when Carl and his friend's step in. Carl said to the guy's in question "get your hands off the ladies, no means no". Jade and Racheal have already stepped away from their dance partner's moving towards Zara and me. The guy's are drunk, and are starting to get angry. The one who has a hold on Cara, shout's out in anger "she wanted it alright; you've seen her outfit. She's asking for it!" Zara moves, so fast that she punches him in the face, blood splatters from his nose. Zoe, takes that moment to take a hold of Cara, pulling her toward's us. Out and away from the guys angry outburst who is now sporting a bloody nose. That's when all hell breaks loose fists begin to fly, we are pushed and pulled with in the group of people on the dance floor. Cara grabs a hold of my hand as Zoe has a hold of her hand, Racheal and Jade are each holding onto Zara. We have been pushed away from each other as we try our best to not get caught up in the fighting. Carl has more men in black pushing through to help break it up. As wolves, we try and defuse the guy's who came over to us. I grab the one who Zara has hit and Zoe helps, as Cara has pushed her way closer to the guy's in black uniforms. She pushes a guy there way to restrain. I can see my other friend's helping Carl and his group grab the rest. We hold them steady until the men get through the crowd and hand them over. Carl said "thank you ladies for the help". After they are taken by Carl's team and leave, the place calms down and the dancing continues as we all check on each other. We walk to the bathrooms to help Zara clean-up she has blood on her outfit. We are a little shaken up, especially Cara, "are you ok"? We all ask at the same time. Yes, I told him no funny business, I am not out for a hook up. He seemed fine and was whispering about his year at college and what he has been studying. Once the music changed to a fast song as I tried to pull away. You saw the rest, what an idiot. "Thank you, Zara, for saving me." No problem", you could have hit him yourself, but I saw that you were trying not to cause a scene. You were hoping to break away and return to dance with us. He thought he could touch you, so I made him bleed. I will always have your back, all of you girls. Nobody messes as she lowers her voice and says "with the Ashwood pack." We all hugged and left the bathroom. Carl asked if we were alright. "Yes, we all responded and thank you. We did have fun." Carl said "good, I hope to see you here again." I hope you don't mind but my driver can take you home free of charge. I don't want anything else to happen tonight." "I have my car though", Zara said. Racheal said "I can come with my car tomorrow and drop you off while you collect it." "There is no need, Carl said "I will have my brother take your car back". "Who is your brother?" I asked. Mathew who answers from behind us." I am Carl's brother, I will have to take one of you with me anyway, with there being six of you." Zara started arranging for us so we could all travel back home. Two would travel with Mathew and the other's were to ride together with Carl's driver. He was older and smiled at us as he asked us all to follow him. We are driven towards home, we can see Mathew in Zara's car behind us. It was midnight when we finally pulled up outside the gym. Zara collects her car keys from Mathew who shakes her hand and said "that was one hell of a punch back there, be safe ladies, good night." We all waved goodbye and thanked our nights in shining armour. They drove down the street and away from us as we stood waving. "Who the hell were they?" we all jumped. "For fucks sake!" Zara yells back, "Adam, you nearly gave us an aneurism". "I think we should take this inside" I said. Adam did not say a word until we were walking towards Zara's home after we had collected our bags from the boot of her car. Adam has rage written all over his face, he is barely holding back his Alpha power, he has gotten stronger. I mean, I understand being mad at what the terrible two's did, but this rage is new. He has never shown this much of his power, especially in front of the pack. He is being a little dramatic because we went out. Why? for the love of patients everywhere, I need more of it to deal with Adam tonight. Once we reach the private entrance to Zara's flat, Zara freezers. "Why do I smell your brother and, before she can even finish her sentence, my other brother has turned up, and interrupts Zara. They were all meant to be out of town. Why are they here? Abel, as I am having my inner dialog, said to Zara "Because I am here awaiting your arrival, and that is why because you" Zara. "How the hell did you get in here"? Racheal said, "Calm down boy's, we have been out, as you can see we were dropped off safely by friend's who happened to be guy's." They were gentlemen, wanting to ensure us ladies arrived home safely. We are all tired and have a busy day to get up for. So why don't you chill out, we are old enough to do so." "We've had an amazing night, can you for once not spoil it please." Racheal and Zara are blocking the boy's from seeing us Cara, me, Jade and Zoe we each walk towards Zara's flat. We're almost there, and as we do Abel is never the one to shut up or back down. Growls! "I was about to ask Zara why do you smell of blood!" Cara interrupts by saying "Girl, let's get out of here." I am not listening to these two morons, not tonight anyway. We all look at both of my brothers with fury, as they can't help it, they can't let us go anywhere without following then giving us all a lecture or nosing on what we were up to they could see we were not hurt. Zara opened the door to her flat as she allowed us in. She was about to shut the door on my brother's but they grabbed it before it closed. Adam and Abel stormed in after us as. Zara replies okay I am not dealing with either of you tonight I am going to bed, ladies ignore them lets go. She throws the keys at Adam with a "let yourselves out" and he catches them in one hand.

Adam's eyes were shooting lazor beams at all of us. Adam, takes a deep breath and asked "why do I smell blood and guys all over you?" We don't even respond; we keep walking with our heads held high following Zara to the bedroom. I turned around to take a hold of Cara's hand when I noticed Adam had a hold on Cara's arm. "Hey Adam, what are you doing"? I can see over Adams shoulder Abel, who is shooting daggers at Zara, who just gives him the middle finger salute as she wiggles her arse at him as she carries her walk to her bedroom. Cara holds my gaze as she told me "I will be fine Anna, I'll be with you in a minute". I know she will defend herself against Adam, he would never harm her. I think he thinks he can find out all the information we haven't told him. I know Cara, she won't say a word no matter what he says or does. I nod my head and look at Abel again who looks like he wants to follow Zara by the look on his face, he has words he wants to say. "Zara!" He shouts. She ignores him, just as she is about to shut the bedroom door behind us, he puts his foot in the gap and tells her this isn't over. "Believe me Zara". She leaves the door open and throws the dress she has on in his face. Saying "ohh Abel I am really scared" She climbs into bed, and we all follow her, we are still wearing our outfits though. As each of us ignore Abel, who has Zara's dress in a death grip. As he storms away, slamming her bedroom door. We can hear him open the bedroom next door. Zara whispers "looks like he is staying over." After ten minutes or so Cara comes back in and she has tears in her eyes." What has he done?". I will let you all know in the morning, let's please just sleep we have school tomorrow. We all cuddle into each other and drift into sleep. I am having my usual dream. I see him, he smells amazing, he is in front of me, and I am trying to lift my head hoping that maybe this time I can look into his face. I managed to lift my head a little higher, but just see his chin it's shaped with a little stubble on it. He has that strong masculine jawline. I inhale deeply as I rest my head on his chest just enjoying the moment. I jolt awake and with his strong warm scent in my nose.

I feel refreshed and warm knowing I got to see him in my dreams again. I didn't realise how much I needed to see him. His presence calms me, his scent surrounds me bringing peace to my wolf and to me even though I know my brothers are here I feel relaxed. I looked at the clock and it is time to get up and ready for school, Jade and Cara have their dates tonight. Zoe and I are going to go to the gym after school to give the girls some privacy. We were all in a sleep pile at Zaras flat avoiding my brothers. We are all looking rough, we have makeup smeared all over each of our faces, and our hair is a mess. Everyone other than Zara slept in last night's clothes. "Morning" I say as each of us wakes up. "What time is it?" Zoe asked. It is 7 am" what is the plan"? I whisper. Zara answers," we get ready fast, and we get the hell out of here." We can eat at the cafe, before I drop you off at school. Racheal, can you distract the guys while we leave via the fire escape. I am not dealing with those two this morning. "Sure, I will make breakfast and put some music on the noise and smell will help". We each shower and dress for school as Zara dresses in her work out clothes lets go. We can hear my brothers rattling around in the kitchen. Racheal opened the bedroom door, just as Zara opened the door to the patio. She has a balcony outside her bedroom. We will have to climb and jump onto the fire escape stairs. Wait until we hear the music. Racheal was talking to Adam and Abel, how about breakfast, the girls are coming out shortly. I think they drank way more than me. I have left them to finish getting ready. I have promised them a cooked breakfast. We each climb over the balcony and jump onto the stairs that are attached to the fire escape door. Which leads out towards the garage area, lucky for us Zara has a spare set of keys. She threw the set she had at Abel last night and he wouldn't think that she had another set. Nor would either of my brothers think that we would through the balcony onto the fire escape either. Once we each hit the ground we know we are in the clear. Zara opens the car and we drive away laughing, as we imagine the look on their faces when they realise we have outsmarted them again. We all order breakfast at the cafe closer to where our school is. We are in a human owned business and we are the only shapeshifters here. While we wait for our order, we ask Cara to spill what happened between her and Adam last night. Nothing I want to talk about right now, if you don't mind I would rather not get into it. Zoe, hugs Cara. listen to me, do not let him see that his words hurt. You are strong you are loved and we will be happy to take his bike next time if you ever want revenge, I have many ideas. We all break out into hysterics as we know the guy's will be hunting us as we play cat and mouse games with them. We had a pleasant breakfast, it was relaxed as we talked as we ate, it was what we all needed after last night. We said goodbye to Zara asking her to let us know the gossip from Racheal about how my brothers took our escape. We entered the school gates with no issues, thankfully we haven't yet bumped into Bradley yet either. We managed to avoid him all day in school. We are lucky as we have so far avoided all of them, we even switched where we eat at lunch choosing to eat in the food hall instead. Where there are a number of students, we thought that would be our best tactic today. To remain within large groups of other students, the scent blocker Jade gave us in the car that she made in chemistry class probably helped too. After school we head over to Cara's house to pick her an outfit out for her date later, her mum is home thankfully Callum isn't here and her mum laughs at our antics. She begins by saying "Callum has cleaned the inside of his car multiple times and still cannot get the smell out." We all laughed as we filled her in on what we have been up to. She is such an amazing woman, she doesn't tell any of us off. She hi fives Zoe and Jade as she knows those two are the ones who came up with the idea. "Go on and get ready for your date. Cara. I bet that will add more fuel to the boy's fury, serves them right". Cara and Jade are on a date with a regular human guy's from our school. Cara's date is hot and has the man bun look down, I hope he treats my girl well. At least they are doing what the guy's do by actually going on dates. How can they be mad when they always go out? Well, except for Callum, he hasn't dated, he believes in waiting for his mate which melts my heart. If anyone will be mad it will be him, he will most likely just say because some of the guy's in our pack date, it doesn't mean you have too, just to prove a point. Cara and Jade both need a boost, and I think it will help boast their confidence. Jade started by applying Cara's makeup, while Zoe styled her hair into loose curls left to fall down her back. She had on a pair of tailored shorts to show off her legs as the weather was hot outside, paired with a cute top in red. Which helped bring out the black tailored shorts. She has on strappy sandals which were comfortable but stylish as they helped complete her look. Her makeup makes her eyes pop, her lips looking fuller with the colour of the lipstick. We then needed to go over to mine and Jade's house. We have avoided the guy's long enough that we still know we are in trouble about the car incident, and us being out last night hasn't gone in our favour. Cara's mum drops us off at our house and agrees to wait to drop both of the girl's in town. Nobody was home, which was lucky for us, we ran upstairs, straight into Jade's room. Jade is getting ready, we put music on and settle in to wait. She comes out of the bathroom wearing shorts like Cara's, but hers is white and she has a Cami top on in a light pink with wedge sandal shoes. Wow girl's you both look stunning they won't know what hit them. Zoe and I switched our uniforms for gym wear, we are going to jog to the gym. We all leave Jade's room to go and are talking about whether they will allow the guys to kiss them or not, laughing being girls. We can hear a motorbike pull up to the driveway, it is a little early for Adam, he should be at the office. We all leave the house as we do we see Adam, who looks up he has his helmet in the crook of his arm. He is staring at Cara, intently I see him as his eyes slowly rise from her feet to her head, is he checking Cara out. Cara is too busy talking to the others to even notice, when I turn to the girl's Zoe can't help but comment knowing full well it will piss Adam off.

Adam has already turned the opposite way towards Cara's mum's car. Zoe said " now listen girl's if they do kiss you just try to enjoy it, Anna and I are happy for you, those guys are hot." They are two hot, hot, hot, guy's. I mean hello, man bun's and muscle what else could you ask for. Now don't do anything the guy's of our pack don't do and please remember every detail because I want the details." Cara, answers a slight smirk forming her lips as she replies back "We will, and you are correct they are hot, and I promise I will enjoy every minute with Liam." We each turn to walk the girl's towards the car, as Cara's mum is waiting. Adam speaks "So you have dates, when did this happen?" I answered my brother, "why? The word's you are looking for Adam, are girl's you look beautiful and have a good evening." Adam ignored me completely, and focuses his attention towards Jade. "Hey, Jade make sure you behave, and remember it is a school night, do not come home too late." He then smiles widely and said "Remember Abel and I, have things we need to talk to you about." We all looked over Adams way, when Zoe decided to say "why yes, Adam we will be spending time together here." We won't have time to chit chat with you or Abel, as we will be too busy getting all the juicy details." I see her wiggling her eyebrows suggestively. "We won't have time to listen to you or Abel, you will have to just wait your turn." Cara's mum interrupted, saving us from any more discussions from Adam. As she asked "are you ready girl's? We don't want to keep your hot date's waiting now do we?" She is smiling as she said it, but I know she is wanting to laugh especially Adam's face he was glaring at Cara and Jade, when they reply "yes, let's go we don't want to be late." Once they were in the car and pulling out of the drive way. Zoe and I saw our cue to run, as Adam stood still watching and glaring daggers at the car as it drove away. We started at a steady pace jogging towards the gym. Zara is teaching us and she knows how to put us through another tough session. After our training had finished, we asked Zara if we can hide in her flat until the girl's are due to return.

We are staying at my house tonight we know we can't avoid my brothers forever, but at least if we are all together we can each have a say. Zara gave us her keys and said she would pop up soon, to fill us in on what happened after we left that morning. Zoe and I get showered and hang out, we watch a couple of shows on television. We ended up falling asleep on the sofa, as we were woken up by Zara, who has come back after work. "Coffee anyone?" she asked "yes please" she was in the kitchen making our drinks. Sitting up from our nap, Zoe and I asked Zara to fill us in on what my brothers said to Racheal while we had all snuck out this morning. "Not much, according to Racheal they thought they heard something, but Racheal distracted them with music, and her cooking. After the guy's waited a while, Racheal asked them to serve up breakfast while she checked in on us, to see why we were taking so long. She too escaped using the fire escape." We couldn't believe it, as we all including Zara cracked out laughing, none of us wanted to deal with my brother's behaviour so we all ditched them this morning. Zara said "when Racheal came in earlier, and told me. I couldn't help myself, I cracked out laughing I couldn't help it, we both just laughed as all the guy's in the gym looked over at us as if we had lost our minds. I bet they are pissed.""Have either of you two had a run in with them yet?" "No we saw Adam for a few minutes earlier, he didn't get chance to say anything as the girls had dates he didn't look impressed, we saw an opportunity to leave as he was deep in thought glaring at them leaving. We jogged over here, as soon as Cara's mum drove off. We will most likely have to face them tonight though." We all hung out, as we were chatting, and were laughing, the time went by quickly when we heard a car horn. We knew our avoiding the tongue lashing from my brother's was over, it was time to face the music. We gave Zara a hug goodbye, as we got into the car with Cara and Jade, who were back from their dates. We had Cara's mum drop us back over to mine and Jade's home. The driveway was empty, as we walked towards the house and we were greeted by Ethan who was talking fast, telling us about his day and asking where we had been. We have been with Zara studying, and we picked up outfits for the weekend yesterday. "Where is everyone"? I asked him. "Dad has a pack meeting with both of our brothers. Dad told them that they had to attend." "Thank you, Dad," "where is Mum?" I "than. She is making snacks as we are playing games. Will you play with us? "sure we will as I ruffle his hair, Jade picked him up and kisses his face after she has pappered his face a few times, she puts him back down. Let's go say hi to Mum we all go into the kitchen Zoe and I haven't eaten yet. Mum has made a few snacks, she has cookies, with little sandwiches, crisps, and sweets. My mum said "Evening ladies, how was your trip to Deadwood?" did you buy anything nice?" We did, we each bought a lovely outfit with a few other bit's you will have to wait and see. "what time will Dad be home?" He has a meeting with Adam, Abel and Bradley. Dad needed all hands on deck so I think it will be later on tonight. You're safe for now as mum laughed. That was a mean trick you pulled, by the way they are furious, Bradley has said quote "I know that minx took my key's Gerald I told you one more thing and she's mine to punish" Zoe looked over at my mum, and said "I would never ever do such a thing he has no prof therefore he can't punish me." My mum said stick to your story but it was a good one f.y.i as she ruffels Zoe and Jades heads "Are you hungry?" I left you some food in the oven just in case. How were your dates? Jade answered "mum it was great, Andy was shy at first, and he was a little uncertain, but once we started to get to know one another he relaxed, I had fun." 'I am glad you enjoyed yourself,' Mum said. How about you Cara?" Mine was good, he talked non-stop, he was a little bit handsy. Which I had to remind him it was a first date. I would like to get to know who he is first. After that, he was better and had me laughing a little and the conversation was okay." We plate up some food and sat down with mum and Ethan enjoying time together. We each began to talk about if we found our mates, what our life's would be like, would we live at their pack in their town or city, or will we stay here. I don't want to leave my girl's I would be lost without them. We have grown up together, we always spend time together. Mum joins in as she reminds us all that we have a choice, and that all will be well. "You will be matched with your soul mate, and life will be filled with joy as you learn to understand each other and you grow as a couple. Ethan asked "can we play a game now Mum?" "Okay we will play a game of hide and seek." I will be the one who has to find you," my mum said. We each run and begin to find a place to hide as we hear my Mum counting, Cara takes Ethan with her as they hide in a storage cupboard. We play a few rounds and we each have a turn. Afterwards Mum and Ethan go up to bed. Cara tells us more about her date, where he took her to a posh restaurant, he pulled her chair out and opened all the doors for her. Liam has been making her feel more comfortable as the date progresses. Zoe is taking each word in like she can't wait to hear the juicyier details. Zoe then says, "And did he try to kiss you?" Cara goes bright red and nods yes, he was trying to stroke my leg when we ate in the restaurant and wanting to hold my hand I want to find my mate welwell him find me. I asked him to ease off and I allowed him a kiss at the end of the date. There wasn't any tongues or anything major, just a small touch of lips. Jade then went ahead to tell us about her date, he took her to a different place to eat, he was quiet at first and Jade had to help the conversation move along. He has a football obsession and would like to play professionally. She then said that he kept giving her funny looks as if he wanted to say something but chose not to. They did not share a kiss, but Jade does like him, and he took her ice skating, which helped to break the ice, pun intended. We all laughed as Jade seemed so happy having been able to go on an actual date. Cara is the same happy to have just gone out with a guy and have fun with no strings attached. We all hi five each other and started laughing as we got ready for bed, each of us sleeping in pair's me and Cara in my room and Zoe and Jade sleep in Jade's room. We normally just share but I am so tired I don't care. I am back in the woods in the middle of the tree's as the birds sing their songs, and the leaves blow in the breeze, I perk my ears back as I listen out for him, the guy I always find watching me. I used to be scared of the first few dreams I had, as he never showed himself straight away. The forest would continue to go quiet as if there was a threat nearby. Now I know I am dreaming as I can smell him he is out there watching me. I keep walking along the path that is made from the endless footsteps of all who enjoy walking here. I continue on heading towards the noise of the River which is up ahead. The sun shines high in the sky it is another hot weathered day. The way the heat warms my skin it is as though I am really taking a walk I hear a ruffelling sound behind me as I turn to look I slam into a warm body. It's him, my dream has brought him out to me. He is bolder in this dream he puts his arms around my body and holds me tight against him as though he is afraid I am going to disappear I can feel his heat warm my body further with the sun and him, I am toastie. I can hear his heartbeat as it beats a steady rhythm, he inhales deeply as I feel his nose on top of my head he is scenting me. It's a wolf trait, it's how they put their scent on their females. He is already acting possessive and we haven't even looked into each other's eyes yet. I feel him relax as he feels as though by scenting me blowing his scent onto my hair has calmed his wolf down. He is saying you're mine. I can feel myself waking up as I feel him tense against me.

CHAPTER SEVEN

Anna

I woke up and had slept well, we only have two more days left of exams this week. Zoe and Jade headed over to Jade's room to get showered and ready for school. We have a full day ahead today full of exams. Cara and I are talking to each other, while we each have a shower. Preparing for school, I asked her how she felt this morning, I know we laugh and joke around, especially after Zoe and Bradley had their drama, the last time we were here. As well as the pranks that were pulled, we still have to see what happens about that, hopefully luck will be on our sides. Once we were all ready, we sat on my bed talking as we did. We all agreed to start and live a little bit, more like the guy's but not to the point where we feel we have disrespected our future mates. None of us think it is fair how we are treated, our brother's have their own lives in this pack we deserve the same treatment. Each of us believe it's not my dad's fault, but it's our brother's along with a few others in the pack who are friends with them. For Cara to go on a date was a big deal, and I am proud of her, she has really started to embrace who she is. Cara told us about her date. "Liam was nice, he put me at ease he talked and listened to what I had to say, after a while he came on a little strong as he tried to kiss me when I wasn't ready as I told you last night. I am glad that I went as it felt good to be normal for once in my life you know." "I sometimes feel out of sorts, within the pack as all of you can change shapes from human to wolf. I can't, I am human all of the time, yes I can fight and have the abilities that normal humans don't process, which is the only benefit I have. So for me I felt like I fitted in, as Liam and I did normal date stuff, he was nice and it was ordinary which made me feel like I fitted in. It's like when I dance, I feel like I move my body and Mattio knows what to do to help me bring out the fire that I have inside of me. The part that I hide away, due to feeling I don't know how to explain it but I feel like I'm not, you know, good enough." Hearing Cara as she opens up, this is the most she has ever spoken about her real feelings. I hugged her and kissed her cheek. I love you Cara, just the way you are as Jade and Zoe each gave her the same hugs and saying how much they loved you two. 'This is what we were all waiting for, Cara, to open up about her feelings, as we will always be here for her and we will help her remember who she is, which is a member of the Ashwood pack. She is the most amazing sister to each of us as we would not change her as she is who she is meant to be.Jade spoils our bonding session by saying "girl's I love each of you, but come on before the guys eat all the food." Trust Jade to think of food and remind us all that we have to face Adam and Abel. Here we go as we all head downstairs towards the kitchen, we walk in with our heads held high as we enter, it's just Adam and Abel with my mum in the kitchen. "Morning girl's how did you sleep?" "Great," we all spoke at the same time. "Go on and sit down and I will get each of you a plate." What are your plans after school girl's?" Zoe, answered "who know's maybe find a date each, for the party this Saturday?" "You know, now we have invited a few friend's from school." Adam and Abel just sat watching each of us as though we were prey. Mum brings each of us a plate and sets another place where dad normally sits. "Mum, is dad here?" I thought he would have taken Ethan to school." Just at that moment when I spoke our Beta, Bradley, walked in. "Shit," we all whispered under our breath. I am not feeling great, I am not feeling relaxed at all, what is going on? My girls and I each look at one another as though words are not needed to act normal. We all act cool, as though it is just another morning having breakfast before school starts. I know that none of my girls will crack. No sir, we are not letting these arseholes rock our freedom, I am not going to receive a punishment nor are my sisters from another mr, we will not break. I keep this marta running through my head as I hear. My mum ever the star. "Girl's Bradley wanted to join us this morning.

Your dad has work and has taken Ethan to school. The guy's have asked to have breakfast with you girl's this morning to mend some bridges, isn't that nice." Like you girl's I found out this morning just before your dad left the house, that we were having Bradley over and that we would have a small meeting as we ate. I refused to leave you here as this is meant to be a conversation not a argument so I offered to join in and be the calming influence." As the marta is still echoing in my head I look over at Zoe, Oh no, my sweet beautiful friend, is on the verge of receiving Bradley's rage, as he zoned in on her. We can all sense the power coming from him and the anger, all the males in the room including Abel. Who has added him to the mix with Adam who is pushing the strongest vibes into the kitchen. We now have a kitchen that is full of pure testosterone, pure annoyance, and most of all rage. I am not going to let it push me down, and I can see that each woman, including my mum who is fighting it off too. Mum is making up another plate, "who else is coming over?" Adam was the one who spoke to ask, as the front door opened and in walked Zara. I am relieved by the looks on the guys faces they were not expecting her, win for us girl's as we all smile towards Zara as she enters the lions den. "Hi, I see that I am just in time for the interrogation,cough cough I mean meeting of course." "We all just need Callum to come in and we can have ourselves a party." Zoe muttered under her breath. Of course we can all hear her as she said it. Bradley chairs the meeting, "I am glad you are all here. Callum wanted to be here but he has another errand to run and sends his condolences, cough cough I mean apoliges. We will all tell him about the results from this breakfast meeting." Zoe said " why are we having a meeting sir?" "It's not a normal procedure." He ignores her and said instead "when I was here the last time, we had words, as you may recall I wanted to punish you Zoe, then afterwards you stormed upstairs, like the mature soon to be adult you are" When Alpha Gerald and I discussed your punishment, which I am definitely going to proceed with. We were in the office discussing the matter. When you girl's decided to have a pool party, by the state of your nearly there swimwear, you looked as though you were having a party on the Keel island. The volume on which the the music was being played, we thought you had the whole town over. You seemed in high spirits compared to the performance that was displayed earlier that day. When I left here that very evening, my car was fine. When I got home and I woke up the next day, I noticed that my car had been messed with." Zoe said "really sir, I am so sorry that happened to you, but why is that our concern?" "As you said we were here having a pool party, you know with barely there swimwear, dancing and having a fun time. After which, our pack mates had hurt us all, but as you clearly said we were here and we didn't even leave the house. So do tell us, how we could have possibly been involved with what happened to your car. I mean, with your track records. I wouldn't put it past it being a spawned lover, you know, as you all think women don't talk to each other. Perhaps they know when they are being played or being used." Bradley carried on with what he was saying as though nobody spoke a word. "After I had woken up, I found that my car had been messed with. When I came over her I heard that all of you had woken up and had already left very early that morning. During which I found out that another three members of our pack had, indeed had their car's messed with as well. Some to more extremes than others. We ended up spending the whole day sorting out our vehicles. Which took me away from school duties, as well as pack duties. Adam and others had businesses to tend to that were important, yet they had to miss them due to what we know was a prank aimed at us from you." "We then after not being able to track you down that morning, we found out that you all went to Deadwood after school that afternoon, avoiding us were you? You left where none of us could ask about your possible involvement. You went there shopping, and apparently went out that evening to enjoy yourselves. Then we found out that you were involved in some trouble, and had strangers who drove you home. After you had gone all day and night Adam who will be your future Alpha, and another enforcer Abel came to Zara's home to speak with you all as you would normally return home. They found you, and tried to ask where you had been and gather information about your whereabouts that day. None of you would let them know what had happened, and if you were safe, which is a reasonable response to ask you, regarding the position of pack structure. You avoided any questions that night, the guys stayed over to ask you that morning again you avoided being asked anything by escaping via a fire escape and you spent another day avoiding us all. Now here we are, we have had to go to these lengths to be able to speak to you all. Have I missed anything out?" Adam said " I think you have covered all of it Bradley." "So I am asking each of you to start from the beginning. Let's start with you Zoe. Did your plan start with the pool party, to throw us of your trial?" Zoe ignored him, and his questions and began to eat her breakfast ignoring him completely. We all stuck together, and didn't respond we each followed Zoe's example and ate. Ignoring the guys,and there questions as well as watching them as each of them starred daggers our way. My mum hid her smile behind her cup as the three of them just stared at us. After we had finished eating, Cara, was the one who broke the silence by saying. "I know that you all think that you are the smarter species being male, and that each of us are stupid, but this meeting is total bullshit. None of us planned anything with your vehicles, me and Zoe haven't even passed our driving test yet, so that rules us two out. The others were here with us the whole time. We had a pool party to help us relax. We had a ton of revisions, and had exams all day. We had to go buy outfits for our birthday party just incase you forgot it is on Saturday. So yes, we went to Deadwood to buy some things. Zara came with us, she is a trained enforcer as is Racheal and Talia. They also hold high ranks just as Abel and my brother Callum do. We were smart, as we had three pack enforcers who accompanied us. After Zara drove us for an early birthday gift she had arranged with Zoe to pick us up early to plan our night away. Zara dropped us off at school, and kindly picked us up afterwards to take us shopping." "Where we met Racheal and Talia, at a restaurant for dinner, Talia had just gotten back from her honeymoon, and it was an unplanned last minute decision to go and try out the new cocktail bar. We had a few cocktails as we each caught up with Talia about her mating. We talked about her wedding and how fabulous her tan was from all the sun. She told us that she had the best time with her mate. Who had recommended the place to his mate, he was also there with others who belonged to our pack. They left a little earlier than us, as they are newly mated and wanted sexy time." I am trying so hard not to laugh, after I heard Cara say sexy time. She is on a roll, and as she hasn't gotten her wolf through yet the other's can't sense her twisting the truth. All that I can smell is honesty as well as astonishment of us all being accused. Cara continued and said "We were having fun until a few drunk men got handsy, and Zara sorted it out.Carl and his men kicked them out and offered us a safe ride home. Zara arranged for each enforcer to be in one of the cars so that we had one in each. We have not avoided you out of guilt or to avoid you. No, not at all, quite the opposite, we have been avoiding you because you continue to protect us by sufficating us. Now, unless you have proof that we have indeed done anything wrong, please have our Alpha punish us, but until then we have school." Adam said "not so fast, Zara, you should have been on shift that night?" "I would be but I had my dad cover my shift. I had planned to take the girls and I told them over an early breakfast. That I had arranged a surprise that Talia was back and wanted to see us all. After we had been shopping, Racheal came too as a friend of mine and Talia she wanted to come not just to see us but also to help with protection. I didn't think shopping was your thing Adam and I did have permission. I okayed it with your dad Adam." Abel then had to say something too. Come on there my brothers, they will try anything to get us to admit fault. "listen, I know you were involved. I

might not have proof just yet, but we grew up together. I could smell blood, as well as multiple scents that came from men who had been all over each of you. I know my sister Jade, and I know your sister Zoe, they are both menaces with pranks and revenge plots and you can pretend you had nothing to do with it but I know you have and I know you had help planning this. "I will get that proof, believe me.”
"You do that, and while you do I am glad you got a whiff of multiple men, there scents on my clothes on my body must be driving you crazy. Now you know how each female feels when you all reek of so much human pussy we can't smell anything else. At least us girl's know how much it bothers you, maybe we should do it more oftan." Zara said back to the guys, to us she said. "Girl's, let's go." We each got up and stepped away from the table after thanking mum for breakfast. As we were leaving I noticed Bradley, who has a look in his eye's I can see it as he catches Adam's eye as though calculating something of his own i know this is over but for right now they have nothing. Zara drove us to school on the way we each were talking about what just happened. What was that all about seemed to be the theme from all the conversations taking place. We all concluded that we were not off the hook as we could see the guys were up to something of their own. Adam with each of us, especially Cara. Abel was with each of us but Zara was his main target. Bradley is all ready to take Zoe down, by the way he kept staring at her his eye's held a promise of repution I am happy he was staring at her and not me, because I know he has something up his sleve, and Zoe will need her wits. We have his class to take as well this morning. Which is not going to be awkward at all. We all agreed though Cara was on fire this morning she called bullshit and stuck up for each of us. Zara told us all to be good, keep our heads down and it will blow over. I don't know, something is wrong with them, they are acting strangely, being more possessive and territorial they have always been that way. I am confused why they are hell bent on cageing us knowing we will fight back. As we all walked into school, we each

headed towards the math room. Zoe stayed quiet the whole time we were in math's, she has been an angel in today's three-hour revision class. I don't think she wants to piss Bradley off anymore after the showdown at our house and I know she is smart, she knows he has a plan but I know Zoe she will have a counter plan to piss him off more. Mr Anderson taught the class and we listened even though he glared in our direction every so often, as if he thought about something. Then he would scawl and focus his glare at Zoe. Who kept her head down and avoided eye contact during the whole class. We met up for lunch. With our friends Lisa, Natalie and Becca, we asked them what they were planning on wearing to our party. My dad has arranged for buses to take us all down there. The bus for all our classmates and friends leaves at 6 pm and the bus is coming back at 12.30 am. We talked about outfit's and who will be going and who had dates or were taking boyfriends. Lunch was fun talking to our friends and gossiping helped us release some of the tension from this morning. That afternoon we each are ready to go through another three hours of science exam. We managed to cram in some last minute revisions in on our last ten minutes of lunch break. As we headed into the large hall and we all took our seats, by the time the buzzer went off at the end of the three hours, we have each completed the exam. We all left the hall as we walked down the corridor towards the exit. We were all saying to each other how hard the exam was, but felt as though we had done our best. We managed to answer all the questions and did not leave anything unanswered. There is nothing we can do about it now, but wait and see, it has been such an exhausting day. Math and Sciences has been a total brain mash of a day. After school it's time to practice our dances we have a solo and the duo, along with our group one. We are doing our individual one's in class tomorrow. Sunday was our last practice session and we have been using the gym to get in as much practice work as we can. Zara let us use the spare space at her gym as we perfected moves and fitted better chography in some places to fit it together more. Our dance school lets us practice there too but our time is limited as other students use it for dance classes and shows. We each put on our leotards, this is to replace this Sunday's practice with us being away. We had arranged it with Mr Mcbride and Miss Kelly as we have to get in as much practice as we can when each of us are free. The school is the easiest place for our group performances to meet. My duo routine with my dance partner Simon is a hip hop routine. We synced it to look like he is in the mirror, and he was my reflection and I his, if I was a boy and he were a girl. We both added a little fun to our performance. He mimics my moves, he acts more girly with moves as some hip rolls and backflip split. I mimic him by doing more masculine moves, grabbing my crotch area and making my moves stronger and my movements are different. I have to lift him on one part of the rountine where I am the male lifting him higher and vice versa we have it perfected and I am happy with it as we both hi five each other afterwards, as we have nailed it. Zoe has a routine with her dance partner Luke, it has some really good moves in it. She has some fast moves where she is thrown up in the air, and lands perfectly. She slides across the floor as Luke jumps over her then he grabs her and spun her through his legs. He has her, in a lift using one arm while she poses in the splits, they have really put a fun, high energy routine together, they have the routine down. Cara and Mattio wow, they dance so well with each other, it has a little bit of hip hop with Latin infused moves. The way their hips move together is quite sexual, and I need to fan my face while I watch. As she flips her hair and crawls on the floor while swirling her hips around, Mattio slides under her thrusting his hips upwards as she continues to crawl. Cara then twists away and backs up as though they are having a lover's tiff with makeup sex. It's amazing the whole routine uses the beat of the music and they use their bodies by entwining with the sexual fineness of Latin. Meanwhile, the hip hop moves show the anger and the hurt that is fitting with the routine making it into a masterpiece. Jade and her dance partner Dale, are extremely passionate dancers, and their routine is full-on chest bumping and arms hugging as he rolls her down his body. Where Jade drapes gracefully and then she spins with pure grace on the floor. He lifts her up into the air while she is thrown high, she does a triple spin and as she comes out of the third spin Dale catches her. Dale has one arm holding her legs, while the other is holding her upper ribs. It's breathtaking to watch as he holds onto her and lifts her high up above his head. They are all dances, the guy's, they each come from a dance background, they are amazing. These guy's have been adding in Sunday mornings training since the spring term. We have all been putting the work in, even Zoe, it is her way of telling our P.E. teacher, bitch I have some moves too. We practiced the group dance at the end of our duo routine. It's a fun, with lots of comedy added in to help make it special as we add in lifts spins and tricks we add in humour to the moves to make it pop. We each have different parts to play, from one of us pretending to fall as though we are to heavy to lift, to another tripping over their partners foot it is a fun routine and we each laugh as we practice. The school play is Beauty and the Beast, it has humour in it along with fight scenes, a lot of drama and a little love along the way. The students have made it there own by adding a classic story, but adding a modern twist it is going to be one hell of a bang the last day of school. I am glad I am dancing, as drama is not for me, or my girls we prefer music and movement. Not having to remember lines and having to fake love and kiss in some plays with all that you have to do to perform and not mess up is big, with dance it is about remebering steps but not talking which I know I prefer.I feel excited, but also scared, as we all move on to other ventures Cara, Zoe, Jade and I all hugged at the end and tell each other how we nailed it and we have all of our routines down. After training we hit the gym to burn off the tension from the past few days. After training we all went out for dinner and headed back over to mine and Jade's house for a swim session to help ease away the soreness from a killer day. The weather is still warm with the skies getting darker as we have had a full day it is later than our normal home time. The pool area has lighting so it's nice to be able to go late and still enjoy. Ethan joins us as we splash about and play with him, he is our little brother and he is always welcome to join us any time he wants to. We raced each other and had a diving competition where Ethan could judge who was better by letting him mark us all, as he got to choose the winner. When we get out of the swimming pool, we wrap our towels around us and put on our dressing gowns. Mum takes Ethan upstairs to get a bath and get ready for bed we have helped in tiring him out he has energy and we made him race each of us he shouldn't take long putting him down to sleep. The girl's and I head upstairs too each of us have a shower and get ready for bed. Were all in bed with Cara and I are laid at the top of the bed, Jade and Zoe are laid at the bottom of the bed and in the middle of the bed in our sleeping pile is Ethan. After his bath he wanted mum to bring him in here, we are all reading him a story one of his favourites, his mum used to read to him when he was little, each night before he could fall asleep one of us has always had to read to him. It helps him to relax and for him to feel sleepier. He nods off halfway through the story, and once I know he is fully out and sleeping I turn the light off and get comfortable. I know today has been a full day from this morning's meeting to now so it doesn't take me very long before I fall asleep. When I do I know I am dreaming as I am in my favourite place, and he is there waiting for me. This time, the only difference is that it is darker, the sun isn't high up in the sky the heat isn't on my face, but I can still see everything the path the surroundings as he is holding me to his chest I love his touch it is calming and I don't know it feels safe. He is taking deep breaths as though memorising my scent, I still can never look up to see his face I just can hear the sound of his heart beat and the scent with the heat of his body as it presses closer to mine. He managers to mind speak with me again, but this time he is more growly as the words spoken to me are a bit scatchy as though he is fighting back his wolf, as if he has been stressed or thinking too much. He said I have to be patient, and that he was going to find me. The words he said were "I am coming to find you soon. Nobody else can have what is mine do you understand, you are meant" I awoke suddenly before he could finish the rest of what he had wanted to say. I could already guess what he wanted to say to me, but I couldn't focus as I woke up hearing my family singing. Happy Birthday I must still be sleeping, I am not fully awake either, what I am is confused and I could have sworn it was Thursday when I went to bed. Meaning today is Friday. My birthday isn't until Saturday, because I am still half asleep and my brain isn't working properly. My family are continuing 'loudly' singing Happy Birthday. Cara is the only one like me still confused about what day it is, and we are both in bed rubbing our eyes trying to wake up. Our other friends are not in bed with us, they must have snuck out while Cara and I slept on. Because they are with my family singing the happy birthday to you song. All of them are dressed and singing so loud I want to cover my ears, I look towards Cara who is still rubbing sleep from her eyes with her cheeks flamed red, from all the attention. Adam and Ethan each have two trays of pancakes, toast and bacon, with a glass of orange juice. We both sit up to be served breakfast in bed. Adam hands his tray to Cara, each with a big smile on their faces, and he makes sure it's resting on Cara's lap fully balanced before he bends and places a kiss on her head. We both look at each other, thinking what is happening here, he was mad at us, and especially Cara, he never kisses our heads it's a soft loving gester. He would normally rub our heads to annoy us, especially when we have styled it ready for School. Cara is speechless, Ethan steps in by telling Adam he was meant to give me his tray, and he wanted to give Cara her breakfast. I feel like I am in the twilight Zone. I said to Ethan "ahh thank's am I not worthy of your trey?" He smiled and brought my breakfast tray over, and said " I am sorry Anna, I love you too." I made the toast and I poured the couldn't believe the content, she has been so thoughtful "it is amazing Jade, thank you!" She has a little tear in her eye too. She has made me a photo album of us, from being babies to us now. 'We all hugged the four of us this is true friendship we have pictures as babies there is one of Cara and I leaving the hospital were in our mother's arms Cara is tearful beside me Jade whispers to her, "I have made you a copy too with some extra pictures." I flip it open and I see pictures of us in nursery, on camping trips at the park with our families. We have pictures of us having picnic holidays, all the beautiful memories stored for us to remember our lives so far. I love it. Now it's time for Cara, she has to open all her gifts. Her mum and dad gave her a hug and said "Callam is outside he has a gift." He wants to show you. This is your family gift. Then hands her a box, in it is a locket of all of them, that is beautiful. When I see the gift I bought with the girls we bought this gift together, as Cara reaches for its Jade explains this is of your girl's, we love you both very much. Zoe pretends to gag and adds Cara come on open it. Cara unwraps the packages we have bought her, a few items, and the bags take her a few minutes to open. Cara's jaw dropped as she said "you bought every outfit I tried on in the shop, all of them girl's wow, thank you." Even now she hasn't noticed all the shoe boxes and matching bags. We all chipped in to buy her the other outfit's as they all looked amazing on her. We have to tell Cara there is more to look down, she does and said "girl's wow you really went to town didn't you" as she opened all the extra boxes and started to cry. Jade then said to Cara, "Don't cry, we love you, but here this will bring a huge smile to your face, and she then pulls out another bag." Hands it over to Cara this bag has no label even I don't know what it could be until I see Jade and Zoe winking at each other. Jade said" as I know you are little miss goody two shoes, Me and Zoe decided to buy you something else to help you with your second date tomorrow night." Cara interrupts erm Jade "thanks can I open this in private as I know you two, it will be something I don't want anyone here to see." Jade ignores her and said for the whole room to hear "okay but, you can model them for us later, we will all help you pick out the best set". She lowers her voice, but we can all still hear her. "If your date sucks, we have bought you a little Zoe," chimes in whispering, relief if you know what I mean as she winks that I am sure will tingle in all the right places Cough laugh Cough tickle. "Ok! Erm, yes, erm Anna, a little help here." Jade, and Zoe "will you both please behave." They take no notice of me, and just start cackling like idiots. I can see Cara is extremely uncomfortable, she is going red. Luckily all our parents have stepped away to give us a little bit of pretend privacy. Adam is standing beside Abel, pretending to listen to what Ethan is saying to them, but I can see both my brothers smiling and nodding as they each hide their amusement. Ethan comes running over to say "Cara will open my gift next." Cara says hi sweetie, you have a gift for me, as Adam loses his grip on Ethan. "Yes, I made it myself," as he handed her the box. Ethan has crafted a wooden jewellery box; he has added shells to the casing and gloss over it. You can see that it shines, as Cara opens it, a ballet dancer is inside dancing around with a mirror in front of her. He even grafted drawers to put her jewellery in. I have to agree it is stunning. Cara bends down and kisses Ethan's cheek. I love it, it is the best gift ever, thank you. Ahh little man how can I compete with that, Abel hands over his gift it's a beautiful charm bracelet in silver for Cara to add charms onto it, thank you Abel, I love it wait Adams gift goes along with mine. Adam then hands her another box inside the box are attachments to the bracelet Abel bought, he added a wolf and number 18 to attach to the charm bracelet. I love it thank you guys its lovely. Ethan interrupts but Cara it's not as lovely as mine. Cara smiles kissing his cheek and whispers in his ear, "You're the best, but we don't want Adam or Abel to cry, do we?" Mum comes over while Cara is hugging both of my brothers and tells Ethan it's time to leave for school. Mum wishes us both a happy birthday and told us they all wanted to give us both their own birthday wishes while we were at home. Tomorrow everyone else will be there. This was just us, we both hugged our parents and said thank you. Ethan is going to school with Adam today as mum and dad want to see our faces when we see our brand-new cars. The girls and I took our things and put them all back into the bags and boxes. We have another hour before school, so we drink our coffees and grab all our school things, then we find our parents and head outside to see my car, and what Callum has waiting for Cara.

CHAPTER SEVEN

Hayden

It was early morning and our Alpha had us in a meeting, to explain the reason why we must travel to another country, crossing overseas in a boat to see another Alpha. It's delicate and we will find out once we are there, but the new Alpha has important news that is required to be given in person as early as possible. Our Alpha has received word to send over a small crew of trusted pack members to hear some new evidence that has been uncovered by the new Alpha as the previous Alpha Max had died recently, but we do not know any details just that an incident occurred and they are still piecing together what transpired. My team includes my dad our beta, my younger brother Leo, who is twenty. Delia, our friend who is one of our strongest enforcers, is twenty-two. Then her dad,

Phillip Moss, were a small team, but we are good fighters. Phillip is good with hand-to-hand combat, he has knife and sword experience, as well as weapons training. My dad trains us all in diverse levels of fighting techniques he and our Alpha have trained us to take down any beast that can cause harm to humans or to any of our vulnerable pack members. My brother is good alongside me at tracking, were both good hunters and we work well as a team. We're talking about our travels and what the mission will entail and how long we may need to stay for. Making sure we blend in like any other tourist, we stick together to catch up on what happened after the club incident with Tommy and Sophia. Delia tells us all that after the club nobody has seen either of them, Delia just says that I hope she is getting treated the way all mates deserve to be treated. With love, with care, with compassion, and respect. Tommy has a lot of wrongs to fix and explaining to do, which he is most likely trying to do with Sophia as we speak. I hope he does, he has been a total jerk lately I love him like a brother he is my best friend, but even I can't excuse his behavior this time. Sophia deserves priority over getting his dick wet with random girls. I asked dad how Maisie was and he told me she came home with Leo, which you know already as he gave you a lift home after the drama that went down at the club. She has not touched a drop of alcohol and is making sure all her homework is finished on time, so far she and her sidekicks have started to behave. Dad also told me he had enforcers watching over her and her friends as he does not trust some of the guys they were with, especially as they got too drunk and are too much of idiots, for any of my pack girl's to be around such idiotic men. Leo adds that all the guys leave at the end of the school term, hopefully college girls will be more interesting to them. We don't want Maisie to keep pushing boundaries, we hope it's just a rebellious stage as she is a handful at times, she isn't the first sixteen year old to want to push their families lucky for us Maisie does have a good head on her shoulders as do her two pack friends. After a few hours travelling on the boat we pass by Beast Island. We land at the port of the seaside town called Westshore. It's a beautiful town. The sea breeze tickles my nose with the salt in the air and the birds are flying in the sky are dive bombing at the sea to catch their dinner. It has a huge port in the marina with plenty of big ships carrying trade from island to island and the boats that we all use to travel from each of the islands are docking. It's busy, with plenty of residents walking around getting on the boats that are ready to sail out of the marina. Further ahead there are residents relaxing on the beach playing with their children, some of the children are playing in the sea splashing and having fun being young. It has sandy beaches as far as the eye can see. Here on Vale island near the port of Westshore there is a line of shops, with plenty of cafes and restaurants. It has some stunning homes In the area all facing the sea with its high cliff tops, the birds nesting in the faces of the cliffs its such a beautiful place. Some of the thunderbirds we call them that, nest in the higher cliffs striking lightning when the rain comes it is a beautiful site to see the whole sky lights up, they tend to fly high up in the sky amongst the clouds. We have Phynix birds close to the seaside as well, they like to hunt fish, and they try to stay hidden they tend to fish at night when the sky only has the moon to light it up. They are huge, they tend to be shy birds, they have been known to fly over to the island of the beast that we call Beast Island, they are large enough for residents to ride on. So far, we haven't had any reason to chase them away or relocate them as they do try to avoid interaction. Beast Island is a place where no residents live on it. We had a pack of our kind that used to inhabit the island, but with the creatures and beasts were larger in numbers. They have been known to kill the packs that did live there, hunting them in packs even as the strongest shapeshifters working together struggled when attacked in a pack. Once we could travel using boats they came over and interacted into the packs on the other islands. They told our ancestors that the land was hard, and the wildlife was overrun with all types of creatures that even they couldn't fight against as the numbers were too great. They lost family members and finding fated mates twindled as they were not finding any amongest there packs. With numbers being low, those who were left have not been able to find their fated mates. They had no choice but to leave and try to build their packs back up. From the stories my dad told us, and his dad told him there haven't been any residents living there, and the packs that did leave the last that did stay were the Hastings pack and they left over fifty years ago. It is too wild for any of us to live on, we let the population that do live there alone. After walking off the boat we take in the area and find a bus ready and waiting to take us towards the city called Evergreen. It is over four hours' drive to get there we take in the land around us, looking at endless lands of crops, trees, forests, woodlands and the valleys. There is a huge waterfall in the dip of the valley heading closer to the city, and we see the lake and rivers with bushes and trees around the edges. It has so much land we can see a field filled with wild horses as we get closer to the pack house. Once we arrive at the Alphas estate, we are taken to our rooms to freshen up a little bit before we are greeted by the new Alpha. After freshening up we all meet in the living area where the Alpha and his family are seated awaiting our arrival to welcome us. The new Alpha say's "Hi welcome to my home, I am Brock Steel, and this is my mate and wife Belinda, our daughter Rebecca, who is six and this little rascal is Robert, who is three." We all introduce ourselves by shaking hands, and embracing each other we all take a seat on the comfortable sofa's. Belinda asked how our travels were? I told her" it was good how beautiful the trip over was and how the coastline and seeing the vast amount of land made my wolf want to explore." We all catch up on our packs and any updates from each of our islands while we are waiting for dinner to be prepared. The children are telling us about what they have been doing today, they are polite and adorable. Delia is having a girl talk with Rebecca who is asking her what Delia what her pack duties are? and how much fighting is involved. Robert is staring at my brother Leo, and asking him what he eats? as he is big and does he have a mate yet? Meanwhile I enjoy watching my brother say in return I eat the same as everyone else, I train hard. Did you see my brother? He is older than me, and he hasn't got a mate either. I am in no hurry, she will no doubt be around here somewhere. Belinda asked us to follow her to the dining room as dinner was ready. She has arranged for a few of the pack members to make dinner, I can smell the cooking from here it smell's delicious I can see my dad's eyes light up. The pack brings in plates as we all take a seat and they join us too, as we each load up our plates. The pack has made a lovely roast with potatoes and vegetables. We all participated in some light conversation about the next gathering which will be held in our city this summer. We all laugh and have shared stories. It is such a pleasant evening where we are light and just enjoying each other's company. After we have finished eating Belinda excuses her and the two children, to go watch Roberts' favourite movie. Alpha Brock thanks the pack for cooking a lovely meal and asked us to follow him as he leads us into the pack's meeting room. He asked us all to sit, as we all take our seats. Brock pulled out a big box with files in, he hands us the contents to read, allowing us time to swap files between ourselves. While we were all reading, Brock started speaking, "Max could not understand how the Sanderson couple died, especially how they were found, knowing the mother was with a child who had been torn apart. Max knowing the pain of losing someone you love was hard on him. He found it strange how they were laying the lack of scents, the fact that the blood and wounds were not adding up to being attacked by Animal of creature. Alpha Max had our beta look into the deaths, taking pictures, gathering evidence and piecing together as much information as possible from the scents that were found, noting information on where the location was of all the creatures and beasts were, if they were still in their homes, re-checking land they visited for hunting, if they were looking to mate, checking every detail. Every animal that we knew who could cause harm, were all checked, and they were where they should have been. He had collected data before Julie and Jimmy arrived, to help them collect what was needed. By giving them a babymoon so they could use the time to relax instead. He had the location and numbers where each dangerous species were. Max had pack enforcers going over the files every year, checking each area, seeing their patterns, if any changed behaviour. He wanted to see if he was correct in his hunch. He did not want to come to the other Alphas, with what if's, he wanted to have some evidence to prove something was not right. He wanted to gather the packs and work together to produce a solution as a team." What is in those files is years of work that Max had worked on, he had data to prove that the area was free of anything that could kill the Sanderson. He handed us another file with photos inside and a device it was small it was something I had never seen before. Don't open them yet, I warn you the contents are grim, let me explain what I have found while taking over as Alpha. Max believed they were killed, that the Sandersons interrupted something, that morning they had left to watch the sunrise with a breakfast picnic. Max saw them that morning and had written out the map to point out where the herd of Unicorns were and that is where they were going. Max had patrols on but that area is checked every few hours to leave the herd in peace. We know there are no creatures nearby that can hunt them. Max found that the area had been sabotaged and there were no prints left as though cleaned away. The area had been cleared of scent blocked somehow, I was there, I saw it myself I could not smell anything other than what was on the body, which was a Lion or Neeman lion but it smelt wrong. It wasn't fresh, it was old as though dead. Julie had her baby torn out and that was the toughest thing for all of us to see, it broke our hearts. Max had us on lock down afterwards and he sent me home and asked that all pack families and those expecting to be in here the pack estate, or at our beta's home. Max was spooked by it, Jimmy had a wound on his throat to look as though it had been torn out. Yet there were no protection marks, Julie had bruising on her knee and fist as though she had fort. The buggy Max gave them to use, was left but in the area. That is what gave him his first clue, this device, and scuffeled earth in the woodlands nearby. After going through the herd's numbers there were some missing, an expected mother and two of her previous children. They were all that was missing Max had involved another Alpha Jax Dean, he is Alpha of the town Clayton he helps share resources to patrol the land his father and Max worked together until last year when he died and his son took over. I remember Jax Dean I met at the last gathering that was held on The Flame Island. It's a huge, beautiful island. The City's Alpha was so gracious to us all that his pack held one hell of a party that year. There, Alpha Nate Wicks, was hosting it with him being twenty-nine, he thought he wouldn't find her. He found her all right, she was from one of the smaller pack's, she had been visiting family a few towns over on the previous one and he had missed her by a few days. He was greeting all the visiting pack's when her group came in they had fifteen members who were there to find their fated mates, she had come along to support her cousin, who was ready to find her own mate. As there group were walking into his house he smelled her straightaway. She got a huge surprise when Alpha Wicks walked over picked her up, nuzzled her neck and said wow your hear it's you, I have waited so long for you, I was losing hope. She was open mouthed, staring at him with pure shock on her face. She was nineteen and called Gia Hastings and had not expected to meet her mate just yet. Nate had other ideas, he put her over his shoulder and carried her away to his private suite. He excused himself by saying drink be merry and celebrate I have found my mate, Excuse us why we get to know each other. They mated that night, he married her within a week and now they are expecting a baby any day now. It was a good celebration and everyone was so happy for them. I met with Jax's that night and he was hoping his mate would be there too.

We all got drunk and had a fantastic week. We all stayed for the wedding as Nate and Gia wanted us to help them celebrate. I wish it was like that for all of us, but sometimes it's not the who it is, but it is about the timing. Brock carried on telling us more, it was horrible having to listen as he was grieving for all that had been lost. Max has collected bank statements for the bank account Aiden Huntsman user's he runs a hunting business where they have competitions on who kills first, the winner gets to win the prize money and take a trophy. The animals used are game and bears, Lions, tigers, wolves, and wild dog's the toughest animals. He also runs holiday ventures where families go and stay in log cabins by the lake that has a beach and boats, fishing, games, and swimming. With a zoo with lots of animals in it. Max found the missing herd via a spy he had put in to work there and they had them offering rides out to the children that visit with their families. Max had lost contact with the shy and has sent another to locate them The other sent in was a lone shapeshifter he is part of our pack, but after his mate died he chose to secluded himself awayprotecting land furthest away. Only Max knew about it and our beta. The day Max went missing he was going to meet up with him, he left he was alone after putting the pack on high alert. He was gone that morning, and he never returned. We found his car dumped miles away from a cafe truck stop place that is in the middle of a rest stop. That day his daughter Ali was taken from school, her caregiver was found tranquilized, who was put on guard duty and told to watch her. We have been searching now for over two weeks, all the packs on our island have all helped search every inch of land. We have had no luck, we couldn't find any trace of Max or his daughter Ali either its like they just vanished, she is only twelve. We found Max a few days ago. When we sent word to all the Alpha's that he had died we didn't give any details, as we have had to sort out me becoming the new Alpha. I was chosen to be the strongest from our pack. Max had given his blessing and if Ali is stronger when she becomes of age she will take over and I will become a beta. It is time to bring all our packs together we will need each other. We are in danger, we believe we are being watched and that this Aiden knows who we are. We found Max beaten, we found that his heart had been carved out, and his head had been cut off. We found his head was dumped over thirty miles away. It looks like he had been taken there after being killed. We found tyre tracks but no scents, we could not smell any traces of who, or where they had taken him too or where Ali could be. In that file are detailed pictures of Max's death, the scenes of everything we could collect. The last picture that was taken is of Ali with her dad. He worshipped her, he loved her so much as do we all she is only twelve years old. We have been sorting through this whole island to find no traces of her, nothing. Max was kept and beaten daily by the report the healer gave us, he was a strong Alpha he had battled through, we think Ali was taken to make Max talk. Here is a map of all the locations Brock points out the area of land where Max was found, where the Sandersons were found, where the packs of beasts are located, and the neeman lions are living and any other animal we thought could cause the damage done. Max was smart too he also had another trump card he sent in another spy to inforate there ranks Aiden has sons and Max sent a spyin to befriend those sons he is the best kept secret we can have on our team, he is working undercover he can not be discovered, if we are being monitored like Max and I believe then we need to check all areas for listening devices, we have never seen an invention so advanced on the whole planet. I am listening to all Alpha Brock is saying, and I must hold my wolf back, he is angry that someone harmed pack. That a little girl could have been hurt or have been killed, the longer Ali is missing, the higher the stakes are we will find her dead. We will not allow that to happen, we must find her we have to all band together and stop our kind from being discovered most of all being hunted. We now understand why we had to come in person as we need to get this information to take back home. We each read through the files with the maps in all the data, where all the creatures are all the land searched and the photos collect one is Max and how brutally he was killed I feel sick Dela hands are shaking as Leo puts his arm around her to comfort her. My dad has anger set in his face as does Phillip. We sit there taking in everything we have learned and Brock fetches in Jax's who introduces himself. He wants to find Ali, he has a file of his own and place's it on the table as he said" I know you have a loto take in but my pack have been garthing information on Airon Huntsmen, we have pictures of him and some men he has working for him we think he has fled to another island and is hiding out." We all sit and plan my team is staying here to help with intelligents being new they may be able to find out more. I am travelling back to my island Griffin to catch my Alpha up, on what we have discovered. I know there is an eighteeth birthday party at the hotel and the Alpha's daughter is one of the birthday girl's that means other Alph'as will travel to celebrate. As I am travelling back to the port I have all the information swirling around my head and I am feeling frustrated and worried. I wish I had my mate here once I find her I can guard her and have the strongest warriors surround her to keep her safe. Once I am on the boat home, I fall asleep in my cabin. I booked a private space to sleep, I have travelled all day and now am ready to see her. I dream of her, it is darker than normal,the sun is normally bright in the sky, maybe it has to do with what time it is on the boat it's dusk not quite full dark. I want to hold her to get some comfort from her smell, to know that she is safe and that she will be protected. I hold her tight just breathing in her scent as I tell her that I will find her. I say into her mind, as I try to tell her to be patient, I am worried the news I have found out about has me wanting to grab her make her stay with me. Never to be alone or ever put her at risk. I try to warn her to be vigilant to be careful and most of all be patient the thought of another touching her makes my wolf growl as he is unsettled. To be good, to be safe, and not be alone. I wake up and I still have her scent on my nose. I'm ready to meet my mate. I love her scent, dreaming of her has helped me calm my wolf from all I have learned today. Her, she makes me want to fight, she makes me want to keep her by my side. Her hair was loose in tonight's dream, she had on cut of shorts and a vest top with trainers on she was smiling as if she knew I was coming, she breathed me in as I breathed her in just before I woke up. I am again throbbing my dick is rock hard as I pull out my hardness I hold my hand and grip the base slowly pumping my hand up to the tip. Precome is dripping from the head of my hardness, as I gently brush my fingers over my wetness, sliding it onto my dick as I move my hand up and down. Using a firm grip I imagine her scent is all over my senses as I relive my dream, I can see her clearly, I have her scent right there and I know what she looks like, my mouth water's as I think about her lips how they might taste as I slip my tongue in and out of her mouth as I tease her. I imagine myself nibbling her lips sliding my mouth down her neck and onto her breast. I suck her nipple into my mough as I twirl my tongue all the way around her tight peak. I imagine myself opening her legs as I look at her most intimate part, seeing her pink fold's glistening with her juices, as I lick my tongue to taste every inch of her pink fold's. My hand moves faster as I can feel my ball's tightening as I lose control as a come so hard that I see stars, and feel lightheaded from the release. After I have drained every drip I enter the bathroom and wash up. As I look at my reflection and I look into my own eyes I imagine she is there staring back at me, as I tell her I will take each of you first as you will take mine, I will have you spread beneath me as I put my bite on your shoulder and claim you as mine. I can't wait to join us as one as I give you the release that you deserve soon.

CHAPTER EIGHT

Anna

We follow our family outside to the driveway, where sat in a red car is Callum who has a big smile on his face, he has the window down, as he shouts "Cara, happy birthday! This is from me, mum, and dad." Thank you, it's amazing! Cara has a full beaming smile upon her face, but I have my driving test next week. I might not even pass, and now with this car which I love, by the way. It might jinx me, because now I might fail. "Cara, you will not fail, you are a great driver," her parents told her. Callum has agreed to drive you anywhere in this car until your test on Monday night. You will pass have faith. I am in shock as I look at the other car, that is parked next to Cara's. My parents have bought me a silver car the same style as Cara's, we have a matching set just in different colours. I love it, I will no longer need to rely on my brothers. I passed my test in the spring, me and the girls celebrated. I didn't want a car, until my girls passed their test too. Cara has her driving test on Monday, and Zoe does, so they booked them together. So, they had moral support and as Zoe failed her first test, she blames her short legs, telling us that she struggled to reach the peddles. We convinced her to try again and to adjust the seat as it does move. Jade already passed her driving test several weeks ago, she wanted to wait like me, so we all could have cars for our eighteen birthdays' by then we were all hoping that the other half of our girl squad would pass their driving test as well. Zoe turns eighteen in two weeks' time. Jade is already eighteen, but she has held off getting her car until my dad said, "hey Jade" yes dad, "can you just take these keys and unlock the garage door, just press this button to open and this to close it." Will do dad what I am getting from the garage? I have left my brief case in my car, and I need to pack it with my belongings for the weekend. While Jade helped dad by retrieving his briefcase, me and Cara are checking out our new cars. We only have another two weeks to wait then Zoe will have had her birthday, and her parents will hook her up with a car Mum and dad have gifted Jade her parents' house for whenever she is ready it's been looked after by a pack and has all been re done as a gift from her aunt and uncle. She doesn't want to leave until she has her mate, which she is not ready for. She wants to be with Ethan and stay with us, but at least she can move in when she is ready too. We have a girls only weekend where no boys are allowed as it's Zoe's birthday, she didn't want a party she wanted quality time with her girl's. We are making it a three-day weekend, as we are all doing different things in the summer holidays. Cara is going to work with my dad and Adam straightaway. I am too but after I've had some time away. Zoe is taking over training as Zara is off on holiday, with me and Jade, as we are heading to the city. Zara has planned some nights out with the twins Sally and Sara. It will be fun, I did my best in trying to get Cara out of having to work all summer as we will both be starting there after the holidays anyway. Adam said they really needed her now, he said that they have their P.A. off on maternity leave and need help organising as the current person has been struggling. I didn't think it was necessary for Cara to miss out. The plan was she was coming along with us on holiday, then Adam pulled rank and said he needed her right away. I told dad it was unfair, and he could not do anything about it. My dad said he tried, but Adam wouldn't budge but for the three-day weekend trip. He said he would drive her there himself if he had to, regardless of what Adam said. What is taking Jade so long, she seems to have gotten lost I hear another engine and we all look towards the garage mum and dad having the biggest grins ever. When Jade comes speeding towards us all in her dream car. It has a soft top which means the roof can be folded down into a convertible. She has talked about it for the past year, it's a lovely soft metallic pink, custom made, she leaps out of the car leaving the big bow on and the key in the ignition. She leapt on our parents, she has tears rolling down her face. "Thank you, I love it," I can't believe it the colour is my favourite nobody will miss my pussy wagon I said, "Yeah Jade, what a nice way to say you have a nice car." We are all laughing, she is happy, it's amazing to see. Dad hugs her tight while mum wipes away Jade's tears. "We had a little help from your uncle, he wanted to give you your dream car, so he paid the difference as we love you both so much." We knew you girls had a pact, your uncle had it shipped down last night, so his girl's could all share this day together. Zoe pipes up "hey, where's my car?" I reply your eighteen in two weeks, hunny, let's see what you get." It's best we get going to school, we are going to be late. We got a ride from Callum in Cara's car, as we have two more weeks to wait, then we will all have a car hopefully. Callum drives us to school and said "I know it's your birthday but really doing my car over, the only reason I haven't had a word with you, Jade and Zoe is because I understand partly where you are coming from" I see why you get frustrated from my point of view Cara hasn't got her wolf, and I worry I don't want anything to happen to her, or any of you. Who would jump in to protect her? I know you are strong and fierce, but I am a guy, and my wolf rides my arse daily so I will try to back off. If you promise not to hurt my car again. Zoe answers back "we may or may not be responsible, but if you really mean what you are saying then maybe you can have a stress-free life, I am making no promises" Jade said, "you are a good brother, but please remember if the rolls, were reversed how would you feel". "I hear you ladies; I will try to rein it in from this day forward." We enjoy the fun lightness after speaking with Callum, as he drops us at school and screams "Happy Birthday" as he drives away, as all the students look our way. We have a day of endless exams, by the end of the first three hours. When it's time for lunch, it's so nice as we can take in the fresh air and refuel by the end of the afternoon session. My brain is burning from sitting six hours of exams. We finish the day off by going out for a run in our wolf forms to blow the day away. Zara picked us up from school, wishing us a happy birthday and said she would be giving us our gifts tomorrow. Zara decided to join us on a run as our wolf shape, she seems a little off today, I can't put my finger on it, but we all sense a storm is brewing. Watch out for anyone who has ever upset her, she is going to kick their arses. The forest that is owned by the pack is where we do our pack runs every full moon, Cara always joins in with us. She can run fast, and it helps her feel free, even though she hasn't received her wolf, just yet she still enjoys the freedom of it like we do in our wolf shape. "We change shapes in the blink of an eye," Cara told us, and said "we each sparkle gold one second your human the next our wolves." She said it is beautiful to watch as the colours are so bright, and it seems easy to switch from shape to shape. It is once you learn how to control it. We started off by playing tag, my wolf is the same colour as my hair a light golden-brown that is the colour of my furry self too, with my blue eyes. Jade's wolf is deep brown like her hair, with bright green eyes. Zoe, her wolf has white fur it is so pure it takes your breath away, she has deep brown eyes. Zara's wolf is a little bigger than Zoe's, but the colours are the same. We run and play for hours, it feels so good to be able to do this. It is a rush to be able to share this gift with our pack it bonds us, it is a beautiful thing to see all the pack run and play. Even with Cara we all chase her, play games, tag is a good game, hide and seek is another one we play. Zoe, Zara, and their mum are always found quicker with their wolves being white. They stand out, they all have blonde hair as human but being a wolf they are pure white it is hard for them to hide with fur that colour. The run as wolves helps as we all feel much better even Zara has lost the tightness of her shoulders and her smile is back. It help's us shake off all the stress, were, free, a few hours of pure bliss. After we return home our bus is ready our bags have already been loaded as Zara drives of she has decided to bike down with Adam and Callum it helps them feel free so they say. We all jump on the bus as we talk about the plans we are all going to the city of Darlington. Mum has arranged a pamper day with all our mums and all the girls. We have booked massages, facials, pedicures, and manicures to look forward to. Zara has arranged an afternoon lunch with a few drinks. Zoe has booked us hair and makeup to be done by a makeup artist and hair stylist. I can't wait, Jade's excitement is catching she loves all the girly stuff. Cara on the journey over has fallen asleep, as we are talking about all the surprises me and Cara have to look forward to. Jade can catch up with her family, the twins will love the day we have planned. Abel and his friends chose to drive behind us in Abel's car, as Zara along with Callum, they are both twenty-two. Adam is almost twenty four, they keep over taking the huge bus, dad arranged showing off. Abel is right behind us, we can see him through the back seat window. Tom is sat up front winking at us all, and the twins Drew and Logan who are seated in the back. They are cute, I know me and Cara melt when we see them, they are hot. Drew is the party animal of the bunch, he is always flirting with us, he likes especially to flirt with Cara to see how red she can go, it is even worse if Logan joins in too. It's like those two boys got the sexy gene. Their dad is an enforcer, he is okay, an average looking guy, but it is their mum who is the hottest one, she is stunning. She has long amazing legs, dark curly hair, green eyes, with brown skin, there dad has black hair with sunkissed skin with brown eyes. The twins both have black hair like their dad, but they take after their mum, they have green eyes and brown skin. Logan is taller by three inches, but they can both fight, they have they have washboard abdominal muscles, with tight thighs that ripple with muscles and their arms are toned. They are also known amongst the college girls. You can hear them talking about them in town. The guys love the attention, just like my brothers they are the biggest players ever. Yuk! Tom is the opposite, he is waiting for his mate, he has blonde hair, blue eyes, he is tall but lean, he has a swimmer's body shape, he is fast, as he moves with speed. He is handsome, smart, and such a loveable person. Callum, Cara's brother is like Tom he is waiting, he has been on dates, but I do not think he is the love them and leave them type. He is so nice and polite to me and my girl's. Callum has red hair but it is darker than Cara's, he is tall and has muscle he looks hot, he has hair that is slightly longer but cut into a style that you can see the girls swoon. He is waiting and whoever is his will be a great catch. I nod off for a little while on the bus as does Jade who I am leaning against, with Cara on my other side, she has Zoe on her opposite side. We are bunched together in the back seat, being lulled to sleep by the movement of the bus. I am back in the woods behind my house when I see him, but he is a lot further away than usual, I cannot make out his face it is blurred. I do however hear him mind speak, he says I see you mate; I will track you, and I will hunt you; you will be mine, do not mis behave I do not share. I jolt awake as I hear Jade whimpering in her sleep, I hear her say, "Do not leave me please, I do want you to go." As the bus pulls up to our hotel. I nudged Jade awake to tell her we had arrived and wake her from her dream. It seemed like a nightmare from the way she was talking. Cara is still fast asleep as Zoe has woken up she has Cara fully laid against her as she cuddles into her further. Zoe smiles down at her and says "girl's look at her isn't she cute." Try and wake her, by nudging her and calling out her name. No, she is fast asleep. Zoe tries by resorting to holding her nose to see if that wakes her, the running and trip seem to have knocked her out as Zoe can't wake her either. Her mum comes over and tries to wake her, her dad is at home watching our pack and keeping all of the town safe, along with Zara's dad John who is keeping an eye out as we always leave trusted members on pack land. Her mum told us I would be back and I will ask Callum to see if he could carry her in, right as she was getting off the bus. Drew steps on the bus and says" hi all, I hear you have sleeping beauty on board, she needs a prince to kiss her awake and carry her to bed." We do not miss his innuendo. Zoe and Jade start cackling like two witches honestly those two. Drew comes towards the back of the bus and in one swift motion picks Cara up, she snuggles into his chest snoring softly. Abel, Logan, and Tom are unloading the bus with our luggage on. There are just us girls left with Cara and Drew. Zara is walking into the hotel whispering to my mum and Cara's. Adam and Callum come on to the bus, what is the hold up? Callum sees that Drew has his sister in his arms, around the same time as Adam does, but Adam's nostrils are flaring and his face changes. Drew has her in is arms as Cara sleeps dreaming about, wait is that a soft moan we all hear as Drew stands stock still. They can smell her arousal flooding from her. Two things happen at the same time one Callum yells for Drew to put his sister down, that he is to stay away from her the pervert. Secondly Adams eyes flash to his wolf and he has Cara in his arms in less than a second, as her sleeping body gets man handle, away from Drew. Adam frog marched her off the bus and began storming towards the hotel entrance. What was that all about,? Drew brushes it off and puts his arm around my shoulder, Callum looks confused, Zoe and Jade are too busy doing an impression of a goldfish watching Adam leave. Enough strange behaviour for me, I said, okay "the first one up to our suite gets to pick the best room." The shock on all their faces turns into, I want to pick a better room. We all take our belongings and meet everyone in reception to collect our keys. My friend's and I have a penthouse suite where our parents and brothers, alongside the rest of the pack, couples and males have the floor below. Zara and the twins are staying in the room across from us. Along with most of the pack's female's it's a floor for the ladies. Which suits us fine, not having to deal with our constant spies. The hotel is run by the Darlington pack. Once we were all checked-in which was fast, we were handed our keys to our rooms as promised, we have the penthouse suites. The room is stunning, we have a bar with drinks, and a fridge full of bottled water, fizzy drinks, juices, and a few bottles of champagne. A small kitchen where there is a proper coffee machine, the living space as two huge sofas, and a giant rug, a huge fire place. Above the fire was a giant television. The bedrooms are tastefully done with a huge walk-in wardrobe to put your clothes and cases in. The main bathroom has a jacuzzi bath which is large enough for six people. All the bedrooms have a on suite. We have three large bedrooms, but we tend to share beds anyway, so we put the beds together to make a big enough sleeping nest for later. As you open the door to the balcony there is a small swimming pool which leads to a view of the whole city. Wow, it is just amazingly stunning. Adam has put Cara in the opposite bedroom to the master, he had removed her socks and taken her shoes off, she was even tucked into the covers. We are still a little shocked at Adam's behaviour, those two haven't been getting on this past few week's. After we have checked on Cara, we silently leave her to rest, we decide to make some drinks and order food from the room service. Zara joins us after checking on everyone else we all get cozy on the sofas, while Zara puts the fire on and dims the lights. Our food is delivered, room service sets up our food on the table in the living area after they leave, we get a plate and pick out an old movie, with comedy, pure light-hearted entertainment. Afterwards we clean up our mess and go to bed. It has been a long day with school and travelling here tonight we were all ready to sleep, we each took turns in the bathroom. Once we are all in the beds, we pushed together earlier we get into a comfortable position, and I fall asleep not long after. I slept so deeply I can't remember dreaming. I woke up to find some of the girls are still sleeping. I go to the bathroom and take care of business. When I come out, Zara has woken Jade and Zoe by jumping on the bed to wake them up. I lay on the bed with Jade and Zara as we sat on the bed. Zoe has gone in to wake up Cara and they each bring a tray with coffee for each of us. They pass us one each and join us on the bed. It's early morning and we each take a sip of our drinks. Cara asked why she wasn't with us, "why was I on my own in the other bedroom? I can't even remember how I got up here." Zoe and Jade rushed to explain how she had fallen asleep and they both thought the guys were going to fight on who would carry her. Adam won by taking you of Drew, "No, your making it up, Adam carried me, he tucked me in." Why he has been a pain in my arse for several weeks. Zoe said " erm, do not freak out okay, but you were stuggled into Drew who was loving it by the way." Jade wraps it up by finishing saying " Cara you were sleeping deeply Adam saw Drew had you in his arms and he was annoyed, then you moan and they all smelled your arsoual" Zara said, "girl's really you had to tell her didn't you it is okay Cara we all dream and we all get turned on we are just not like the boy's dishing it out for anyone with a crotch." We cracked out laughing as Cara was having a mini meltdown. "I have never been so embarrassed, hide me, can I hide in here, tell them I am sick tell them I have left anything." She is mortified, as she continued with "No", how can I face them after this?" Zoe told her not to worry about it. Jade asked Cara, "I just want to know who you were dreaming about give us some details?" Whatever had gotten you so hot and bothered that Adam started growling." Which makes Cara hide her face in her hands." Zara saves Cara by asking us all to finish up as we have places to be. We all get ready, after were all are dressed, Zara said "Cara and Anna your coming with me to a special breakfast, girl's the rest of the pack are having breakfast in the dining room." Zara took a hold of both our hands and said ladies let's go as we were taken to our surprise once we arrived. We were greeted by each of our mum's ahh they have made us a special birthday breakfast with glasses of orange juice, and a glass each of Champayne. There is a mixture of everything, I fill up my plate, as does everyone else. We all sat down, talking about each of our childhood's, what our mother's did for their eighteenth birthday, it's so good. We were there for over an hour when our mum's told us to close our eyes, we did as we were told as we are both blindfolded. We were guided back the way we came and as we could hear whispering, with someone else asking them to shhhh they will hear you. Our blindfolds have been removed and as I open my eyes "surprise!" is shouted at us both. We have been led back to our suite, we both look at each other as our friend's have decorated the suite with balloons, and a huge birthday banner. It looks tastefully done, they have even more gifts waiting for us to unwrap. Cara and I said " thank you, this looks amazing." They each have gifts and cards to lavish on Cara and me, and the girls have booked us all another weekend away, as a joint gift as a surprise to a log cabin for us to chill, rest and relax just what we need after the school holidays to reunite. Cara and I embraced all our friends, as we thanked them. The log cabin weekend away will include Zara, Sally, and Sara as well and us four it will be our last weekend before we all return to a new start we all have jobs. With the three-day weekend we have booked for Zoe's birthday, where we are taking her to the coast. Cara is going to do some work at dad's company helping earlier than was expected, I will start after the holidays. Jade is undecided and wants to wait for her results, either way she can work with us or join a team who work on inventions, as a new starter she is smart and is good at science she may even attend college as she pursues that type of work. Zoe will be working at her family's gym,and working at being an enforcer. With two weekends to look forward to, we have a long hug fest. Adam and Dad are here, alongside Abel and Callum, they are hovering in the kitchen, waiting until we have finished hugging our girl's. Dad comes over first giving me and Cara a kiss on our cheeks as he gushes about how we are now adults and he hopes we each find our own happiness. I can see Cara over Dad's shoulder as he hugged us both, she is smiling and relaxes against my dad, then she notices Adam, who is waiting his turn to wish each of us happy birthday, and she looks away as soon as their eyes meet. She has gone a little red so I put my arm around her reminding her that I have her back and we are going to rock this party tonight. Cara tries to ignore Adam, she speaks to Abel thanking him for being here, and for all the gift's and cards. How great her and my birthday has been so far. While the girl's let themselves be buffers so she isn't alone with Adam as we know she feels embarrassed. Adam kept on looking at her, like she is a puzzle he needed to solve. He did manage to give her a hug as he waited for his turn and got her attention. He wishes her a happy birthday, as she is thanking him Adam's face changes if I wasn't invested in being so nosy. I would not have seen the way his body stiffened up. He moved away and stayed on the outskirts watching and scawling like he had somewhere else to be. Once the whole suite began to sing happy birthday. My mum claps her hands, and says" it's time to go ladies, we have places to be" were off to the spa. The guy's left us and told us to enjoy our day and they would see us tonight at the party. Sally and Sara are meeting us there. All the girls each have a bag with swimwear in and hand a bag to me and Cara as we leave the suite and get into the elevator going down to the lower floor where the spa is. Sally and Sara have dressed up the room with birthday banners, balloons with drinks and snacks. The day at the spa was pure bliss, it was so relaxing, we were spoiled, we had our nails done to match our dresses, and our feet were done too in the same design. Zara came over to us both and said "right girl's remember yesterday I said I had a special treat planned, well come in boy's" O.M.G. in walked two male masseuses who were going to do our treatments. Zara, introduced us, Cara meet Zack he will take you now so enjoy as he guides her to a room Cara's face is a picture. Zara introduced mine, this is Zanda please take care of her. Zoe has taken pictures of our faces and the male gods who have us for two whole hours. I had the most amazing massage and he did a facial where I walked out feeling totally zen. When I returned to the group they too have had treatments all by women. Cara is the last to come out as she thanks Zack he smiles and walks away talking to Zanda. Zara, asked how was it? 'Really good, I feel refreshed too,' Cara said. We all leave staying in our dressing gowns as we are sat in a salon having our hair done and make up. Once we are finished we each go to our suites to finish getting ready. We have a drink and toast to a good night. My hair is styled into an updo with pins that hold it into place, with a few loose pieces of hair hanging down my face. My make up is done with gold shimmy with a black eyeliner to make my eyes pop I have on a lipstick that is as bright as my dress. My dress makes me feel good, sexy, it's comfortable the colour red suits my skin the whole look completes it. Jade had my hair styled to the side when I tried it on in the shop, but this updo is perfect. Jade is flawless, she really suits the colour she is wearing, it fetches out her brown skin. The way in which the make-up artist added gold to her arms was with a light glitter that finished her dress off. Her boobs looked unreal as they have been shimmered, her hair is down in lush, loose curls, with a side elegant hair gripped with jewels. Her dress is white with a gold encrusted detailed corset top. Jade's date is going to want to kiss her tonight. Cara looked just as she did in the shop, breathtaking, her hair is simply perfect, she has had it styled how it was styled in the shop, her dress is showing off her toned legs. Her dress and style, of which is clinging to her body making her boobs look good, giving her a womanly shape. Cara's date will have his tongue hanging out. Zoe looks stunningher dress, is short but the heels make her look taller than she is it is sleeveless and hugs tight on her body her make up is natural but her lips are bright red which adds danger to her whole look. Her hair has been styled in an elegant updo like mine. She has had some hair left to fall around her face. With her blonde hair she is the ultimate hottie and Zara in her outfit and how her hair is down and in waves across her face she looks fierce but in a sexy kind of way. wow, they both look incredible and sexy as hell. We each look at each other and say "cheers heres to a good night" as we click our glasses together and take a sip. Cara keeps tugging the dress she has on down, she even has on the matching underwear Jade and Zoe made her wear. I have my own set on, and they are red pure lace with nothing to hide my butt. Cara's is a green set laced with black, which is a thong she clearly feel's a little underdressed. 'Her silver heels and updo with her ears showing encrusted diamonds, she really does stand out, we've heard the door. It's the guys who have turned up. Jade, Cara and Zara's dates. Yes, Zoe made sure her sister had that date too. They have really dressed up smart, Liam's brother drove them and has agreed to take them home tomorrow, they are staying in a hotel five minutes away. Both are handsome, and tall, Liam's brother has already started eye fucking Zara. Zoe lets them in, we start to introduce them to Zara, as we know Liam and Andy from our School. Liam's brother is twenty-five and he works in some sort of security for their dad's firm. His name is kyle, and I have to say he is attractive and charming you can tell he works out by how snug his outfit is, it shows of his tone physic. We pour them all a drink, and we toast to new beginnings, we drink up it is time we left. We come out of our room towards the elevator as Kyle being a gentleman holds the door open for us. Once we are all on the floor of the party we can hear the d.j. playing some of our favourite songs, the party is on the second floor. The room is decorated with white covered chairs and drapes, there are pink and gold balloons, that make the room look elegant and banners wishing me and Cara a happy eighteenth birthday. All our family and friend's cheer. Our friends from school come over and say we all look beautiful, we say they scrub up well too, they hand us a drink each along with a shot and we click cheers and drink them down. We walked over to the bar and ordered a drink, as we needed to losen up after another round of shots we hit the dance floor and we all started dancing in a group. We to Kyle, Zara, Sally and Sara as they brought over another shot for us. We really love the music that the D.J. is playing. We are all following Simon and Dale as he asked the D.J. to play some of our favourite songs, he started doing this really good hip hop dance, and I jumped in as did Dale, who added some more dance moves in, and we all just started to add our own piece to Simon's original. Jade and Cara started doing a hip hop two piece we paired up to follow them, it was so much fun. Zoe, started another solo bit in as we all break apart copying Zoe, she then asked if we should add in some flips for the peanut gallery who were giving us all death glares. I told her "Zoe we are wearing dresses less is more, we are having such a fun evening ignoring them I am they won't do anything dad has warned them all to let us breathe." The peanut gallery is Adam, Abel and Callum who has been dragged over by Abel who was heard saying "brother's stick together." Tom who is stood with Drew and Logan, I think they were just there watching what would happen, and the twins were checking out the girl's on the dance floor being the ultimate players. Jade's date Andy this time, actually kisses her he spends most of the night spinning her around they are laughing it is so good to see her happy. I am dancing with Zoe in a slow dance as we keep our eyes on the other's dancing near us. Simon and Becca are slow dancing, getting a little bit too hot and heavy, Dale and Luke have been dancing with their dates, thankfully not putting on a sex show. Like Simon oh and Mattio is not one to be left out, he is currently french kissing Natalie over in the dark corner which us wolves can all see. Zoe is more like stalking them all following there every move, she is such a pervert. Zoe whispers in my ear O.M.G. Mattio, he is not getting a blow job over there is he? I say" is he no way!" Zoe, started laughing and said, "See who's the pervert now." They are just kissing, but because I looked like I was now the pervert, so I said "let's just observe, and see how far people from school go." Jade is in front just over Zoe's right shoulder dancing with Andy, Zara is dancing a slow song with Kyle to my left, on my right I see Cara getting up close and personal with Liam he has her body pressed tightly gripped to his front. I can see that he is about to go in for a kiss. When I look at Zoe her eyes open slightly, she has a smile on her face. I look around to see what has her attention, then I see the peanut gallery. which is Adam, Abel, staring death glares at my girls' dates. I see Drew and Tom dancing with Sara and Sally, they are laughing and trying to add a little bit of tango into it. Drew has a flower he has taken from the centre pieces on each table in his mouth honestly, they are so much fun. They could teach my brother's a thing or two, Zoe whispers so quietly I could just hear her "what is their problem? They are acting like they own them or something." I agree with her by nodding my head as we stop dancing, we watched to see what our girl's do. We are secretly hoping they give the boys a little taste of their own medicine like we had agreed on, let's see how they like it. The girls do not seem to care at all, they are blantly ignoring the guy's from our pack. Zara grabs hold of Kyle's bum, and starts to caress it while moving her hips closer. Kyle is typically man he does not miss a beat as he goes in for the kill. He picks Zara up, and wraps her legs around his waist and towards his left, there is a pillar, he slams Zara into it and devours her mouth. Zoe and I gasp, as we had never ever seen her with a date or anyone, Zara wants to hold out for her mate. Zoe shout's" go sis!" What in the hell, then in the blink of an eye the next thing we see is Drew and Tom. Zoe says the obvious "where the hell did they come from?" Last time I checked, they were messing around with the twins." Both were beside Abel, grabbing hold of him with each arm, one hand holding his shoulder, the other gripping and pulling him back. Whispering in his ear, Abel has his fists clenched and he is shaking. Kyle has his back to the room thankfully, but me and Zoe see Zara open her eyes as she looks Abel dead in the eyes. She gently pushed Kyle back. He takes it well, he twirls her around and carries on dancing, as he twirls her again, after a few more seconds Zara let's go of his hand. I see her mouth "ladies." He nods and walked towards the bar for another round of shots. He has been giving us these drinks he calls magic shots. He hands over one each and said "drink up ladies the night is young." They are sweet in taste but lethal as I feel the effects instantly. Cara looks more affected by them than we do as Liam is holding her up, he has got her to drink each shot he has bought. I look at Abel and he follows Zara what for I do not know, he is one strange guy tonight. "What crawled up his arse" Zoe said, I replied "I do not know" With Abel, I can never figure him out, he has double standards by the looks of it to me. We both laugh and carry on enjoying the evening, I ignored my brothers for the rest of the evening, eventually all the girl's came over and joined us for the fun dance routine we made up in Zara's living space. We all fall about laughing as we try to teach Sara and Sally the move's, even Drew and Tom join in Our friends never left other than Mattio to kiss Natalie, and Simon slow dancing with Becca he locked lips the whole dance. They came over after they noticed how drunk we were getting, they kept us dancing which helped the effect as Kyle and Liam have been buying us drinks all evening. We were being idiots, but we did not care if we were having fun. Zara came back from the lady's she has reapplied her lipstick, taken her heels off and joins us in all our dances she even joined in for a group dance. She downed both shots in Kyle's hand and said "let's get fucked up." Meanwhile, Adam, Abel, and even Callum are watching from the edge of the dance floor. Dad is with them, whispering in each of their ears, probably telling them to chill out. I can smell their wolves the power of it is making me dizzy. Callum's mum walks over to the grump group as we have decided to call them, loudly. Even Elle, Becca and Natalie join us in Chanting it's the grump group tra la la la la. It's the grump group tra la la la, it's the way they look tra la la la like there going to have to suck it up! We look at the guy's as we are all chanting and all the girl's are chanting looking across at them and laughing. Even Zara, Sara and Sally have joined in with us all. The guy's face's say it all they are fuming, even mum has to tell them to step away or leave. They are not spoiling the girls' fun. We are pulling our tongues out at them all, they all fully deserve it. The grief we get from them is stifling. Zara catches all there eyes and puts her hand as if she is adjusting her bra and rolls out the middle finger, as she grabs Kyle's face and gives him the most X-rated kiss I have ever seen. Abel is just staring her down as if he can make her submit to him, she turns her back to him the ultimate bitch slap. We all kept on dancing with our friend's, just us wolves can sense the guy's and their strong vibes of bitterness. Liam has been watching as Cara joined in our chant and seems off, annoyed maybe, as he grabs Cara a little bit aggressively, as he has spotted Adam's death glaring at them. Cara moved away and I heard her say," ouch Liam that hurt." I only spot it myself as Drew and Tom join us to dance to the new song playing. They grab a twin each and start spinning them around. Liam holds Cara against him, it's a little bit of a she's mine kind of move that a wolf would do. Cara though after she spoke to him he said "sorry baby, I am a little drunk, those shots are making me clumsy. Maybe he is just drunk, we are all feeling the effects, but we all just carry on. After we are all dancing Liam has pulled Cara further away from us and he leans forward to kiss her, she gives him a small kiss but Liam wants more as he holds her to him he has her in a position that I can't see fully. Our human friend Luke must have seen though as he went over and asked to borrow Cara a bit. Kyle went to the bar again while this interaction went on and he brought a tray of shots for everyone I down it, as did the others. Luke has Cara and they are dancing with us, Cara's mum grabs Callum's hand as she makes him take her for a spin around the dance floor. My mum and Zara's mum are dancing with a few of our pack members. Jade's aunt is doing a move that my mum is trying to do. It's funny, we are just embracing the moment enjoying ourselves. kyle takes Zoe for a spin around the dance floor, as Liam takes me. We switched partners with some of our pack, and our friends from school by the end we have all danced one song each with each other. Drew takes Jade for a daft tango routine, they are milking it so much, they keep swapping flowers from each other's teeth. Andy started cutting her shots off after he cut in earlier, I have to admit she seems a bit better. I really think Kyle giving us magic shots hasn't helped she drank loads more than us, Luke bless him handed us all a bottle of water he wouldn't let us dance until we all including Zara had drank one in front of him, then Andy came over and said let's play a game. Kyle and Liam had gone to the men's again they went an hour before, that's when Liam chilled out a bit and asked me to dance. They have been gone a while, Andy gets us in a circle and hands us each a bottle of water whoever can down it the fastest win's he counts us down on 3,2,1 drink Zoe wins, I want a rematch, we go again Zara beat's us that time. Cara, wins the third round after four bottles of water in twenty minutes we all need to pee. We all head towards the ladies, just as Kyle and Liam are back. "Hi girl's I we will get you all another round," Luke cuts in, "no its ok they have me and my boy's who have yet to buy the birthday girls one." We've got them covered, Simon is with him, yeah, boy's, let's treat our dance partners and our friends, you can't keep hogging them. Now let's dance, Sara and Sally said they want a dance from each of you. They both go back to the dance floor and take the twins for a spin. We all pee and re-apply our makeup, I do feel a little better, no more magic shots for us, we all made a promise to Luke and Andy to not have anymore. The guys were being really sweet, they didn't leave our sides as we started joining our friends. The twins are still dancing with Kyle and Liam. Luke brings us this cotton candy looking drink that has candy floss on top. Wow it's so good, Mattio buys us a blue one with ice in it and its like a slushy but it's refreshing. All our friends are leaving as the bus has arrived and it's going to drop Liam, Andy and Kyle off at their hotel on the way back home to Ashwood. We say goodbye and thank everyone from school who came and our closet friends, each with dates, planted a kiss on their lips. After they left we were dancing, it's just our pack left, now. We are all at the bar having another cocktail and we buy a round of normal shots that taste good. Zoe orders another shot, and we head back on the dance floor. I start feeling the buzz from the drinks again but it's not as bad as it was with those magic shots earlier. Zoe starts to clear a space on the dance floor, it takes her 2 seconds from removing her shoes, in the direction of their intended victims. One hit Abel on his head, as another hit Adam in the face. Their faces are a picture dad has to warn them not to react he said, "let them have fun, only the packs are left nothing will happen in this hotel it's guarded." So relax boys, go grab a beer." We are all watching Zoe clapping her on, laughing at the music she has picked, this one is our Jam we love this song. We all form a circle as Zoe waits for the beat she wants to start on, and she shocked us all. She does a double back flip, holding her hands above her head to prep for her next move. I mean two backflips in her dress, she has not got any underwear on. I am open mouthed and shocked that I am looking at Jade open mouthed. Cara and Zara the lunatics are still encouraging her, chanting, go Zoe, cheering her on, clapping and shouting "go sis! Go Zoe." Zoe laps it up and she then decides after another back flip to go into a front flip followed by her signature move, and she is about to show the crowd her front flip into a cartwheel then into a jump spilt her boobs are almost hanging out of her dress, not to mention she has indeed not worn panties. If I can see her bits, the whole room can we are wolves, oh brother, Cara is still laughing her arse of clapping with Zara. The music build's as the clapping is just fuelling Zoe to just go for it. I can see that she is going to do it, as she's about to start the next part of her routine, when I spot a very red, very angry beta, walking her way he look's absolutely fuming! I've never seen him look so enraged, this is one pissed off Bradley. I have not seen him all night, where the hell did he come from? I thought he stayed home to watch over the pack. Oh no he is heading straight for Zoe, this is not going to be good. His face is like thunder. "Oh shit," Cara and Jade say in unison. Bradley storms over just as she has reached her arms over her head: "He just picks her up, puts her over his shoulder, draping his jacket over her body to hide her bits and bobs from preying eyes and says to dad, "she needs to go to bed right now!." He hands her over to my dad with his jacket draped over her waist to hide her flashing the whole pack he then walked out as fast as he walks in. Luckily people started clapping as if it had been the best entertainment ever. Dad has a look on his face as though he read something on his beta face. My dad carried Zoe to our room as we all follow, it looks like the party is over as we are led back to the penthouse. Sally, Sara and Zara join us as we bid dad a goodnight. As soon as he closes our door the party is back on as we go even wilder in our room. We end up downing more shots and going skinny dipping in the pool. We play games and listen to music. Zoe joined us as when dad had carried her up she had fallen asleep in das arms. Dad put her to bed while Zara stayed with her. She seems less drunk than two hours ago, Zara is with her as she woke her up and said Zoe come on lets party! We started up the karaoke machine our pack mates bought us as a birthday gift as we belted out songs until around 4am. Adam and Abel, along with Callum Tom and the twins, entered the room, thankfully we all had underwear and dressing gowns on. They must have got a key for the room, as they were knocking when we were in the pool skinny dipping. Zara told them to stop being the grump police and bugger off. When they first come in we don't even bother to acknowledge their presence, as we ignore them most of the party, but after we all do a group performance where we start adding in jumping and out of tune melodies, that's enough for Adam. Who turned the machine off as we all carried on without it, that is how drunk we were we didn't even notice until each of the boys picked one of us up. Throwing us all on the large sofa's that Callum had put together to make a big sleeping arrangement, Drew pulled the pillows and bedding from our room's to make a bed for us all to snuggle in. Once we are picked up and laid down, Abel does the sweetest thing he tucks us all in. They turn the lights off after Adam uses his Alpha tone and says "sleep now no more, its almost 5am."

We all must have instantly nodded off because when my mum and Jade's aunty came in to wake us up it was 10am and we were all feeling the hangover from hell.

CHAPTER NINE
Hayden

I arrived at the port Saturday, mid-morning I travelled all night and managed a few hours of sleep in the cabin on the boat. I know my Alpha has family plans today, and they are having a party at the hotel tonight. The news I have will have to wait until morning, I want my alpha to enjoy this evening before I drop all the information I have collected onto his lap. It will be hard news for me to tell him and having to show him the files will be even harder I know it will devastate him hearing about how his brother died was not down to an attack from a lion or any other like it. That, by all the evidence gathered, it was most likely a murder. Why was Julie killed? and why was her womb cut out as though her baby was stolen, if that is what happened could the baby be alive? Or was Julie killed so her baby could be taken away and watched as it grew? Did they kill the baby if they had, where is the baby's remains? After leaving the estate last night and travelling home, I have been thinking about the details repeatedly. Reading the report Max had done, it showed the baby was not inside Julie's body, it had been removed. If any creature or animal had attacked and killed Julie and her baby, there would have been some remains. Is the baby still alive? and if the answer is yes, where was it taken? those questions have been swirling over and over, Aiden has two sons, but I do not have pictures. There was no mention of a daughter, so why kill Max? And kidnap his daughter, surely, they would know we would look. I need to tell Henry and the others, and we need to produce a plan. When I do tell him, I know that Henry will be devastated having to reopen the death of his loved ones. I am still in shock myself especially knowing how capable Max he was a strong Alpha he was one of the strongest we had so far, an Alpha as strong as Max had been savagely beaten, then killed in such a manner is pure evil. I have never known evil amongst us, we all live as peacefully as possible. To be able to do what Airon and his employees have done is pure inhuman behaviour. I left my car at the port when we boarded the boat, it is a few hours' drive to arrive home. I enjoy the fresh air on my face as I sit at a cafe on the beach and think about things, I have learned through I need time to process and gather my thoughts. I order a meal and try to think of anything else. The only thing that I know will ease my heart from the pain and memories is her, so I eat thinking of her, I picture her, carefree in the woods I picture her and I meeting and how we can spend time getting to know one another. I know we have not met in the flesh, but just thinking about her calms my thoughts and eases my worries. I pick up my belongings and get into my car I need to drive home it will take a few hours as I drive, I think about my family, how I would feel if anything happened to them. I think about Max and how scared he would have been as he took pain and knew he would most likely die. I think of his daughter and prey, she is safe and did not have to witness the cruelty of what her father went through. The drive home is a thoughtful one. Once I pull up at my house, I take a deep breath. I live in a townhouse with three floors, a garage, and a garden off to the side. I have four large double bedrooms all have an on suite, I have a large kitchen with a huge center part where I cook, I love to cook, my mum taught me, I find it relaxing. Tommy has a house next door we all live close by. Our pack prefers the outskirts of the city as it's quieter and we have open spaces, and our forest, with the woodlands that surround us it is home. We have mountains that are pure and unspoiled nature at it's best. Our whole city and the surrounding houses that head more towards the natured areas, are protected by our enforcers and the beta, my dad. We all have homes around the other side of the city to make sure we have the pack all around our territory to watch over where most of our residents live. That is great for us, as we learn to adapt using our wolf, when we need their abilities. To be able to tune out the noise from the city, it can feel too much at times hearing all the cars, buses, and trains with the hustle and bushel the city makes daily. We do learn to tune it out, which is why having all this nature around us is the perfect blend of busy and tranquil. We would go crazy if we did not have that ability. I have made arrangements for my Alpha to come to my home tomorrow morning. I left him a message with our head enforcer on my way into the city. Making sure that Henry knows that I am back and that I need to see him. After I enter my home, I head straight to the kitchen I am starving, and I feel the stress of the past twenty-four hours. I decided to cook, to help me relax. I cook a meal from scratch, and I make some breakfast cinnamon rolls and pastries for the morning. I leave everything wrapped and secure to dish up once Henry arrives, I eat my freshly cooked meal, wash the dishes, take a shower before getting some sleep. The morning comes around quickly, I wash up and get ready for the day, just as I am heading downstairs, I heard a car pull up outside my driveway. It's my alpha Henry, he has brought Alpha Gerald with him and two others.' I let them in and am great with my guest. My Alpha introduces Gerald as we shake hands, his beta Bradley, and the Alpha's son Adam. I greet them by asking them to take a seat. Hello, my name is Hayden Hawk, and my dad is our beta. My wolf has perked up, he is trying to tell me something important, as my wolf says on repeat smell mate, they smell like mate. Why? I ask them to sit down as what I am about to tell them is not pleasant, I take a deep breath and tell them everything I know. I speak, about everything I have learned from Evergreen about Alpha Brock and what he has had to deal with. Once I got onto the death of Jimmy and Julie and how much Max had put a lot of resources into investigating it, he had left evidence that showed that they were believed to have been murdered. That Max had been building up evidence of where each animal, creature, and the beasts were all accounted for and how nothing was left behind from tracks to scents. How Julie suffered bruising and the fact her baby may have been taken, and a reason she may have died. The scuffle marks that were found near the abandoned buggy. I showed them the listening device, and that Max had found it near to the scuffle marks. Max believed Jimmy stayed in the area to help the herd of unicorns and sent Julie to get help, but somehow, she was surrounded by the scuff marks and the dirt found under her nails she was in that area and put up a fight. Her body was near the herd he believed she was moved and could have been used to bait Jimmy as he was found a few feet away from Julie's body. I handed over the files with all the evidence for them to go through. I went to the kitchen and made coffee. Once I returned, I handed each a cup. Henry has gone quiet as the others are still reading the files. He asked, "What happened to Max?" Max had died, he knew that he just didn't know the details. I said to the group" Max was beaten, tortured, and missing for a couple of weeks before they found his body which had his heart taken out and his head removed and dumped." Brock believes they are being watched and that they are dangerous. He couldn't tell you or anyone over the Radio after he found all these files in Max's fault in it was a letter to gather the Alphas we have an enemy and he has knowledge we exist" This file here is graphic I warn you all it is disturbing and it has pictures of your family Henry, and Max's death. I must also tell you all that Max's daughter was taken on the same day Max went missing, she is twelve and we think Max was taken and hurt and that

Ali his daughter was used to get information. Brock discovered that a businessman called Airon Huntsman owns land between Evergreen and Clayton. They have pulled their resources together and all the packs on Vale Island have searched every inch of the island and have found nothing. I hand over the final file and allow them time to process. I have information that Airon has two sons and many employees he runs holidays for hunters. We know that the winner, not only pays a huge amount of money he runs a profitable operation, where each person pays, and the winner wins prize money and to have a picture with the animal they took down. If their winner can take a trophy which is normally the head or heart. Max collected bank transactions and has been tracking this guy's whereabouts over a five-year period. Max found out this Airon guy has also just purchased land on Flame Island. Max had gone to meet a lone shapeshifter who chose to live away from the pack after his wife died. He had information but was too sensitive to say anything over the radio incase it was overheard Max had gone that morning to meet him and had left the pack on high Alert. Ali was taken from the school and her caregiver had been tranquilized. Max's car was found halfway between the pit stops where residents fill up their vehicles and can eat. Max had a trump card he sent a spy in six months ago to befriend Airon's sons and the men who are on his payroll. He had him deep undercover, but Brock could not risk him being found out. Max's letter included details of who his spy was and only Brock has that information. Airon has knowledge of our existence, and what we have learned from these files is that Max strongly believed it all started and is linked to how the Sanderson died. We just need to gather as much information as we can about who the hunters are, who are his associates. Why kill Max and take Ali, she is a child. We believe Airon Huntsman has surveillance and has been tracking our movements, he has been watching over the Vale Islands. He has been listening with devices that Max found at the scene they had left, and we believe he has been watching out to see if there are more of us, he has been watching out for strange behaviour. Brock would like more trackers sent over just to see if they can find anything and get onto the land Airon owns on Vale Island. We also need to keep all conversations under closed doors as he has staff that may be taking notes. We need to check the area and see if any of these devices can be found. Brock and Jax's have found many in and around their homes and the woods nearby and have given instructions for patrols to stay in human form, in bigger groups and to be armed. Henry, the last thing I need to tell you is that Max believed that Julie had her baby cut out, may have been taken, and that from the evidence no traces of blood were found that belonged to the baby other than Julie's. Henry and Gerald stepped into action mode, and I allowed them to sort out where we went from here. I entered the kitchen, and heated up the bakery and remade fresh coffee, as I brought it in and placed it on the table. Removing the files as we will need to show them to the other Alphas and their beta's. Gerald and Adam have her scent around them, and they must be close relatives. I know she is near their scent held me together as I had to tell them the horror I have learned. I just need to follow the scent as I know finding her will get me through anything. I handed a coffee to each of them, as I do Alpha Henry speaks to all of us, "we need to gather the other Alpha's immediately. We need to train the pack's and prepare to fight, if this man has kidnapped Ali and killed Max, I want his head. If I find out that he stole my niece or nephew, I don't know if I could hold my wolf back." Gerald speaks next "I agree with you Henry. "I think we should use my land as it will be the best as we have too many eyes here and if we are indeed being watched we need to move to an area where it is a safe environment away from humans. Henry said, "Your land is the most secluded around our country and we know we can keep our kind hidden while we train." Gerald agreed and continued to say that the enemy could not spy around his land as he will increase all patrols and have all his pack sweep the area for any listening devices. His land is large, and they can all train without being interrupted. Adam will make sure all is planned and that all will continue to help in any way they can. Bradley explained that the younger one's have one week left at school, so we will need to arrange what there role will be. Alpha Gerald said, "we will discuss with the others." He told me that they had an eighteenth double birthday party earlier for his daughter and her best friend. Who is also part of his pack, most of the other pack's came to the party and are staying at the hotel until later tonight. Adam and his Beta Bradley want to put details on all the pack's children and any who are not able to fight to be able to protect themselves by being issued guards. Alpha Gerald and Henry do not want to scare the pack's just yet, to keep it amongst the need to know for now. We all talked some more and agreed we need to produce a plan and send a team over to help with Alpha Brock as soon as possible. We all decided the best action we have is to prepare the only way we can do that is to train. Adam said, "we need to do a two-week training program starting tomorrow if we can get an agreement from the others." It is decided that I will go with them and make sure we have small teams working well with each other. We need to be smart, if the Vale Island Alpha's haven't located Ali in four weeks, sending more pack members over won't help. We need one Alpha and Beta to do the training as we need the other Alpha's alongside their Betas to be able to run their pack's and keep an eye on any human interactions that seem unusual. We need to locate Ali, she will be able to transform as soon as her wolf comes in, the first week that happens she will need to be taught control. While she and her wolf bond. After finalizing a plan I want to ask about the scent, I know she is here somewhere as I know my wolf. From Gerald's and Adam's scent she has to be at the hotel. I am following them back to the hotel as that's where Gerald's pack are staying. I use my car to follow, as I am driving, I know the hunt is on for my mate, it is time to find her. As we arrive at the hotel, walking towards the meeting room's the hotel has a few. We are taken to where the sound proven one is so nobody, but us can hear. Adam went with Bradley to locate the others who had to hear what I had brought back. As we waited for them to arrive, we swept the whole room as a procaution, we knew we needed to be careful. The door opened, with all the Alpha's who enter along with their mates and betas, even Henry's and Gerald's mates have joined us. It looked like the ladies refused to sit this one out. I retold everything I have learned along with showing each of them the files with the device. The mate's wives are shocked it has saddened the whole room we all sit a moment taking it all in, some of the wives have openly cried, as they can imagine how the girl must be feeling, scared, hurt maybe even dead, along with how Max died that alone makes the room fill with power. Telling them the rest, with the possibility Julie's womb was cut open and made to look as though it had been torn open, that maybe the bay was taken and could be alive has the room filled with power of everything inside the room. It makes everyone in the room unsettled and everything is becoming harder to make sense of. This changes the whole atmosphere in the room and what upsets the females of any pack, the men are just as hurt and upset, and most of all the scents in the air is of pure anger it's coming off all the male's in the room and the women's scent is of deep despair and pure rage but also sadness. Taking any pack member is terrible but killing an Alpha is tough, they are stronger than any other pack member. They do not die easy, to find out how Alpha Max died, as well as the Sandersons' anger surging through the room in waves. Now to take away Alpha's daughter, our wolves demand we protect, we love our pack members, they all mean everything to us. The human part loves this about us, we are stronger together than alone. Calmness enters the room peacefully as we all produce a plan on how we can start to gather evidence to see how many are involved. Why? and put together a defence plan. Sending over our peace enforcers across the other three countries to make sure each and every pack member is accounted for, no one is missing. We iron out the training program details' with Alpha Gerald wanting his Beta Bradley and John amongst the training teams, alongside Adam and I. Adam will be an Alpha after his dad and he is powerful the whole room sense's it Bradley has power too he is new to his role but he is just as strong. I suggest that Sam has the best nose I've ever come across that he should help with learning how to use scents and track, Alpha Henry agrees he is the best I have ever seen. All the others agreed to step up training for all pack members, even our youngest members need to learn to protect themselves with Ali being taken. We need all our young to be fully protected with more fighting techniques and how to watch over each other. We also don't want to panic any pack members, the older ones whose fighting days are over, will be with the youngest pack members where they will be the safest. We protect our pack, our elder members are still skilled, we decide that our pack care givers will train our little one's to make it into a fun game. The elders will provide knowledge and experience to our young them spending time together will help both groups as they love the children and the children love them. The juniors, all aged twelve to fifteen, will team up with them to strengthen their abilities, learn more skills, to learn to be vigilant, trust their gut instincts, as well as those who can change shapes, they can learn how to hide and how to defend to escape. All adults will increase their training to five times a week, including weapons being used. So, each pack mate has enough knowledge to know when to fight, and when to hide, and most importantly to hide and how to cover their tracks. All the sixteen to twenty year old pack members will train before or after school, or college as they have a week left and they need to have time to study. Those who work will train with the Adults. We have a plan now, all we need to do is put it into practice, and we wrap up the meeting. Some of the pack's coming over for training will start arriving tomorrow morning, Tuesday night the latest. I follow my Alpha and the others up to their suite, their families want to take the girls to see a show and it starts at 1pm. Their mother's have planned it as a surprise they have dinner planned afterward's, before they all head home as school starts tomorrow and the girls have another week of exam's. Bradley will head back early to plan the training and prepare the details as he is covering at the school for another week. He is in charge of the sixteen to twenty year olds, as the school kid's travelling from other pack's won't be able to arrive until Saturday. He and Adam will train their pack and the Deadwood pack in the mornings or evenings after school. Gerald will lead the training of the Adult's along with John and Zara, we will help to train each group to mix the training up. Bradley and John will set up hunts, tracking, fighting, and weapons ready for tomorrow night. Adam and I are going to find his brother Abel and their friends to accompany the girls. We take the elevator to head up to the floor below the penthouse suite to find the guy's. It is still early morning around 10.30am apparently the girl's had a wild evening. I see Alpha Henry and Gerald shaking their heads now and I am interested in what these girls got up to. As we enter the lift, we stop off on the floor below the penthouse floor to allow us alongside both Alpha's as they have a lot to organise. We all head out of the elevator as the mates of both Alpha's say they will give the girls a fair warning before we all arrive. We carry on towards the large suite where I can see a few of the pack members of Alpha Geralds pack. Adam introduces me to Abel, his younger brother, I shake his hand he looks like Adam but a slightly younger version, he also seems slightly leaner. Adam will be Alpha soon you can feel his strength, he is going to be a tough one to beat. Even my wolf knows not to mess with this one. Abel introduces me to his friends Tom, and the twins Drew and Logan. They all shook my hand as I said, " hi, my names Hayden Hawk." Adam explained what they will be doing this afternoon. I expect the guys to moan a little, but they don't, they know that it is not a request but an order. Adam introduces me to his friend Callum, apparently his sister Cara is in big trouble. I sit down to ask them, "while we have time, why not fill me in on this huge party last night?" As I listened in on the events that unraveled and how it went on until almost 5am this morning. I am reminded of my sister Maisie, this is what me and Leo, have to look forward to. Callum told me how she had a date with a human who kept on giving her shots. My sister is downing these so-called magic shots like glasses of water. Her date Liam, who is human alongside his older brother, were continuing to just be buying and letting our girls down these bloody shots! and I heard a couple of growls coming from my right. Callum asked me if I have a sister? "I do" I reply I have two. One is already becoming a handful, as she sneaked into a club that opened up in the city centre. Marcus owns it, my sister who is known to push boundaries is sixteen and called Maisie. My brother Leo and I have eyes on her 24/7 and she is an utter pain in our arses. Leo caught her sneaking out of school to flunk off with two of her best friends, Voilet and Gemma are a trio of pushers I can tell you. He caught them, all playing spin the bottle with a few of their human friends, all the girls are the same age, along side the whole football team who were smoking and had beer. Leo caught them, he yelled out busted, but they all ran off in different directions, but Leo caught all three of them. He picked Maisie up by throwing her over his shoulder, and he put Voilet on the other. Once he had them locked in the car, he tracked down Gemma. Who was in a cafe hiding in the ladies, he frogged marched her out, and she started causing a scene, by screaming that she was being kidnapped. She didn't know this guy and he was taking her, shouting for somebody to help her. Luckily for her it was a packed owned cafe. Leo managed to get her in the car by picking her up and whispering if she carried on making a scene he would spank her in front of the whole pack. Leo took Maisie, Gemma, and Violet home. Our dad had to calm him down even though the girls hadn't kissed anyone or drank they were still there out of sight. Leo was fuming at how they were all risking being hurt and Gemma needed a good spanking, for being dramatic. My dad grounded all three of them and had them cleaning cars for a whole month. Gemma hasn't spoken to Leo since, and that was fine with him, he says. I can hear laughter, they defiantly have to hang out with the our girls then I can imagine the mayhem now. I mentioned that I have a sister called Jess, who is only ten and she is so sweet now that's where Leo and Maisie are in agreement, we all dote on her. We are worse with Jess all three of us protect her. Callum says smartly, "I need to arrange a plan, tell me all the ways I need a plan of action to produce a way to keep her innocent, a little bit longer." I want her to wait for her fated mate as she hasn't got a wolf yet my sister. I hear Drew say "she is eighteen now Callum, she might just want to experience a little taste first." I can tell he is trying to lighten the mood, as I agree with Callum I would want both my sisters to wait, but I know they have to live and chose their own path which is hard being the big brother. I feel strong angry vibes coming from behind me, it's Adam I can feel how strong he is he is trying hard to hold back his dominance. His anger is either towards Callum or most likely towards Drew. Drew said "well it is true, her date did try to kiss her and he did constantly try and touch her up." Logan nudged his twin and said, " shut up," Abel said, "What about Zara, she had kyle the brother of Cara's date practically dry humping her in front of everyone!" He got them so drunk with his magic shots that none of us could buy. He took full advantage of Zara. She has never behaved like that, ever she has always wanted to wait. I wanted to punch his lights out, but these two idiots stopped me. Abel was about to say something more, but Tom interrupted and siad, "that he did buy the shots but the girls chose to drink them they could have refused." Drew joined in by saying "yes and they kept on calling Adam and Abel the grump group, and the peanut gallery we got tied in by helping our boys not lose there shit" He looked at me and told me about Zara's sister Zoe, who decided that she was going to do gymnastics in the middle of the dance floor in a dress! She, cleared a space on the dance floor while the pack surrounded her those dancing anyway, we all thought she was going to do a dance show, as it is her best friends party Cara and Anna. The girls are trained in dance, they have an event on Friday all of us are going. But Zoe decided to add some flips where he whispers so low I just caught it, she had no underwear on. Bradley, our beta, lost his shit and marched over to her, tossed his coat over her bare legs and told Gerald to take her to bed. Zoe normally trains each Sunday, with three friends their dance partners are human Dale, Mattio, Simon and Luke all have their own type of dance they are best at. We thought she might have planned a surprise for Cara and Anna, but she did have a surprise alright. First off, she purposely kicked her shoes off, aiming one that hit Abel right on his head, and the other hit Adam in the face . Drew then tries to joke about it and said,"with a set of boobs like that, and everythingI would" Adam slaps his head and says, "She is our pack mate, do not speak about her that way." Drew says back, "chill out Bradley's not here, he probably wanted to spank her if you know what I mean." as he wiggles eyebrows." Abel slaps his head on the other side. Logan then adds in what all the girls were on fire, and they probably had enough of the double standards around here. We are all guilty apart from Callum and Tom, we do not keep it a secret we hook up and enjoy ourselves. Maybe the girls wanted to teach us a lesson. Jade was a little minx too, she was on a date with this football nerd called Andy. Callum then proceeds to tell me about Henry's niece Jade, their prankster of the pack. He told me about some of the prank's she has pulled, I know Jade, I have met her a few times over the years. I bet she keeps the pack on their toes. so far the girls have really riled up the men, well, the three brothers mainly and there beta. The more I hear about the party the more I look forward to meeting them. Apparently Zara and Cara were cheering Zoe on, clapping amongst the pack, while their other friends Anna and Jade were open mouthed catching flies. I bet the beta saw her flash the crowd and went into protective mode. I most likely would have ended up being in the grump squad too. I imagine as the Alpha of the pack Gerald felt he didn't need to go over and collect Zoe himself. He would have known Bradley was their already and wanted to leave him to deal with it, maybe to not embarrass his daughter in front of her friends. Tom seemed to be waiting for us to be calm and happier with the stories I know I feel better it has helped with all the heavy stuff. Tom asked that the guys listen as he needed to tell them something important. He warned them that what he had to share would anger them but to stay cool. Apparently 'Luke heard Kyle talking to Liam in the toilets, Andy was there too, but they didn't see Luke, he was hidden in a cubicle listening, protecting the girls. He heard Liam say to Kyle that they were running low on Jungle juice, bro, what are we going to do? I want to fuck Cara, she'll be mine, but I need her to have more she keeps pushing me off.' I want to be the only one who gets to play with her, as my reward. Kyle told him to shut up, and told him no more drinking for you, little brother you need to chill out. Andy stayed behind after they left, he told Luke it was safe for him to come out as he did Andy told him, Tom stops what he was saying as we can all feel Adam losing control. I can see that Adam is shaking with rage, as Abel strokes his arm and calms him by saying "we won't let anything happen Adam, we will set up a watch ok." I asked Tom to finish what he was saying as this could be important, "go on what did he say?" Tom finished by saying "Luke was told by Andy, to get water into the girls, to wait until both the brothers came back to the bathroom to try and not let any more magic shots pass their lips. To encourage each girl to dance as much as possible and I will help you as much as I can, but I have to be discreet. He told Luke he had to share a room with them and they might beat me up for not letting them win the girls over tonight. He asked if I could get any of her brother's friends to help watch them. Luke told me when he went over to the bar to buy the water the girls drank, he whispered it in my ear. I couldn't tell you Adam or you Abel nor you Callum as you would have spoiled their party and upset everyone. Kyle is the worst as he works in security, he takes in everyone's posture and can see if it's too obvious. We made sure they all danced and had fun, without knowing their dates were dickheads, wanting to loosen them up for their pleasure by the sound of it. The girls were drugged, Andy had drunk some and he noticed that he felt freer. He and Jade started kissing, he knew from their previous date she wasn't as full on nor was he. He cut them off and hid the shots that were poured into the flower vace's he played up to it so Kyle and Liam wouldn't know that he was the one who warned me. That the girls were being loaded up with something to losen them up. Luke told his friend's and they danced and swapped partners and they were the only ones who provided the girls drinks. That was why they had a water game to help flush it out of their system. Tom says "the girls don't act like Zara, Jade and Cara were on dates yes, but none had ever acted like that, Cara was hit worst as her date Liam kept on loading her up with them, I watched as she kept on stopping him from kissing her and trying to manhandle her repeatedly. Jade and Andy helped her dance with the group more so he wasn't dragging her away from the group. Adam took a deep breath, I need to tell my dad and Bradley this information especially with the news earlier. As he heads towards the suite to speak with the others. We all chat a little Abel is deep in thought and all seem shocked that their pack mates were being drugged right under their noses. Adam returns and they want a watch on Kyle and Liam, Tom and Drew and others will take turns having to keep them under surveillance. I share ideas to help tab these human males to make sure none of their pack mates get hurt. They all form a plan of action, as they decide who will watch which girl as a precaution, what they don't know is I will keep an eye on their sister as from the scent ive picked up from Abel and Adam, their sister Anna is my fated mate, I know it. I just hope we can all get along, as fated mates were welcomed. Our kind understand that being able to find your mate is a gift. To actually know a little about her and her friends and how she spent her birthday makes me happy, I want my mate to have friendships and be able to have fun. It's just no fun with males who want what's mine. Her pack has a good leader, and my mate having two older protective brothers which is a bonus. I know she was has been well protected until I came along and I will take over that role. Alpha Gerald along with Bradley came to join us and they told the guys everything I had told them. What will happen and how we will be training on their pack lands. The girls will fight us if we restrict them which will cause them to make mistakes. Adam wants Cara and Zoe to be kept at the Pack House that way they are safer. All agree, Abel asks if Zara would be better off at the pack house as she lives alone. Gerald agreed, but he asked us to leave it with him. He would be the one to tell the girls. He said, "They are adults, and we have to trust them to be able to live as well." They sleep at the pack house alot anyway so it shouldn't be hard to keep them there. Zara may rebel, but as we need her skills to help with training, Gerald will make it a request, that she can't say no to. He will tell her about everything as she needs to know. "Adam you are strong son, you will be able to help me." The peace enforcers will travel to each island, and with each Alpha they will send over teams that we will train. We will do two weeks of training with each team. Once their team has completed training, we will be sending over the next team and so on until every single pack member has had the training. Alpha Brock will arrange for his pack and the other packs to be trained over here as well. Alpha Jaxs will remain on Vale Island with your dad and your team. Peace enforcers are warning the Alpha of Flame Island to be vigilant as Airon Huntsman has already purchased land on their island. Bradley is going now as we have to prepare for a large number of guests. Alpha henry wanted to come along with his wife and there daughters, he has his beta already over at Vale island, he has to stay here and protect everyone here. After school finishes, he will send his daughters down along with all sixteen to twenty-year-olds on Saturday, disguised as student backpackers visiting different parts of the island. They will be split into teams and throughout the holidays all will have had the training.

We have a busy couple of weeks ahead and I need you all to be prepared. My sister Maisie be one of them, oh brother, I have to go home and tell my mother. Henry wants extra patrols on, and all land to be swept for technology that shouldn't be there. At the docks, we have arranged extra enforcers to check each cargo, all humans will have to sign in there details, what is their business? Where are they from? Why are they here? Who are they delivering to? to check there whole paperwork and check out all warehouses and land will be monitored. Sound equipment will be put over every inch of land to check on any intel we can find. The listening equipment Max found will be duplicated and hidden by our intelligent pack force. We will add any packmembers who have any experience with technology, learning how to listen in and use any technology we already have to help amplyfy to advance it in anyway we can. We need to protect our way of life from whatever evil we find along the way. We continue to plan and that we all add in ideas about who we know who can help. This takes us all to lunch time, after we are all on the same page we all have orders it's time to go upstairs to the penthouse suite we have given the females plenty of time to be ready it has just left midday. The guys and I have gone on up and security have been told not to let on, we are going to be protecting, we are just tagging along as we all want to celebrate their surprise. As we enter the elevated up towards the penthouse suite. I know my mate is behind that door, her scent is stronger here once we enter the suite via the door. I can smell her even more but I know she isn't in the living space Adams' mum and Wendy are still here. On the sofa's are Sara and Sally who shout, "Hey guys, you're ready to whisk us out all afternoon." While smiling my way, these two are not stupid they know all too well we are on guard duty, they just don't know why. Zara and her sister Zoe I know who they are by the guys description. They look a like and are both glaring daggers at Abel and Adam who are getting frosty vibes from them. Jade is sitting with them and she has the look of the twins I've seen her about when she has visited.

They all look ready to go, I can see Adam and Callum looking around the room both seem to be looking for either of their sisters. I can hear a little bit of talking from two voices in the bedrooms, but as we all just entered. I think I need to introduce myself, everyone comes over to shake my hand. I'm getting appreciation vibes coming from all the new girls that I haven't met properly. Abel is staring a hole in my head as Zara gives me a hug, she asked what I do for the pack and how she hasn't met me up close just from a distance. I know of her, I've heard of her fighting skills, her sister is another strong female she is known in our pack for some of the fights she has taken part in. Some of our pack enforcers have said she is small but mighty. That her sister Zara has handed them their arses many times, her sister is just as fierce. That is when I notice her, she enters the living space alongside her, is a red haired girl who is both wet from showering and has just a towel on. I only have eyes for the vision stood in front of me. Nobody else matters here but her. She smells divine and her eyes I can't help but stare at her in a daze. My mate at last I can finely relax as she is here, she will be mine and I can't help but go in for a kiss I want her to respond and she does. It is pure perfection as her body presses into mine as her lips mirror mine as I hold her closer towards me as I part her lips to get a taste as my tongue explores her mouth. Inside my wolf relaxes and has gone silent as though sleeping, I feel content for the first time in my life. I feel at peace, that I have found the other half of my soul that she and I are destined to be together. I can feel her heart beating against my own as I bend down lower so I can reach her, I want more as I continue my assault on her mouth. In the distance I can hear a throat clear as I am brought back to where I am stood holding my mate as I notice we are in a hotel suite where everyone is staring at us.

CHAPTER TEN
Anna

I was woken up by someone knocking on our door, it feels so loud and too loud for my ears this morning, Girls wake up, we have more surprises planned for today you need to let us in. Sally bless her heart answered the door, she has underwear on as do we all. We must have been too hot during the night as we took the dressing gowns off. I remember the guys coming in and putting us to bed, my mouth is dry. We are all slowly trying to wake up yawning and stretching coming around Zoe, Zara, Sara, Cara and Jade are looking at each other with pure do we have to, I ask what time is it my mum answers me, it's 10am sweetheart we have arranged a surprise for you all come on girl's lets wake up. Mum and Wendy have asked room services to send breakfast up, they each hand us all a bottle of water and two pills. We all drink the water and take the pills, as we each grone we all start unravelling ourselves from the bedding, where did we put our dressing gowns. We all started searching through the pile of blankets, no luck, what the hell happened, I have vague memories. We all leave the search and head towards the big table and take a seat. We all sat around the table in a daze as Mum and Wendy answered the door and brought over two trolleys full of breakfast.They made us a plate of bacon toast scrambled eggs with large glass of orange juice each. I look at each of the girls Cara has on the underwear she wore with her dress last night, we all seem to be suffering. My mum and Wendy Jade's aunt are tidying the suite as we have made a mess. What a state we are all in, we have make up smeared all over, some of us have pins hanging on the tips of our hair. We just sit there sipping orange juice, nibbling on our plate of food slowly trying to eat as much as we can as it will help our wolves burn off the effect's faster. What the hell was in those shots, Zara says what I was just thinking,"What the hell were in those shots? I have never felt this rough before." Sara and Sally agreed with her as they are older than us, they have been on many nights out and have drunk before normally it wears off after a few hours of sleep and food helps. But this morning the food is making us all feel sick. I look over at Cara who is trying her best to eat some toast, to help line her stomach. I asked her how she was feeling as it affected her more than us. She answers by saying, "No, I feel like I've been hit over the head, my tummy feels like a washing machine and my whole mouth tastes nasty. I can't believe the number of magic shots the guys kept giving us. Zara, what were Kyle and Liam thinking?" Zara responded with, "Who knows I have never felt this bad before" Sara and Sally said "us either." Those guys were happily supplying us with them. Jade said "I drank different shots after a while as Andy kept on taking mine away, that the guys bought and replacing them with the ones he had bought instead. I remember Luke and Andy giving us more water." Zara said, "yes, he did. I felt better for it until we started on shots again after they left." I added "I can't remember if they had as many as us, but at first I think they had a different type of shot to us, there's smelt different." Zara continued by saying "I don't know I remember seeing Abel, who kept on staring dagger's my way and I remeber allowing Kyle to kiss me and he was grouping me too, and I remember that at the time I didn't even care." "After we all danced and drank the water the effect's wore off

I didn't kiss him until he left and he asked me out on another date." Cara added 'I am so ashamed of myself I was having to calm Liam down he kept on trying to kiss me and he grouped me many times, the more I resisted the more shots he gave me. Even then I kept on thinking about the conversation we had where I said I wanted to hold out for my mate. He had his hands all over my body and I swore in my head I was screaming "no get off me." Zara says "girl's don't feel bad it's nothing the grump group hasn't already done, and rubbed our noses in it too." "I hope that they enjoyed the show, it taught them not to be such man whores. It's ok for them to do as they please even though they have mates waiting for them they don't seem to care they just say use the excuses of a man has needs what and we don't. Well fuck them, I am going to meet up with Kyle I will just buy my own drinks or as he said the bar is free il order my own. Abel can kiss my arse, I am so sick of him he came into the bathroom shouting horrible things at me. He told me if I dare go out with Kyle again and I let him carry on kissing me, I will regret it! He was in my face, spitting threats, the whole matcho bullshit! I was stunned, he never ever gave me anything but grief, so I smacked him and told him that he is being a selfish prick, he has a nerve." Luckily, our mum's are in the bedrooms music as they tidy round. I think they wanted to leave us for a while to talk and come around. We all sat in silence a little, taking it all in, piecing our night together. Zoe seemed really quiet though, which isn't normal. "Girls did I do anything bad I can't remember much, if I am being honest. Kyle handed me this drink and told me to down it before they left it was a home brew he said he handed it to me as he left. "I can't remember anything, the only the part's I remember was when we came back here afterwards, but there is a blank space where I must have blanked out." Sara told her what she had done, as we all sat and watched Zoe, as her face morphed into horrified as Sara told her each detail. Zoe is hiding her face in her hand's saying "no frigging way, I am never going to live it down, I need to hide I am going to avoid him and your dad all the pack other than those in this room." she looks mortified, "Zara dad will kill me, and I will be grounded for life." "Bradley already has it out for me, this will make it ten times worse." "He would love to give me a punishment. I bet he has one lined up, if he can prove that I arranged the car stuff I am dead. Kill me now." I told her "not to worry, the kids from school had left by then." Zoe whispers as we all just catch it. "Oh shit, I did not have underwear on, I didn't want to have lines showing." "The whole pack will have seen my nun," " you're what now?" We all spoke together. Zoe lifted up her head and says "my girly bit's my hoo ha, my pussy, my nunny as in its nun territory." We all laugh so hard, it helps, it really does. Cara went really quiet as I tried to reassure them "girls it is ok, you didn't leave with them, you didn't do anything wrong. It's nothing to be ashamed of, put it down to being drunk." Both girls say together "yeah, I think you're right." Cara doesn't want to see Laim again, he isn't her mate, and after how he behaved at the party she does not want him to think she has lead him on. "Last night he just kept pushing me, you know. I felt it after Luke and Andy made us drink water, Andy helped me by every time Liam went to the toilet with Kyle. Andy would give me water and tell me to drink it fast." Jade said the same as Cara, she wanted to wait until she find's her mate she want's what her parents had, which brings tears to her eyes as we all got up and hugged. We love you Jade its ok they will be proud of you no matter what. My mum and Wendy broke up our moment by shouting from the bedrooms "girls, you need to get a move on!" Go and get showered and dressed we are taking you to a show and out for dinner afterwards the guys are coming with us. So chop, chop, move already." I shout back "Mum, please give us a minute we are not well, and we are feeling rough the water you gave us and the tablet's are not working." "use your healing abilities, at least that would be a kind gesture as were all ill." My mum says "five minutes girls," she totally just ignored my demand to be healed. We each played rock, paper, scissors, for the showers. The twins win, they go into the bathrooms first, while we all wait. While we were waiting we moved on to the gift's that are unopened in the living space. I opened a few from the pile as does Cara, they are all nice and thoughtful gift's the karaoke machine from our pack was best we already opened and used it last night. The twins come back out all dressed and looking pretty again. It's Zoe and Zara's turn next, as we wait for them the twins make us all a coffee, it's so nice it warms my whole body. Once Zoe and Zara have returned looking better than earlier. 'Me and Cara are the last to go in, we decided as we are pretty much joined at the hip, we will share,' Jade jumps into another shower in the opposite bedroom across from us. I take a shower in my room and Cara jumps into the bath as she feels the worst out of all of us, and she is hoping the jacuzzi bath will help bring her round. As I am just coming out, I have a fluffy towel wrapped around my hair and one big fluffier one around my body. Cara is still in the bath, I sit down and talk to her for a while we talk about being eighteen now, how our party was and how we feel about going back to school. I know from our chat earlier that she is embarrassed about her actions. Cara started to open up telling me how she wants to find her mate, but is she ready yet is he ready? "I know I am vulnerable without my wolf Anna, but I don't want to rush into it because of fear." "I want a mate who thinks I am worthy as I want him to want me, and sees me as a good strong mate, not as a weakness or a burden that he feels he has to protect me you know." None of us know what will happen when Cara mates how she will cope with being to shapeshift. "If I am able to adjust quickly like the kids do. It's tough being the only member of our pack not to be able to shift Anna I feel it as the pack looks at me I see it in our brother's as they feel I need protection as though I am not capable it hurts to see it in there eyes." bu Cara is tearing up and sharing her deepest, darkest fears. I hug her tight as she starts to cry deep painful sobs. "Come on Cara, let's get you out of this bath," I wrap her in matching towels like how mine are and we sit on the bed. We can hear talking coming from the front door and my wolf perk's up. I am just about to comfort Cara, with word's when Jade and Zoe enter the bedroom closing the door behind them and locking it. They both sit on the other side of Cara, they both embrace her from the side Jade has her arm around her, Zoe has her hand in her's I have my arm around her other side we sit and comfort each other. We all ignore the noise in the reception part near the door of the suite. 'I am ignoring my wolf, as I know Cara feels pain, upset and afraid for the future,' Zoe says "Cara what is it? what has been bothering you, we love you, you can tell us anything we will never ever judge you, sisters before Mr's and all that" Cara whispers, "We are all being quiet, so none of the others here can hear us." They are talking so they most likely have tuned their wolf hearing down, we all do it as its to keep our privacy. Cara begins by telling us, "I have always felt different, you know, I know my pack love me and I see how our brothers look out for us." I just feel like I am just not going to be good enough for my mate, what if he see's me as less, as though he wishes he had a better choice? I don't have my wolf I can't tell who my mate is, you all will know once you are ready you will know. I don't know any others who are born like me. We have only our history books to go on." "I have nobody to ask who is like me how they found their mates, I have only learned once's mated the wolf comes out via the mating bite. Will I know him, will he know me, will he want me." With Cara as she opens up her heart and soul to us all as big fat tears fall down her cheeks breaks my heart. "I just don't know if I should date, or wait at least if I wait, he will be pleased especially if he is the possessive type. I crave wanting to meet my wolf fully." Jade tells her, Cara Hunny, "You are a true wolf shifter, you are more than worthy, you know we will not let any wolf mistreat you." Zoe chimes in, "I will cut his balls off Cara if he doesn't see that you are the worthiest mate ever." I agree. We are interrupted by Zara come on you three we have places to be. Zoe is the first one who gets up after hugging Cara one last time as she opens the bedroom door to Zara. "You know sister we were having a beautiful moment, that you spoiled with your tactful interruption." Zara just hugs her and whispers "hurry up there is a new hottie to meet, he is frigging cute, plus Abel is pissing me off, by staring at me constantly." I just gave him the finger and walked away to see you girls." I tune them out as I heard a voice I have not heard before, my wolf is going crazy. I heard him say to the twins "Sara, Sally I heard you had quite the night." Sara replies with, "If it isn't Hayden how are you?" He must be part of Jade's uncle's pack. I have met the Beta before and he had his daughters with him, but I have never met his two sons. They were always on duty, or travelling whenever I came with my family to visit. Zoe and Zara head out of the room back to nosy on the newcomer, as Jade practically flees out of the bedroom leaving the door open as she chases after them. I smell a scent that has me slowly walking towards the open door of the bedroom. Cara asked me "where you are going? you're not dressed. Wait! I will come with you, as I know full well the boys will start telling you off." I wait as I wait for Cara to join me she is right though I am only in my towels, I can't get dressed I need to see why that scent smells familiar. I can barely wait as I see that Cara is following behind me as she says, "Let's make it a double dose of what the hell are we thinking, and both just walk out with just a towel in our hair and another around our bodies." "I don't know what's happening Cara, my wolf is pounding, telling me I'm going outside now; "Ok I will be your ride or die let's do this I'm right behind you, I have your back." I am grateful Cara has my back as I know my brothers will have a hissy fit, at us both. We both reach the living area where everyone is talking, near the suite's doorway. At first nobody spots us, but the new male though see's me as he is looking right at me, he has spotted me, and I have spotted him right back. It's him, the man from my dreams, his scent makes me want to roll around in it. I gape at him, and he gapes at me. I don't remember moving, but we are almost chest to chest. I have gone into a trance, and I can't hear anyone but him. Mate, that's one word we both speak at the same time. "Hi, my name is Anna Harris, and I am the daughter of Alpha Gerald Harris." He responds by holding my face in the softest of touches and says, "Hi, mate of mine, I am Hayden Hawk and I know who you are I have dreamed of you." I am then kissed with so much longing, it's him he is here with me kissing me. Wait stop thinking and kiss him back you fool, I follow his lead and kiss him with the same passion that I am being kissed. He gently encourages me to open my mouth and I respond and open my mouth allowing him to taste my mouth. His tongue gently caresses mine as we both delve into pleasure knowing we have found each other. He is mine and I am his. I follow Hayden's movements with my own and I sink into him, allowing his soft touch to warm my skin, the softness of his lips molding against mine, his tongue, which teasers mine. His taste is pure, haven he is everything, he dominates the kiss, taking full control, and I let him. We pull apart and I rest my head on his chest just taking in his scent, he is kissing the top of my hair holding me tightly to him. We stay entwined until I hear a coughing sound, someone is clearing their throat to get our attention. Sorry to interrupt, it's my mum, I look around the room Cara, Zoe, Jade are all smiling and sighing like they have just watched a romcom. Zara is in front of my brothers, while Jade's aunt helps her keep them back. I then felt my whole body being moved behind Hayden's back. He has gone into full-on protective mode Oh brother, here we go, the male arsehole moves, protecting the little women. I notice the other's watching from around our group leaning in as if awaiting the fireworks. The twins Drew and Logan are leaning against the wall, Tom is standing next to Sara and Sally with pure joy for us on their faces. Callum has his sister Cara behind him to hide her from viewing eyes. I started to laugh, I couldn't control it as I just started hysterically laughing as my girls joined me. Cara smacks her brother and dashes in front of Hayden with Jade by her side. Zoe grabbed my arm and pulled me to her side to the center of the room. I hear Hayden growling, Cara, and Jade block him coming towards me, all the while Zoe started talking. "Now we all have eyes and we can see that our girl has gotten herself a fine good lucking, hell of a hottie, my sister's words but I have to agree." Jade joins in to say, "yes, he is a hot piece of arse," fanning herself as she is talking. I see what my girls are doing, they are distracting the room to help ease the tension I love my friends they are awesome. Cara hi-fives her Jade in agreement as my mum is hiding a smile. My brothers look on in shock, Zara then proceeds to add "Hayden welcome to the family, ignoring these two cave men. I am happy Anna has found you. You are going to be a good mate for Anna congratulations." My mum asked if everyone would clear the room to enable us some privacy. As the girls say congratulations Anna and Hayden were so happy for you and are walking back towards the bedrooms. I notice that Cara is being grabbed by Callum, who is giving her a lecture, "are you seriously walking around naked! What is the matter with you!" Just as Adam was heading her way, he also had to open his mouth as my girls were trying to leave. I heard him say "Cara what in the hell were you playing at?" "Really your breaking the rules, pushing my buttons these past few months you are becoming more and more like Zoe and Jade, a pain in my arse!" "HEY!" Jade and Zoe shout together. "She is a fine arsed woman, you two idiot's need to remember she is eighteen now not a child, she is her own woman." "Hello, your sister found her mate, have you ever thought that Cara may find hers too you know." Adam response is to say, 'I didn't ask the peanut gallery, I am talking to Cara, not you she is without her wolf, meaning that she is vulnerable just as the children are in this pack therefore she needs the protection." I saw her last night with Liam the way she drank every drink he gave her, and how cosy they were! Not to mention the clothes you all wear. What you wore last night was more like you had on a top, you were all drunk and therefore vulnerable. It is my job as a future Alpha to protect you. Cara was not making smart choices nor were the others. Now look at Cara now walking in here, where the guys are, in just a towel!" "If she carries on being such a disobdiant girl, all those who brought dates to the party who were clearly just there as they wanted to fuck you, then you all clearly need protecting." Oh no he didn't, the room falls silent even my mum is shocked when she told Adam,"You can't treat them like that son, they are not property they are women who are growing up. Just like you have been able to, I know you are upset, especially with everything going on, but you need to calm down." I can see the moment when Cara's eyes tear up, then her fist cletches, it all happens at the same time, but to me it's in slow motion. Abel has a hold of Zara, as she looks like she is about to punch Adam. Zoe trips Abel up and moves his hand away from her sister. Once they escaped his clutches they made their way towards Cara. Zara and Zoe charge at Callum, knocking him over flat on his face. Jade is about to take a hold of Cara's hand when Cara shocks us all by punching Adam in the face, as she knees him in the balls he goes down to one knee as he wasn't expecting it. After he is down looking up at her in confusion. Cara takes her towel off, and screams at his pained face. "Now I am naked you arsehole!" She held Jade's hand and all of them walked to the main bedroom and locked the door. The girls are laughing their arses off I can hear them saying you just kneed our Alpha to be in his balls. We might need a healer to help him retrieve them. Cara, that was impressive I am going to replay it in my mind to cheer me up. Adam is glaring daggers at the other men in the room. I hope you all everted your eyes. Callum lifts his head and mutters that she is dead as he helps Adam up. Adam spoke to the room, including my mum, that he was next in line and that nobody touches her or looks at her. He will deal with Cara, as he asks everyone in the room are we clear. We all said yes, as he is giving off you must obey as he has made it an Alpha order that even mum agrees with him. He shouts for the others to follow him and stormed out of the suite. My mum is chuckling as she spoke "sorry about that Hayden, they have not been getting along this weekend. I think the girls wanted to teach the men of our pack that they will not have double standards. Which from the display you just witnessed it has not gone well. Now please, can you two take a seat." We all sit down in, me and Hayden sit together holding hands. "First of all congratulations, we are happy for you, it's fast for a mate bond to snap so suddenly. Both of you must be ready and it is an honour Hayden, to have you join our family." I love my mum, she can see we were just as shocked as the rest of the room was, but also trusts us to make our own way. "I will take everyone along with us to watch the show, tell your dad the good news and I shall be speaking to both of your brothers. I want you to spend time alone without us all in the way. "You both need time to get to know each other." "Thank you, mum, that would be great." "Hayden I will be back as quickly as possible, I just want to get dressed and check on the girls." Hayden nods his head in agreement and I leave him and my mum to talk. I am greeted by my girls who are sat on my bed waiting for me. Cara is now dressed, and I hug each and every one of them as they congratulate me. Zoe bulldozes straight in with "how was that for a first kiss?" I whispered "it was everything I can't believe how I just met my mate in the hotel after my birthday party." "Let me get dressed real quick and I will let you know the details. Once I was dressed I spoke to the girl's about how earlier my wolf was unsettled like she knew he was here, as soon as Zara opened the door I could smell his scent more. How my body just wanted to move and see him. "I want to learn more about Hayden, everything about him." Zoe being Zoe "how much do you need to know he is hot, strong, tall, and looks wow I would so jump him." We all started laughing at her antics, she knows how to lift the mood, especially after the boys reaction which helps us all feel better. "We wanted to hide in here away from the guys we have had enough of them, with there I am a man I am bigger and stronger, you need us to protect you." "follow me because I was born with a dick. They had no right to be that way with us. You found your mate and they had to make it about how we behaved please." Cara moves up of the bed and hugs me tight "I am happy for you. We will all want more details later."" We best go, I am playing my music all the way there and back. I am not talking to either my brother or yours Anna." "The grump group are not in our good books, so let's do this one last fuck you!" They all cheered and left me to enter the room I left my mate and mother in. Each of them are wearing earphones and are going to ignore the main culprits all afternoon. I know that Adam is mad at Cara, but he has been so much more angry with Cara than any of the rest of us. I think he secretly enjoys Cara pushing back, but maybe kicking him in the balls and punching him in the face might have changed his view point. I will still laugh about this day for many years to come as that moment when she did that and flashing the whole room, was a little win for her in mine and our friends eyes. After our chat earlier I could tell Cara was feeling low, once we get home we have a weekend away that I am looking forward to, I will make sure she has fun before starting at the office. With a plan in mind to cheer up Cara I feel better, especially finding my fated mate the day after my birthday. I know I am lucky, I am excited I am ready to see Hayden's beautiful face, while we get to know everything about each other to meet his family and introduce myself away from everyone else. I am nervous now the girls have left I can hear them talking to Hayden. Not long after they wrap up saying goodbye and congratulations, the door to the suite opens then closes. I have alone time with my mate, the guy I have been dreaming about. Hayden is tall, handsome, and his muscles being a shapeshifter makes us look more sporty. He has hazel eyes that look into my soul, with brown hair cut in a trendy style it suits him. I take a deep breath and walk back into the living space where Hayden is sat waiting for me as I say "Hello,"

CHAPTER ELEVEN

HAYDEN

I am sat waiting for Anna to get dressed, her mum has welcomed me with open arms, we talk a little, while we are waiting. Her mum, Annabelle, apologised for her pack's behaviour. She said: "I am embarrassed about the boys behaviour, Adam as you can feel, is strong, he will make a powerful Alpha, he is extremely dominant and very protective." Abel's the same, especially when it comes to Anna and the girls in their group." "Callum is just as bad but he calms down once he thinks about their point of view." "Adam hasn't found his mate yet, and has been more grumpy than what is usual for him, I think as the girls are becoming adults he has struggled even more." "They were all in shock, it's a first for any of our pack to find their mate this fast it normally takes a few years for fated mates to find each other, or at least be mature enough to handle being bonded." Adam wanted that he was set on finding his mate once he was eighteen, and he attended all the gatherings but had no joy." "once he turned twenty one, he started dating and hooking up, Abel and the twins were not interested in finding there fated mates, they have continued to hook up whenever they can. I think Adam saw what they were doing, and the others in our pack, I think he got frustrated as he was actively looking, the others were not. They go out a lot, and the girls haven't been able to go anywhere without them following. They are so bad that even if the girls have a sleepover they have to tag along. The only escape they get nowadays is if they stay at Zara's place as she won't allow them in. Zara sticks up for them, she tells them off. Adam being the next in line though he use's that to get his own way. Which is why my girls have been giving them hell this past week, they have grown tired of it. Anna's friends are really good girls, they have been that way since birth, to be honest with you they are more like sisters than friends. They are good and kind towards every member of our pack. As you can see, Cara is normally the good one alongside Anna, but I have to say these past few months from spring time to now." "The girls have been teaching them lessons this past week. Jade she has been through so much already, she is our prankster she likes to have fun knowing her she and Zoe are the main masterminds behind payback. The guys cars were decorated this week, ask Anna she will tell you all about it. They will definitely keep any mate they have on their toes, which is a guarantee they are both bundles of fun. Jade, though she does struggle, she has a fear of losing the people she loves. She is protective and will not let anyone hurt her friends or those who she loves. The news earlier as she lowered her voice and whispered that will cause her pain, I am hoping that we can uncover this mess without involving them. Zoe and her are like two peas in a pod they are alike, put them together and things will happen. Wait until you meet her brother, our adopted son Ethan, he is so loving Gerald and I will do everything in our power to find out what happened and help to uncover the truth. Losing Jimmy and Julie hurt us deeply. 'We're hoping we can end whoever is responsible. I hope we fined Ali and as for the animals that killed Max they will feel the full force of how our kind look after one another. They will receive death as that is the only way we can protect all of us and all of our children from future danger. Zara she is a big sister to all the girls, she is a damn good enforcer her skills are fantastic, she can fight her John her dad and Zoe are the best fighters I have ever seen they have speed and they can think as they fight. Her and Zoe learned to fight at four years old they are very protective of all the female's they do not like to see them hurt in any way. You will love them all just as fiercely as we do, especially all the guys you've just met. You will fit in perfectly, the pack will welcome you openly, at that moment the girls all came out of the bedroom. "hi, Hayden it's nice to meet you, congratulations. Look after our girl, you are one lucky guy, she is the best of us treat her well." that was Zoe as the others all said, "see you love birds later, bye" Anna's mum Annabelle followed them to the suite door to meet up with the guys who I can hear through the door. I smile to myself and say goodbye as they wave back, and Zoe wiggles her eyebrows telling me to behave or else. I have to laugh she is going to be a handful to whoever her mate is, I can tell she will defiantly have him turning grey early. 'Before they open the door to leave they all say Mrs Harris please forgive us, for earlier and for our next lesson we are going to teach the boys. We are not listening to them bitch all the way to the show. 'We are not speaking to them either," Annabelle laughs and says 'girls I don't blame you," laughing harder when she sees the girls' tactic on how they will ignore them. All the girls put in their ear phones to listen to music loud enough not to hurt their ears but also loud enough to drawn out the outside world. I say to myself, good luck guys, you're going to need it with those four. I am awaiting Anna to come back into the living space, after they leave. She reacted well to me earlier, she was open to being mates which I wasn't sure if she would be ready or not. I had a plan that maybe she wouldn't be ready to mate just yet. I was going to charm her, to use seduction to draw her in, to play and have fun. Anna responded to me, her lips, her taste I don't want to rush her just yet sex can wait. I will spend time letting her adapt and learn about each other as in a few weeks we may have a fight on our hands and I will need to check in with Brock and my team. I want to make sure Anna is safe and mine. Before that happens the training will keep me with her and hopefully she can stay away from the investigation with any luck. I have a mission to go on and I do not want to be separated from her but I won't let Anna come with me. Anna walked in from the bedroom to the living space where she stands and said hello,."come here and join me" she sits beside me on the sofa. She is wearing jean shorts and a vest top that is comfortable but covered. She looks nervous, taking her hand in mine, she responds instantly relaxing against me. I reached over and pulled her closer towards me I touched her face and pulled her against me for another kiss, her lips with mine moved softly at first, then I deepened the kiss wanting to taste every inch of her mouth. I nibble, lick, caress, tasting her, and teasing her. I hear a soft moan of pleasure which makes me pick her up and straddle her over my thighs. We stay like that for several minutes lost in each other, exploring one another's mouths until I feel her need to breathe. I pull away, landing soft little kisses across her lips. I move us back to sitting against each other on the sofa once again, holding one another's hand. I tell her how I have been dreaming about her for so long, how I've been able to watch her for a few minutes in each dream. The way her hair blew in the breeze how she would be carefree how much I just liked to see her relaxed. "I wanted to meet you, as the dreams kept on coming each night and as I thought about it, I would find myself in front of you. I was able to see you, but you could never see me. I knew you were younger and must not have been ready to meet your mate just yet. I wanted to find you after the first night, but I knew it was too soon each time I dreamed of you my need to find you grew. I thought that if I searched for you, that maybe the reason you never saw my face was because you weren't ready." "I know some of our kind do not wait, but I want you to know that I have waited, for you. My fated mate you will be my first and I am honoured for you to become my mate. I am ready to wait until you have finished school, your mum said you have another week to go. Just know I have longed for you, I have dreamed off you, and that I want you." "I want you to get to know me as I will get to know you. I will protect you and I will warn you now I am possessive not just my wolf but the man too, you will be mine and only mine from this day forward. Now that I have found you their is no turning back. My full name is Hayden Hawk, I am twenty-five and I am next in line to be the beta of our pack." My dad is the current Beta, I work on missions as an enforcer, and I accompany our peace enforcers on some of their travels, as well as track and take care of any potential threat. I have a brother called Leo. He is twenty, and I have two sisters. My sister Maisie is sixteen and my other sister Jess is ten. I am currently in the middle of a mission from my Alpha, I live on the outskirts of the city along with most of the pack we have surrounded the city and spread out nearer to the woodlands, and mountains we have a large forest that we use for pack training and for our pack runs, we have some beautiful lakes and plenty of unspoiled lands to explore. I own my own townhouse, it has a garage, a fantastic kitchen, and I relax by cooking. I am an amazing cook and look forward to being able to cook for you. I am going to really enjoy feeding you I have a large master bedroom with a full bathroom attached. Along with another three bedrooms for friends and pack mates. I also have a comfortable living space with lovely views of both the city and the surrounding beauty of nature its amazing to have the best of both. The whole lights at night are breathtaking, then the views from the mountains and forest on the other side are perfect. I drive both a car and motorbike and my best friend lives next door. His name is Tommy. I will introduce you to he has been a naughty boy which I'm sure you will hear about once you meet my other friends Delia, Sam and Sophia, we all work as enforcers and they accompany me when we have to leave to complete missions. Delia's dad Phillip is another team member. We have had to work as a team with the beasts, and not to mention the Neeman lions they are stubborn and hard to persuade to move further away from the residents living area. We are called out a lot to the towns to help move them away to help protect the farmers and their cattle. My parents live nearby and they will fall in love with you. They will be so happy I've found you at last. That is most of my basic information, sorry if it's too much I want you to feel at ease and I want you to know what I do sometimes I have to travel but we can sort out arrangements as and when they happen. I know I am not leaving you after today I will be accompanying you to Ashwood we had a meeting earlier I was already going there tonight anyway so I call it fate us meeting like this. What about you, Anna, tell me everything? I listen as she tells me about herself, she tells me about her home life, her friends, her brothers, her last week at school. How nervous she is and how Jade and Ethan live with them and are her family, as her girls mean the world to her. That she has a weekend away booked after school finishes as it's been given as a gift it's girls only. I might have to see about that nearer the time as I want her to enjoy her trip but I also want to spend time with her. She has a holiday planned here which is great as once the training is completed I can come too, but after the news today her plans might have to change, it's something we can figure out together I'm sure. I want us to build a strong relationship where we can be everything each of us needs. I want to take her right here, right now on this sofa, I want her so bad the urge is powerful. I have to fight it. I want to take my time and get to know her and her me. When we do take the next step I want to make our first time together last. I want her to feel precious and taken care of her whole body to buzz from my touch, I can't help myself I need to touch her to hold her, I need to kiss her again more slowly teasing her lips playing with her tongue I can hear her intake of breath as I begin my slow sensual kiss I nibble, suck, lick tease , taste her whole mouth. I need to hold myself back as my wolf, he wants to claim her as his right now to bite her, as the man thrust home into her as I break her barrier to enter deep inside her warm, wet, pussy as I do. She will take my virginity, as I her's. I will have to settle for her mouth as I push my tongue inside her mouth to taste her as I gently hold her face as I take every ounce of pleasure from just kissing her. I slowly move my hands to her shoulder's down her arms to hold her hands in mine. I allow our kiss to naturally end as I cup her cheek, I look into her eyes as she looks into mine, she is perfect. I want us to have more time to get to know each other. It's been a couple of hours since the others left, we talk some more she tells me about her subjects and what she plans for cheering her friend Cara up. I don't want to suffocate her. I know she has been battling the protection she has around her now. I shall plan with her brothers and their friends to watch them without them even knowing about it. I think it will help us guys bond too with what has happened and the danger we are facing, it makes sense that we want them protected but I also don't want kneeing in the balls either. I can do it without them knowing I do it all the time with Maisie, as my brain is formulating a plan I hear the other's getting out of the lift, how quickly the time has gone by. I held her hand as we waited for the endless questions, when the door opened it was her parents and my Alpha, and his wife Wendy. "They sat down across from us," Hayden, my Alpha, says, "can I congratulate you on finding your fated mate Small world we live in isn't it." "As we discussed earlier I want you to get to know your mate, and help with the new training we all agreed to try out earlier today. It will help us all improve and be better at and what we do best protecting our pack lands and human kind." Alpha Gerald shakes my hand squeezing slightly, you take care of my daughter you hear. "Congratulations to both of you, and welcome to our family Hayden. I know that you are going to make Anna very happy." I want to take Anna to meet my mum and sisters. Before we leave, I take Anna's hand in mine, as we say goodbye and tell them we shall see them soon. I am going to be taking Anna back to Ashwood in my car. We leave the penthouse suite, taking the elevator down to the car park basement. I open her door and get into my car driving us towards my house. We talked all the way to my home. She asked me what that was all about with the Alpha's, I told her earlier today we had a meeting to try new training mixing our forces and learning better techniques from each other and that everyone had to partake the two weeks of training. We thought it would help keep us fresh and help us improve alongside each other. It's so easy to talk to her that she nods her head and says" it does make sense we do hold fights at the gym, but you are paired up with each other and being able to train with others from all the packs a few weeks at a time will help us be at a better protection for humankind." She has one hand resting on my lap, and I hold it every time my hand is free. Her scent is intoxicating, the car smells wonderful. Just pure Anna sweet flowery heaven, my beautiful mate. I am glad we have found each other fate must have had a hand in entwining us to meet on my return and blessed me with her. When we pulled up outside my house I noticed Tommy wasn't home yet and he must still be either with his mate Sophia as an actual mate or on patrol. After the night club he would be an idiot to not try and win her over. I opened Anna's door for her, as I took her hand into mine, opening my front door and took her on a tour of my house. She likes how my kitchen is set up, I promise her I will spoil her with my cooking. She laughs and says I will like that as she takes in every detail, I show her the living space and the view out of the windows. She could see the city on one side beginning to light up, and through the opposite side of the house through the larger window she could see the land, trees the natural part of Darington. I show her the spare bedrooms which are on the third floor, the views are much better. She takes in everything from the windows, the decor, the bedding, and the artwork I hang on my walls. She takes extra moments to look at the art I have hanging. She told me she loves art and has been painting our dream setting as her art exam piece. I can't wait for her to show me it. As I then proceeded to hold her hand and lead her to the master bedroom on the top floor. I show her the floor to ceiling window that looks beyond into the woodlands and landscapes, I show her my large on suite, it has a jacuzzi bath, a double shower, everything you might need. I take her to my walk-in wardrobe so she can see how unorganised I am. She helps me pack a suitcase with my belongings in, she picks me an outfit for her final day at school she told me they have a performance for all parents to see. Her family and most of the pack will be there to cheer them on as she continues to tell me they are marked by the exam board on the first routine, she refuses to give me anything else. She just said, "it's a surprise you will see, my family haven't seen any of our practices we all want to blow them away, and I want to impress you with my smooth moves." She teases me and I really like it, that she feels comfortable. I gave her a quick kiss and asked her if she would make us both some coffee to help herself in the kitchen to anything she wants. As I finished adding my boxer's and packing my razor and toiletries. I also want to retrieve the gift I bought her, I bought it just after the dreams started. I will give it to her after she finishes her exams on Friday after her performance. I can't wait to see her beautiful face light up, I had thought of what I could buy her, I wanted her to remember the moment to treasure the memory so when we are old and grey she can look back on it. I had her gift custom made it's a necklace with my wolf on, so she has a part of me with her always, even if we are apart I am there with her. A pack member of ours is talented at making unique gifts. She can take the smallest gold piece and put so much detail into it. The detail with how much it looks like my wolf, each stroke of my fur is there and the added jewels that are the same colour as my eyes. The details of my fur and my face are a perfect portrait of me in my wolf form. My wolf likes the idea of our mate wearing us around her throat to always have that reminder if were ever apart, that I am there in spirit kept close to her heart a little part of me. I grab my things by bringing them to the living space where Anna is making us coffee, "do you have sugar? I'm making you a latte with me is that ok?" "perfect, thank-you and no sugar for me." i watch her as she enters the living space and sits beside me. I can't stop, I have to have her again. I need my fix I go in for another kiss this one is more heated as we end up with me laying her down on the sofa and my body on top, settled between her parted thighs which brings us closer together. I parted her lips and took a hold of her tongue, touching caressing it with mine I moulded my lips with her's as I encouraged her to open a little wider. She is holding her arms across my back moving her hands upwards towards my hair. Where she started to slide her fingertips through my hair. My wolf has me wanting to purr, I stroke my hand down her face across her cheek towards her hair, which is loosening from the loose bun she has it in. As I grip her hair, pulling her head closer towards mine. I can feel my erection pressing into her belly. She moans into my mouth the sweetest moan yet, I can smell her scent getting stronger the more aroused she is becoming with the longer we kiss and touch each other. I need to pull away as I gently end the kiss and slowly pull my lips to hoover above hers. Anna whimpers, wanting me to keep going, which isn't helping me when I am trying to slow it down and pull away. "Anna, you are everything I could ever imagined, you can feel how much I want you, I do so much." "I want you to get to spend more time with me before we take the next step. I want to take my time with you to make it memorable and unforgettable. You will be mine for the rest of our lives as I will be yours. I want it to last, I want to taste every millimeter of your skin from your ankles to the top of your head.'Soon', that's a promise." "I want you," she whispers quietly, as though shocked it came out from her lips. I rest my forehead against hers and tell her "can't you feel how much I want you?" As I breathe in her scent, she takes in my scent too. I gently kiss her lips one last time, a small touch of lips as I move, pulling her up with me. We sit up as we do, I put my arm around her shoulder as we pick up our coffee's that are cold but we drink them just the same. I know she hasn't eaten since this morning when she was telling me all about her party and how late it ended. I want her to meet my family before we head back. I told her I would buy us some takeout on our way back. We rinse our cups and go outside to where my car is, I load my stuff into the boot and drive us over to my parents home. It takes less than five minutes I hold Anna's hand after opening her door. My sister swings open the front door and says, "hi Anna, great to see you, how are you?" While running to hug Anna, Maisie kisses her cheek as she welcomes her new sister to the family. She hugs me too, "wow I gather with Anna being with you fetching her here means you have found your mate." "Anna, congratulations he will annoy you with the protective macho bullshit, but he will love you just as hard. He is my hero, I am so happy for you both." Thank you, we both say as my sister is leading us towards the house, I can tell already mum has made dinner. Our pack honestly is nothing secret, I bet Alpha Henry's wife told my mother we might be visiting. My mum came out of the kitchen, my mother is a beautiful woman she is almost fifty now, but she is still stunning. My dad always spoils her rotten, he treasures her like I plan to treasure Anna. They have given us all the best examples of how amazing finding your fated mate is, what kind of love they have for each other. How to build a life together, having children together, how it is such a blessing, we are lucky. "Hi Anna, welcome to the family, you are simply beautiful, my Hayden is one lucky boy." She embraces Anna and kisses both of her cheeks. My mum comes over to embrace me and whispers in my ear "I am proud and I am very happy for you son," as she holds me and kisses my cheeks. "Come on in I made some dinner, I heard you had quite a night Anna you had a lovely party, but didn't get much sleep as you girls carried on the party until 5am I heard." Anna, smiles happily at my mother, as she asked if pasta was okay. "I wanted to make you my own recipe as you need comfort food to help. Wendy told me about last night, how I miss those days. Me and my girls, before the children were born and before I met my mate. We used to hang out and have the best fun, I remember skinny dipping in the sea my father was not very happy with me ahhh memories of being carefree and embracing your youth. We still do enjoy fun times, but we are a little more tame nowadays. You are going to be spoiled and loved by my Hayden, and I can't wait for the rest of my family to meet you." Just as mum is talking to Anna, my little sister Jess comes flying down the stairs" Hayden!" She jumps into my arms and I pick her up while the ladies talk." Hi their Jess, what have you been doing today?"" I have been playing with my friends while Maisie watched us, we played tag andI won Maisie because as she lowers her voice runs too slow, I am faster."I laugh, "are you. "How about the next time I'm home we race and get Leo to join in?" She laughs, and says back, "I will win, I am fast." "Mum took me to watch a movie and bought me some new clothes yesterday. We had, as mum said, a girl's day Maisie did my hair see" I do see she has braided her hair into two side braids on either side of her head. I introduce my mate to Jess who hugs Anna and says "I know who Anna is Hayden, I play with her brother Ethan and sometimes Jade will play hide and seek with us." "I like you Anna, you're really pretty my brother is lucky." Anna thanks Jess and gives her a kiss at the end of her nose. Mum asked us all to take our seats and dishes out the food. It was so good I had a second helping, Mum even made us an apple pie with ice cream. By the time we have finished dinner it's starting to get late. "Mum, thank you for dinner I am doing some new training with the packs I'm sure you already have heard if you spoke to Wendy. We will be back in a few weeks." I heard I know Maisie will need to pack and will be heading to Ashwood for two weeks to train, I know you will keep an eye on her. I love you and have a safe ride back to Ashwood I will see you when you return, I will cook us a nice dinner to welcome you home hopefully your dad and brother will return safely and we can alll have some family time getting to know Anna more." We should both be back in three weeks as Anna willl have completed her training and I may need to help with the mission, Anna willl be staying at my house with whoever she decides can stay, my home is her home. "We all embrace each other saying goodbye. It's always good to see my family, we are close as is the whole pack." I opened Anna's door as we headed back to the city. "I could stay with Henry and his family, you know." I know, but you are mine Anna, I have a home I bought for us, and I will feel happier knowing you have privacy and you are amongst the pack. I know the Alpha's home is well protected, but I would like you to put your own stamp on our house here too." She kisses me and says thank you. I want her in my space, my home is now our home, I want her to leave her scent everywhere I want her to feel comfortable and I want no other man to touch what is mine. We drove all the way back to the hotel once we arrived at the hotel they were loading up the bus. Gerald came over to my car and let Anna know all her things were packed and on the bus. "The girls packed them for you, along with all your gifts both you and Cara will be busy opening them all you got quite a pile." she thanked her dad. "You will have the pool house to stay in it has privacy and your brothers can leave you alone to enjoy getting to know each other. Ethan will no doubt want to meet you Hayden, by the time we get home he should be ready for bed, but I know my son will want to wait until we are all home safe." see you back at the house. Once the bus left, I followed behind it as three motorbikes drove beside it and another car is behind mine. Anna said Abel was driving and it had Tom and the twins Drew and Logan inside. Adam, Callum, and Zara were on motorbikes. She begins to tell me about Ethan." I think he will want to have a movie or story first as he will want some time with us all before he goes to sleep." We should be back by 8pm so I will be able to meet him before he goes to sleep. I have met him before when he played with my sister Jess. I can see the girls waving at us out the back window pulling funny faces and making Anna and I laugh at their anics. Cara keeps giving Callum and Adam the middle finger, as Zoe and Jade are at each side of her doing the same then they mix it up by pulling their tongues out. Anna is laughing so hard I can't help but laugh along with her. The ride to Anna's town was fun, we chatted all the way back, she told me all about her friends and the guy's with what I am hearing I think perhaps there could be a mating between one of the group with how hard they fight. It does remind me of my own friends. The girls are harmless, they are making me laugh out loud at the way they wide up the guys. It's funny, at least it will be entertaining watching them all as we train. It will be lighthearted relief after training and when we start hunting to find our missing member Ali. Anna was telling me more about the town and the school, her favorite place to eat and where they all go to to hang out. When I pulled up onto the driveway the girls all jumped out, as we got out of my car I opened Anna's door. While her friends asked "hey you two, we are going to see Ethan." "We were told to crash here, we have to stay until training is complete. The Alpha's think we all need to step it up on the training front." Cara is muttering under her breath but we can all hear her as she mutters. "I could do with it now, I have faces I need to punch!" okay someone was in trouble I am glad I am in the poolhouse with the tension I can feel coming from both groups, time to meet Ethan. I take my things out of my car, the guys take all the girls stuff inside and up the stairs. We are all talking as we head inside the house towards the living area, the house from the outside is huge, it is similar to our Alpha's home. They need to be bigger to house any pack members and guests. The girls have not spoken one word to any of the guys, they have just listened to music, while at the show and they refused to sit near them. The show apparently had male dancers in it, so having the guys there having to sit through it. They said as we all sat down how worth it it was, to see their faces as they hated it. Jade had her camera and began to show us some pictures, I can't help but laugh. The guys faces say it all with no words needed, they are angry and very much pissed off. Wendy and Annibelle had planned on light-hearted fun by taking the girls to see human men with their shirts off dancing. One of the men did a dance routine using a lamp post with rain coming down and with the music and skill it was so good they had really made the show a good dance performance. Zoe was saying how they were shocked, that Wendy and Annibelle booked it in the first place, as both their mates are Alpha's and Alpha's are the most posessive males of our whole pack. Beta's we are protective too and can be possessive, but it can sometimes be hard on our female pack members. For our mate's we can get into deep heated conversations to where we will follow or have our mate's followed as that is the only way to calm down that part of ourselves. The females will push you and hide from that protection and that is why arguing takes place as we are stubborn even I can agree to that. Anna's dad seems calm enough I doubt he knows, if he doesn't it won't be for much longer, by the looks on Adam's and Abel's faces. Zoe: 'Yes, did you see this one Hayden, this is what my girl missed, I hope you were worth it,' and she again wiggles her eyebrows. Anna playfully taps her round the head while they all laugh like idiots. 'It's cute, it reminds me of my sister and her friends.' Looking at just the first few pictures I am very glad I met Anna when I did. Out of nowhere this little spitfire of a boy wearing blue pjs comes running at Cara, the red-headed girl. He avoids his own sister to leap at Cara, just as Anna's family walk in to join us. Anna's mum fetches hot chocolate and cookies in on a large tray for all of us as Alpha Gerald help's his wife. I am holding Anna's hand I haven't let go since we left the car I like touching her. We sat with Cara on my left and Jade sat beside her, Zoe is on Anna's side. Adam and Abel are sat with their parents. Ethan hasn't even noticed me yet, he has just leapt on Cara, he is whispering in her ear we all can hear him though he seems to think we can't. He is saying how much he has missed her, and while they were away he had lost a tooth, he has saved it in his box with his other teeth. He asks her, "If she liked any boys and if she did that she could tell him, Cara, I can keep a secret, you are so pretty you don't need a mate yet" I won't see you as much if you do, he might want to take you with him, away from me. Cara hugs him tight kisses his cheek and whispers back, "nobody will take me away from you little man, I won't let them. If I do find my mate, he will have to love you just as much as I do, and stay here or I won't be his mate." I have to say she is good with him. I can see the bond they share, he then jumps on his sister Jade telling her "You won't leave, I won't let you mate until I am older to protect you first." "Remember I won't leave you, and you won't leave me will you?" "Ahh Ethan, I could never leave you I love you so much it is you and me buddy always." I am holding back emotion as I look at those who saw the files earlier. I can see their eyes are misty, you can see that the siblings fear losing each other. Finally, as we all watched his sweet interaction he notices I am here, as he looks around the room. Finding Adam and Abel did you protect my sister's this weekend. We did little man, even though they are not speaking to us. Adam then looks at them all and then looks at Cara a beat longer before he settles his gaze towards Ethan. "I will always protect my pack mates, even if they think they can misbehave, or not speak to me or punch me and knee me where no man should be hit. When they know that it will entail a punishment." Cara, rolls her eyes and smiles "Ethan hunny" Ethan nods his head. Although he has just jumped up and ran towards Adam and Abel, hugging their necks, he says in a whisper, "I will help you as soon as I am as big and strong like you." Cara waits for him to finish speaking to them as she finishes saying you know Ethan, girls are just as strong, don't listen to them two they will keep you in the dark ages. Chuckles erupt around the room from just the women as they try to hold back their laughter. Ethan moved over to give Gerald and Annibelle hugs as he told them, "I miss you the most mum and dad I want to go next time, did you save me cake. We sure did, and Uncle Henry and Aunty Wendy can't wait for your visit next week." We have a gift for you with some new stories but before we take you up to bed do you want to see who Anna has brought you to see? He looks over, as Zoe says "hey, Ethan what about me?" Am I not getting any sugar over here? He runs over sitting on her knee looking at me. He answers Zoe, by saying "I already know you can fight and protect yourself, especially having Zara there who can kick even Abel's butt." Ahh little man, you say the sweetest things. Abel had just been burned by an eight-year-old. Abel pretended to be hurt by holding his arms against his heart. "Hello Hayden, I know who you are, I remember your sister Jess we played tag when I visited and Maisie joined in." He then asks me if Anna is my fated mate, as he says I have never seen Anna hold a man's hand before and Adam hasn't hit you so you must be mates. The whole room laughs I am, I will be staying a while, and I would love to play tag with you. I will even show you how to beat my little sister and her friends. He hugs me and whispers "I like Jess she can win, she smells nice." He sits back on Cara's knee as Anna hands him his hot choculate, be careful it's hot she says to him, He answers back "I will thank you, I will help you open your presents if you like you and Cara have so many gifts." Both girls agreed that he could help them unwrap them tomorrow night. We all drink our hot chocolates, afterwards it's time for Ethan to go to bed. He gives each of us big hugs and follows his parents upstairs, as he leaves he asked them if he can stay with them as he has missed them. "They like to spend time with him," Anna says, as they don't like leaving him behind, but knew he would have been better here than at the hotel. We all like to read or watch a movie Abel takes him swimming alot, us girls bake and do movies. Adam takes him on adventures with dad on weekends and he enjoys Jade reading him storys until he falls asleep. Mum takes him everywhere she goes if she's home and not at work. He doesn't like to be left alone. Jade, Zoe and Cara all agree and say they enjoy doing activities together. He adds a little cheer to there days. The girls ask if they can borrow Anna for some much needed girl time as they head upstairs to Anna's room. I sit with both the guys and we start talking about our roles in the pack, what they do training wise, they tell me how the afternoon went, they start with how annoying the girls have been and watching the show their mum and Wendy booked was pure hell. That they were planning revenge as they were not getting away with all their antics. They told me all about how the girls went skinny dipping, and the manager who is pack asked if we could rein them in as it was 3am, they had knocked and the girls refused to open the door. They then started singing they had to get a key to their room and ended up putting up with them all singing until almost 5am. That's when Adam and the guys put the girls to bed. I can see these girls don't half enjoy torturing the guys, especially as they have both hooked up with humans to scratch an itch. They asked me about my friend's. It's nice to be able to just talk freely. When Anna returns from her catch up with the girls and I can see she is tired she has had a long weekend. We say goodnight and head towards the pool house. Anna gave me a mini tour and promised me after school she would give me a tour of the town as we will most likely be training tomorrow. She has a study session planned with the girls while Zoe and Cara take their driving test afterwards. I have to plan training and I have meetings with Gerald while Anna's at school. Adam has offered to take me on a tour of the house and grounds. Adam has work Tuesday him and his dad have to arrange their schedules with their business to run smoothly. Adam will be boss at the company to free up his dad and he will train his team at teatime and in the evenings while his partner does the day training so they can work around everyone's home life. They have a large task force and they do have others who can step in, but Adam wants to and he has asked that Cara be there bright and early the following

Monday. Her punishment, part one he told me while smiling he is going to really enjoy being her boss. I will be her Alpha soon, and she has to learn I am boss! We have a lot to do over the next two weeks to get in all the training and get the our kind here who will be travelling down. It gives me something to do as Anna has a full-on week at school, I want her to have time to do what she needs to do. As we get to know each other as well, we decide to spend our first night in separate bedrooms as we are both tired and we need to feel comfortable. I give Anna plenty of kisses before we turn in for the night. I am looking forward to my week with her and her family has made me feel so welcome and her brothers are good guys, they just have fear of something happening to the girls. Maybe it's because they have lost two members from their pack before, and wish to continue to hold on to the ones they love a little tighter. To keep them safe away from any danger they are strong wolves, both brothers you can feel there strength they love their pack, especially the girls they are fond of each and every one. I'm sure they will balance it out over time.

CHAPTER TWELVE

Anna

I am in a dream surely, I have never felt so overjoyed after I have found my fated mate. My dream with the guy I have wanted to see the face off, for weeks had turned up the morning after my birthday party. I couldn't believe my eyes when we met back at the hotel suite. I was shocked, but happy he is tall, handsome and muscular in a I work out body type. I kissed him in front of my friends and family, I don't even care that I was in my towel, or we had witnesses he has the most incredible scent I have ever encountered. When we kissed my toes curled, he was dominant in the way he made me open my mouth to let him in. We were lost to each other, and I wouldn't change it. The whole weekend has been amazing, I have just been given the best gift by him. The guy I have smelled on my nose for the past couple of weeks, is now in my pool house at my home in the next bedroom across from me. We spent the whole afternoon getting to know each other. He is on some sort of mission and it is on a need-to-know basis. I get that Alpha's and Beta's only share what they want us to know. We are always protected by our enforcers and have patrols checking our land is safe that nothing can attack, we have never had any serious issues. Because our enforcers, my dad and all our leaders have managed to keep the ones that do stray onto pack lands or too close to where we all live away. I never question my Alpha, I trust him and our pack to know what they are doing. We held hands all the way through when we talked, in the car he held my hand, or I put my hand on his thigh. We had physical contact from leaving the hotel to arriving home. My girls will want all the juice details, I can see them all now gossiping with each other asking each other what is she doing? Is she happy? He opened every door for me from the lift to the car to his home, he showed me his house, it was nice it had a really good thought-out plan. Where the bedrooms were to the living area, the garage and the kitchen. I couldn't contain my awe of the place, he had art that took my breath away, he has the best views over Darlington. I loved his house when he told me I can stay there that it's our home now, I wanted to cry I feel like any minute I will wake up and this will all be a dream. I wouldn't change anything about Hayden's home. He has taste, he has decorated it beautifully, tastefully. I would pick something similar myself, he has art hanging on the walls that really fit into the whole feel of the house. I am going to have the painting I have done of our dream, framed and I will hand it to Hayden as a gift. I can't wait for him to see where I grew up and see me at home, meet my whole pack who will make sure he feels welcome. He has made me feel so welcome at his house, I felt it was like my home warm loved and comfortable. When he kissed me and laid me down, I wanted him to take me right there, my wolf was up for action. My human part agreed when Hayden suggested we get to know each other more first. I melt as I know he is right, how sweet and thoughtful he is to be willing to give us both time to get to really know each other. I am now sitting in his family's home having dinner with his mum and two sisters. His mum is a wonderful cook. The food melted in my mouth. I was starving. I haven't eaten anything I was hung over this morning from my birthday party. I ate then, but that seems like ages ago Hayden was already going for a second helping. I know his sister Maisie, me and my girls have seen her around town with two other girls, she isn't that much younger than us. I think we shall be spending a lot more time together. She reminds me of a mixture of Zoe's attitude and Jade's zero fucks given attitude and prankster vibes. She will be a handful, that's for sure. I have also met Hayden's dad as he is the packs beta. I've yet to meet Leo, but I am sure he is just as nice as the rest of his family. Jess his youngest sister is so sweet she has two braids Maisie put in her hair she looks like Hayden with his eye colour they have hazel eyes with brown hair he wears his short but long enough length to put your fingers through and be able to let the soft trussells slide through your fingers. Jess's hair is a shade lighter than Hayden's, she is ten years old. She has many friends and enjoys playing games. She loves my little brother Ethan, and hopes to see him soon. Hayden has told me about Deila, one of his friends. They all go on missions together and she lives at home and has a sister. Tommy is another friend who lives next door. He is currently grovelling to his mate as he has not been kind by sleeping with human girls when he knew Sophia was his mate as she had told him. He wasn't ready and has played around, oh him and Zoe will not get on she will take it upon herself to teach him some manners. I smile thinking of her and Zara meeting him. I hope Sophia enjoyed the payback prank, she and Jade needed to get together and get some ideas together, well her and Delia since she was the planner for it all. I already love her with the things Hayden has already told me. He has also told me about Sam and how he has been down and as he is running out of time to find his mate I told Hayden I have seen him he stayed at the gathering when my dad hosted it he is such a kind man he is very handsome too he is big ripped and has the most gorgeous face. That was a few years ago though so he must be worried. After dinner I thanked his mum and hugged everyone goodbye, I will look forward to seeing them all soon. Hayden drove us back to the hotel. My dad came over and told me that we had the poolhouse to ourselves, which is great news. Privacy. We are now driving to Ashwood, my hometown. On the bus as we are behind it Cara, Jade and Zoe are pulling funny faces, Cara started it by giving the middle finger up towards Adam the others do the same. Hayden and I are full on belly laughing. Adam will not be happy he is wearing a helmet, but I swear the visor is steaming up. We head home talking and laughing. I know the girls will want to talk and find out how my afternoon went, as I want to know what their afternoon was, like. After I excuse myself to go upstairs with the girls Hayden is with my brothers, they start talking to each other as we head up to my room. We all sat and relaxed on the bed and I told the girls all about my afternoon, how the kissing felt amazing, how turned on I was how his lips were soft. After filling my girl's in on every detail. I asked how the show really was. Jade let me know how the guys were grumbling and folding their arms a lot, giving the mums a glance, as they kept on saying really dad was ok with you booking this show. They were not happy about any of it, they looked unimpressed with our swooning and telling each other what we would like to do with each of the dancers. I can't help but laugh as I can imagine each of their faces. The girls told me they had ignored them all afternoon and all evening due to their theatrics earlier. I asked them all if they were excited about our weekend away, we are leaving after the show and leaving Sunday teatime. Cara has work with Adam the next day, apparently dad left him in charge. I bet that is going to be fun for her as she knows he will try to boss her around. Zara has gone home to pack up some belongings as she has been asked to stay here. A few pack members will be using her place as we have a large number of our kind coming over. They want to put some in town and around the area to keep it more subtle. Without the town folk knowing that there would be a lot of visitors to the area. I told the girls that Hayden knows about the trip and that it is girls only, I know we are mates but I just turned eighteen I need to experience living as well. I need him to know that me and my girls can protect ourselves, that I don't need permission or approval and that I do not need to be watched all the time. We will need to go to Deadwood as we have all our outfits to buy and we need to collect all our costumes for all the performances we have. Zara will drive us all we need to collect our costumes from vera's shop we can then go find an outfit each and have some dinner. The guys will be training, we will only be there for two/three hours at the most. I will tell dad to schedule an earlier morning training session with us, as we have to pick up our costumes for the show. After arranging everything we all hugged each other and told each other goodnight. I head back to Hayden and as we head over to the pool house, I am grateful he is putting me first, with only kissing and cuddling stage. I feel like I will explode if he doesn't claim me soon. I really want to be his in every way possible, he is mine and I am his. I want to claim him, my wolf is going crazy with need, he makes me all hot and wanton my body craves him the more we explore and get to know each other the more I want him to take the next step. Once we are both ready for bed he kisses me goodnight I fall straight to sleep it's been a long day, exciting, but long. The next morning I am awoken by soft kisses on my forehead, I can smell Hayden, his scent alone makes my mouth water. I open my eyes to my mate looking down at me with so much want, he is holding back. I know he wants me I could see it, but he just asked me if I am ready for breakfast as its almost 7am. Hayden pulls me out of bed to embrace me, he kisses my head and holds me close for a few minutes. We are both just enjoying the comfort of relaxing and being peaceful while we remain in each others arms. We pull apart, he holds my hand and leads me to my own suite, I will let you get ready. I will make us a coffee and we can head into the house as I know you have to go to school. I have a lot to organise with your dad and need to get ready for those arriving today and tomorrow who will be training with us for two weeks. I take a fast shower, clean my teeth, style my hair, and dress in my uniform. I feel refreshed and ready to take today's exams. We have a full day ahead as it is the day my friends will pass their driving test. We also have training. I see Hayden, he has a coffee waiting for me, I sip it and we talk about what we have planned for today. I know he has a lot to do, and we will have a date night Wednesday evening. We have our evenings here together, and we are having a movie night tonight, cuddling up on the sofa will be heaven. When we finish our coffees as I turn back from the sink, Hayden has me caged in with his arms on either side of my body as he leans in and kisses me with so much passion I go a little dizzy. He then says now that's a good morning, he takes my hand and we meet everyone in the kitchen mums home today she has a few days off work and has to train with dad. My mum and dad are skilled fighters, they are a great team, they can take down many in both forms, being the Alpha couple, they work hard to be able to fight many opponents, as well as how to deal with the beast. I love watching them train, I hope Hayden and I can become like my parents a strong powerful team. The girls are all sat with some books out studying while my mum and dad serve breakfast Ethan has already gone Adam has taken him. Hayden sits next to me while my dad serves us a plate it smells good. I have Jade on my other side, she is reading notes for the exams for today. Zara is helping Cara by asking her question on the revision she is doing. Zoe has been taking notes and seems distracted. "Are you okay?" I asked her. "Yes, I couldn't sleep, I kept on waking up with my driving test paper which said failed on it. Every time I woke up and tried to sleep again I did something else like crashed the car, or the pedels kept moving further away. I gave up and revised instead today is going to suck." Zoe, you will have a great day you will smash through today's exam and you will pass your test afterwards we are going to pick up our costumes and we still have training so you will be busy and it will be a good day because you have us who will always be here for you." While Hayden is in deep conversation with my dad, my girls and I test each other on the notes we have taken to refresh our minds. Zara needed to leave as she has to help with my dad and Hayden. They have a busy day ahead too, they have to get the guest suites ready and some of the packs are each taking in at least two to four guests in each. If there are any mated pairings those will be paired together. Dad asked if we were going to drive or did we need a lift to school. We do have an agreement that we would wait until all of us have passed our test, but as we know there is a lot going on with everyone Jade said, "I will drive us as we need to hurry and we can cut the time to get these two to the test center." we alll leave together Hayden takes a hold of my hand and kisses me right there in front of everyone, as I can hear gagging noises as my girls tease us. "See you later and goodluck" Hayden gave me one final kiss before letting me go with the others. My dad, Zara and Hayden head straight to the meeting room as the others have arrived to go through what their tasks today will be. Jade jumps into her car as the sun is out, so takes off the roof blaring music as we are driven by her to school. We sing along to the music and enjoy getting to school independently which feels good. Hello, adult life we all shout as we enter the car park laughing at how lame we are being. Once we were in school we walked towards the main hall. We see our other friends as we catch up who all are still buzzing after our party. We each wish each other luck as we enter the hall and are seated. The buzzer sounds as we each begin I complete it just in time, as the last buzzer sounds to say that our time is up. I had just turned my page over and it was close, I answered each question as best as I could. We all leave and go to eat outside our other friends join us today, we are all talking and getting the gossip on what the others got up to on the way home. Luke is telling us that after they dropped Kyle, Laim and Andy off at their hotel which was posh according to Ellie, they seemed disappointed but tough as you were to good for those arseholes. Luke is sweet him and the others really did look after us, which I am grateful for. As we ate our lunches Zoe asked Mattio how he was after the pda he and Natalie pulled. He put his arm around Natalie and said as you can see it went well meet my girlfriend. Whhooo we all screamed and cheered as the rest of the school stared at our table. They have been eyeballing each other for a couple of weeks so it's a case of about bloody time. We all finished lunch as we had another exam to take we all walked back towards the hall, for round two again we each best on good luck as we are seated and hear the buzzer after it sounds to finish. Thankfully, I did better, as I had finished with time to spare I can see most of the room have completed their own papers waiting for us to be able to leave. Once the buzzer went off everyone rushed to leave. We saw our friends, as they each gave us a thumbs up. We were all leaving as Jade showed our friends her belated birthday gift. They knew that we had a pact and told her they loved it. Our friends are having a study session at the library Jade and I agree to meet them after we have these two for their driving test. All the guys wish them luck giving each of us a hug. As soon as we are about to get in the car we hear "hey wait up." It's Liam and Andy "where are you four off, to in a hurry." Zoe told them we have to meet friends and we couldn't stay and chit chat. Laim is holding the door to where Cara is and asking her if she's ok, she told him she was but how exams today have kicked her arse. Jade revs up the car as Liam closed Cara's door. Jade sped off as we could see Liam's face as we did. We all started to laugh, he looked shocked that Cara hadn't fallen at his feet. He is a handsome guy, but he has an ungly centre, so he will have to get used to rejection as Cara has clearly given him the friend zone vibes.We finally arrive at the driving test centre and Cara looks green, Zoe looks scared as we all get into a group hug, you have this we are going to celebrate your win. Jade and I wave them off and we drive to the library. Jade and I hoped that they pass with flying colours. We could tell they were thinking they had failed before even entering the building, but I know they are good drivers they have nothing to fear. Jade parked the car as we headed towards the doors as we entered the library most of our year are here cramming in as much study time as possible. We found our friends tucked into the far corner, hi we both whispered. All of our friends wave for us to sit and we each start to study. Jade and I stayed an hour and waved as we left, we walked over to the coffee shop over the road. I feel eyes on me as I poke Jade, who whispers, "I know." We both inhale but smell nothing, if dad as us tailed it's nothing new. The last guys who tailed us, we went into a lingerie shop and Zoe and Jade kept walking out in underwear so they had to hide better. I laughed so hard that the owner thought we were in their stirring trouble. We had to all stay in a week after that episode because we were causing an unnecessary scene. After ordering Jade and I sit outside it's a hot summer's day we have another thirty minutes before we have to pick up Cara and Zoe. Jade is telling me what they got up to as we left last night. They all had gone into her room and locked the door ignoring the guys they even managed to dodge them this morning as Adam had to go to the office and Abel had taken Ethan to school and was going to help Adam as they had stuff to do. We each bought a latte to takeaway for our friends as we drove to pick them up, both our friends were sitting on the pavement with sad faces. Jade and I rushed towards them "no, you didn't pass how come?" they then jumped up off the pavement and shouted "we passed!" We were all jumping up and down as we celebrated with them hugging and screaming with such happy smiley faces. "Come on let's celebrate lets go we head to the Italian restaurant which is human owned, so at least we have privacy. Some of the pack should be in training. We should be too, no doubt we will have to make up for it but come on we have our best friends who passed their test. We were seated near the front windows, we order and Zoe says "I hope after all this stress and taking my test twice that I get a car for my birthday." Well you have us for now, so let's just enjoy the success. I asked Zoe if she had seen Bradley as none of had seen him since he carried Zoe over to my dad. No," which I am pleased about the longer I can avoid him for the better I just want to get this week over with go away with you girls and forget that a whole room of pack might have seen my ho ha, my bits." we know we all said back. He might be busy with the pack stuff and training so at least you have a better chance to ignore him or avoid him until you are ready. "I hope so, but I know he is waiting, I know he will enjoy whatever he has planned, he really does want me to suffer." Zoe you might get him for training so we can't avoid him forever. We are looking out the window watching residents walking by as we notice a motor bike across the road. Zara is here, she is smiling at us. "Hi ladies, how did it go?" We passed "well done, I want to help you celebrate, but I came on my way back from getting a few more belongings. Really it was an excuse to give you all a heads up leave now as you are busted they are sending pack to pick you up with orders that you get your scrawny arse back now." "That was Adam by the way, as you are late you should have returned a hour ago they don't care they are coming in here and will cause a scene to teach you a lesson." what a butt head bloody hell how do they know where we are, I knew it we have a team on our arse nothing ever changes. Zara embraces us all and said "I was never here, your tails have gone for a toilet break so move." Cara said, "I say we ignore him, let's just enjoy our meal and see if he comes to get us." Zara, whispers I wouldn't do that they are sending the twins and you know how Drew and Logan are. We were out the door in two minutes, and in Jade's car as Zara speeds past us. We were all moaning about when do we get a break from these guys, we were eating, not out partying. I am so mad as are the rest of my friends as we pull up outside the centre where the training is now going to be. We had no choice, it was to come now or be humiliated. We all get changed as we go towards the training floor, we have two stoney faced males. My brother Adam the utter arsehole smiling at us like he has won. Then there is Bradley, our Beta, who we have managed to avoid until now, he has a matching smile as he said "you four have missed training." Zoe and Cara both glare daggers at them as Jade tries to smooth things over, "they have just passed their driving test. Give us a break, it's training we missed one session. Why is it such a big deal." Yes, I add, "they haven't even had a chance to tell their parents. We had dinner shoot us why don't you." Adam steps forward towards Cara as Bradley steps towards Cara, what were they up too, they are being mean they both want payback you can see that this is the only way they can get some. "Congratulations" and they both say it at the same time, which is freaky. "It's about time" Bradley said too Zoe. In my head I am repeatedly saying don't fall for it keep quiet they are goading you to get a reaction. I know it is pointless as a reaction is exactly what Zoe gives him by shouting back. "Hey! I can't help it that I am short and my legs struggled to react as the seat was too high." "Excuses you are full of them aren't you Zoe," "Adam why don't we take two each as a reward for being able to drive." " sounds good to me, I will take Cara and Jade, you can have Zoe and Anna." I am fuming at both of them but Adam really is being a dick. "Adam why are you being such a" "don't finish that sentence?" I am angry as he just cut me off and used an Alpha tone which I have to obey, I can feel the anger of the other girls, too. This is why I do not feel guilty about knowing they had their car's were decorated because they are both dicks. They have us doing sprints, burpies, boxing, skipping, more sprinting, then they have us kicking, jabbing, attacking, defending for over two hours. I take everything they throw my way without saying a word, I know the girls feel the same way as neither of them moan, act out of breath or slow there movements they keep going, Cara even pushes through too she has determination in her eyes as she follows ever command shouted to us as if we can't hear them anyway. We were dismissed as they looked at each of us, we smiled back as we walked away. I must admit what got me through it was chanting arseholes in my head as they tried to kill each of us off. As we walked away we skipped the showers, we just grabbed our belongings and left as Jade broke speed limits to get away from the centre as quickly as possible. We all started cursing them as we both headed over to Cara's and Zoe's homes to pack up and tell them the good news. Cara's mum hugged her after congratulations, then told her she needed a shower. Zoe received the same reaction from her mum, as were back in the car Jade has a plan a prank of all pranks.

As we all listen as she tells us what she has planned, it's childish, but what the hell Adam was a arsehole in there, he pushed Cara to breaking point, he was harsh just as Bradley was harsh on Zoe Jade and and I are working just as hard but without the glares and the nostral flaring as if they both enjoyed being arses to my friends. As we entered the house, Abel and dad were in the living room as we joined them. "Where is Hayden?" Dad said "Hayden would meet you in an hour at the pool house." "Okay, well we are off to shower Bradey and Adam, who killed us for daring to have a celebratory dinner for us passing our driving test" the Zoe and Cara told dad and Abel. Who each, congratulated both of them. My dad said to us all "I know Adam and Bradley seem harsh, girls, but they really do want you all safe. I know we are normally not this mean but we have to be vigilant. We have to keep everyone safe, we are just preparing you all. We never know what dangers we face, all we can do is prepare you to the best of our abilities." I know dad but that was just revenge if you ask me, yes Mr H that was revenge and pure power playing. Cara and "I got death glares the other two didn't." Dad just replied with "I know, it seems that way, you will understand soon enough." I have to go Ethan is waiting for me to pick him and your mum up from the centre all the kids had a training session of their own. My dad hugged us all and said "girls behave, I know you all so well, whatever is in your heads no." Jade smiles, "Of course not, we are now almost all adults anyway." Zoe laughs yeah well im a child for two more weeks. Dad chuckles and shakes his head, Abel then stands and says, "Do not touch my car! I mean it i know you were behind it I swear if you even breathe near my car. I will decorate your own cars with the bitches of Ashwood and I will have my face engraved on your seats!" After leaving that parting shot of Abel we go to our bedrooms to shower and get changed. Afterwards I leave to go see my mate as I head over to the pool house. Hayden is waiting for me. He has lit candles and has a table full of freshly baked snacks. He has a movie ready to be played and has set up a cosy cuddle sofa for us both. I walked over and he kissed me holding my face, he said how much he has missed me, I have missed him just as much. I told him all about my day, how we had eaten out. He already knew as he asked Zara to give us a heads up as he heard Abel talking about it. "Thank you for doing that." "No problem" as he moves us towards the sofa he has made into a comfortable nest to lay on as he puts his arm around me. He told me all about his day, he has been busy settling in with the new pack members. He has set up training and has taught a few one on one sessions. We cuddle and get comfortable as we press play and watch the movie. Hayden feeds me his homemade snacks. "How did you find time to bake?" He answers, "I wanted you to taste some of my cooking skills. I knew you had eaten, so I thought comfort food would be a nice treat." "Thank you we were out of the restaurant in two minutes flat, they trained us hard and I dread to think how much worse it would have been if Drew and Logan had come in and dragged us out. Honestly it felt like they were after revenge, especially after the girl's ignoring them Bradley was really hard on Zoe, and she can take it as she is tough, that girl is no light weight when it comes to training let me tell you but that workout was pure hell. Adam had Cara and Jade doing the same as us but he barked out the orders even though he knows Cara has no wolf, he pushed her so hard I knew she could tap into the ability of a wolf but its not as powerful as it would be if she had a wolf like the rest of us, he was extra mean." "Cara did well, she took everything he gave her and gritted her teeth like we all were. I don't know how these two weeks of extra training will go down with those two training us. I'm telling you Hayden, two hours with those as our trainers, someone is going to blow. It was hard. We trained a lot anyway, and I have never missed a session, even with studying and dance prep." Iknow I am moaning as I told my mate about today, we are fit but they wouldn't let up at all, it was like we were going to war or something. They were on one today, I just hope it gets easier as the days pass something is going on that we do not know about but all I can do is trust my dad and know that he would never put us in danger. Hayden kisses me and the the training session of pure hell is forgotten about, the movie is soon forgotten about, as we get lost in each other. No words are needed we just enjoy exploring each other, with touches and kisses all night we cuddle and kiss, he strokes my face my arms my belly moving his arms up my ribs. I stroke his neck and back and feel his belly tense as I stroke my hands below his shirt to feel his body. I can feel how much he wants me as I can feel his hard length pressing against my belly and hip. I have no doubt in my mind he can smell how much I want him, he is just perfect. I've forgotten everything that happened today, I am just enjoying my mates touch, how he soothes me. We stay like that for most of the evening exploring each other enjoying each other while not taking it too far, we lay on the huge sofa in each others arms he is stroking my hair I am laid on his chest. We fell asleep like that until morning and I woke up to Hayden gently shaking me away. "Morning" we both spoke to each other. I asked Hayden what time it was, as he told me it was 6 am." I wanted to wake you as I know you have earlier training this morning. Your dad said you and the girls had errands to run and Zara is joining you to run those errands." "Yes, we have to pick up costumes, we have a few items we have been waiting to come in. We shouldn't be too long we need to try them on, if they need any adjustments there is another shop nearby hopefully we can grab dinner while were there and study at the same time. I want to be free to spend our evenings together. Maybe we can have a swim and spend some time with Ethan, as he loves the pool." Hayden kisses my hair "that sounds perfect, I have a lot to do with John with training. I am going to be busy while you are at school." I will be in training until 6 pm if all goes to plan today. I have something to tell you, I will be training you this morning." "I am happy it's you and not my brother or Bradley, that is great news to have first thing in the morning." I placed a soft kiss on his lips. I haven't seen Hayden train so we can see what he has to teach us and he can see us girls aren't to be messed with. "Will you be as harsh as those two were yesterday Hayden, or are you going to be normal?" "I will try to teach you, but not finish you off to be too tired for school but please remember we are doing all this extra training to help our packs and to keep our way of life safe." I understand what Hayden, is saying and I will put in the effort as us girls always do. "We have had so much to do. It's been tough with the exams and studying the last minute plans. There's a lot on our plates." "I know, but let's go train and I'll cook breakfast for you afterward's how is that for a deal." We both get dressed for training, this one is in the woods near our home. Hayden and John are training us this morning. We have to hide our scents as we run. We have to use our wolves' abilities to help, but we need to stay in human form. There are a few of our pack mates training with us in this session, which makes it more fun as it's not just Jade, Cara and Zoe. We have five minutes to try and get as far away as possible, the enforcers are watching the perimitor so we have privacy. Cara hides in a bush, she is quiet and makes her body move in a way it doesn't make a sound as she hides in there centre. Jade has chosen to hide high up in a tree she has wrapped her body as close to the large branch as possible. Zoe and I head further away we head towards the river. I could hear a few of the others who had been spotted, but if the pack weren't so unhappy about how quickly they were found we wouldn't have known. They were silent in tracking and the hunt is on for the rest of us, once we have been found we are to run laps until everyone has been tagged. Zoe points at a tree near the river she leaps up and claims as high as she can while hiding amongst the green leaves at the top to help her desquise herself better. She has thought this through as the river is hiding any noise she makes. It's a good spot, I head a little further away as light as I can be. While turning down wind, as I crouch near the sand where the river bank is, we hang out on this part to fish, swim or just relax. I find myself thinking on my feet I can stay on the sand and I know Hayden will spot me, he has my scent as much as I have his, John's out here too. Well it looks like I shall be getting wet. I am trying to find a path where the current hits the stepping stones nearer to the side of the river. Stepping on those until I reach the last one I place myself slowly into the water it's up to my waist. I crouched down hiding behind the last stepping stone. I wet my hair in the water to help me blend in. I noticed a few stray leaves with smaller branches heading towards me. I grabbed onto those and placed them in my hair to help my disguise. From here I can't hear much as the water takes the sound, me and my girls used to play this as a game with my brothers and Callum and Zara used to find us. I wait, and I am still waiting I use my wolf to help keep me warm in the cold water I stay as still as I can, using my ears to pick up on the smallest sound. I try to slow my heartbeat to help mask me as long as possible. I hear someone approaching they are quiet but I hear them, like I can't scent anyone just yet it seems like they have tracked me to the beach part I hear them walk away I hear Zoe ahead shout "how the hell did you spot me, I was in the hardest place ever." John laughs and says, "I know your tricks daughter you forget I can find you and your sister anywhere." Just at that moment as I hear John talking to Zoe I am manhandled quikly out of the water as I am face to face with Hayden as he said,"found you mate." I am aa little bit annoyed that he found me as I was careful and thought my scent was hidden being in cold water. Hayden must have noticed I was annoyed that he found me as he places a soft kiss on my lips and whispers "your my mate, I will always find you." Ahhh that helps to brighten my mood because how can I be mad when he says such sweet things. He and I walk back towards the path where we meet up with John and Zoe. "May I ask did you find everyone else's or are we heading to do lap's while you find others'" "We have found almost everyone we have one left to find." "Who?" Zoe and I say together. "Go back and you will see who we haven't found yet." We left John and Hayden to find them. John ruffled both of our heads and told us we both did well. We both run I'm wet so the sun will help me dry, as running will keep my body warm. We find that Jade has been found too "hey, girl's" she smiles and comes over as we all jog in a slow lap amongst the rest of the pack. As we are running we noticed that everyone but Cara is here. "No Cara, they have not found one of our team. She has outsmarted them score one for our girl." Well, I am happy one of us outsmarted them as we keep running for at least another half an hour. It is getting late its 7am now and we have school to get ready for I am starting to worry. Jade tried to assure us both that she will be fine as she says, "who can take her? We are on pack land, all the enforcers are around the area, we just need to tell them where she hid." John came back as we were planning on finding Cara ourselves. "hey everyone your dismissed we have strict instructions that you all go directly to the pack house for a shower and food. and there are clothes waiting for you." He points to us as he asked that we follow, I am panicking something is wrong. Zoe whispers to Dad, "What is it? Your scaring us" "wait, love, let's go further into the woods before I say anything as we get further." We all told John where she hid, we will show you. John shakes his head, I hear more of our pack further a head. Thank god I could see Cara who was with them, I didn't realise I was holding my breath until now. Adam, my dad and Hayden are with her too. "What is going on?" We all say together, we run and embrace Cara. "Are you ok?" Cara asked, "Can I tell them?" my dad nodded his head giving her permission. Cara told us that, while she was hiding in the bush she found this, as she opened her hand there was a small device. "What is that we all asked?" Hayden answered our question. "Part of my mission is to do with finding these devices, we are checking all the Islands that our kind live on. We are learning as we go, because these devices can hear conversations and are something we haven't seen before. We believe these have been used to collect information on us, we now have to speed up arrangements with search teams. Which will take up a lot of pack members and as we find one another can be put in it's place. We are training you so hard to be prepared for anything, as we believe that those who made these, and those who planted them are dangerous to our kind. We can't tell you any more, as we are still looking into it." My dad, our Alpha, then adds, "We just ask that you trust us to keep you safe, and you go to school as normal. You have a trained enforcer with you when you're out of school." Zara has agreed to be with you girls after as your own personal enforcer. That is why we have had her moved here, and why we have put enforcers on duty. Do not talk about it, do not tell any others, this is a need to know, as we find out facts first. Trust me, as your Alpha, that the choices we make are to protect the packs. Zara will be helping us with the training, but she will travel with you mainly if you leave Ashwood. We will check in with you via Zara every two hours she has her own radio, that she will be using we have had them shipped down by Nate who is an Alpha from Flame Island. He sent them back with some of his pack members as a quicker way to communicate. It's a project that the invention team have been concentrating on, we are the first to have them, and will be the first to use them. We have enough to manage with until more are made. We ran a test during the night and they are clear and the channel is 5 if you are in any other area other than home. This is an order we will have enforcers watching you in and around town, not just you but all of the pack. Zara will be your main bodyguard as I said when you are out. Don't make me regret it as others would have preferred you to be kept at school and home that would be it. So please, no antics Jade." Why me? "I am good as gold dad," you are my dad said, but "I need you to take this as a threat to our way of life." My dad told us that a team would be travelling with us tonight until they know the areas in which these devices are hidden. "I can't, and I won't, have anything happen to any of my pack. Anyone who wants to leave town for any reason has to run it by me, Adam or Bradley. Understood." Yes Alpha, we understand." "Good, now Adam is taking you to school and I am having Ethan stay home today with your mother. Cara and Zoe, both of your mothers, will be staying here. We want all of our females in the pack house with the little ones until we know more. The center is closed until further notice and I have arranged to have the kids be taught at our home. Where I can control it with so many pack members around it is the safest building we have the caregivers will be inside to watch everyone else. I know it seems extreme, but trust me when I say it's needed and I do it out of love." My dad embraces each of us as I think this device has really shook him up. Hayden pulls me away and whispers in my ear, "hey, please Anna don't try and rebel and listen for me." I need to know where you are? Who is with you? Is that going to be a problem Anna, as if it is. I will drop my orders, to watch over you as is my right as your mate." I take his hand, and pull him towards my lips and whisper "I will do all you ask if you do the same, I worry too you know." "deal," we kiss and hug goodbye. Adam walks us home it's now 7.30am, we make fast work of getting ready. We were all silent as we didn't want to talk in the house we could hear all the children arriving. We will have one busy house, it's big enough we have a larger room that can be used as a school for the kids. All of our mothers have made breakfast and have the pack setting up a nap room for the smaller children room to watch movies and toys and all the kids will need are being prepared as we all sit and eat. The kitchen is busy, we all make do. Some are sitting on the kitchen benches, we have a large dining room that we normally use on Sundays when the pack comes over for dinner. Everyone fetches over a dish, and we all hang out and play games. We have a games room for the older children, and another that the is for the smaller children. We have a football pitch and tennis pitch in the garden as well as a pool. In the summer months, we have a barque and set up picnic benches for all who come. I love Sundays, we have missed a couple of dinners as we have been dance practicing and doing revision, but those we do make we always have fun we all have friends and we like to gossip. Once breakfast is done and we are ready to go Adam drives as we all hit the books as we have another exam we still need to be prepared for. Adam is quiet which helps I see him looking at Cara through the mirror as if he wants to say something but chooses not to. "Have a good day and be safe, if anything looks strange to you, tell Bradley you hear me." Yes sir! We will sir! "Adam calls Cara's name, "yes Adam?" "Look I know we have not gotten along lately, just please be careful no dates. Stay with each other, and don't go off to prove a point." we all say yes. but he is not looking at us, he is waiting on Cara, "Promise me." As we all wait for Cara to answer before he blows a gaskit. Cara is holding off and I don't know why. Adams' temper is about to flair, we can all feel it, he wants a yes from all of us and she is not giving it to him. The bell rings and Jade and Zoe save her by answering for her by replying, "Yes." "She promises we have to go in Adam." He wanted to say more but when we rushed off he sat in his car until we entered the building. To then find Bradley, I mean Mr Anderson waiting for us alongside another pack member, Mr Mcbride. "Girl's we will be watching you ok, no tricks, do you think you can manage that?" "Yes sir", we all say that together. As we walked towards the main hall for our first exam we were all whispering lunch time we needed a meeting to be at our table outside as we are all in agreement. When we feel eyes burning in the back of our heads we hear "hi girl's wait up" it's Andy with Liam and a few others. "Are you ready for this exam then lady's?" "The library must have been fun, I heard all of our year was in there studying. What are you doing later?" I answer "we have to go to Deadwood for costumes, then we have even more studying and some family plans." I asked them, "What are you guys doing? Do you ever study?" As we all laughed Liam said, "We will be late as we have practice. We have a game tomorrow night, you girls coming." I can't, as I have other plans, but the girls will be there got to support our team." Zoe adds "yes we will be as our other friends Ellie, Natalie, Luke, Dale and all the rest will be coming with us." "We have to win this time, I hope you guys win." Liam sais, "we should do, we have practiced all season too hard not to give it our best shot." "I will dedicate any goals to you Cara, you being there you can be my goodluck charm." Luke, Mattio and all our friends shout, "Hey girls, you're ready." "We are. Let's do this," we all answer together. Heading down towards the hall as we were saved by our friends, Cara looked relieved to have not had to respond. Liam looked hurt, disappointed maybe I can't put my finger on it, as he hides it so quickly that I can't figure out what the look he gave meant. I put it out of my mind we all smile at each other as we take our seats and the exam starts. We just finished our morning exam and wasted no time getting to our table, Jade and Cara bought lunch today as it was there turn we saw them heading over I could smell lunch and I was hungry it smelled delicious. Zoe and I were talking , as lunch is placed in front of us we all dig in. After we have all eaten we want to finialise our plans later. We know that Zara had a date arranged with Kylie but with her picking us up and escorting us she probably had to cancel. We still want to know what happened with Cara, I know we were told not to talk to others about it, but we already know. Spill I told her all of it start from the beginning. Zoe plays some music from her music player as Cara whispered low that no way could anyone hear her with the music as a distraction. Once Cara had told us that the device was in the bush she was in and how the leaders came out and she had to wait as Hayden changed to scent the whole area. Ho my dad and Adam had a plan and were putting it in place. It was Adam who wanted to lock everyone down as he wanted us to go to school and home for him or Hayden to drive us. It was Hayden and my dad who convinced him Zara was enough. That she isn't weak and would protect us all without us feeling babysat. That is why Cara could not answer Adam, as he was happy to make them all prisoners. Now I understand why she didn't reply, because she could not make a promise if she could not keep it. Zoe started to add in her theory and said 'with the extra training, finding the device and Hayden on a mission things are not adding up'. "Well," Jade said, "all we can do is watch out for each other, and try and enjoy tonight, it's our last week in school." We have to trust that dad has it all under control. After lunch we are heading back towards the main hall we have another exam to complete, and we saw our friends as we catch up quickly as we are walking towards the doors to the hall. We have all agreed to do one last dance rehearsal even though we have it down, the guys want to go through group one, we all agreed to stay in school just before the game as the whole school will be cheering on each team, there's a game on Wednesday. Mr Anderson and Mr Mcbride should be okay with it as we need to practice and it should take half an hour for all our dance groups to get together. Plus with it being in school it was a protected space. After yet another exam we all went to find Bradley Mr Anderson, as he has to be called in school. We were close to where his office was when we bumped into Liam and a few of the football team members. Who was heading towards us from the opposite direction to their practice session before the big game. Andy isn't with them "Hey girl's how are you?" we all said good and spoke a little about the exam, we all asked the the team if they thought they did well. They all said they tried and did their best and what will be will be. They were telling us how they had college and some were travelling to attend college in other towns. They all said they are looking forward to cheering us on at our dance performance. We are just about to ask if we can have a practice session before your game. "Are you all ready for it?" Won't there be some football league watching out for talented players? this was Zoe as she continued firing questions at them as she was clearly flirting. To be honest it was nice to talk with the guys about football, they work hard and I have seen how much practice they put in so I am listening to what they are saying. While Zoe carried on asking them about who is the toughest team to beat? have they got it in the bag tomorrow? What do they do as a pre-game warm up? do they where lucky socks? Then Liam blurts out "Hey guys have you met Cara, she is going to be my girlfriend?" "She just doesn't know that yet, but I can be quite determined when I see something that I want." okay that just killed the conversation we were all having as every one looks towards Liam and Cara. Mr Anderson's door opened as the door is behind the football team they didn't know. We do though, as we have good ears and can smell. The team are all taller than us so it hides their faces but we know who is there in that doorway. Adams is here, why? And Bradley. We could hear how fast the door snapped open as well. "Cara", Liam said, "you were going to agree to another date." as he put his arm around her and was pressing his lips to her ear and whispering "don't turn me down again sweetcheeks, the guys will give me some stick." "It is our last week at school and I am going abroad for a while. My dad has work he needs me to help him with." "Tomorrow after the game, just a hotdog and maybe sit up on the benches for a while, nothing major." Cara shocks me as she says. "Ok yes sounds great my girls will be with me though, ask Andy along for Jade they got along well. "He is speechless. I think he thought she would have blown him off. What he does not know is that two of our pack leaders are hearing every word and this has revenge all over it. I know it is bad, but inside I am doing a happy dance as it's in town on school grounds so none of dad's rules have been broken point two for smarts goes to Cara. My thoughts are broken, as this tall handsome god walks forward and asks Zoe out. He said, Hey, Zoe I know you are single as I have been watching you, not in a stalker way ah I'm messing this up well if you are free tomorrow night il hang around and be your plus one. I've seen you fight and I admire a woman who can take care of herself. I think you're cute and I would love to get to you better? Zoe is stood there after all her flirty stuff she has actually gone red and stands quite a minute. When the tall guy said, my name is Travis and I promise you I am a Teddybear I swear no funny business. Cara answers for her, "oh she will be there won't you Zoe." Zoe looks up at travis and says "yes il be there it's going to be Hotdog date, I am all in Travis." "Good so it's a date then?" "Yes Travis it is.""We can drive you and your friends home afterwards if you want to have a couple of drinks during the game?" Adam the protective arse, makes himself known as the football team watch him walk towards us. "hey guys il be at your game, so I'm sure I can take the girls home after." Liam is not so easily swayed as he cuts in "isn't your sister on a date herself? I heard she has met someone. Why would you need to watch over these three?" "Were not going to hurt them," Zoe said, "well my sister will be picking us up afterwards so we can catch you at the game or in exams tomorrow guys. Travis, see you tomorrow." "You will, but I have this for you, will you wear this? It's clean, but it has my number I play in and I'd love to see you wearing it" Liam hands Cara his top with the number eight on as he passes number twelve to Jade. "Andy wanted you to wear this, it's for luck as we take on the Deadwood team." They are good players, and we will need all the luck we can get." Travis hands his number 5 shirt to Zoe, As she takes the shirt Travis leans down as he is so much taller than Zoe it is comical but when he kisses her cheek it is so sweet. Zoe has gone a little red. Mr Anderson interrupted the sweet moment by saying: "Your late Mr Mcbride is waiting." "Bye girls," the whole team said, ignoring Adam completely. Before he can give us all grief, Zara comes running towards us, "Sorry, we need to get a move on." I asked her to give us a minute, as we wanted to ask if it's okay to practice in the hall before the game tomorrow. All our dance group want to perform as a dress rehearsal to practice, we will be no more than an hour. Adam answers "well I will be here as will Bradley and Mr Mcbride, we need to stay. If you are here and indeed watching the game. The dates, though not a chance." Zara jumped in 'what dates'?" Zoe happily informs her, Jade and Andy, Cara and Liam, Yes, "Me and Travis are going on a date. I am going on a date with the captain of the football team!" She actually squeels, as she said it I hold back my laugh this is just too funny not to soak it in. "He is the cutest boy in this school, and he is not a fuckboy, like some I won't mention. Yes, I have a date, lets go,

I need to shop, I need nice underwear, nor plain boring underwear but dam girl that underwear is hot, bye all she said as she turned and walked away with an extra bounce in her step," Zara said, "Well, I can watch them if they have dates. I'm coming with Kyle as he will be here supporting his brother, I had to cancel tonight. We are meeting tomorrow, so it's a win, win situation. Gerald has okayed it as I know the girls normally stay and watch. Hayden's going to pick Anna up, he may stay to watch the game you never know, and head into town after the game has finished with Anna." She winks at me. I know her well and I respond with "well yes which sounds like a plan." Bradley responded with "yes its fine I will be here as will Adam." Maybe we should ask if Abel and Callum would tag along. We should all go and watch it too Adam. You know, support the team. As Adam nods his head with a stare down as he is pissed that Zara just saved our arses again. Dad did say she was our personal enforcer so Adam can't do anything." Zara huffs 'low blow Bradley even for you." Zara can't help but add, "I heard you have been dating yourself some cute p.e teacher." "I also heard that you are not very discreet at all. I am sure my sister will have a really good time, I hope Travis makes a move of his own. Seeing as Zoe deserves a nice loyal man as do all my girls this has been fun boys. Let's go girls catch up to Zoe before Travis grabs her and heads into a cupboard." I can't help but chuckle that the Sanderson sisters do not like to be treated badly by any man or boy without a hit back. We catch up to Zoe, as we leave behind a fuming Bradley, his eyes are full of anger, and were now burning the back of Zara's head. We have another angry male, my brother Adam, following behind us shouting, "Hey!" "I'm coming with you, so wait up!" We waited until we were in the car and Adam and Callum are going to be along to watch over us on their motorbikes. As we head out of the school we see another member of our pack, Tom, he is in his car following behind us. "Really Zara dad said if we left town only you were needed, oh and thanks for the save we were about to start a scene back there if you hadn't arrived when you did." Zara said. "I know but this morning has freaked everyone out. This was your dads way to compromise, as he had Adam and Bradley chewing on his arse before you left this morning. Here radio Hayden he has one of his own hit 3 as that is mine and his radio, he wanted you to check in. Oh and ask him to come to the game you can go out afterwards as I lied to Adam and Bradley now it's your turn to cover my arse." It takes me a while to figure out the radio but I managed. "Hey, Hayden it's Anna." click the button when you talk or he won't hear you. I did and repeated my words. Hayden answered" back are you ok? And how were the exams?"After a few minutes of back and forth we have arranged that he would come to the school to watch the game and we can go for a meal in town afterwards. I love him, he is so sweet, he puts my needs before his own and who can't be happy about that. Zara said, "I am sorry you had to rearrange your plans but I am glad he is coming, because Gerald would have had to add more enforcers with two beta's and an Alpha that is enough with me there as well. Under the circumstances Adam and Bradley are not bringing Abel after your eighteeth birthday party, I am not dealing with all their bullshit. It will be like your party all over again if they all come." Ok, me and the girls agree she is right with everything that has happened, perhaps it would be better if we stayed together. I feel better knowing Hayden will be there as he will see the fun side of our pack and get to meet my friends as he has been busy helping with arrangements and I know he is worried after this morning. The girls started talking about what the hell just happened at school as we were catching Zara up on everything she had missed her timing was perfect because it was going to end in a huge fight as the guys had been throwing their power at us and we could feel it too. What was wrong with them being blatantly rude, we are meant to be acting in public like any other human not pissing all over us as if we are there property they were acting like cavemen. They both act like they can do whatever they want but no, not us girls. We need rules, and big strong men to protect our weak arses. Zoe pulled out the shirt Travis had given her 'I don't care, I am wearing this shirt, I am going to make it my own by wearing it as a belly top, with my new bra under to boost my girl's up I will still have Travis' number showing, but have I will show off my abs with a little bit of bra showing when I scream go Travis!' We all crack out laughing as we know that she will do just that to prove a point. Jade will encourage her more and maybe join her to help her with her mission of pissing off the soon to be Alpha and our Beta and anyone else from our pack who tries and cock block them again. Jade agreed, as I knew she would, but what I didn't expect was for Cara to say "well I may as well join in with you two, and make it the three of us."We might as well if we can't leave town, or go in town for a date, we can at least get revenge by wearing less clothing." We all started laughing. I can picture it now and I know it will cause a mini tantum. Zara has the music on as our jam starts playing she turns the music up, as we all start dancing and singing as we head to collect our costumes and pick up a few items.

CHAPTER THIRTEEN

Hayden

Once Anna and the girls head inside for breakfast and to get ready for school. Gerald arranged a meeting with his top leaders which included Adam, Zara and Bradley and I met the twin's dad, and Callum and his dad. There are others here who are head enforcers who need to know the full extent of the threat we are under. I have the files and we are going through everything that was spoken about yesterday, it is to stay in this room as Gerald and the other Alpha's do not want everyone in a panic. There is shock, disgust, and fear for Ali, who was kidnapped as the room falls silent as I speak. I explain about the Sandersons and Max that it is hard for me to keep having to give the information, but I know it is important for all in charge to know that there is a threat, and these are the lengths in which these humans have gone to. Gerald took over after thanking me, he addressed the room "I have had to tell my daughter's and there two best friends limited information. They know information about the devices and have given me their word that they will not disclose what Cara found this morning. I have told them that as agreed earlier that Zara will be their own personal enforcer. If they leave town or want to go into our town that Zara is with them, she has a radio and will check in on channel 5 which is the main station for us all to communicate with. They do not know any of this that has been talked about, I do not want this discussed outside of this room nor do I want you telling anyone else. We need to research and get as many details as possible, that is fact based understood." Bradley will be keeping an eye on things at school as will Craig McBride. "I have arranged training, and we will prepare our pack with every possible sinero. We have no guarantees, and this is a precaution, and I know if it comes down to a battle, we will be ready." "Any questions now is the time to speak up." Adam has plenty to add as he wanted to lock up everyone and keep movement to a minimum, Bradley wants more enforcers on any who do go out especially He doesn't think that Zara alone is enough security on Anna and her friends especially as she is an Alpha's daughter after each person has a say it is agreed that for every group of four will have three enforcers and everyone has to have permission to leave town. He will arrange extra patrols nearer town, and he will make sure that everyone has the same. Permission and enforcers are all to go through him, Bradley or Adam, nobody else has authority. After the meeting Adam is taking the girls to school. I want to see Anna before she leaves after spending a few moments with her and knowing she will behave as will her friend's makes me feel better. Once they all leave for school. I caught up and had breakfast with Sam who has just arrived, and he looks better. I told him about Anna and how I found her and that the dreams were real. He has been taking notes and has been looking into it via our history books to see if he can see anything that can clue him in on her whereabouts. He has also been looking through data on all the names from each pack. I briefed him on what we are looking for before we need to head to another meeting, this is for the whole group of enforcers and those from other areas to help search. The house is busy as everyone is moving in here with their families. The house will be used to tutor the children as this will be their school for now, at least until we know where the devices have been put. I am aiding Alpha Gerald and John on tracking down any more devices that Cara found this morning, one that is close to the woods nearest to the pack house that has us all worried. We need to be searching in teams, to comb the whole area. Gerald has decided to set up all training in the building in the forest and surrounding forest land, as we have that area secured and heavily guarded. Zara and Tom along with Adam and the lead enforcers are to do all the training for the rest of the day. Gerald, John, and the rest will train the other groups tonight. All the children have completed training this morning. Anna and her age group also trained this morning, so we just have some of the adults left to train. We have arranged a meeting to make sure each pack member has learned as much as we can give them, without causing too much panic. We have set up a few teams, each has five members as human and three in their wolve form that is eight members in each team. Sam arrived this morning and we will use his tracking skills to help track with the B team. We are each placed into groups of eight working across the whole of Ashwood and Gerald radioed the other packs across Griffin Island to do the same. Once everyone is caught up on what they are looking for and why each team has a radio between them we have not got enough for all of us to have one each. They are new and are being made in a factory as we speak. We know the enemy has better technology than us, as these devices are the first any of us have seen. The technology invention team are working on it and how it was made. They will be using the design and duplicating it with an adaptor so that we can play it back. If we can listen to music, then there is a way to design how to do the same for the device. Anyone who wants to leave town and visit anywhere else must come to me, Bradley, or Adam as we will need three enforcers per group, if your mates wishes to go out you will double date or travel in pairs as I know you are capable of being careful. Anyone else, especially the younger adults or anyone with children will still need to go through us. I am doing this to protect you all and as you are all highly trained, I trust you to set an example. Adam has a radio, and he will deliver one to Bradley later as he will be escorting the girls with Zara and Tom. I need you all to watch out for anyone who is watching us, where we live, any vehicles that you don't recognise, anything that your gut says isn't right, you radio in, or you see me. Let's all get searching, we will meet back here at 2pm for lunch. Everyone moves out to search everywhere I have Zara working in my team as we get to sweep the area closest to the house. I asked her, to radio me as soon as she picked the girls up from school and ask Anna to check in regularly. I know she has to check in with Gerald, but she is my mate and as her mate I have just as much right. That is why I have my own radio and I have one that I will give Anna tonight as I want her to check in when nobody is around. We fan out and search everywhere the tree's, bushes and paths under areas that would be the best spot to be nosy. We have three in wolf form as our noses are heightened even more as they go through the lower ground to check on any scents that wouldn't mix with the area were in. After getting up to the river checking all around the area, we have only come across two more, but all were near to the area that leads to the back of the pack house that is a short cut to the woods. We head back toward the house as it is close to lunch time, we have the lake to do where a lot of the kids go to swim and hang out. Each search group has different areas some need to search near to where the creatures are kept. Where they have been relocated to. The whole area and around some had to drive to them as they are too far away from the town. The fields where the unicorns are kept are being checked too, that is how Max had found that one, I brought with me. The town school and colleges are being checked as well as the hospital and any businesses that we go to. All the land is large there is the town, the surrounding area and then the valleys, and lakes, where everything is furthest away, as we know Aiden Huntsman has stolen unicorns who knows if he has taken anything else. Once we return to the house lunch is ready and we all eat in the large pack dining hall the house has changed since this morning as all the tables and chairs have been set up. The nursery is in another spacious room that has been finished, the playrooms have had extra toys delivered, games equipment brought in. The children have chairs and desks to work on for school. Later, Annibelle told Gerald the children needed fresh air and he has already searched the garden and outside areas they hadn't found any, so he agreed and suggested that he would join them later, as would some of the others. To play football and teach swimming lessons. They did an amazing job in the hours that we have been searching and it seemed less chaotic than earlier. Once lunch is over, we all head back into the meeting room. Each group maps out the areas that have been searched, and where they still need more time. With school finishing soon. Gerald called off the search for today and we will resume tomorrow after everyone leaves for school. He wants us to sweep through and check if the devices are still there. We haven't removed them, as we know that would give us away as they will know we are on to them. We are marking where each device has been found and awaiting news from each of the packs. To see if we can gather a clearer picture. Some of us decided to head over to train, before the adults tonight came over for there sessions. We arrive and each of us begin with a warmup and afterwards we break off into groups to spar. Sam was in another group to me as we picked to fight in any style we wished, as we even had things, we could learn from each other. After fighting one on one we break off into two on one, and so on until we each had five on one. It is brutal I have blood coming from everywhere, we had a timer on to making sure we swapped over in regular intervals, but it was good as we all held our own. With me being a beta and being stronger, we had larger groups. I was up to seven in my group. I have a shower and as I am in the car driving towards home my radio clicks, it's Anna she and I are watching a football match tomorrow night which is fine by me some are having hotdogs and hanging around a while afterwards. Which means with all the rules in place we would have to double date. I will stay afterwards and make a meal for us tonight. I told Gerald I would patrol the gardens as the children were using the space. Once I parked up Gerald had already got pack members roped in with helping with the children. They are going to have a barbecue for dinner tonight and have some fun. I patrol with a team we each are focussed on the job at hand. We agreed no pack business was to be spoken about and that we were just there to observe. We swap round, and I get to play football. Ethan is playing too, in my game as we have swapped the children over, so each has a turn. so, it is nice to see him having fun, he has the biggest smile on his face. After an hour we swap again. Once the barbecue fires up Abel and his friends are back. Abel was covering for Adam at the office, they have a contract coming up and are in the middle of a large building job. So, somebody needed to help run things. He has on a suit and looks smart, I hope the office has middle aged women in it. I could see not much work would be getting finished. He sure knows how to work it. He and the guys got changed into swimwear and started up a game of water polo to the delight of the kids. I have noticed more of the sixteen and college girls have noticed. It's a good job that they are pack members. We have a rule, nobody touches pack that is the one rule, we all stick too, you can't hook up with any of our kind. I waved, as I headed over to the pool house where I had ingredients, Annabelle made sure Anna and I had food and drinks so we could get to know each other alone. I start off preparing everything ready to cook once I get the radio message saying she was on her way home. After making up the table and baking fresh bread and dessert. I take a shower and get dressed. I have a bottle of chilled wine, and as I finally heard from Anna, she is on her way home. I started cooking it would be ready as she entered the pool house.

CHAPTER FOURTEEN
Anna

Shopping was fun, our costumes looked amazing I can't believe how good they turned out. We had a good time, the guys were discreet, thankfully. We bought a few pieces of clothes for Friday and Jade insisted on me buying a sexy nighty with matching underwear. Zara kept the boys out, Zoe and Jade bought matching underwear Zoe had a a black set. Jade had her set in red it looked hot against her skin tone. We all bought new pieces for our weekend away. I hope we can still go. Even though Cara bought a few items, she bought a light pink matching underwear set. She bought a glitter set to match the outfit she wanted to wear on her birthday. She looked hot, in it with the underwear to finish the look she looks like a sex kitten in the silver one, she bought a red and black set too. We all bought a few sets of nice matching sets, with nighties and silk dressing gowns. The house has male pack members who are visiting from all over, you never know if one will be a mate to these four. We bought a few chill out clothes for our trip and we are taking swimwear as it has a natural hot springs area and a fresh watered lake. It's a relaxing break that we all could do with. Once we have finished, we load up the car, the costumes look great, we all have bought one for our individual piece, another for our partnered dance, and one for our group one all are dance costumes and eat fitted better. Each outfit fits in perfectly with each performance we need to look professional and dress appropriately for each dance. Once we were on our way home, I radioed Hayden who told me to come straight to the pool house. We all sing and start body popping to music in the car. Knowing all is here and fits is a weight being lifted as the last thing you want while dancing is a boob falling out. Once we are on the driveway, we unload our things. Cara, who has dropped her handbag with the contents under the car, told the girls to go on in. Zoe took her bags with her. Callum and Tom headed back out of the driveway as soon as the others entered the house. Adam looked my way and mouth's go on I have her. I know Hayden's waiting for me. I leave him to look after Cara. Adam bent down and was helping Cara pick up her lip gloss and other crap we girls had in our handbags. I leave them to it; I can smell the food Hayden has cooked. He meets me at the door" hey, I missed you. He pulled me in for a kiss as he walked us both backwards into the pool house as he shuts the door. He then pushes me up against it and we just start heating up the kiss where I have my legs around his waist. He breaks the kiss and places his forehead against mine. Are you hungry, Anna? I will have dinner served in five minutes while you freshen up." "Okay" I say as he taps my bum as I walk by him to our room. I brush my teeth, take a quick shower, and I notice he has placed my bag on the bed. He is so sweet I decided to put on some of the sexy underwear I bought the last time we went shopping and I found a nice summer dress in the wardrobe. When I head back into the living space barefoot. Hayden took my hand and walked me over to the table, and he pulled my chair out. I am seated as I would have been in a restaurant. Hayden has made us a lovely meal of steak with potatoes, and vegetables. He has lit a candle and has placed a vase of flowers in the center he has put napkins and even has placemats, he pours me a glass of wine. It is so thoughtful he has really gone all out as if we have gone into town enjoying a meal together as a date. The food smells amazing, it looks tasty, and it smells so good.

Hayden sits across from me, he pours himself a glass of wine, as we both take a sip, and we begin talking about each of our days and what we both have done today. The conversation flows easily between us. I feel so comfortable in his company. It was so nice to be able to share a beautiful dinner and have an easy conversation with no awkward moments we just fit. Hayden told me about my dad's plans for our pack, how we need to be in small groups, those like me and my girls would have three enforcers regardless of if we were in town on another. Even families had to have enforcers and couples double dated in pairs to be more protected. Hayden planned this an indoor date which suits me fine. I told him about what happened earlier with the girls, how they were given shirts to wear, and Bradley and Adam were rude about it. I know scent is important for our kind, but the guys have had other women I only know Tom and Callum who have chosen to wait to find their mates the others have not. Hayden understands my point of view, he told me about his best friend Tommy, and his mate how many times he slept with other girls when he knew his mate was waiting for him to be ready. How Delia has slept with multiple guys she wants to have fun while she can. If it is good enough for the males of our kind, it is good enough for the females too. It was such a pleasant evening he told me how he played football with Ethan, and Abel and his friends had come back and played water polo with them. He came in here to make this for us. I told him about the game tomorrow and that Zara had a date with Kyle and he knew about the other stuff. He told me we could stay as we had this place just for us which is why he doesn't mind. Hayden pours me another glass of wine, and after we have finished, he has made a desert. I asked if we could have it later and just let it settle after he gave me extra helpings, I am feeling full. We chill on the sofa, and we are watching a movie that Hayden picked, we have been cuddling just enjoying being alone and getting to know each other. I excuse myself to go to the loo, I freshen up and decide to put on my new nighty with my silk dressing gown. I do not know why but I am feeling brave. I headed back into the living space, and I noticed that Hayden was not there. He must have gone into the other bathroom; I felt a breath on my neck then his scent surrounded me. I was about to turn around when he said, "Don't." Why? I asked," if you turn around Anna, I want you to know that my control is weakening, that gown you have on leaves little to the imagination." I can feel his whispered words tickling my neck. His hands are on my waist, his chest is pressed against my back. I told him, "What if I don't want you to be controlled, what if?" Hayden stops my words with a kiss down my throat as he takes his hands from around my waist and slowly moves them across my stomach slowly, I feel his thumb brush under my breasts as I take a shuddering breath. I whispered his name softly. He then asked me "Are you certain Anna, I will want to mark you?" I nodded my head in agreement as I said, "If I bite you back you won't be able to turn back either." "True," he says, "why don't we take this to the bedroom and just see how far we go. If at anytime you want to stop, I will I promise." "I know that, and I trust you Hayden," and he takes my hand leading me to our bedroom. He closes the door and locks it; just incase I do not want anyone to intrude on this moment. He pulled me towards him and kissed me with so much passion, I could feel liquid dripping into my pantie's. Hayden gasps, and he shakes with anticipation. He can smell my arousal, I hear him breathe me in. Omg I never knew kissing could make me feel so wanton. I want him, I am feeling a little nervous too. I know we have not done this before. So, I am excited, as much as I am nervous. Hayden rubs his nose up from my chin to my neck, he inhales deeply. "I want you Anna I'm trying my best to be slow and give you gentle as you deserve my wolf though he wants to bend you over and have you against the dresser over there while your naked body is bent as I view you from behind and watch your reflection in the mirror to see your face as I take you. How does that make you feel, Anna? Do you want me to stop?" I know he is trying to see how I reacted if I would pull back or if I had any doubts, but I know what I want and I want him as I I tell him. "I want you so make me yours now." "I'm flipped over his shoulder and he throws me on the bed. "Anna, I need you to take your gown and nighty off in the next thirty seconds or I will rip them from your beautiful body." Okay well I am not going to argue I am so turned on by that I do not hesitate. I try to tease him a little by taking my time. I want to see what he will do if I do not obey his order straight away. I am watching him as he is watching me, I slowly undo my belt, that is holding my gown together, looking him in his eyes. There is no awkwardness as I lift myself upwards to my knees, as I start to loosen my robe off, I remove one arm at a time then I place it on the floor. I could see Hayden's eyes tracking my movements as he grabbed my arms in his and kissed me, slowly teasing my mouth." I said hurry Anna, I think you are being slow on purpose, let me see if I can persuade you to hurry." He kisses my neck blowing on my sensitive skin, I feel his finger tips trace circles up from my knee to the top of my thighs. Oh he is good he makes my whole body tingle where every touch and every kiss is making me shudder, I can't take it I need more, he seemed to be satisfied that his own teasing has worked as intended. I pulled the nighty above my hips. Hayden's eyes flash bright he is so still his hands are fisted to his sides as he has on jeans and a t-shirt. He tracks the material as I tease him by removing it above my hips to show him my panties, which I know are now soaked. His nostrils flare, I can see his eraction underneath straining against his zipper. He watches my reaction and asks me, "are you certain Anna?" I will walk out if you are not ready? I will have you, but only when you are ready, but you need to be all in. If we go any further tonight." I do not give him time to finish as I carry on taking my nighty off. Once I have it over my head, and I throw it at Hayden's face." Hayden I am ready now stop asking I am all in." Hayden starts to remove his t-shirt revealing his upper body, he has a light dusting of hair across his chest as I look him up and down, knowing that he is mine. Hayden licked his lips. "Wow Anna, you are a gift of pure perfection." I responded with "as are you Hayden, I am lucky you found me." "I will always find you Anna knows that I promise you I will always find you." He opens my legs and just admires what he can see "did you buy this with me in mind Anna?" "I did, I wanted you to see it. I was hoping we would maybe move our relationship forward a little." "I like it" as he crawls onto the bed as he strokes his fingertips from my ankle towards my knee, he bends down and kisses my thighs slowly, nipping his way from one thigh to the other as he inhales deeply. He slowly whispers "I can smell your sweetness Anna, it is so much better, knowing I make you feel this way." "I am honoured as your mate to have you here with me Anna. I want to take it slow so please lay back and let me make you feel good." I do as I am told as Hayden started his slow seduction. I am kissed all over my leg and belly and he works his way upwards towards my breast. He caresses each breast, and as I am laid there, I can feel my heart beating faster. Every single sensation Hayden is creating upon my body. He moves to my neck inhaling behind my ear, where he nips, sucks, and kisses working his way to my jaw. "I'm going to remove your underwear now," Hayden whispers to me. He kisses my lips with such care and passion I am burning for him. I do not even know what I am feeling. I feel like I am going to explode, I feel a burning sensation across my lower belly, and my core feels hot. I couldn't help it but let out a whimper of need. Hayden removed his mouth away from mine. He looks into my eyes as he says to me," sit up Anna." I obey, he places his hands behind my back and undoes my clip to remove my bra, as he gently removes it from my body as he just looks his fill. Hayden lays me back down on the bed and instructs me not to move. He puts my nipple into his mouth and his hand slowly massages my other breast. He switches between each breast, giving them both the same attention. He proceeds downwards, where he hooks both thumbs into each side of my panties. Hayden removes them from my body, and he gently opens my legs wider as he is knelt between my legs admiring my whole naked body. I am exposed in a way I have never experienced before, yet I feel wanted and cherished as though I am a gift and not just a release, Hayden has only removed his t shirt as I am laid bare as he whispered "You're so beautiful Anna, I need to taste you now, I feel Hayden stroke one finger down my most intimate part. I shiver, as he lifts his finger to his mouth and sucks my juices from his finger. I want to touch him so badly, "Hayden I need to touch you too. Please let me touch you." Hayden looked back up to my face into my eyes and shook his head. "soon" I am sure he had not said those words out loud, but I swear he just told me soon. I forget to ask him about it as he licks my centre, o.m.g I am lost to the pure sensation as he licked me from the top of my pussy to the bottom. His tongue feels good as he works my centre licking, and nipping as he works me up into a moaning mess. I can feel something building inside me, a tingling burning sensation, as if knowing I am close to something. Hayden inserts a finger inside me. At first it feels strange, but with his tongue moving around my clit takes my mind away as I am getting used to the intrusion. I feel even more closer to exploding Hayden is reading my reaction as he adds another finger inside me and then curls them. As I explode so fast, I swear I feel like I am floating into utter bliss. As I rode out my orgasm as that is what it was. I remember Talia talking about it. Hayden removed his fingers as he had rung every last drop of sensation from me. I am still riding in the glow as Hayden removes his jeans and his boxes, he is breathtaking as he lays between my legs, I felt him nudge his length up and down through my juices he lines up at my entrance as I am still coming down from my pleasurable induced moment, he pushes himself fully inside me. When I inhale a sharp breath, I feel something pop inside it is a sharp shock of pain. Hayden holds still above me, and he rests his forehead against mine "are you ok?" I nod my head to let him know I am fine. "I need to move now, Anna." he began to thrust slowly at first. He tried to ease me in gently as he continued kissing my lips and kissing my neck. He began to move faster after he knew I had adjusted as he really started moving. I feel full, but the pleasure too, the more Hayden moved the more the pleasure increased. He lifts my legs across his arms and repositions me, as I feel him more deeply in this new position. He nibbles and kisses my calf's as he moves deeper with each thrust. Sweat is glistening on my skin as he makes my insides turn to jelly. I can feel my wolf wanting to bite and claim her mate. Hayden flipped us as he said, "one more Anna and I will bite you as we both find our high." I am on top of Hayden as his eyes rake over my body, taking in every inch of my skin as he massages my breasts and squeezes my nipples. I moved my body with each flex of my hips. Hayden's thrusts match my own, him with every push of my hips, we are connected, and I feel my orgasm building. Hayden changed position to where we moved entangled as my knee's hit either side of his thigh's. He kisses my lips and my as I ride him moving my hips to a good rhythm. As we both enjoyed the feeling of each other, being connected as we rode each other into bliss. Hayden and I kiss and touch, exploring each other with small tastes of skin on skin as I am about to peak, he bites into my shoulder where my neck connects, and as I explode around him, I felt my teeth expand slightly as I ride through my pleasure. I could feel Hayden release his own pleasure, as I bit his shoulder in the same place he had bitten me. We both enjoy the eutrophic release as we are joined together in body and soul, and the bond between us snaps into place. As we ride out the blissful haze of our claiming. After we each came down, I removed myself from Hayden's impressive manhood and rested my head on Hayden's chest. He strokes my back as we hold each other. Hayden speaks first, "Anna that was amazing, are you okay?" "I didn't hurt you?" "No, you didn't hurt me that was wonderful I am happy, and I am satisfied." "Hayden, was that just as good for you as it was for me." "Anna, as he straddles me over his naked body and kisses me with so much passion. I want to go again. Can you manage another round?" My answer is to reconnect us together as I tease him as I slowly lower myself onto his hardness inch by inch. He feels amazing as my inner centre clenches and holds and moulds us together. I move my hips and find a rhythm that has Hayden starring as I do. "You are beautiful mate of mine and when you're ready I will marry you." I am too lost in sensation as Hayden tweaked my nipples harder to get my attention. He wants an answer now. "Anna" "yes, yes, Hayden, I will marry you just do not stop," I feel him as he tweaked my sensitive nipples again. I can feel my clit rubbing against his pelvic as he thrusts his hips which enables him to thrust deeper as he keeps up the strong, powerful thrusts. I hit pleasurable bliss as I exploded and my muscles twitched, holding Hayden tighter as he too climaxed. I stay where I am as we catch our breaths. I let my hands slide up onto his shoulders and down his chest, circling each pink nipple through my fingers as I heard Hayden gasp. I continue onto has belly feeling his abs tighten to my touch. He shivered as I continued exploring Hayden's body. I asked him if he was enjoying the view. "very much so it is a view I hope to see for many years to come" You will as I will with you too. I love you Hayden, and I am happy that we have found each other." Anna you are my everything I love you so much. That it scares me as I look upon your beautiful face, I see my life and I would not know what I would do if you were not in it" I lean forward and kiss my amazing beautiful mate. He has the most delicious taste as we enjoy being with each other Hayden helped me remove myself from his body as my body felt like a bowl of noodles. I laid in bed holding onto my love. We both just talk softly into the quiet space where we broke a lot of first. I am happy that I chose to take Hayden as my mate, he was a surprise. I didn't even know I was ready for and he has been everything I could have wished for. He has taken my first kiss, my first touch, and the first ever who has seen me naked and vulnerable. He has taken my body, my heart and my soul, I am laid beside a man who will be my everything and so much more. After we have rested after our love making. Hayden carried me bridal style into the bathroom as he sat me down on the closed toilet seat and started the shower. It is a huge shower that we will both fit into comfortably. He checks the temperature as he carries me inside placing my back against the cold tiles as he devours my mouth and lays his forehead against mine. I love you now, let me take care of you and show you how honoured I am that you are mine. He places my feet gently on the floor as he takes a loother and fills it with soap. He slowly washes my neck and shoulders adding small soft kisses in their place. He takes the loother and moves it across my chest and as he gets to where my breasts are he slowly teasers as he massages the loother over each breast. He takes his time and as he moves closer to my nipples he swipes over them gently as he waits for the water to rinse away the soap. He takes a small bite and swirls his tongue around each peak. I am slowly gasping trying not to die from the anticipation, as he looked up into my eyes and smiles at me. Oh yeah, he knows what he is doing to me. "Stay still he demands and I will make you happy you listened." He lowers the loother across my belly and over my hips as he takes a hold of one of my legs and he rests it on his thigh, as he knelt before me. He massages and circles it from my hip to my toes. He repeats the motion on my other side. I am breathing deeply at this point, as I am trying really hard not to grab ahold of his hair and move him to my centre as I feel it pulsing wanting his touch. He then kisses my ankle, tasting every inch of my skin as he takes small bites and licks and teasers, each sensation building tingles in my body. My belly has butterflies as he takes his time. He asked me to turn around slowly. I do as I am told as I want to see what he plans to do to me next. After I am facing the tiles he said, "hands on the wall Anna and open your legs." I stand still not following his order fast enough. he stands up behind me as he takes each of my arms and puts them on the wall. He brushes his lips down my neck and whispers in my ear, "Anna do you want me to stop or carry on." He wouldn't dare no way, he wants me just as much as I want him for now I will listen as it is our first night together. I open my legs as my answer who can talk when my body is feeling hot and full of tension as it wants something more. He kisses my neck and continues washing each of my legs starting from the bottom to my butt. He makes slow circles as the water pours down my back and rinses away the suds. He nibbles, bites and kisses all the way to my butt he takes each globe into his hands and touches and pintches as he massages each cheek in his hand he slowly washes each globe as he slides closer to my centre I tense. "Anna it's okay trust me I am not into taking you there so relax." I do I mean it is not something I have thought about most of our pack haven't had sex so we only find out through those who have newly mated in our age group. I Wait, to see what he has planned next. As he continues washing he slowly moves up towards my lower back as he bites more firmly on my left butt cheek. I can't help it, but move. It took me by surprise as he kisses away the sting, as he repeats the action on the other side. He loothers my lower back and I can feel his hardness pressing against my lower back. Hayden is taller than me and he towers above me. He gently wipes the loother up towards my upper back and licks my clean skin. I am full of sensation from his licks, kisses and bites. I really wish he would do something to ease the ache that has been building in my core my whole skin has heated up from all Hayden is doing to be he reaches the top of my shoulders and kisses my neck as he reaches the side where he bit me. He licks over the bump of teeth as he soothes away the ache, it sends shivers down my spine as he gives me more sensation as he bites down on it I can't control the moan that comes out as he said. Anna do you want me to ease the ache away I nod my head he has a hold of my hips and pulls me back towards his hardness as he thirsts home into my center. His thrusts are harder and he is less gentle and more rough with the need to take me. He pistoned in and out as I felt every inch of his manhood as he kept up the pace. Skin slapping against skin as he kisses my neck he brings his arm around my front and circles his fingers around my clit I come apart and almost lose my balance as I feel my orgasm warming my whole body with pulses of pleasure. Hayden is still thrusting when I feel him climaxing. It releases aftershocks as I can feel him pumping his seed into me. I am spent as Hayden removes himself from my body and turns me around to take my mouth again. We just stay like that, kissing for a couple of minutes as we come down from the high. Hayden bends down in front of me as I ask him "what he is doing?" He smiles at me as he lifts my leg over his shoulder and says. "I missed a bit" as he licks and kisses my centre until I beg him to stop, as the sensation after all the love making is too much. He stops and looks up at me. I relax again as he stares deep into my eyes and I can see the love in his eyes. I didn't expect him to pinch my clit and insert two fingers as he curled them and I orgasmed all over again. I don't think I can even see straight as everything feels fuzzy. Hayden waits until he has rung out every inch of pleasure before he places a final kiss at my centre and stands up. He washes my hair and as he rinses out the suds. He adds conditioner and massages it into my scalpe. He moves me away from the showers spray allowing the conditioner to work into my hair as he makes quick work of washing himself he rinses my hair. Grabs two towels. He dried me and wrapped a towel around his waist as he carried me to bed. He drys himself as he finishes, takes the towels and leaves them in the wash basket. He climbs into bed and holds me as we cuddle into each other and fall into a deep fitful sleep.

CHAPTER FIFTEEN

Anna

I awoke the next morning to Hayden wrapped around my body as I felt him kissing my back and shoulder, he has one arm around my waist. "Morning beautiful" he whispers to me "Morning" I can feel his hardness poking my back and he said, "How do you feel, are you sore? "I feel good Hayden" "Good because I really need you again" "then take me I'm all yours" He lifted my leg and wasted no time entering my body he thrust slowly and takes his time as he strokes my skin kissing my neck and should as he massages my breast and lifts my leg higher as I can feel each thrust taking me higher Hayden doesn't stop he poistones into me I feel him getting closer to his orgasm and as mine is building he pinches my clit as I go over the edge and scream out his name as Hayden pulses his seed into me he slowly releases my leg as we move come down from our lovemaking he holds me close and we enjoy the peaceful moment. We stay there relaxing and hang onto the moment as long as we can. "Sorry Anna, but we need to move we have training, and you have school.""I know I just don't think I can move." He started to tickle me, as I was laughing and screaming against his tickling. I jumped out of bed and took another shower. Hayden is cleaning his teeth and having a shave. I know he wanted to join me, but we have no time. We swap over as he showers, I clean my teeth and we both get ready for training. Once we were both dressed, we headed towards the main house. We were greeted at the front door by my girls alongside Zara and Adam. We are training in the center from now on Zara will drive you in while I follow you on my motorbike. Hayden and I kiss goodbye. I don't care who is watching, he is mine and I am incredibly happy Anna this morning. He took his time releasing me." I will see you at football tonight. Have a good day Anna,"" you too Hayden." he kisses my nose and walked into the house. He has some work to do this morning. All my girls are looking at me funny. Adam is standing still, "why are you all staring at me? Jade shouts out "o.m.g you are officially mated, and you have bonded." I am so happy for you. I can't wait to hear the details." Zoe being Zoe, "you had sex was it everything you hoped for? I am so jealous of the way he was looking at you?" Adam found this conversation uncomfortable by saying "girls discreet isn't in your vocabulary, talk in the car this isn't a conversation I want to be hearing." Anna, he said, "I am happy for you." I hope you and Hayden have a wonderful life together. You have a good man there and as your big brother I only wanted to see you happy." I love you and I am proud of you." as he walked towards me and embraced me, we stood like that for a few moments as we broke apart, he put on his helmet and walked towards his motorbike. My girls are smiling but a little shocked at how sweet my brother has just been. Jade said, "See I told you my brother loves all of us. He is a big contradiction." "Now let's go I want to hear all the details from Anna." Once were in the car heading towards the center. I told the girl's how special it was, and I told them some of it not all, how it hurt a little at first but after a couple of thrusts it eases into pleasure. I would like to know the details if any of my friends had sex especially as none of us in this car have ever had any until now. After I have given them enough even Zara, is listening as she is older than us and has always wanted to wait. I told them it was worth it, and he makes me happy, and I look forward to getting to know each other as we explore our mating. Jade handed me breakfast mum did us a pack up as we had uniforms over at the center as dad arranged it last night. Dad wanted us to go straight to school from our training session. There are more of us here this early in the morning and a lot more older adults are training alongside us. We are an exceptionally large group, so we have been split into four groups, Adam has my group, Zara has the other half of our age group. Across from us is Bradley, who has the twenty to thirty age group. John, alongside Axel, was training the rest of those above thirty. We are put through a fast warm-up, we are then split into smaller groups of three. It is a combat fight of two against one. I have Zoe in my group, Cara and Jade are working in Zara's group. I have two pack mates who are from another pack. We all have mixed up who we fight with each round lasting two minutes, both your opponents are to attack you and you must defend each hit. We swapped around once we have completed each round. Each time we swap we have no rest until all three of us have spared. I got hit a few times but nothing major, I defended the worst ones. Adam's approval of admiration helped as we are told to stretch out, he was watching us all and checking each of us up on skill and damage. Some did well, some struggled to hold a good defence. Adam made some changes, swapping a few of us around this time we went again but we had one minute in each round. I have two guys this time around, both were strong, capable fighters. I defend as many of the worst attacks off. I could see him try to aim a kick to my face. I crouch as the other guy see's my counter move, he attempted to sweep my legs from under me. I see it coming, though I stay low, but jump as he sweeps out his leg to get me on my back for me to lose my footing. I miss his footwork to floor me, while still managing not to get kicked in the face by the other one. I heard Adam call time, excellent work everyone, we are going to now add another attacker, this time you will defend and hit back. He makes adjustments, I see my girls, they seem to be doing well, I can't look while in combat but when each match is over, we all check in on each other. Zoe is in her element she is good; Cara has a bloody lip, but I can't see any other damage. Jade looks good, no marks that I can see. I have been moved to another group as I now have two guys and a girl in my team. Zoe has three guys against her, I look over at Cara she has two girls and a guy, Jade has pulled three girls, but I can see they have skills they had won both matches. "Ready," Adam says to our team, "go." I attack, I have a fist swinging to break my nose, which has been forbidden. We can mark, we can attack but we need to limit the damage. We are sparring, not fully going into kill mode. I backflip to move quickly, as I tumble backwards, I go straight into a front kick, I hit his chest, he lands on his arse. I feel his pack mate behind me. She holds me steady, so I use her body to push against her, as I lock my legs around the guy in front, I flip him using my thighs to perform the move he lands on the guy I kicked to the floor. With them two down, I had to deal with the girl holding me from behind as I landed back on my feet, and I used my head. I headbutted her backwards after hearing her curse "you bitch, you broke my nose." Serves her right, those two worked as a team to cause me damage to perform the move they were aiming for. I have no regrets. Adam calls time, he gives me a slight twitch of his lips I know he is proud of how I handled myself. Take five everyone while I talk to Zara. My girls come over, "you, ok?" I asked everyone. Zoe won her fight, she is fine, Jade answers with" "I'm good but those three are from the same pack." "They're strong, they got me a few times, but I managed to handle everything they threw my way." She has no marks neither does Zoe, I have a bruise around my chest where I was grabbed as she tried to squeeze the air out of my lungs. "Cara you, ok? I am, I think in my second match one of the guys punched me so hard I thought I would lose some teeth, but I kicked him in his thigh, and punched him in his cheek, he had a nice bruise, so were even." "How was it with three Cara?" "I won't lie I found it hard just trying to keep most of the worst attacks from connecting she lifts her vest up to show us, but as you can see, I have a lovely bruise forming on my ribs." She isn't kidding she has a bruise all right. "You ok to continue," "I am" her response. We all hugged and were then teamed together both our groups Zara speaks. Right Adam and I have decided to mix it up three against one. You have one minute in each round. I am going to team you with a winner from each round so you will each have at least one winner against you. Some of the strongest fighters will have two winners to fight against. "Great, I mutter, let's do this." I am partnered with one of Jade's girls who is good according to Jade and two guys I have not had the pleasure of fighting with yet. In this round I need to focus fully on holding back as many hits as I can. When I am attacked, and I manage to hold my own, I get a good few counter attacks in. However, these are strong fighters and I get a few hits of my own. When it's my turn to attack, I watch each fighter as they try to use kick and jab combinations to get at least one hit to counter my movement. I switch to a side attack, and I get a few jabs on their ribs, belly, and a good few kicks in. After time is called, we get to spar one on one with a winner from each round will fight another winner. We do longer rounds, we each have three rounds lasting two minutes per round, when you are tired another will take their place. By the third round your body starts to fatigue it hits you. That is when you can start to get sloppy. I manage to hold my own until round three with my third opponent, before I tire, and time is called. Zoe is on her fifth opponent before she gets tired, and her time is called, she is good her skills are fast strong and brutal she does not mess around. Adam and Zara continue this pattern until each of us have fought at least three rounds with three fighters. We rest in between, before we have another winner to fight, and so on until each of us have fort everyone in our group has competed. It was close to 8 am, when time was called and we hit the showers, as were all heading towards the showers. I am dripping with sweat I have aches and pains a few bruises which have started healing already thankfully. I have a bruise on my chin from my last match, he got me with a left hook. Zoe has a few bruises but her's are not too bad she is a good scrapper. Zoe told us she loved it and felt like she achieved knowledge she could use if ever attacked. Jade looks like me, but her face isn't marked she does have a nasty bruise on her thigh though where a guy dropped her to the floor with a kick to her right leg. She seems ok, though no limping just a few hisses escape her. When we are in the showers once the water hits our bodies, we all sigh in relief. Cara is so quiet she seems to be deep in thought, maybe she is thinking over her fights we all learned a lot from each one, we gained different techniques from each other. We dressed and Zara drove us to school. We are quite on the way to school I have managed to hide my mark we heal where bitten, but it will leave an impression just not a visible one to the human eye. All our wolf eyes will see I am claimed. I want to keep it to myself a little while longer. I am deep in thought and thinking about Hayden. The way he touched me and kissed me. He worshipped my body, I feel differently stronger, loved and most of all secure. I know Hayden is mine and I am his, I feel protected, and I feel amazing after we connected last night. Zoe and Jade break me away, from my thoughts asking, "are you ok?" "Yes, why?" "We are at school, and you haven't even noticed we have been calling your name a few times now." "Oh, sorry I was thinking, let's go we have to get our brains in gear for exams."" We thank Zara who told us she will see us at the football after school it's at 6pm so we will get changed at school I brought my clothes in my school bag it's hot out. So, I bought jean shorts, and a nice vest top with a zip up hoodie if the air chills later. Cara has been really quiet, and we are all looking at her with confusion. "Hey earth to Cara," Zoe says." Sorry I am miles away I will tell you all about it later, I just wanted to get through this morning first." "Okay" we all replied. We will catch up properly at lunch time. We see our other friends in the car park as we were all walking in "hey girls" we all smile at our friends. Dale puts his arm around Jade's shoulder and Mattio does the same to Cara as the others are talking about practice. We each have got our costumes fitted and ready so we will be doing a dress rehearsal. At least we have the football afterwards to look forward to and I hope our guys win then we can take the trophy. We are all going to hang out together later tonight were all going to support the team and the school, we explained how we all have dates. I told them I have a boyfriend that I met on my visits to the city, and how I have kept it to myself. I have to say something as Hayden, and I are all over each other. It has only been a few days, but our friends won't understand it as we mate for life. To them it would seem weird as humans take longer to get to the stage were at. Luke warned the girls not to allow them to give them any drinks as he believed that our drinks had drugs in them as he heard them talking. I know they helped us, they are good friends, we know that they had messed with our drinks, we were told of the twins as they told us all about it. We will be careful. We all agreed we would buy our own and not take one thing from them after Saturday. The conversation before we got to the hall has helped even Cara is talking. We wish each other luck as we head into our morning exam.

CHAPTER SIXTEEN

Hayden

I am in a good mood, after kissing Anna goodbye this morning I start my day by rejoining my team on finishing searching for anymore devices. I am deep in thought as I drive towards John's gym we are meeting there as training is now being held at the center of the forest away from any spying eyes. I can't help but remember the way Anna felt. I cherished every touch, every kiss and taking her as my mate. She felt pure perfection every time I heard her moan it sent tingles through my body. When I tasted her mouth, it was amazing but when I got to taste her pink flesh that glistened with arousal. It was worth the wait the reward from her taste and knowing I was the one who turned her on as she moaned my name I have never felt as connected to another the way I am to Anna. When I was deep inside her, the pleasure that I felt being inside her as she gripped my dick was heaven. When she exploded, I felt her muscles gripping me as my orgasm hit when I bit into her shoulder it heightened the pleasure where I saw stars. I thought I would pass out from the euphoric feeling. She is everything I told her I wanted to marry her, and I meant it, I know I love her, and as I drive to meet the others I am not bonded to my mate in all ways of our kind. I look forward to every day we get together. This morning as I woke up having Anna naked in my arms was the best morning of my life. I am almost at the gym as training is going off at the center the gym John and Zara owns is the next best thing. I clear my mind as I am feeling aroused thinking of Anna. Which is not good walking into a meeting with an eraction. Once I parked my car and entered the gym. I have calmed down enough to not have a tent in my trousers. Alpha Gerald is there "hi Hayden welcome" we walked inside where a few others are taking a seat. Gerald went over what was discussed in the meeting I missed last night as I wanted to spend time with Anna. I was caught up on everything I missed. Gerald started the meeting. "This morning we are heading up towards the mountains to check on the creatures there and check each area for devices. Aiden Huntsman likes to hunt, if any are missing it might give us an idea on where he has gone to. I have heard back from the other Alpha's who are doing the same as us. Nate has his mate due any day now, so he needs to keep his pack close by to be safe. He has asked if we could send any pack over to help search the land that Aiden has purchased on Flame Island. He has had to put up extra patrols and so far they haven't come across any devices. So I see that as a good sign. The Vale Islands and Everygreen in particular have been Aiden's main focus point. However, he has left the devices here and I want to know why? After these first two weeks of training are complete, we will need to send out the best of us over, because Ali is short on time. We need to find her. We will meet at lunch at 2pm and everyone has their duties. Let's get to it." He has breakfast out on the tables around the room and we all pile our plates. "Gerald called me over. "Hayden follow me," he takes me to an office area and closes the door. "Alpha Henry has received word from Alpha Brock Steel from Evergreen. He needs you back at Vale Island. Your dad has been hurt and they have left you a message to head home as soon as you can. They will give you more information when you return." "What about Anna I can't leave my mate, we just found each other." "I know son she has two more days left. I will protect her like I have all these years. Hayden, I promise you that she will be safe." "I know that I trust you, I just don't like leaving her. If I have to go to Evergreen, I would prefer her to be here amongst her family. We have bonded sir and my wolf will fight me. He is wanting time just as much as me. He hasn't seen her wolf yet, I want to have more time."" I feel like I am abandoning her when we are just learning about one another." "I am happy for you Hayden, you are a good man and I am honored to have you become part of my family. It's unfortunate that we are having trouble after centuries of peace. Your dad is the Beta of your pack, you are needed if he's hurt, and they have asked for you, it has to be bad. Plus, you knew this might happen; Anna will understand the sooner you go the faster you can return to her." "Ok I need to say goodbye and explain before I leave." "Hayden, if you go now, you will be in Darlington by 11am you could be at Vale Island and in Evergreen tonight. Anna has her show on Friday and she wants you to be there. Speed is your best choice besides, she has exams she can't walk out of. I will make sure she knows why you had to leave so suddenly." Alpha Gerald hugged me take your radio I will give Anna one of her own, so you can keep in touch I will even have Zara get it to Bradley to give to her at school at lunch time. Use station 3 that is private and only you two can talk be safe, son I will see you Friday." "Thankyou I head towards my car I don't bother packing anything, I can grab what I will need at home. Driving like my arse is on fire every mile I take is hard as both the man and wolf wanted to remain in Ashwood with Anna. I feel a pain in my chest the further away I get my wolf and I are hurting. I am also worried about my dad if I have to return, he must be in a bad way. I am in Darlington faster than I thought. It's still early and I broke speed limits to get here. I park at my Alpha's house. He is at the door awaiting my arrival. He brought me in for a hug, "sorry Hayden lets go inside." We go into Henry's office, "I have spoken to Brock, your dad has been involved in an accident. Leo was with him as they were tracking one of Airon Huntsman's men near the edge of Airon's land following a lead. Brock thinks it was a trap luckily Delia had Phillip and another team alongside them. Your dad fell into a pit believed to be a trap and has been impaled on sharpe bars of steel he has been severely injured. He is in hospital awaiting surgery. They asked for you to go over as the oldest son your next in line to be beta you will need to sign paperwork. A healer is with him also. That is all the information I have" With Aiden Huntsmen having advanced technology, we are being extra careful Brock used the main radio. Each pack house has one that is how we communicate. Luckily, Nate has a team who are just as smart and have enabled us to speak without having to go to the pack house to save time. Who knows what else they may have invented that we have no knowledge about just yet. "Hayden, I have a boat ready to go I have had a bag packed ready for you, and I have packed some food and water go now get back tomorrow so you can reunite with your mate." "I don't care I want my friend and my beta to get the best care possible. I am sending Sally with you as she is the best healer, we have take care of her and please keep her safe and be careful. Sara wanted to come but I need her here, we found a few devices of our own near the house this morning. I need to make sure all is well. Brock has sent enforcers to meet you. It is a private boat with just you and Sally on board, and after hearing that my brother and sister-in-law caused a lot of pain knowing how Max suffered brings me anger the only bit of hope is finding Ali and I am hoping that Jimmy and Julie's baby is with them and safe. That is all I hope we need to be able to travel at a moment's notice so I bought one and Jason knows how to drive it, he will dock and wait for you. I have teams reporting to me this afternoon and I couldn't spare anyone else as most are on duty or training in rotas with Gerald's pack. I have asked your mother and sisters to stay here with us. They are safe here with us, I give you, my word. I have followed in Gerald's footsteps, and we are in the middle of moving our pack around to protect the vulnerable. Hayden, I will see you soon." I leave the office and drive to the dock. I noticed Sally's car is here. I walk to the dock, and I can see Sally waving at me "Hi Hayden I have your things on board." This boat is fast, so hold on." Once we were on the boat, we were catching up. She was not lying, this boat was fast. She is telling me about where they found the devices and how she is going to be working on Nate's team after training she is good at technology, her Delia and Sophia will make a talented team. Once they are shipped over. Sally has been practising her craft for a few years working alongside the other healers, she is a natural and her power has grown this past year. Henry due to him losing his brother has kept Sally and Sara close and on pack land. For him to send her with me speaks volumes of his worry about my dad our pack Beta. Sally has news to pass on to Delia regarding her friendship with Sophia and that she will tell us both together. Sally and I have always hung out when we cross paths, her twin Sara and her are powerful in their own right and one day I will be Beta as Sara will be the next Alpha. Out of the two Sara is stronger, her wolf is formidable as she grows in strength. She fights well, and she has handed me my arse a few times. Henry has sheltered them and it frustrates both of them because they are both powerful and each may look alike but both have different strengths. Sally is a healer and has grown in power and has been able to heal bones when broken it tires her out but she has done it and she is smart. She likes to explore medicine but is really good at adapting quicker to new technology. She can fight too, but she prefers to heal than fight. Now Sally is a fighter she has spared with Zara and she wins many fights she has. She has been taught by her dad and mine. She has different styles down to an artform. She is a fast learner and when the time comes she will be a good Alpha. They both like to go to the clubs but I have never seen them with anyone. They are both passionate about making sure when they step up they will help the other. I can't wait to find out who their mates are. She asked me about Jade and Ethan as I told her about the prank they pulled and how Ethan is adorable but protective. She and Sara are taking a break during the holidays, both work for their dad. He has companies all over Darlington he provides well for our pack. He helped build the city to what it is now. "You have a weekend away I hear are you looking forward to it," I am dad wants to have guards so I have no doubt in my mind him and Gerald have a plan." It doesn't take long before we arrive in half the time it normally takes. We thanked Jason who is a member of our pack. He docks the boat, he will wait to take us home. I was surprised to see Brock waiting for us, "Hayden hi, Sally nice to meet you. Let's go. I have a lot to speak to you about." we walk to where Brock has left his car and there is a man sat on the dash watching as we make our way over. "Let me introduce you to my soon to be beta, Noah Hayden, whom you have met, "nice to see you again" as we shake hands. Noah is biting at the bit to become beta, his dad decided to retire after finding out Max had been killed he has been helping Brock with the pack. His son is taking over after he has completed the training we are hosting in Ashwood. He is young around Abel's age he great Sally "hi Sally it's nice to meet you." Sally shakes his hand as they stare at each other. "You alright Sally we need to go. "Yes I am" as we climb into the car I am at the front with Brock, Sally and Noah are sitting in the back. While we were in the car driving Brock told us what had happened." I'm sorry Hayden your dad is in hospital recovering and he has been put into a coma to help his injuries heal." "What happened?" I ask. "Your dad and brother alongside a few others were tracking a lead, we believe the lead was a false trial, and we sent two teams, the first one had your dad and Leo in with six others. The second team went as back up Deila and her dad and my best enforcers. They were rushed in to help. Your dad had struck a trap set by humans we believe are working with Airon and they left fake trails. Your dad saw prints but no scent, he knew something wasn't right he and his team back tracked to warn Leo and his team." They caught up to the team and Leo was up front and saw Leo was about to step into a trap similar to the one he had found and he changed into his wolf on the fly. He managed to push Leo out of harm's way, but your dad landed in a pit and his back legs entered swinging your dad downwards. It had been covered to look like the earth, with a scent left on leaves mud and branches to get there attention. He dropped in as he was in his wolf form, and impaled his leg onto metal spikes along with his chest and front paw. He remained in wolf form, which is most likely what saved his life." "This is where the story gets interesting, a young woman jumped from the treetop and went in after your dad. She jumped in with him avoiding the worst areas, but she got hurt with a ruff landing breaking her arm. Leo and two others helped get him out using equipment as they lifted each impaled limb and his torso from the spikes. Our new helper is a healer. She is called Maria and she is one tough cookie. She is our missing link to the information we need on Airon and his men. She helped heal your dad, enough to help him not bleed out. She is young and untrained, but she is one of us." "I need you to know she is scared and has trust issues Delia has taken her under her wing and we have her staying in the Hospital. She wanted to make sure she was there incase anything happened to your dad, she is also injured and has been healed herself. She has broken her arm and has a cast on in a few days she will be fully healed. She looks like she has been living in the wild. She has not said much but I managed to get her name and where she came from. This is the interesting part she is from Beast Island. She has been searching for her family. They were taken by men who killed some of her pack." "She hid and has survived many years alone, she tried to find any pack mates that she could. Most had fled years ago and were taken in, as you know, by packs years ago. However, she alongside her grandparents stayed, Delia is still talking to her but that is all I know. I have asked Alpha Jax to watch over the hospital until we arrive, I am taking in all this information, and I am shocked but grateful she risked her own life for my dad. What happened on beast Island and how she survived proves to me she has strength. "How has Leo been?" "He is by your dad's side, he has not left him since it happened. Your dad is stable, but we are unsure if he will lose his leg, the damage and blood loss hasn't helped at all. He is lucky Maria was nearby, or it could have been sad news." We sit a while taking in all we have learned so far. Sally asked Brock "maybe I can help, I can heal, and if she lets me, I can help her heal her arm." I am strong and I can help David too, he is our beta and we do not wish to lose anyone else. He is family to us, and I might be able to help Marie if she will allow." "We have suffered at the hands of

Airon Huntsman. My dad told Sara and I last night that we are to not say anything to Jade and Ethan until we gather more information. I want that arsehole to suffer as he made my aunt and uncle suffer. I want him to feel the pain my family has gone through. I will do anything in my power to help." To hear Sally speak and feel her pain has my wolf whining for her to sooth her, Noah comforts her from the back seat and holds her to his body. It must be helping because she calms down. Noah holds her until we reach the hospital, I am speechless. Brock gives me a smile and nods his head at me. Where here as Brock parks, we all get out Noah pens Sally's door and guides her in with his palm on her lower back. We all go up to dad's ward and we are taken to the room my dad is in, I see Delia and Phillip. We all hugged, I have so much to tell them. Delia explained that Maria had taken up sitting besides my dad. She has ordered Leo to go take a shower as he is stinking up the place. I can't help but laugh. I bet that didn't go over well. He did as he was told she also told him to rest, that she would stay with him, he is currently laying in Maria's room on a spare bed the nurse brought in. She has been a breath of fresh air wait until you meet her. Brock asked "where Alpha Jax is?" "You might want to wait until he calms down before you speak to him." "Why?" We all asked at the same time. "Let's go sit in here," we follow I want to see my dad but I also want to know what is happening. Alpha Brock informs us that the room is sound proven. Phillip stayed to guard my dad's room. Delia told us "Maria is protective, she feels responsible for what happened to your dad Leo picked up on her scent." "She was hiding nearby when the trap was set. She watched as a number of men dug out the earth and came up with a plan to capture the wolf people as that is what they have chosen to name us. Marie had been watching the men from a distance after she remembered one of them who came over to their Island and began loading up the creatures that lived there." "She has agreed to tell us all her story but would like it if we can calm Alpha Jax down first." "Why?"We all ask. Delia responded with "because

Maria is his mate. He has searched all over for her and he has been dreaming about her. As soon as he laid eyes on her, and took in her scent he said it's you."The problem is, Maria had no clue who he was to her. As her dreams have been filled with endless nightmares. Her wolf however recognises him as her mate, but as she has been alone for years her human half wouldn't except him trying to touch her. The way she is underweight and has been living in bad conditions has sent his wolf into protective over drive. Maria asked him to leave as she doesn't react well to anger and he was pushing off anger in waves. I have spoken to her and tried to explain that he is not angry at her, but as an Alpha he protects pack. Seeing her injured and underweight has distressed his wolf. She has agreed to tell her story once you returned." We heard a knock on the door "it is Alpha Jax, can I enter." Alpha Brock answers "of cause, come in are you ok?" "That must have been a huge shock for you." "It was, Brock, I can't believe there was our kind still living on that island after all these years. I took one sniff and knew behind the door was my mate I have dreamed of her. I wasn't expecting to see her injured, underweight and living wild as if she hasn't had the luxury we have gained used to. I know she has been through hell and I was angry at myself for not knowing she had been here years and none of us knew. She knows how to hide her scent and how to blend into the nature around her. I had to have a run in wolf form to calm down I was careful I just needed to be free for a moment. I want to hear her story. I know she needs to tell her story to us all to help us find Ali, who is still missing." "I am calm and I will try to hold back." After hearing Jax and knowing we all would feel the same I introduce him to Sally to Jax we all go back to see my dad. Phillip remains outside, I shake his hand and he opens the door to dad's room. I am hit with the scent of dry blood and pain, my dad is covered in white blankets with a drip set up and a machine monitoring his vitals. He looked weak and pale. I walked over to his bed and sat in the chair by his side as I took his hand in mine. "Dad, I am here, it's Hayden. I hope you can hear me, I have so much to tell you. The others sit down on the sofa against the window. His room is big and Jaxs is leaning against the wall close to where the on suite must be. Sally came over nearer to the bed and asked if she could have time once Maria came to help in anyway she could. The on suite bathroom door opened as I saw Maria for the first time. I looked her over and I told her thank you for saving my dad's life. "You must be Hayden, I am Maria and I have met your very stubborn brother already." She is thin. You can see bags under her eyes. She is small like a child, but has a face that has suffered pain and loss." Alpha Jax have you calmed down "she asked him. "I have indeed I am sorry if I caused you distress mate, that wasn't my intention." Marie turned to look his way, "I am just as shocked as you are that I recognise you are my mate as Delia has explained a lot to me this past day. I just need you to be patient with me. I have spent so long battling alone" "I am ready to tell you my story. Hayden, your dad is a brave man, I am sorry he got hurt, I am untrained but I do have early memories of my childhood, my mother was a healer and I remember she had healed very injured pack mates throughout my childhood. Your dad is lucky, another healer came from Brocks pack no offense but he believed your dad could lose a limb. I am not going to let that happen. I know I can help him recover his heart is strong I will work with your healer. Sally, I am maria and I can sense your power. I will try to explain what I did to heal David." I" need time to fix the injuries he has gotten, but I will use my gift to keep the blood flowing freely. I have just healed the worst of the wounds and that is why you can smell blood. I have cleared away the infection and helped put fresh blood to flow to his most injured parts. He will sleep a few more hours and by this evening he will be awake. Another day and he will be able to walk out of that bed. I can promise you that." Sally speaks to Maria "Hi, I am happy you were there Maria, I can sense what you have done." "For you to have power, I am the strongest healer we have on our island I can mend bone which nobody else has been able to do in one go." "I can tell David our beta has no broken bones, you have cleaned his blood and helped his heart pump a fresh supply into his body. You must be tired and you need to eat. Please take a seat. I would like to look at your arm after you have eaten and had some water. Is that okay?" "Yes, please that would help. Should we leave Hayden alone to spend time with his dad?" They all leave and I don't know what to say she is new thats for sure, she doesn't sugar coat things. She is blunt, but to the point. I like her already, she is going to be hard to tame as I look over at Jax as he leaves. I think he knows this to be true himself. The door opened and Leo entered the room. He embraced me and he pulled another chair over to join me. "Have you met her." "I have she is special thats for sure." "I was ordered to go shower and sleep, she wasn't taking no for an answer," Leo said. "What happened Leo?"" Dad and I had split into two smaller teams. The tracks we followed were of the beast but the scent was strange as if the beast was dead, those were the tracks dad had followed to the pit he saved me from. My team we were tracking a human, but other than a few footprints there wasn't a scent it was blocked. He had back tracked and when we found another set he backtracked again. After the fourth trial, I knew these prints were a distraction and raced back to warn dad." "However I could smell Maria but it was very faint I got a wiff of strong earth with just a hint of her scent she had covered herself in the land around her and had blended into the tree she had leaves and branch's all over her flesh hiding amongst nature. I could detect a scent of human near the pit but it had been hidden to look like the floor of the forest surrounding it. As I got closer to investigating, dad leapt at me, pushing me out of the way. It was strange I could smell something familiar on the leaves they had placed upon the pit. I couldn't figure it out dad smelled it but he knew something wasn't right. I couldn't help it I needed to get closer I felt I was in a trance next thing I knew dad had changed into his wolf on the fly that was amazing. It was as he jumped and knocked me backwards that he slipped as he couldn't grip the earth properly, he couldn't get enough traction his back legs dragged him downwards into the pit. It was a trap to harm whatever fell inside. Maria leapt from above into the pit and kept dad alive." She was covered in dirt, everywhere she had covered her whole body with the landscape but we all knew that she was one of our kind our wolves recognised kin." After hearing how it happened I am more interested in hearing Maria's story. Leo asked who the chick was, that he could smell. I told Leo that chick was actually my mate that he could smell on me. I told him and hoping my dad would hear me as I told Leo all about Anna and how we met. How incredible she is. I told him about the meeting and the plans we have put into place over the last few days. I told him that she has met our mother and both our sisters. He listens and congratulates me on finding my mate. Phillip entered the room "are you both ready? Maria wants to tell you her story, I have enforcers keeping an eye on your dad while we all go to listen." We say farewell to our dad that we will return shortly, we go back to the room where everyone is waiting. There are refreshments and dinner is served Maria has a plate Jax made for her with instructions to eat every mouthful. She nods her head and takes a seat we all eat and drink while Maria has a few moments to gather her thoughts and eat she needs it. I have a feeling Jax will make sure of that, by the way he watches her. After we are all fed and have a hot coffee each. Sally wants to help heal Maria while she has eaten it would help her find strength to continue. Jax's is hovering over them as he starts to pace closeby Sally hasn't even started yet. Maria asked Jax if it would help him if she sat on his lap, Dario told me that touch help's. "Will that help you?" Jax stares at her in shock for a second, then he said "it would yes, I promise I am trying to be calm I won't hurt you?" 2then come here" he picked her up so gently that Sally and Dario make asound of "ahh"Noah looked over at Sally as though he can't stop himself. He even brought a chair over for Sally to sit on, close enough to reach Maria. Sally smiled and thanked him. Maria is sat on Jax's lap, she has pulled both legs to sit on him like a lady would a horse. She is still as Sally helps remove the support from her arm. "This will feel tingley like a warm bath, are you ready?" Maria nods her head as Jax's leans her back against his chest and rest his head gently over her shoulder to watch. Sally puts her hands over Maria's arm and closes her eyes. We are all watching as it is amazing to see. Her hands glow and Maria is watching observing. After a few moments Sally removes her hands and said,"all fixed I healed the break and I have helped restore your energy." You used a lot to heal David. I have given your body enough, as though you have had a really good rest. "How do you feel?" Maria is moving her body as she sits on Jax's lap"I feel great this is the best I have felt since. Well, you will know from the story, thank you Sally." Sally returned over to the rest of us as Marie started her story. Her grandparents, alongside her parents, lived on Beast Island. They lived deep in the cave system they had set up homes within the mountain. Where for centuries each pack family, had made homes within. They have homes high up using only rope ladders to climb each one. It's how they have stayed safe from any of the dangerous animals that live on the island. They had no trees inside which helped, as the creatures would climb or jump up to reach them. The stone walls are smooth, they use the mountain to keep the dangerous creatures from being able to climb using their claws. Many had left the island, but some did stay behind as it was their home. That was all they knew. They didn't know there were more of us out here that other places existed. Her grandparents were only children when there people left, they had lived high in the trees but after more of their pack were being hurt and at times killed. The Beast were large and had increased their numbers alongside the Neeman lions. Who could climb and would attempt to attack their food supplies. Her grandparents stayed with their own parents, and a few other families who lived at the caves, as both of her grandparents came from different packs. Her grandfather was from the Hastings pack, her grandmother was from the Stirling pack. They lived building homes into the rock and would set traps for the beast and use them as a food supply. It wasn't until her parents along with the others would go to fish on the south side of the island as it was free of the most dangerous creatures. She and her baby sister, alongside her grandparents, stayed behind with the pack's children and vulnerable members. There were five other children, the others were teenagers, two were brothers belonging to a mated pair and the other three were a cousin and sibling set. They lived together with their mother and aunt as the men were killed by being attacked gathering fruit from the trees. One was attacked while the other tried to take down the beast, Other pack members helped but he had already been killed, he had bitten him in half. His brother fort alongside the rest of the pack to help in any way they could to get the rest of the team to to safety. They managed to escape but lost one member to the attack. When you reach thirteen your wolf would normally come through. That is when the adults of the pack would teach control. They would allow the wolf to run free in the cave system. Once they were with their wolf for twelve full moons they would be taught to hunt, to track and how to protect. They learned how to set traps around the cave to trap any creature who would kill them and would harm the pack. They had fruit and berries and had learned how to live of the land. They had a water supply that ran through the mountain that they used for bathing and to drink. But whenever they left they got hunted and they lost two other pack members, one being the surviving brother to an attack from a pack of Neeman Lions who were trying to find mates. It was a dangerous place we had our wolf to help us defend ourselves and we made arrows and weapons with spears attached but when the male's teamed up we couldn't always escape without losing a pack warrior. Who would stay and fight while the rest of the pack had found safety. This is how she lost her mother, she was a warrior who stayed to protect the teenagers. They had gone to teach them to set traps, hunt and hide their scent. Again they were attacked them, my dad was with her and he was saved by a healer, who was one of the teenagers who had the gift. That teenager was me and I managed to help heal my dad enough to get us all to safety. My mother I couldn't reach her without being killed she stayed and protected us to leave. That happened when she was fourteen. Not long after that incident my dad wanted to leave the island and take us with him. My grandparents agreed they lost there daughter in law that day. Most of the pack had agreed to leave and try and see if there were any others. My dad was Alpha and made the choice it was time to leave we wouldn't survive if we didn't we had less than twenty pack members left. Her world changed when a ship came by and they watched as the team came on the island and set traps to catch the creatures. We watched them and managed to stay hidden as my father wanted to see what type of people they were, we had seen them return two times each time setting traps and coming back to check what they caught. They would put them to sleep and carry them off in huge cages. My dad decided as they had a ship to introduce themselves alongside a few of the pack warriors to see if they would help us leave. When they returned, my dad, alongside my grandfather and four others two single men Lyle and Kenny, who were unmated, and one of our warrior girls. Nera, who was twenty-two, she was the best fighter we had alongside her mother Rose. The men who came had their leader with them. We had a few others hiding in the trees incase anything went wrong, my Grandmother alongside the older teens who were men now they were there with their mother, leaving there cousin and aunty behind she was watching my sister and I. She was the youngest of her three cousins who were twenty three and twenty five. They were called James and Jack. She was eighteen and her name was Poppy after the flowers that grow over the island and we all loved her. She was kind and loving, she had not found her mate nor had her cousins. It was one of the reasons why we needed to leave. We had no mates amongst ourselves and we had become too small. We took a lot of hits over a two year period, we lost my mother, the cousins lost their fathers. We were dying out, we were desperate to leave. The visitors were not kind, the leader was evil. He pretended he would help us all leave, my dad was smart he had them meet only a few of our pack. He hid the younger members from him and his men. Jack, James Poppy, me and my sister Ava were hidden as they had already met Nera and her mother Rose and both my grandparents. Lyle, Kenny, and a few more of our older pack members. We were hidden with Poppy's mother Sunshine. Dad refused to show them where we lived but he took them to the old homes we had years prior to the tree homes. The man introduced himself as Airon Huntsman, he had introduced us to his eldest son K, something he only visited once. I can't recall his name but I do remember his two henchmen Toby Morris and Mark Duncan. That's why I was in those woods. I had tracked down Toby was the one who set the trap that your dad fell into. He was the one I hoped would lead me to find my sister and the rest of my pack. The men who came to our island told us they rehabilitated the creature on a reserve of some sort. To help increase there numbers and keep them from hurting others. They could be free and have a home where he planned to open a reserve so everyone could enjoy there beauty. They were not to be messed with, they were not endangered, they are wild and they are dangerous, my dad knew he was lying and decided not to trust him. He had a plan to steal a boat they had one they used to carry the creatures to the ship. They had arranged a plan while the visitors went to collect the cages. The team would take the boat back to the ship and return to upload the rest of the men to the ship to rest. They docked on the beach with two men who stayed behind and the driver. With the plan made they hit just as the sky started to darken we had packed and had provisions. We were to wait on the eastern side on the beach until dad arrived, what we didn't know was Airon was smart he knew what dad had planned and had set a trap to capture us. He has seen us change into wolves and had been watching us and listening to us the whole time. He knew where we lived and he had arranged a cope to take us before we even got to the beach. My dad had grandfather, Rose with a few of the older adults. My dad had left Jack, James, Poppy, her mother and Rose's daughter to help us leave and head to the eastern beach. My grandmother held my sister Ava, as she was our youngest member she was eight that was almost four years ago. They killed my dad, my grandfather and the pack that went to get the boat. They had set up an ambush and my dad and the others were killed as they fort hard they showed no mercy they were fighting for us to save us. My dad sent Rose to warn us, he fort hard to let her escape. She managed to get close but we had already been rounded up, we were all caged like animals they had put most of the pack to sleep. I healed from whatever they used to put us to sleep, I saw Rose follow us behind, she used the trees to hide while masking herself to not be seen. As we were loaded up to the awaiting boat I saw the bodies of our pack dead on the beach. Butchered by these men with hunting knives and weapons we didn't have. "My dad had his head cut off and one of the men, Mark, kept it as a trophy. I heard him say spoils of victory," Alpha Jax comforts her by nuzzling her neck. She calmed down and told us the rest of her story. I was with Rose's daughter Nero they had us in a bigger cage along with my sister Ava. They had Lyle and his brother Kenny, who had injuries but were alive in another cage. Sunshine and her daughter were kept in another. They had my grandmother alongside two other older pack members they were talking about using them in tomorrow's hunt. I was slowly coming more alert, I opened my eyes. That is when I saw the horror around me, the guy Toby saw me waking up and he was about to lift me aboard the boat. Aiden was alerted as he came towards my cage and he un did the cage. I was fourteen. He grabbed my chin and told me to take a good look around as he said" "that is what happens to animals." "You will be my prisoner. I may even let my sons play with you, as you seem like a good lesson for them to learn." I was terrified, I was discusted seeing my pack butchered my father and my grandfather I saw red. I changed into my wolf, and I bit the hand that held me and I tore a claw down Aiden's face. I ran as fast as I could. It was turning dark and I have never ran as fast as that day""Rose grabbed me, covered me in dirt and we hid in a hole in the ground that housed a pack of animals who had vaccated. She had hidden us deep within the air, it was hard as there wasn't much. We stayed all night not moving until we heard the ship leave. We were left to bury the bodies we gave each a funeral and cried until there were no tears left. We knew we had to leave, we knew they would return. Rose and I made that hole our shelter, we slept in our wolves. We fished, we stayed together and we planned our escape." "They returned and we waited until we heard them leave to find the traps. We set some of our own alongside there traps to capture them to give us time to grab there boat. When we heard our trap had worked, the men watching the boat ran to help leaving the driver to watch the boat. We crawled along the back of the boat staying low in our wolves, we swam as humans in the sea to climb the boat. We held the driver hostage until he agreed to take us to another Island where they came from. What we didn't know is that this driver had replaced their regular driver and he was a spy working with a guy called Max. He smelled like us. We believed him as we got to know each other. He explained that Max was his Alpha and that he lived here. We were clothed and he helped us settle in. His name was Mitch and we were kept a secret. "We lived in his cabin in the middle of nowhere he owned the cabin. It had been in his family for generations, he had mated and after his wife died he chose to leave and live in the cabin where Max was the only one that knew about it he had no children Mitch. After a while Mitch and Rose fell in love, and we told him everything that had happened on the Island. Mitch was shocked, he had no idea we even existed, he and all of the packs thought we had moved years before. That nobody stayed behind, we had a visit over a hundred years ago when peace enforcers came over as they did they took pack who wished to leave with them. Every year more would leave the last who left were my ancestors. It was deemed too dangerous to live on. My great grandparent was the last family that stayed. After that, no boats came as the pack was reduced and it got harder."" Mitch said how we survived is a miracle. Mitch told his Alpha about what had happened on the island, how devices were found and creatures taken, and that a pack had survived but some were killed and some were taken. He never told his Alpha about us, he knew we would have to speak to all the Alpha's and he knew we needed time as we had been through hell". "Max knew that his pack was being watched as he had found a device on his own land after he spoken to Mitch. Max, knew that Aiden Huntsman was behind it due to the device and what Mitch told him. Rose and Mitch were heading to meet up with Alpha Max to explain everything we knew that was a few weeks ago and I have not seen them since. Rose and Mitch spent time trying to look for our missing pack members. Rose tried to find Nera. Rose and Mitch had enrolled me at a school and Mitch was trying to get me better educated with me being in school Mitch and Rose took turns following leads. As the years went by, and we lost hope and feared that they would all be dead, we started to live. Until Mitch found a lead that Toby was in the area, and that was the guy I was following that day in the forest. Rose was ready to tell Max everything and Mitch was driving to meet Max, because Mitch had found a lead that Aiden and Toby were in the area. We needed help and wanted to find out if any of our pack, was still alive. "They arranged to meet away from the city. That was the last time I heard from Rose and Mitch and they never returned. I still don't know what happened but Mitch and Rose have a file that has pictures of Mark and Toby, and a few others they believe were there that day. There are places they looked and found a dead end, but if you think it might help I will get them for you. I hid them with my belongings before I found you. I packed a bag and packed supplies I could carry. I walked across the land until I came here, and I followed the the signs I knew Evergreen was where Mitch came from. I waited until the next day and have been on the road ever since." "I slept undercover in wolf form at night and walked every day until I reached here. I had been watching the area a few days and trying to smell pack members. Then I found Toby at a warehouse shaking hands with the owner, he had loaded his truck with equipment and I followed him, staying close to nature in wolf form. I watched him as they used feet they had on wooden spikes to mark the land." "They sprayed the earth with scent blockers to mix up what you would be able to smell. I saw them dig those pit's they have had men watching you. They set traps and you followed I stayed behind to watch I tried to lead you away from the trap. But when I saw Leo heading towards it. Your dad had already figured it out and knew Leo was going to be hurt and saved him.He reminded me of my own dad, I saw him change as he knocked Leo out of the way and I didn't think I just reacted. That lead me here and I have found pack members who come from different packs all working in peace and together. That was why I stayed, and why I helped. When I came here I met Jax, well he kind of found me first. I am here to help. I have the location of the men you have followed and I can help your dad Hayden." I can't help but admire her she has been through so much in such a short space of time. Yet with it she has given us leads to help find Ali, and hopefully help her find her pack if they are alive. "Thankyou the file will help let Brock and Jaxs look through it and afterwards I will take it with me to inform all the other Alpha's." We all discuss where we need to go from here. Jax will escort Maria, Daria and Noah will go with them as soon as we have finished this meeting. Alpha Jax addresses the room," I think we need to gather all the information we have and we all need to plan our move. I will gather the file and we can meet afterwards to see where and what to do next. We all agreed and they left to retrieve the file maybe there is hope, if others are missing maybe Aiden has kept them I can't think of them all being dead not until we find bodies. Leo and I go and spend time with dad as we each talk to him about our adventures and our childhood memories. I use the bathroom to freshen up and Leo fetches us each a drink. There is a knock at the door, Jax is back and they are ready for a meeting. We all went back to the other room to read through the file Maria has. Jax has put Maria on his lap again and I think he needs it to keep him calmer. It can't be easy for him knowing your mate has spent weeks living outside tracking an enemy who killed her family and pack. We use the table to spread out all the information that Rose and Mitch had found out, on it are pictures of men, Maria pointed out who she remembered from the attack on her pack." Mark Duncan and here are the places where we believed he had visited, over the years and last town we believed he lived." We read through the notes that Mitch had written down last home address no leads nobody had seen him for over a year. Promising led to his old workplace, a warehouse over at Haletown managed to get a photo from the employer who last saw him six years prior he had left as he found employment working for a man named Airon Huntsman ltd. Toby Morris, who comes from the city and has family in the area Brock is going to check it out. "That is why Rose and Mitch knew they needed to tell Max, as they knew he was a risk to Mitch's pack." "when they first started tracking they couldn't find anything. Where he lived. where he worked before nothing, all were leading to deadends. It was a friend who Mitch knew, who recognised the name as his son who went to school with his brother his name was Jude Morris, which led to an address where his brother lives who is older now and has a family of his own. There were places where they had found the others but they moved away, but we had names and where there were names, was a place to start. We can reach out to the other packs to find out any more information. This was our first solid lead. Mitch was smart, he didn't want to tip anyone off that he was looking, he tried to ask those he knew. They had maps of Airon's land where the holiday homes were the zoo, and new buildings which gave us places to look. Every inch of land had been searched but nobody had been able to check his land without help. There are a vast amount of places we needed to look. Brock and Jax had tried to gain access to his land but were told he had left. Their sources have led them to believe this to be true. That he had travelled to Flame island dealing with his new purchase. They also collected lists of creatures that Rose had seen taken by Aiden from her homeland. They found evidence that they were using them for hunts and what led them to think this was what they were taken for was finding out that a hunter was found ripped apart, and Aiden had covered it up. Aiden's land had armed guards on patrol, electric wiring in certain areas, with extra guards that is where they thought the creatures could be kept. There are guards who man the main gate, it's all fenced off on the outside. Mitch and Rose had found nothing else, they couldn't excess the land, but had gathered evidence that they were ready to share with Max. After we had read all through the file we had formed a plan we wrapped up the meeting, as we needed to inform the other packs. Jax's asked if we could leave him and Maria could have time alone. Maria agreed that she would be fine and wanted a moment to process and talk with her mate, I am sure her parents would be proud of her, everything she has been through is proof of her strength and courage. Once we left the room we checked in on dad and he was still sleeping. I wanted to stay with him and Leo too, we agreed to spend the night here. Brock needed to get back to his pack and the others were going to radio in and let Henry know we had arrived and everyone including dad would be okay. I asked for a moment alone as I wanted to check if Anna was alright, the others are going for a coffee and would be back hopefully Jax and Maria will be done by then. Noah wanted to speak to Sally and she agreed she would check on dad before they left. While everyone had places to be, I went into another office to radio Anna. It was the end of school and I was hoping to catch her before practice. "Anna you there", "Hi Hayden I'm here hows your dad?" "Anna, I am so sorry I had to leave, my dad will sleep a few hours and hopefully if he is healed he will travel home with us. Thankfully he will be okay thanks to someone you will meet tomorrow when I return. I have so much to tell you all. How was your day you alright?" I am now, I managed to answer all my questions in exams today and we are heading into dress rehearsal. I miss you and I will see you when you are back. Please send my love to your family and I will be waiting. I love you Hayden be safe." "I love you so much Anna. I will see you soon." After talking to Anna I feel better knowing she is fine, and her day was good. I head out of the office bumping into Jax and Maria, Jax asks for a minute to talk, he explains that he has to organise his pack and his Beta will take over while he travels back with us. Maria has agreed to accompany him as long as Dario can come too. She needs time as she knows he is her mate but she wanted a friend to come along. I told them where the others were in the hospital cafe grabbing a coffee and if they would bring me one back. After they leave in search of the others I go and sit with dad, he seems better he has some colour in his cheeks. I sit down and talk to him about Ashwood, the pack members I have met and all about how I met Anna and the funny story of her friends and the grief they give her brothers. The nurse came in wanting to check him over while she was doing her job and I heard the others coming back. Phillip waited at the door of dad's room while we all went to talk in the other room I had a a coffee that Jax's handed over. He seems calmer, as does Maria. We talked for a few minutes. Daria and her dad Phillip are going to be staying over at Jax's home. Brock has some errands to run, and has decided to follow in the footsteps of the other packs. Housing everyone closer together and stepping up security, a team will be arranged once the other Alpha's are aware of the situation. Maria will tell her story as she wants to be able to help and maybe there is hope she may find some members of her pack. Sally and Maria checked in on my dad as we all asked Jax how he was, he told us. "She will need time and has agreed to mating once she has spoken to everyone and I will be patient what is best for

Maria is to get used to being in a pack again it's been six years and she needs to feel safe. I can do that and I will allow her the time she needs as long as I know shes willing I can wait. Maria wanted to know that if we did find any of her pack, if I would let them join my pack. Which of course I would they are her family. I am sad she has been through so much hell and I have been here not knowing where she was. I am happy I have found her and I know my pack will love her. Speaking of mates, I still do not know what has happened with Tommy and Sophia Sally wanted to tell Daria and me together. Sally and Maria return and the news is great, dad is healing and after a few more hours of sleep he should be okay to travel. We all part ways as Leo and I go back to sit with dad. We each take turns sitting beside dad and getting a few hours sleep in between. Dad slept through the night and woke up early asking for water, Leo was watching him and called the nurse. After a few sips of water he asked if he could go to the bathroom. I came in to relieve Leo and when I saw dad awake, having nurses escort him to the bathroom where he took a shower and came out dressed as if he hadn't been asleep for two days. The nurses were part of Brock's pack and agreed once he had eaten he could leave but to take it easy for a few days. Once the nurses left I held my dad so tight, and Leo joined us as we could have lost him. He held onto us and said congratulations Hayden, I heard you have a mate. "You heard me?"" I heard everything and I need to thank Maria and Sally. Where are they both?" Leo and I sat dad down and told him everything he had missed and as we get to Maria's story my dad feels pain as he hears how her pack has suffered. When he asked how mum and my sisters were, I told him as the threat seemed to be narrowing to our island too. We have found devices and Henry chose to keep my mum and sisters at his home, my dad seemed relieved. Breakfast is served, we all have a plate each and once we have eaten. The others have arrived Brock wanted his beta Noah to travel with us to join in the training and once I have updated the other packs we will need to have search teams to enable us to plan how we deal with Aiden Huntsman and his dealings. Once we arrive at the port we are met by Jason who spent the night on the boat. He greets us as I introduce him to everyone who is with us. Once we have all boarded. Jax is holding onto Maria as she is watching the sea and enjoying the creatures swimming in the sea, her boat ride over when she fourteen, wasn't pleasant she had spent it heartbroken. This time she has a little bit of hope in her eyes. Jax has not left her side, he has his hands around her waist and is happy just watching his mate enjoy the ride. The boat is faster than any I have been on so watching the frill on Maria's face is worth it. I miss Anna I hope she is okay and last night was good. Speaking of mates I asked Sally to spill the beans on Tommy and Sophia. Daria and I have waited long enough and my dad and Phillip are talking to Jason up ahead of the boat. Jax and Marie came over, "can I listen it would be nice to hear of another mating" Maria asked. Sure, I just didn't want the older members listening. In a low voice Sally began to tell us what happened between Tommy and Sophia they have mated and are planning on getting married. After Sally has told each of us what happened after the night club I am glad my dad wasn't here. Leo, commented on it by saying "it took him long enough." Jax asked the group if any of them had found mates or dreamed like I had. Leo hasn't he is young so he has time. Sally is too but by how Noah and her keep staring at each other it makes me think maybe, Daria I know hasn't looked she wanted to study and her and Sophia are wanting to help the invention department and I have a feeling Sally will too those three are smart girls and they would be a credit to Nate's department. We all enjoy getting to know each other better. Once we dock at the port I know something is wrong when I am met by Tommy and Sophia, they have horror written all over their face and have weapons tucked on their person. Tommy greets us, we all ask what is wrong. He escorted us to a waiting bus and I noticed mine, and Sally's car were missing. The cars were taken back by two of our pack, let's go we need to go to Ashwood immediately. Once were all n the bus, my world tilts as we are all told that they only know that the radio's can not be used we believe they have been tampered with. That my mum and sisters are in Ashwood awaiting our arrival. There has been a lot that has happened that he only knows that Henry, Wendy and Sara left late last night taking my mum and sisters with them as someone has been taken. My heart sinks into my feet, I want to demand to know but if it's an order we will know when we arrive. I just hope everyone is okay and my mate is. Maria has gone white, and Jax's is holding her tight whispering comforting words. My dad speaks" until we have facts and details. Let's just wait and see we know where Aiden has land. We need a plan and we can have faith in our packs, we need to be strong and keep our heads." I know that but all I have in my head is Anna and fear pure rage if anyone has touched her. My dad rests his hands on my shoulder. I can see Noah holding Sally for comfort. We know something bad has happened, we just don't know what and the worry is the worst feeling the not knowing. It was a long journey to Ashwood as we all sat and waited to get there. Once we finally reach Ashwood, we are taken straight to the pack house

CHAPTER SEVENTEEN
Anna

Once I head into my exam the morning goes by quickly Mr Anderson is waiting for me Girls follow me we are led to his office where Bradley closes the door. We all are just standing as Zoe is pretending not to smile as I know where her mind has gone. Anna, Hayden has had to go to Evergreen to see his dad, he was involved in an accident and he is in a bad way our Alpha wanted you to have this. It's my own radio Hayden said he would try to reach you at lunch, wait here and you can eat lunch here too it's private, you girls can stay but I will be taking my car keys. I don't want to leave those in here again. He looks at Zoe and Jade, while they pretend to be innocent. The girls grab lunch sandwiches and things we can eat in Bradley's office. Jade stayed with me, they were fast returning back, we all ate, as we talked about Hayden, hoping his dad would be okay. Hayden hasn't radioed, as Bradley came back and asked if there was any news Anna, no he must be travelling il come back after this afternoon exams are over. As were about to leave Bradley congratulated me on my mating and told me I had a good man there. Which makes me feel warm and fuzzy inside, I am lucky, he is a dream guy after all. As we all headed towards the hall, we saw Miss Kelly as she walked by us and asked if Mr Anderson was in. "Yes he was marking paperwork when we left." She thanked us and carried on towards his office. "Zoe are you okay?"" I am, it's his life at least I'm not his mate, I hope mine is not a whore." We all laugh which is what I needed as I am worried, I try to push it to the back of my mind as we take our last exam. We have the dance Friday, but everything else is finished after today, tomorrow we get to meet the new starters at school. We all have a fun day where we each play games and enjoy the sunshine. Once our last exam is over the whole year started,hooting, and hollaring. I leave feeling relieved as tonight we can just have fun, once I hear from my mate. We all went back to the office as we knocked, Mr Anderson opened the door, "come in." As we do the radio comes alive, it's Hayden. We talked for a few moments and I am so happy he will be home tomorrow which is great, his dad is going to heal which is good Hayden will tell me all about it when he returns he has someone he wants us all to meet. Once I have finished on the radio Bradley and the girl's are smiling at me having heard the whole conversation. I wonder who they are fetching back who ever they are, they can hang out with us maybe it's a hot guy. I laughed as Bradley clears his throat, "I'm going to be watching your dance rehearsal with Miss Kelly." Mr Mcbride has football practice before the game, which is in a few hours." "Go on and get ready I will meet you in the hall." We each leave, at the back of the hall, there is a stage where the changing rooms are for performances. That's where our show will be on Friday. The girls and I are all sleeping at the pool house tonight. Jade, Zoe, and Cara and I we find our dance partner's the entire year joins us in the hall once we have all changed. We each have our costumes on and we have a performance to practice miss Kelly is watching while Mr McBride is prepping the football team, ready for the game later. Bradley is watching alongside Zara and her girls. Miss Kelly gathered us in the center and said, "I hope you don't mind us all being here"? "I thought it was only fair that I helped, and we had a few spectators who would watch. I am immensely proud of all of you. I know you have all worked hard, and I can't wait for you to show your families how amazing you all are. The game isn't taking place until 8 pm tonight, we have enough time to do individual routines and partnered then you can all perform the group activity. Is that alright with everyone" we all agree? I have arranged refreshments and I have let each of your parents know you would be here practicing and then supporting our team." We all cheer, it's fun, we all get to show our year, our performances and we get to do the team performance too. I am excited, as we have worked hard for

Friday's event, it's our last goodbye. Miss Kelly surprised us all again when Mr McBride, and the whole football team and all our teachers walked in. "I hope you all don't mind, I wanted you to have a full practice experience. It will help with the nerves on Friday. All of those who are here to watch, please take a seat, those who are performing let's go.". For the rest of the year, get to sit down and watch until our group perform at the end, each are in costume ready. I am now wishing that Hayden was here to watch, but at least he will get to see me Friday along with the rest of our family. Zoe whispers "oh shit, I am nervous." I hope we don't mess up." We all have hidden our outfit's under a long dressing gown. We have some tight, leotards on now for our single performance and we all have some flesh showing in all the performances, being covered helps us not feel exposed, all the girls have one on. "Come on, we got this, we have worked hard let's show them what we have." We all put our hands in as we are behind the curtain, standing in a circle" one, two, three. We all cheered." We have an order for each performance, the light goes on and we get to enjoy watching each of the performances. Luke, to Lisa, Mattio, and Simon, it's my turn next. I perform my gymnastics routine, putting all my worries to the back of my mind. Once I had finished everyone began to clap. Zoe is next, she takes a deep breath, and you can see the moment she tunes everyone out. She tumbles, cartwheels performing her flips, her whole routine is full of energy. She did an amazing job. We all clap and shout out "go Zoe". When it's Cara's turn for her performance, we all watch as she moves, and I am so proud of her that she has the crowd dancing in there seats during her part of the show we all clap afterwards. I am so proud of her, she smashed it. The guys and I are jumping up and down as we clapped, it was fantastic, her confidence has grown, it's been a journey. Mattio has everyone on their feet in his performance, the music has you all wanting to join in. When Jade starts her performance, her music, is graceful, her body and how she puts all of her pain and her loss into her whole movements of each part of her body is stunning. We all have tears in our eyes Zoe, Cara, and I are holding hands as we cry feeling her emotions through her dance. Jade had blown everyone away, she was breathtaking, she received a standing ovation for it. She takes a bow and runs over to all of us, and she embraces us all and the boys join in. We are a pile of hugs and love as we have learned from these guys how to just let go. We all performed our duet dance, Cara and Mattio looked the part, Cara's costume is red, and she had pinned her hair up, Mattio had on a matching red waist coat and wow they look hot together pure fire. The whole routine has me fanning my face, their dancing is smoking! Once they have finished the whole room erupts in hooping and wolf whistles. We each told them how fantastic they danced togetherv with the outfit's was perfect.It was Zoe, and Luke up next, they have a very energetic dance and you can see the joy in their face's as they perform he throws her up high in the air, as we hear the crowd gasp, Luke catches her and swings her through his legs, it's high in energ,y and fast, with lift's that are hard to perform, but those two make it look effortless. They get a standing ovation as the whole room erupts with noise. Jade and Dale, are the last duet performance, as always, it is spectacular. They each move with perfect synchronisation, each move is danced with so much passion and tecnocality you can't help but watch and feel the dance through your whole soul. My dance with Simon went well, we spiced up our hip hop routine, and had some flips in ours. We too got a standing ovation. It felt really good, but it was Jade and Dale who stole the duo dance, as the crowd were clapping and whistling for a few minutes after the performance. We are all behind the stage, our group performance is next, we are all dressed and ready, we all cheer and hi five each other. We all get into our positions, once we hear the music, we all perform. We have different dance partners throughout the dance, we switch between each other, we add our flips, we do splits, we give it our all. Afterwards the whole year are up on their feet whooping, whistling, and clapping I have to admit I am now feel better after it's over we have all performed and we each did a great performance. I can sleep better knowing we have this, we can perform in front of people. When Miss Kelly came over and congratulated us all on our hard work she said, "I am so proud you will knock there socks off with those performances well done. Now go get changed, we have a team to support." We all were heading towards the showers, when Zara came over and picked Zoe up, and she spins her around. "My sister, you were frigging amazing!" I can't wait for all of the others to watch. You all did so well. I am proud, honestly Zoe, you were incredible." Jade you made me cry your routine and the perfection of movement was stunning and moving." "Cara well, well, the quiet one pulled some serious sexy fire tonight, that was pure hot girl." Anna, wow I can't wait for all the others to see. Go on and get showered, I will be waiting." Zara and her friends hugged us all. The football team went straight after our performances finished, they needed to warm up. Zara is heading towards Bradley as he is in a conversation with Miss Kelly, Zoe said "see he is a man whore, look he can't help it, he is such a guy. She has a fit body tick, boobs tick, energetic tick, beautiful tick. He probably already has her down for another session afterwards." We all chuckle and go to the changing rooms to shower and get ready for the game. The girls each have a shirt on, except Zoe, who has cut her shirt until you can see under boob. "Bloody hell Zoe, how high you can't even make out his number you have cut it off." She then turns around, in short cut-off jean shorts, and on her butt stitched onto each pocket is the missing numbers. I could not help it, I laughed so hard that tears left my eyes. Jade has made her's into a belly top, that just covered her chest, but has on the same bottoms as Zoe. Cara had the same they are all wearing cut off jean shorts, but only Zoe has numbers on her butt. Cara had her shirt in a belly top like Jade, Zoe though has her black bra showing at the bottom with hers. Zoe handed a black marker over to me can you write go team across our midriffs. They each stand in line Jade, has Go. Cara has Team, and

Zoe had !. On her midriff satisfied with their looks. We all headed over to the field. It was so busy the whole town came out, Deadwoods, the away team has their own supporters here too. We have many wolves here too. We have students from both schools and a few pack enforcers watching over us. They are working as a whole team, Zara and Kyle are sat in the stand's each have a hotdog and drink each. Zara has a tray with our drinks on. She must have ordered us one each, "hi" we all said, as we sat down. "Thank's for the food and drinks were starving." Kyle bought them, as I saved your seats." It's really busy tonight." I said as we all were ready to see the game. "This is the last one of the season each town as shown up to offer support to each town,"she said. I could see Adam, and Callum alongside them were Zara's friends. Each of them had spread out around the perimeter. Bradley is sat with Miss Kelly looking rather cosy, they are whispering to each other I could not make out what they are talking about." It is way too loud around us." We are all talking amongst each other while eating the hotdogs and nachos Kyle bought. Simon and the guys are sat with their girlfriends two rows in front of us. I have a couple at my side and on Zara's side is a family. I asked Kyle how the family business was, as he mentioned that they worked in security? Kyle told me "so far, so good, it's a lot of work, but I enjoy it my dad's a good boss." Cara replies by saying "I hope it's like that when we start work." I am ready for the challenged, but I am also going to miss everyone at school." Jade puts her arm around her, she said, "my dad is going to be an amazing boss you will love it, and Anna will be joining you soon." "It's not your dad I'm worried about It is having your big brother bossing me about all day." Zoe is glaring daggers Bradley's way "what is up with you?" "Nothing, I am fine I just can't wait for the game to start that's all." The crowd goes wild as both teams enter the football pitch they are waving at us that's when my girl's stand-up yelling "go team." Travis, Zoe's date to be, waves at her mouthing "you look hot!" and blows her a kiss. Liam and Andy noticed where he was looking and waved at us all. I see that Bradley's head snap in our direction. Zoe is too busy blowing kisses back to Travis who does a turn around chesture to Zoe, while her bra is flashing the whole team blowing kisses and waving. She obliges by turning around and jiggling her butt. Zara hi-fives her laughing at her antics as Travis shouted out while smiling at her. "Like I said, you look hot!" my number looks good on your arse. I like how it looks!", as they see that he was yelling, the crowd went quiet to see what he was shouting. All eyes turn our way those in our stand do anyway. Yep, way to get us noticed. I can see Adam and Callum, are looking at us all now. Taking in each of our outfits, from head to toe, I am in clothes, so I know I am good, but those three are in trouble. I could see each one of them receive a full look up and down and an eye roll, especially as the team all clapped and cheered in our direction. I hide my head and pick up my drink, taking a large swing. Zoe, just waves and laps it up her and Jade both chest bump as the whistle blows to start the match. We all sat back down as the players get into place, as the ball is placed in the center. Our team gets access to the ball first, passing it on up the field to the opposite side as they are chased and tackled, the ball is passed from foot to foot, it's a good match between the teams, they are equally matched as the ball is passed on player to player. By half-time neither team has scored a goal, and we all got a break in-between. Kyle heads towards the men's bathrooms while we each head over towards the ladies. Adam stops us halfway there, "girls are you kidding me, what did we say? You were told no dates, no meet ups, until we have more information." Zara told us all to go ahead while she spoke with Adam. We don't need telling twice, as we head to the ladies, the cue is endless. Jade, suggested we go into the school and use those nearest the pitch. Beat's waiting in this line which is not going down much, we all headed over to the school building as we see a few of our friends ahead of us we shout "hey wait up." We all group together as we walked to the building," hiya, you thought the same the it is too busy we saw some of the guys do the same." They have kept them open with how many have turned out to support the team's." We will be back for the second half we each take it in turns after washing our hands, we are heading back out of the building back to watch the second half. Travis and a few others are walking out of the guy's changing rooms. We will catch up with you. Could you let Zara know where we are and who we are with. "Yeah, see you in a bit." "Hi girl's, enjoying the match?" Zoe walked closer to Travis and told him "yes, you are all playing well." You need to score in the second half, though, for the win." Travis and Zoe are chatting, as we heard Liam and Kyle come in through the doors. "Hi are you ready for the second half?" "We are it's been good so far." Kyle asked us "Did you come in here to use these bathrooms too?" "yes, it's so busy that cue out there is endless." We each said goodbye to the guy's as we need to all get back the second half start's soon. Liam told the guy's he would be there shortly, as they each turned back around and left. We all headed to the door to leave the building that is when Kyle being a gentlemen opened the door as Liam was walking behind Cara and most likely eyeing up her arse while pretending to be nice. I will be with you guys shortly. As Kyle holds the door open, I feel a sharp prick in my neck then the room started to go fuzzy, and I feel like I am in a dream state, I can hear some words being spoken, but I don't understand them or there meaning. What is happening I try to bring myself to be more alert, to wake up. I could not move my body it feels heavy sluggish. I fight it hoping my wolves ability's will help as I try to remember my training, don't go down fight use your wolf I push through and as I feel someone approaching I act I headbutt behind me and run away towards the changing rooms I lock the door putting the latch on as I slump behind it holding it closed. I can hear fighting and muffled screams as I felt the door being kicked, I held my body as close to the door as I could, I thought of Hayden and I was holding on. Until I pass out. I could hear shouting" Anna! Anna! Where are you" Anna please! Someone is shouting my name. Anna!.

I try to focus on the voice, it sounds close and I fight using the Alpha power I have from my blood and start to blink away the bright light's from the room I'm in. I try to shout back "I hear you. I hear you! I battle with all my strength to keep my eyes open. That is when I feel the door being kicked, "Anna it's Adam open the fucking door!" I try to calm my thoughts. "Adam, I feel sleeply." This time Adam put's an Alpha command into it "open the door now." My wolf comes through fighting off the drug. As I obey my Alpha, I crawl and undo the lock as Adam and Abel crash through the door. I am lifted up as both my brothers hold me close. Both saying "thank god." I fall asleep in Adam's arms as my body couldn't stay awake any longer. I could hear voices but I am still feeling foggy, my head hurts as I feel the warm heat warm through my body, I start to feel less fussy and start to open my eyes. It's my mum, she's healing me. "How do you feel?""like I have been hit." I awaken to find my family all pacing as I hear a bus pulling up, my dad leaves the room as I look around as my mum helps me up. I have a few sips of water as my mum is talking to me asking me if I feel sick or have any other issues. I shake my head, my throat is dry, I look around the room and I notice that Cara's family are grimmed faced. Zoe and Zara's parents are all watching me. Ethan is sat with his Aunty and Uncle clinging to them crying, as Sara is crying on Abel's shoulder. Adam is pacing as him and Bradley are further away whispering with so many watching me I feel self conscious. After I drank a full glass of water and took deep breaths, my brain started to work. As I remember being at the match with my girls. That's when I looked up and Hayden ran over to me holding me so tight I couldn't breathe. "Hayden, I am okay, I'm here." he is shaking . I hold on to him until he calms down. My mum hands me a snake bar, "Anna eat this you have been asleep for over twelve hours". "twelve hours that is the moment my skin runs cold as I remember I was drugged with something. My dad and others I haven't met yet, joined us in the living space. My dad asked everyone to sit down as a woman I haven't met runs over to me and places a hand on my head, she closes her eyes and I feel my whole body relax and the foggyiness lifts completely. "My girls I screamed out. They I" Hayden thanked the woman, who had helped me, and he picked me up and placed me on his lap as I have a melt down. "Kyle and Liam were there they were talking to us, as we went inside the school to use the bathroom. We were talking to some of the players. Zoe, she was talking to Travis, and there were a few others there. That went back inside the changing rooms to get ready for the second half of the game. I remember Cara was behind me as were Zara and Zoe, they were laughing and Kyle he opened the door and said ladies, as I was walking through the door I felt a sharpe pain in my neck as I started to slump against the door. I thought I heard fighting, and I heard my girls trying to fight there way out. I think Zara knocked me out of the way. I remember fighting the sleepiness and trying to remember my training as I headbutted someone who had a hold of me. That is it I was injected in my neck, as I slumped backwards, I felt arms grabbing me from behind that is when I hit them in the nose. I managed to get to the bathroom and locked the door using all my energy on keeping them out from grabbing me. Where are my friends? Are they sleeping too,? Would somebody please tell me what is going on?"

CHAPTER EIGHTEEN

Hayden

Once we were off the bus, Alpha Gerald joined us and told us to be patient as there was too much to explain until everyone was together. "Anna, needs you Hayden, she is in the living space." I follow him into the house, and I can feel worry, pain, fear, and deep despair as I enter. Anna was with her mum as she looked up at me I can see the hurt, the fear coming from her in waves of grief as I ran over and held onto her so tightly, until Maria came over and wanted to check Anna over explaining to her who she was and that she would help her. When I look around the rest of the room and see how quiet it is that is, the moment I realise that her friends, her sisters, her girls are not here that they are missing. Anna, can see my confusion and notices we have visitors and everyone who came with me has no idea what has happened. Anna, started to speak, she told us that she had been drugged and that as the door was opened she felt a sharp pinch and that her, she doesn't finish her sentance as she starts to panic and goes into a meltdown as I feel her panic hit me, I place Anna on my knee as Marie sends calming waves into Anna she stops fighting and relaxes into my arms. Jax comes over and picks his mate up sitting beside me with Marie on his lap as I know how hard it is with the feelings we both felt as we came into the house.I hold her tight, as Adam speaks to the whole room. "Everyone please stay calm, I know that it is a challenging time and I will explain what we found, and what we saw, then maybe someone might have a clue where we need to look for our pack mates." Everyone takes a seat, as another pack member comes into the living space with a strong glass of amber liquid for all the adults. Ethan is gripping his aunt and uncle with a death grip. I can't help but see and sense his pure fear and I asked "if it wise, Ethan hearing, whatever we are about to be told." Adam, looked over at Ethan and said, "Ethan, do you want to go play with the other children? I notice movement in the corner of the room and look over, I can see my family. My dad has already holding my mother tight. Leo is hugging our sisters once each have embraced. Jess moved away from them towards where Ethan is sat, she asked "Ethan why don't you play with me, we can play tag with Maisie. I promise you, they will find your sister, our packs will find them." Ethan looked up, as he does, he takes in each of his family members as he looks back at his big brothers, he speaks to them first "You will be able to find them all won't you. Please bring Jade back, and Cara won't you she will be scared and they will need protecting."" I know that Zara can kick butt, but still she will need your help, we protect our girls don't we." Adam and Abel answer him by saying "We do and we will." Zoe too, she can fight I know she acts tough and does fight better than most but her and Zara will get hurt first, as they will protect my sister and Cara, but who will protect them.""I am scared, who will watch there backs? I know they can fight hard, but they love us all so much." I watch him as he pour's out all of his fear's to the whole room, the same fears we have. I watch as big fat tears roll down his face and Anna is crying alongside him as she cries into my chest as she knows that her entire world has been turned upside down. Both of Anna's brothers walk over towards Ethan, and each hold him tight looking into his eyes as they promise him that they will not stop until each one of them comes home. Gerald and Annibelle are next, as they each have to make the same promise as their son's. Henry and Wendy each make the same promise, that they will search until every scamp of land has been searched every Island until they find them. Ethan nods and hugs each member of his family as he sets his sight on Bradley and said. "You will help won't you? I know that you fight a lot with Zoe, and I know that she took your car as a punishment because she was mad at you, and hurt that you what was the words she said." He pretended to think as he has Bradley waiting to hear what Zoe could have said. "Ah that was it, Zoe said that you hook up so much that she wouldn't be surprised if you he lowers his voice and whispered a s.t. something I think it is a bad thing for you to catch, and she was worried about you catching it. See she cares, even though you want to punish her, she took your car because you wouldn't listen and she wanted to teach you a lesson. If you want to punish her back for being bad you must find her first." Anna, moves her head and said "Ethan, you told, little brother, what happened to pinkie swear that you made if Zoe told you." Ethan smiles and for an eight-year-old he sure knows how to get motivation when he responded with "Bradley, really wants to punish Zoe though, I have heard him say so many times he wanted to tan her hide he shouted it the last time to my dad, to do that, he must work harder to find her." Bradley puts his hand on his heart and told Ethan, "I will find her I promise and we all will not rest until we find them all, and maybe you and I can plot a prank together to get them back." Ethan runs over and hugs Bradley's leg then he came over to Anna and holds her face in his small hands and said, "I love you Anna, my boys will get them back I promise," he kisses her nose, and runs towards my sister, and tags Maisie saying "your it." Jess and Ethan run away as Maisie gives chase. The room absorbs what just happened as Adam takes over the meeting. "Zara came over to talk to me, as the girls were in line to use the bathroom.

She had witnessed Kyle dropping something into there drinks they had bought. She managed to swap them as the girls came in, while he was distracted and jumpy. She wanted me to inform the patrol as she had a bad feeling that something was going to happen. As we were talking some of the girl's friends came over and told us they were in the school building using the bathroom as the cue was too long out here. Zara, left to find them as Callum was posted nearby where the school building was, we thought that they would be fine with two enforcers. That is when my radio went off and Callum was shouting code red, which was the word that something was wrong. I shouted Abel, and he and I ran towards the building. I saw Callum slumped on the floor, his radio smashed into pieces. Then I heard a vehicle screeching out of the car park. Bradley was behind us, and he stayed to help Callum. While Abel and I ran towards the building, as soon as we arrived we could smell blood, and saw an empty sack. We knew the girls had been taken, as we could scent them and see evidence of a struggle. Kyle and Liam had been there, we could smell them, and other scents were there too but had been disguised. We could smell that Anna, was nearby and we shouted out her name, we were not getting any response. We followed her scent to the girls bathroom, where she had barricaded herself in. We started banging on the door shouting her name, that is when we heard her trying to move. She had been slumped against the door and could not stay awake. She managed to unlock the door but soon after we got inside she callapsed and fell back to sleep. I carried her and brought her, back home. Two enforcers from the Deadwood pack had followed the vehicle and gave chase, they were found by someone from the game who found the car they were in and we found out that they had been run off the road and both had been knocked out from crashing down the valley into the trees." I can feel the room filled with anger and frustration. Maria stands up as Jaxs holds onto her keeping her tucked to his side. Anna has been taking everything in and is listening as Maria takes the floor. "My name is Maria Hastings; I am from the last pack of Stirling's and Hastings members, who lived on Beast Island." The whole room is silent, as they take in this woman. She is not a big woman. She is meek and has lost weight, but you can sense her, strength. This man, who you all know, is my mate, we found each other two days ago when I was tracking down Aiden Huntsman's Men. They came to our Island as friends, but they lied to us and killed our Alpha, my father. They killed my grandfather, and they stole my sister and our grandmother. They took many of what was left of our small pack. I was fourteen when it happened and my sister Poppy, who was just a young child" The whole room boils with rage, as Maria continued telling them her whole story. She once explained that she followed the man called Toby and helped rescue my dad. Maria is hugged by my mother and thanked for being brave and trusting each of us." I take over after we all are seated again as I explain "I have the file that Rose and Mitch kept and inside are maps and detailed areas of where the creatures could be kept, as well as leads to the men who work for Aiden Huntsmen." We need to try and figure out how to counter act the drugs Anna and the girls were given." Gerald spoke and told us that Anna has had a blood test done, and Nate Wickes has asked for a team to help crack Aidens technology. Nate and the other Alphas will all help aid us in searching and putting a team together to help us fight off any drugs. Zara was able to give a sample of the drink Kyle had bought, to Adam. Gerald and Henry alongside my dad, Bradley and Adam were going to call another meeting for all to inform all of the packs what else they have found out from us that everything Rose and Mitch have collected will help. We needed a plan of action and we needed to finish up the training, while we planned. Rushing in would not do any of us any good, we needed to be patient and we needed to be smart to be able to help all captured.

CHAPTER NINETEEN

Anna

Once everyone started gathering the children for lessons to start, me and Hayden needed time alone, we went over to the pool house, and we talked a while. He told me everything that had happened while he was gone. I was seated at the table as Hayden made us breakfast, it was 10 am and I was hungry, as we ate and talked it helped me feel better and the drug had worked through my body Maria helped me feel less out of it. Hayden ran a bath that we both got into. He took care of me, as I was worried sick about my sisters, we may not be blood sisters, but I loved them so much, we spend every single day with each other and to me and to each of them we were sisters. I am frightened, thinking about what they must be going through. How scared and not knowing where they are, why they have been taken and what will happen next. These thoughts are on repeat in my head as I lay in the bath thinking dark thoughts. It seems like my entire world has fallen apart. I am so deep in thought that when Hayden begins to move his hands up my arms and tilts my head back I am taken out of my head as his lips move over my neck as he kisses me. "Anna, I know you are scared right now, and I know you wish we could have them back this minute, but we need to have a plan, so nobody gets hurt or killed." "I know, Hayden but I just can't believe how we were tricked, and how we were ambushed in school. I can't stop thinking about them, and I feel guilty that I got away. I miss them Hayden, what the hell is wrong with Kyle and Liam, taking them why? What do they want?" I started crying again "I need them back. I need them safe, and unharmed." My thoughts are dark, and each thought leads me to sineros that I think up the worst ones. Hayden holds me and starts to empty the bath water, he grabs a towel for each of us and dries us both off. "Come with me" he holds my hand and leads me to our bedroom as he removes both of our towels. He looks deep into my eyes and says" Anna, I love you, we will get through this, believe in our kind, we will help find them, now let me show you what you mean to me." He holds my face in-between his hands as he kisses every inch of my mouth. He starts to kiss my cheeks, my chin and his kisses lead everywhere he takes each thought, and replaces it with sensation. Hayden kisses every inch of my skin as I watch him, as he is on his knees in front of me. He is gentle, and loving, as he works my body into pure fire. He took his time seducing me, he gently laid me on the bed. I opened my legs to welcome him into my body, he entered my body and started to move with slow, sensual thrusts, each one, adding more sensation. He lifts my legs as he turns me onto my side. One leg is over his shoulder as he looks into my eyes, as I look into his. He increases the rhythm of each thrust becoming deeper, as he kisses my lips and his hands roam and touch every inch of me. He never rushes our lovemaking; He takes his time, as I feel him pick me up and flip me around, where I face the mirror and I ride him backwards. Watching myself as he is watching me. I feel a thrill as I can see where we are joined together as I find a pace and move. Hayden sits up behind be pushing my chest forward slightly I can feel every inch of him as he helps guild my hips back and forth, he pinches my nipples causing my clit to tingle, as I can feel myself building closer to a release. Hayden moved his hands down as he opened my thighs wider so he could massage my clit. I come undone as I scream out his name, he rides me through it until I am breathless and feeling spent. Hayden removes me from his body as he walks us both to the dresser, where He says, "remember when I said I wanted you so much I could have bent you over this dresser, well now is that time." I nod my head as Hayden bends me forward my hands are on the dresser as Hayden lines himself up. He started to move, this time he is rougher, he thrust deep into me as he set a fast deep pace. I can hear our skin as it slaps together, as he pistons into me harder, as he touches my breasts and massages them, tweaking and pulling my nipples each time he squeezes I feel it deep in my core. Hayden does not stop, he is relentless as he takes me, he flips me back around as he lifts both my legs up as he places each leg on his shoulders, as he pistons into me he has the dresser banging into the wall, and I don't care he has us both sweating as he doesn't slow down or stop, he picks me, up and slams me against the wall. He changes position as he lifts one of my legs up as he thrusts deep. I feel myself getting close as Hayden slows his thrust and angles his manhood, I feel his pubic bones hitting my clit as he thrust it hits me just right as I go off into bliss. Hayden joins me as he climaxes too, he bites my neck as though he is reclaiming me as his. Afterwards we lay on the bed and Hayden asked me if he hurt me, "no, that was amazing." he told me "I was so scared something had happened to you, after I had just found you, I thought you were gone." I needed you so much Anna, I needed to know that you are real and were here together. That with you I can fight through anything. I love you Anna, and we will get back our friends back I promise you." As I listen to Hayden, I understand how he felt as he is my everything too, I have to have faith in our pack, that no matter what happens next, we will get through it together. That we will find my girls and I hope that they will be home safe and soon.

The End

The story continues in Fated Dreams: book Two Adam and Cara

BONUS CHAPTERS

Mitch and Rose.

CHAPTER ONE: Mitch
CHAPTER TWO: Rose
CHAPTER THREE: Ali
CHAPTER FOUR: Anya Huntsman

CHAPTER ONE

Mitch

Rose and I are on our way to meet with Max, we are ready to tell him the truth of what has happened and why Aiden Huntsman needs stopping. We spent time training Maria and trying to build a normal life together to heal after everything they have been through, they needed it. We had spent time looking into some of Aiden's men and his company I managed a few years prior to giving Max some intel. Now is the time to tell him about Rose and her pack what happened, how some were killed, and others taken. We still don't know why they were taken and what for we have guessed but we hope we are wrong. We have arranged to travel to a halfway point to meet max at a restaurant where many stop to refuel and rest. We are about twenty miles away from where we need to be as I notice a van that has been on our tile a few miles back, at first, I just thought it was normal traffic, but I have taken some turns to check if I was being paranoid. It is still behind us, I hope it's nothing, but my gut says otherwise that we may be in trouble. I speed up, to build some distance and I manage to gather at least a mile aways this road is straight so I can't take a detour for at least five miles ahead through a small farm village. I decided to take it to lose the tail. I keep my speed high, as I turn and keep going, we wait behind a house and park up hiding behind parked cars. Rose and I leave and walk away we see a coffee shop and go inside to wait it out. We can see the road and if the van goes by, we will wait and go back to the car and carry on our way. We order and wait, Rose asked "do you think they work for him?" "They don't know that were together they don't know you escaped as far as they are aware you and Maria died on that Island." Our order is up, as we watch we see no vans and we stay and finish our coffee each taking a bathroom break. We left and walked back towards our car nothing seemed out of place as we turned back the way we came and started back on the road we needed to take to meet Max. We are almost there as we see the place coming up, I park up in the car park and as we are getting out of the car that is when I am shot in the neck, I feel a sharp pain and am knocked out. When I come too, I see that I am in the back of a van I try not to move I know that Rose is with me, and I can scent Max what the hell is he doing here? I know we have been captured and I know we are in deep shit. I pretend I am like the other two, out and even my breathing I try not to move when I feel the van moved and turn as it hits tough terrain. I have been chained up, I have had my feet and hands tied together with a bag over my head. When the van stops, I have a plan formed. I am lifted and I listen as the men speak one voice, I recognize it is Aiden Huntsman he is here. He orders that Max be held up in another room and us dumped in with Ali, so they have taken Ali the Alpha's daughter what sick bastards they are. I am lifted and dumped hard on the floor, I feel a kick to my stomach and a foot to my face, I lay still gritting my teeth as I take a few hits. Rose is dumped near me as I heard one of the men say leave her, we can have some fun later when the boss says so. They leave and I heard a lock engage and footsteps walking away, none of them had a scent, so I know they have blocked it. I can taste blood from the kick to my face, as I lay there, I know Ali is here, but she isn't making any noise either. I have to assume she has been drugged like us. I know if I move, they will hit me with another shot of drug, I don't know why I am awake, but I am glad that I am as I may need to use it as an advantage. It felt like I had been laid here a while as I am starting to feel numb. I move my fingers and toes and I try to loosen up my limbs the best that I can being tied up. My body is healing I may still have marks, but I feel like nothing was broken, I can hear footsteps coming towards the building as the door is unlocked and I am yanked up off the floor I am dragged to another room I can smell Max I try to remain as though I am drugged. The bag is taken off my head. Aiden is talking to Max making threats and trying to get him to talk, I know Max won't say anything but if they are going to use Ali, he might give them enough to save her. I know I need to move as I know my strength will break the chains and I can hear them saying nasty, sick, stuff to Max. I use my wolf senses to find those in the room from the noise I know two have me holding me up and Aiden may be another guarding the door. Max is awake I know he is strong now I need to wait for the right moment I take slow even breaths listening to Aiden try his best to provoke Max to spill his secrets, when he says the next thing, it boils my blood I move I hit one with my head breaking his nose. I know that Max has moved I snap the chain holding my hands in place and grab a hold of the other as I make him sleep by knocking him out. Max has a hold of Aiden and puts him down, we unchain ourselves as we inject them with the tranquilizer gun we find on them. Giving each one a shot each as we lock them in the cell and make our way over to the door.

CHAPTER TWO

Rose

I feel like I have been hit by a truck my whole body is heavy and

I feel tired I try to move my hands and notice they are tied behind my back, then I try to move my legs they too are tied together. I have a bag over my face. I can smell another one of my kind here, she must be asleep drugged like I was. I listen and I notice that someone is outside pacing a guard. I try to be as quiet as I can as I shake the bag of my head and roll over, taking in the room not too far away is a young girl is laid at the other side of the room. She has no chains, but she is asleep as I take in her face, she is young and beautiful. She will be scared just like my pack were scared when that animal Airen Huntsman came to my island and killed my Alpha, stole our younger members and killed the warriors, leaving them on the beach, they are evil. I know when they took Nera from me, I wanted them found and we hadn't been able to locate them but did manage to find his land and stuck on we drew a map hoping that we would be able to come back with more pack that Mitch belonged to. I was fed up with the dead ends and when we did find information, I knew it was time for Max to hear my story. We were taken I don't know how but it must be from the last lead we had that is the only way they would have known to even look for us, I just hope they don't find the cabin and Maria, we have been through so much. I am not waiting here any longer, I wait until I feel less foggy from the drugs and there is a window at the back of the room high up towards the ceiling, I use to climb trees, that is my escape root I know Mitch was here as his scent is in the room. I just need to get loose first so I can look. I snap the chains holding my hands as I sit up, I go a little dizzy, and I wait until it passes once it does, I snap the chain that hold the cuffs to my feet. I shake the numbness from my body as I quietly take in the room, I make no noise as I check around for devices. I know the girl is going to be okay as I can hear her heartbeat and hear her breathing. I found a few on the walls and under the furniture. I take each one carefully and I see a sink with a bucket filled with water and it has a ladle in it. I take a sip of clean water. I know I need to take a few mouthfuls to help with the dryness of my mouth, afterwards I see a cup and fill it to give the girl. I put each device carefully into the water, making sure each one is under and kill the transmission. I walk over to the girl and try to wake her, I take the cup and force a few sips into her mouth forcing her to swallow. She drinks which gives me relief as I lift her up. I whisper in her ear as low as I can." my name is rose, I was taken like you, and I am going to help us escape, be quiet there is a guard outside and look up she does. That is how we will escape it is getting dark, we will sneak out when the sun goes fully down." she whisper really low "my name is Ali my dad is called Max I am from the Evergreen pack and was taken from school I felt a sharp pain and then woke up to find water in mouth." We talk low for a few minutes as I explained that we were meeting her dad to pass on information. I tell her about my old home as we sit and wait to help pass the time. I told her about the bad men that came and how they took my daughter and many others with them and how I and Maria escaped with the help of Mitch who was uncovered working for her dad. I can see that the sky has darkened, and I hear footsteps I hide behind the door as Ali pretends to be asleep. The guards are talking about a hunt and then us as they swap over Il go check to see if she's awake Aiden must be having fun with her companion as he hasn't come out for a few hours. He must be beating the shit out of him and Max. The anger I feel as I listen to them talk about my Mitch enrages me, we are not fated mates both of ours died and we found love with each other we have bonded as mates, but we are not fated and couldn't have children together. I wait as I see the door open, I wait until he is in sight as I drag him and bang his head into the wall knocking him out before he could send out an alarm. I drag him in using the bag as a gag and tying him up. I jester to Ali, we can try the door now the guard is out I find keys on his belt and take them I take his radio and dump it in the bucket of water. I open the door a crack and I can't see any one I step out and smell the surrounding's I can smell two others of our kind, one is Mitch. I heard a noise a Pepple hits the floor near my feet I looked towards the direction it was thrown from. I can see Mitch who is with another man coming down from a roof from a building further away. I look around as they make their way over, I hug Mitch and hold him for a moment. As I open the door Ali steps out and jumps into the other man's arms, I know that this must be Mitch. Mitch told me that Max knows everything and that they escaped a few hours ago and stayed on the roof until it was dark enough to try the buildings to look for us. We are together that is the main thing, we all go inside the building as I explain what I have done with the devices the guy laid out. We came up with a plan. We need to be quite no talking and we come up with hand signals to speak. We have a plan we and we are going to check the surrounding buildings and make our way through the woods Mitch and I have seen some of Aiden's land so we are hopeful we will recognize a place so we can escape and get help from the other packs. I pour water for all of us into cups to drink before we leave. Once we are ready, we leave via the front door, staying hidden in the shadows. The guards on are near the buildings we sneak up by one going on the roof while the others stay hidden each have a window high up, we search all of them no luck we find nothing.

CHAPTER THREE

Ali

I am with my dad and two others Mitch and Rose, we have checked all of the buildings, and nothing is in them whatever was kept in them before have left now. The adults have a plan we are walking in the woods taking quite steps using our wolf abilities to see I haven't gone through the growth phase, yet I am twelve and have time, but I can see clearly which is a good thing we stay off the path and stay close to where the trees are. We kept going as light started to show we have been walking for hours and came up to a large lake. Just as the sky is lighter, Mitch knows where we are, and he knows we are close to the cabins that the families stay in. We head towards them as they will be cars and we are hoping to take one and leave. We walked a few hours following Mitch and Rose, my dad hasn't let go of my hand the whole way, he is my everything and I am his. By now the pack will know we are missing and will be looking for us, we hope we can get to our land and inform the other Alpha's and arrange to end this man who takes our kind and the creatures who just want to be free. I am tired but I push through as daylight is fast approaching my dad thinks it's closer to 6 am as we are near the cabins. We find that the humans staying here are still sleeping. We are walking towards where the car park is, when Mitch holds up a fist, this is the sign to stop. We can hear someone walking further ahead as it is coming from the car park. We stay still and listen as we hear a woman who is muttering under her breath" Aiden and his stupid men staying out all night while I'm under guard." "At least I have lost them. For now I can take a swim in the lake and have some peace while everyone is still sleeping." We begin to walk closer to the car park as we act naturally. She clearly doesn't know who we are and isn't alarmed that Aiden hasn't come home. We walk up to the car park as she has her head in the back seat of her car, she chose that moment to look up and closers the door quietly, "morning your up and about early, I'm just about to take a swim while it's quiet. Don't mind me." She seems nice, but scared as her hands are trebling as though she is doing something wrong. I look her over she is pretty, she has a kind face and has on fitness wear. She keeps looking around as though someone might jump out at her. My dad is ever the kind and caring man he senses something in her as he speaks to her. "Are you alright? you seem frightened we won't hurt you we just need to have a drive and pick up some things for breakfast." "My family and I have been craving some bacon and eggs. "I looked up at my dad, he is the sweetest guy I know, here we are on land that isn't ours and trying to escape unnoticed and he still worries about others. The woman answered back, stepping closer towards us so that we could hear. Which we can from where she is stood, but she doesn't know that. "Sorry, I am Anya, pleased to meet you all. My husband owns the place as she lowers her voice as though scared someone will hear her. You seem like nice people; I don't know why I feel I can tell you this but here goes. I'm always followed by my husband who thinks that I am his, and he doesn't allow me to go anywhere." she stops talking as though surprised she said it. She doesn't know my dad, he can pursue anyone to talk if he uses his Alpha tone. Anya told us the code to the gate and to keep on driving the way we came. She told us that she doesn't often get time alone to swim and that is all she wants to do. She walked away as we all looked over at each other, my dad knows that with a guard not being on the first gate gives us a better chance of escaping as the only gate ahead after that is the gate house. My dad holds my head as he crouches down, "once we get to the gate house me and Mitch will hide in the back seat. You and Rose sit up front and try not to give us away, act normal by taking deep breaths. Tell them our cabin number is 112 that one had two people in you will pretend that it is you two." Once we are out of here, I will bring fire onto this land and burn out all the evil that is a foot. I love you so much Ali." My dad kisses the top of my head as I hug him tight. I know my dad will do everything possible to get us all home and I trust him to be able to do so.

CHAPTER FOUR

Anya Huntsman

I have escaped from the prison my husband calls home he never allows me to go anywhere without him or a guard. A few years ago, I tried to leave him because he was controlling and I didn't want to carry on living like that anymore. I could see what it was doing to our sons, who were told to follow orders it feels like we are his, so he can tell us what to do and how we do it. He has become a nightmare he never used to be like this. When we first met, he was charming, he opened doors, he took me out we went away, and had fun together, we were happy. We got married, bought a home, Aiden had built a business and had been making a fortune, I never asked questions, I trusted him; I had a job of my own before we were married. Aiden used to support it he didn't mind me working. Once he got more successful and we got married and moved into a huge, beautiful home he wanted me to give it up. He told me I could work from home doing his books for the family holidays. I agreed as I knew it was for our future, he had an office of his own and had me next door to him where I would do bookings arranging cleaners for the cabins. Make any arrangements for any work that needs doing. Once I got pregnant, he changed, he didn't want me stressed, I had to think of the baby. He asked me to stop and hired someone else he had bought a building to use for his businesses and had added hunting trips. Which he knew I would not support. He hid it from me I found out as I checked his files and invoices, I confronted him about it he sweet talked me after our fist born was born, he was over the moon, and he took time off to make sure we were looked after. He was amazing and he took good care of us, once he had a few weeks at home he needed to return to work and hired help around the house and put a guard on duty. I never knew why he told me for safety we do have a lot of dangerous creatures that we avoided as they would rip you apart. We were fine then I started to want to work again and have something for me not just be a mother that was great, but I wanted to work too. I had spoken to Aiden about it, and he told me, once our son started school, he would let me work with him at the office and I was happy as I knew Kyle started school that year. I was happy to wait as Kyle started school and another year had passed by., I asked Aiden why he hadn't stuck to his promise. He took me up to bed and seduced me so I'd forget that was every night he would always make my body scream for his touch. I wouldn't let it go and was due to start on Monday, that week my parents were killed in a traffic accident I was devastated, Aiden helped to take care of everything he took me away and stuck me back together again. I found out I was pregnant a few months after again I stayed at home, I had a guard with me wherever I went. I loved Aiden, I really did, but he got more and more controlling, I noticed the boy's started acting scared around Aiden as though if they didn't obey him, they would be punished. I took my children to school one day and went to see my sister. I asked the guard to take the car to be cleaned as I was in my sister's home and wasn't going anywhere without the car. I told my sister how I was, and that I needed to get away anywhere as long as I took the boys. My sister had money saved and had kept my mum and dads house it was a large property big enough for us all, as she knew Aiden would come here and try to convince me to go back. She told him she sold it and that a family had moved in, so we should be safe. Once the driver returned, I said goodbye to my sister as I put my plan into action I was going to have to pack, and do it so Aiden wouldn't notice. I acted as normal as possible each night Aiden, and I would have sex and every night while he slept, I would pack a few items and hide the cases. I was ready to leave. I got ready as normal, I dropped the boys off at school and went home to gather the cases. Aiden was waiting in the bedroom he had the cases and had opened each one. I told him I wanted to leave, he knew. My best cause of action would be to tell him, as I did, I saw Aiden's face change but then he hid it. He told me he loved me and that I wasn't going anywhere and that I wasn't taking the boys either. The next thing I knew he had me thrown on the bed and he laid on top of me and said "Anya, you are mine and the only way you will leave me is when we both die, do you not see how much I love you how much I need you how each night I show you my love for you." He kisses me and I hold my mouth closed, I turn my head I want him off, me now. I try to push him off I shout and scream how much I hate him, and he can't stop me from leaving. He locked me in our bedroom slamming the door as he broke something outside the door as I could hear glass breaking. I cried all day he had food brought in and had them lock me in. I refused everything fetched into me, I was so mad at him. When day turned into night I laid in bed as Aiden unlocked the door re locked it and put the key away in the safe so that I didn't have excess too. Aiden undressed and as he did, he looked at me never taking his eyes from me, as the low lighting allowed us to see each other. He had a good body and I'd give him that he knew how to make my body scream, but I was mad, and I wanted a life, a job, money off my own. My resolve was waning as he pulled of his boxer shorts in all his naked glory. Damn him, I yelled "I hate you." do not touch me I am not yours not anymore you can lock me up, but I will not allow you access to my body" He looked at me as he walked closer towards the bed, as he pulled the bedcovers off leaving me in my nightwear. He grabs my ankles, pulling me towards him right to the end where he takes each of my ankles and places them in the cuffs that are attached to each corner of the bed. I sit up and demand that "he let's go of me." He doesn't say a word. He forces my body back down on the bed as he takes each of my arms and places them in the silk straps tying them securely. Aiden likes it when I don't move, he likes control, and this is him taking back control as he will now use my own body against me to get what he always wants. I am thinking back and remembering this memory as I talk to the man holding his daughter's hand, he has another man and woman with him. He is tall and attractive. I am so lost when they approached as I managed to leave without a guard. It's the first time I have had a moment to myself and all I want to do is swim. He asked me a question." I am fine, I just want to enjoy my morning swim as I don't have much time for myself. My husband, as I lower my voice, he can be too controlling, he thinks I might run off."" Do you know how to get out of the gate? as the security guard hasn't arrived this morning, it's early maybe he is running late but the code to release the gate is 5532116 once you get through that gate your good you just head up the way you came give the gate hose you cabin number and I hope you have a lovely breakfast goodbye and I might see you on your return." I smile and wave the last thing I need is Aiden turning up seeing me talking to a male guest he would flip, and I really just want to be alone. I can't remember if I locked the car, but I have started walking away now so I carry on walking.

This part will continue as a prequel in book two.

the end

Printed in Great Britain
by Amazon